CODIRECTION

BOREALIS: WITHOUT A COMPASS

BOOK 4

GREGORY ASHE

H&B

Codirection
Copyright © 2021 Gregory Ashe

Published by Hodgkin & Blount
https://www.hodgkinandblount.com/
contact@hodgkinandblount.com

Published 2021
Printed in the United States of America

This cover has been designed using resources from Freepik.com.

Trade Paperback ISBN: 978-1-63621-021-6
eBook ISBN: 978-1-63621-020-9

Codirection, noun: direction by two or more people working together

Shaw's note: Like that time North was trying to drive the golf cart on campus, and then I tried to drive the golf cart because he was doing a terrible job, and he hit the gas, and I hit the brake, and then we weren't in the golf cart anymore.

North's elucidation: I broke my aviators, thank you very much. And I was doing perfectly fine driving the golf cart. Shaw grabbed the wheel because he wanted to see if Howie Gallagher had a stiffy or just really solid pleats.

Shaw's correction: Actually, we both wanted to see if Howie had a stiffy because Howie had this spiky hair kind of like if Pikachu had a special adult relationship with a hedgehog and one time, after I watched Lord of the Rings, I had a dream where he was washing my elbows with water from a silver ewer, oh, and he had great chi.

North's gloss (from shawspeak): He was hot as fuck.

Chapter 1

"ARE THEY WEARING the same boots?"

The housewarming party at North and Shaw's new home was in full swing, and the question came from one of their guests—a neighbor from down the street. Nita was a big woman, her dark skin warmed by gold undertones, her eyes a frank and startling hazel. She wore a sleeveless blouse and a short skirt in concession to the September heat, and she kept lifting the ends of her plaits from her neck, flapping the blue hair in an attempt to cool herself. She was looking at her wife, Breezi, who was currently picking a fight with North.

"Don't get me started," Shaw said.

Nita laughed so softly that it was almost swallowed up by the Jethro Tull playing on the Bluetooth speaker.

"I'm serious," Shaw said after another sip of Coke—his fourth, because North had gotten caught up in the argument with Breezi. "He saw her tool cabinet in the garage last week, and he's spent every night since researching them on his phone. They cost four hundred dollars. He talked about them in his sleep last night; I'm not even joking."

"So much for that wizard's crystal ball you were going to buy."

"Well, technically it belonged to a witch, so I think it's a witch's crystal ball." Shaw smoothed his hair and checked that it was still gathered in a bun. "But yeah, unfortunately, I seem to have forgotten how to say no to him."

Nita laughed again, but that last part was more truth than joke. On the big things, they tended to agree, and so the shift in their relationship had snuck up on Shaw, catching him by surprise on the little things: where to put the weight set in the basement, what types of protein to prep for the week, how much of the grocery budget could be spent on ice cream sandwiches. At least they'd managed to buy a house together—a gingerbread brick structure in the neighborhood known as St. Louis Hills, with high, asymmetrical rooflines and Gothic arch doorways and rubble masonry accents. And it had a garage that could fit both their cars, not common in St. Louis. A garage, Shaw suspected, that pretty soon was going to be sporting a new tool chest.

The party had started an hour ago, and now, with dusk settling over them, it was in full swing. Fairy lights strung across the backyard cast a warm, yellow glow. The smell of charcoal and citronella, of salmon grilling on cedar planks, mingled with the voices of their friends. Puppy in her arms (although at this point, *puppy* was a stretch for the dog), Pari sat on Truck's lap, her bindi goldenrod today, the two of them engaged in another all-consuming conversation. Zion and Jadon were standing together near the coolers, both men in slides, gym shorts, and tees. Jadon's darkly sandy good looks were relaxed tonight; he was smiling as he said something to the other man. Zion kept running a hand over his hair, a tight fade cut into his curls. Whatever Jadon said made Zion burst out laughing, an unusually expressive moment for the reserved man. His hand found Jadon's arm and squeezed, and Jadon leaned in, whispering something else, as Zion laughed harder.

"They're cute," Nita said.

"Um, yeah."

"How long have they—"

"No, really, North." That was Shaw's dad's voice.

Shaw turned in time to see it all happen: North making an impromptu takeaway container of grilled salmon out of two paper plates; Shaw's mother shaking her head and raising a hand; North shoving the plates at her with a manic grin; the plates hitting his mom's hand at the worst possible moment; the plates separating; grilled salmon everywhere.

"Excuse me," Shaw said as his mom stepped back, plucking at the front of her shift dress where the maple-soy glaze was spreading. His dad was casting about, probably looking for paper towels. North was on his knees picking up salmon.

"I'll get Breezi out of his hair," Nita said. "I'll tell her she should send him a picture of that new drill she bought."

"God, no, I want to go on vacation sometime again in this existence."

Laughing, Nita made her way toward her wife, who was offering pointed comments about how North should be picking up the salmon. The main piece of advice seemed to be "Do it better."

"You're the devil," Shaw shot sidelong to Nita as they separated.

He reached North as he was gathering himself to stand. Shaw's dad had found napkins, and he was dabbing at the linen dress while Shaw's mom tried to politely and nonverbally tell him to leave her the hell alone.

"Let me rinse this off," North mumbled.

"North, they're leaving, and they don't want salmon."

"It'll be fine; I'll be back in five seconds."

Shaw squeezed his boyfriend's arm.

"No," Shaw's dad said, his voice tight. "Thank you. We need to get going."

"It's a lovely home." Shaw's mom kept her gaze fixed on Shaw. "And a lovely party."

"Thank you for inviting us, Wild."

Apparently a thank-you was beyond the realm of possibility for Phoebe Aldrich, so she bussed her son's cheek and let her husband lead her to the gate in the privacy fence, and then they were gone.

"Oh my God," North groaned.

"It's fine."

"Oh my fucking God."

Shaw kissed him, but North's eyes were directed toward the sky, and he didn't return the kiss.

"I offered to rinse it off. It fell on the ground, and I ruined her dress, and I offered to rinse off food that had been on the ground and send it home with them."

"I did notice that."

"What the fuck is wrong with me?"

"Do you think Jadon and Zion are hooking up?"

"What?" North's gaze came down. "Why?"

"Well, the way they're standing, and there was this weird moment where Zion laughed and he touched Jadon and it was definitely a thing, like, my nipples—"

"Oh, they definitely want to bone, if they aren't doing it already. I meant, why do you care? Wait, what the fuck about your nipples?"

"Go wash your hands. I'll keep an eye on the burgers."

North eyed the plate of salmon, his expression contorted.

"Don't throw it away," Shaw said, reaching for the plate in North's hands. "We'll rinse it off and toss it back on the grill for a few minutes. I'll eat it. I'll put it in a salad. Oh! Or I can make that salmon-flavored baby food that I saw on Pinterest. Or that omega-3 rejuvenating eye mask where you use salmon instead of cucumber slices and—no, stop, don't put it in the trash!"

"I told him he could use the bathroom," Pari was saying. The party's flux had carried Jadon and Zion into conversation with Truck and Pari, and Shaw couldn't help noticing that Jadon and Zion's shoulders were brushing. "And he did look like he felt better when he came out. But honestly, I think he needed a decent meal and a night's sleep."

"Who are you talking about?" Shaw asked as he joined them.

"If you checked your voicemails," Pari said, "you'd already know."

"We've discussed this. I'm glad you're on board with the voicemail situation. I'm glad that you've finally caught up with 1990s technology. And I appreciate that you want to pass along messages that way. But it gets a little overwhelming when you leave forty to fifty voicemails every day, and most of them consist of things like 'I paperclipped that client report like you told me to,' and 'North's chair smells like a burrito, in a bad way.'"

"This from the guy who once sent me fourteen videos in a two-minute span," Jadon stage-whispered.

"Really?" Zion asked.

"He was very proud of himself for eating ice cream."

Zion's smile was huge, and he angled his body toward Jadon, as though sharing the expression with the cop. They were close to the same height, Shaw noticed, and Jadon wouldn't have to do much more than tilt his head for a kiss.

"I wasn't proud of myself for eating ice cream," Shaw said. "Well, actually, yes, I was. But the videos were because I was excited to find an avocado-based frozen dessert. And then I had to tell you about the flavor profile. And the top notes. And the bottom notes. And the crunchy, pointy part at the end of the cone that had mango syrup in it. Actually, I think I still have those videos—"

"He was a street kid," Pari said. "He came into the office and asked if he could use the bathroom. I know your official policy is to trample the poor and impoverished with your solid-gold heels tipped with the sharpened horn from a murdered unicorn—"

"I said one time that you couldn't let the can lady sleep under my desk!"

"—but some of us have consciences, and I wasn't going to send that poor boy away. He looked terrible, Shaw. And you ought to be ashamed of yourself for making me send him right back out onto the street."

"I didn't—I wasn't even there."

"But you would have. You'd have made me march him right into oncoming traffic. Thank God you were too busy doodling North's penis on my diploma to check your voicemails."

"In the first place, nobody leaves their associate's degree diploma facedown in a pile of random papers. That's asking for trouble. And in the second place, as I've told you literally a hundred times before, it wasn't North's penis, it was an anatomical rendering—"

"Excuse me?" North said.

"It wasn't North's penis," Truck said. "North's penis has that weird angle in the middle, like a pipefitter was in charge of putting it together."

"Excuse me?" North said again. There was a definite tone.

On the deck, Breezi was laughing so hard that she fell out of her folding chair while Nita tried to shush her.

"My dick does not have a—no." North shook his head. "I'm not doing this."

"Prove it," Truck said.

North's eyes narrowed.

"It would be pretty easy to prove," Shaw said.

"You're supposed to be watching the grill," North snapped, "not encouraging my Peeping Tom employees who keep trying to walk in on me when I'm taking a shower."

"Right," Shaw said, eyeing the grill, which seemed smokier than he remembered. "The grill."

"God damn it," North said as he marched toward the Weber kettle, fanning the air in front of him.

"He might have been casing the place," Zion said. He had a voice like someone stirring honey into scotch. "That kid."

"He wasn't," Pari said. "He needed to use the bathroom, and since Shaw's going to fire me for offering him the milk of human kindness—"

"You gave him my yak's milk? Pari, I was saving that."

Pari rolled her eyes, leaned into Truck's chest, and whispered something in hir ear that made Truck laugh.

"You'd be such a great mom, and I could definitely put a baby in you," Truck said when hir laughter had faded. Pari blushed and hid her face against Truck's neck. "I'll put the best baby in you."

Jethro Tull was singing about sandcastle virtues. At the edge of the fairy lights, the deep blue haze of dusk swallowed up the last of the day's long shadows.

"Are you really thinking about kids?" Jadon asked in the same tone he had used when he had asked Shaw if he was really planning on building a Mayan pyramid out of shoeboxes.

"Not seriously," Pari said, blushing even darker.

"Yes," Truck said at the same time.

"I mean, maybe," Pari said. She stroked Truck's chest. "When it feels right."

"We are," Breezi announced from the deck. Nita said something quiet, and Breezi shrugged and repeated, "We are. We're just looking for the right donor."

Shaw's gaze slid to Nita, who brushed something invisible from her shoulder and said, "We're talking seriously about children, yes."

"That's fantastic," Shaw said. "I'm going to do their natal charts, and I'll get them warding crystals, and if they're boys I'll teach them all sorts of manly things like how to shave and be feminists and chop firewood."

At the grill, North made a noise.

"Do you have something to say?" Shaw asked.

"I'm thinking about that apology shrine to a dead tree branch that took up all the walkable space in our bedroom for a month."

"What the hell is an apology shrine?" Breezi asked.

"What does it sound like?" North asked.

"It's not an apology shrine to the branch," Shaw clarified. "It's an apology shrine to the boxwood whose branch I broke. The branch is the memorial part, that's all."

"I came home, and he was curled up on the couch with the branch, crying. He'd gone through an entire box of tissues. So if that's the guy you want teaching your kids to chop firewood, good fucking luck."

"North!"

North shrugged and flipped a burger. He looked up for an instant, a smile in his ice-rim eyes, and his lips quirked into a kiss before he went back to the grill.

"I think we should all take a moment," Shaw announced, "to share with North how his toxic masculinity has affected us personally. I'll go first: sometimes I can't put my shoes on the shoe tray because his boots take up all the room."

"That was your opening move," Jadon muttered. "The shoe tray."

"My boots aren't the problem," North said. "The problem is that you have nine pairs of ladies' saddle shoes piled up on the tray because you were determined to perfect what you called your 'one-man, intersectional retelling' of *Grease*, only for some fucking reason, you think it actually involves grease, so you kept ruining new shoes and piling them up, and you keep telling yourself that Sandy wears saddle shoes, which she definitely does not."

"No, I keep telling you that Danny Zuko should have worn saddle shoes, but you don't listen."

"He's coveting my tool chest," Breezi shouted. When everyone looked at her, she turned redder than usual and mumbled, "Nita said Shaw said he's having sex dreams about it."

"What in the name of fuck—" North began.

"Hello?" The woman stood at the gate. She had light brown skin, glossy hair that spilled to her shoulders, and burnt-sugar eyes. Her blush-colored wrap dress was pinned right below her breasts. Her substantial breasts. Her mostly exposed, substantial breasts.

"Cassidy didn't have a sex dream about your tool chest," Shaw said. "He had a dream about your tool chest and definitely some morning wood, but I can't prove they were related."

"Who's Cassidy?" Jadon asked.

Zion laughed so hard he had to clutch Jadon's arm to hold himself up.

"Thin ice, motherfucker," North said, leveling the barbeque turner at Shaw.

"What's the joke?" Jadon was grinning at Zion. "Why's he calling North Cassidy?"

"Oh my God," Zion wheezed. "Oh my God."

"Don't worry about it, dumbass," North said.

"Hello? I'm sorry. Hi? Hello?" The woman had taken a few more steps into the backyard.

"Go on and laugh about it," North said, waving the turner ferociously at Shaw. "I hope you're enjoying this, because that was the last time I tell you anything about myself. Ever."

"North, no," Shaw wailed, "you still haven't finished telling me about your first kiss. The first one without a hardhat, I mean. When you were twenty-six."

"That's it," North said, "everybody go home. Party's over. I'm going to murder my boyfriend and spend the rest of my life happy and alone."

"Alone with your tool chests," Nita murmured, and Breezi burst into fresh laughter.

"Bunch of treacherous, ungrateful, backstabbing—"

"I'm looking for North McKinney," the woman shouted.

"Jesus Christ, lady. Can't you see what I'm fucking dealing with here?"

"You're Mr. McKinney?"

"Who's asking?"

"Belia Lopez, Channel 6 News Team. I'd like to talk to you about your husband. He said you'd want to comment on the story I'm interviewing him for."

North stared at her for a minute. Then he slammed the lid on the Weber and marched into the house. Ash and cinders whirled up in a cloud, red, then black, then gone. The kettle's metallic clang reverberated for a moment, competing with Jethro Tull, who was asking one more time to be spun back down the years. Then the music on the Bluetooth speaker cut off. Inside the house, a door slammed shut. The puppy leaped out of Pari's arms and began barking wildly.

"I think we should probably call it a night," Shaw said quietly.

Chapter 2

"DO YOU WANT me to tell her to go away?"

Their bedroom was dark, and it smelled like sweet smoke and North's sweat, still with the tang of sex from the afternoon, when North had braced him against the wall after his shower. The puppy squirmed in Shaw's arms, eager to get down. North's breathing was rapid and slightly frayed, but his laugh was solid, and his voice passed for steady when he said, "Pretty good coping skills, right? I run away as soon as someone brings up Tucker. God, teenagers handle their shit better than this."

"If you need time alone, you know that's always fine. Knowing when you need time to gather yourself is an important skill, North. She barged in, wanting to talk about some of the worst stuff in your life; there's no reason you shouldn't have needed some time to process that."

Nothing more a than shadow on the bed, North brought a hand up to his eyes.

"Do you want me to tell her—"

"No, I'll do it."

Neither of them moved. The puppy scrambled down from Shaw's arms and clicked across the boards, and North rolled onto his side and swept the little Löwchen up onto the mattress. Shaw moved to sit at the foot of the bed. His hand found North's leg, the calf muscle hot and tight under his touch. He ran his fingers over the denim.

"Why can't he leave me the fuck alone? He's out on bail, and he's got Biff making sure he'll never do any serious time for the assault charges, and he's getting what he wants in the divorce. Why can't he just go away?"

Shaw knew why. Some of it, anyway. He knew it in that place inside himself, the green-black waters under the frozen crust of consciousness, but not in a way he could put into words. All he could do was stroke North's leg and say, "I'll tell her to leave."

"No." North sat up, kissed the puppy, kissed Shaw, and repeated, "I'll do it."

"You taste like that when I come home sometimes. Do you kiss the dog all day while I'm gone?"

North swung his legs off the mattress.

"If I've got a competitor, I have a right to know."

North made a disgusted noise.

"If you get a furball from licking him too much, I'm not taking you to the vet."

The middle finger waved a lazy goodbye as North padded toward the door.

She was in the living room, pulling her hair over one shoulder, head turned to study the pictures on the wall. A thin layer of sweat glistened on her nape. The blush-colored wrap was darker where it was glued to the small of her back.

"How the fuck did you get in here?" North asked.

"The door was open." She was still studying the pictures. North and Shaw at the Lake of the Ozarks. Swimsuits, sunscreen, Shaw leaning into the plumb line of North's body. North and Shaw at Gulf Shores, the waters tropically blue, the sand white and crusted with salt, the palmetto-thatch hut where they served drinks so cold that Shaw's hand had ached around them. North and Shaw when they were kids, barely more than kids, sitting on the quad of Chouteau College at dusk, North's arm loose across Shaw's shoulders. The picture had been taken from behind, at an angle, capturing them in profile. Whatever they were looking at was lost. Who had taken that picture? Percy? Rufus? Tucker seemed like an oddly strong possibility.

Turning, the woman took them in with an avid gaze. "I came in because the alternative was stand outside by myself. Your friends left. The Indian girl would have clawed my eyes out if her boyfriend hadn't carried her off."

"Datemate," North said flatly.

Belia gave a one-shouldered shrug and a smile that didn't touch the hunger in her eyes.

"You know, you really shouldn't go inside someone else's house without being invited," Shaw said. "North is always telling me that. One time, he made me dress up in this awful disguise, and I had to go door to door, and then I met Lola, and she wanted me to come in for tea because I looked like her grandson, and I said, 'Really? He dresses like a clown too?' and Lola and I got into the weeds about that because she didn't think there was anything wrong with the clothes, and—"

"A polo and khakis are not clown clothes," North said. "Have you ever even seen a clown?"

"Once, when I had that psychic transmigration to the Chicago World's Fair, and—"

"And that old lady pushed you down a flight of stairs because you immediately ruined your cover. She was going to club you to death and bury you in the flower beds."

"She took advantage of me!" Shaw flashed a reassuring smile at Belia. "Not of my body, I mean."

"Yes, of your body. She pushed you down a fucking flight of stairs."

"But I want her to know that it wasn't sexual. She didn't take advantage of me sexually."

"She didn't think Lola took advantage of you sexually. Nobody thought that. Nobody would ever think that. That was back when you were a dried-up virgin, anyway. God. Better times."

"Ok, now that's rude, because this afternoon when someone came out of the shower with his wang like a flagpole—"

"I'm afraid I don't have all night," Belia said.

"It's not a long story," Shaw said. "Actually, that's a separate issue. Staying power isn't exactly his strong suit. Sure, there's a whole Mount Vesuvius situation at the end, but sometimes a guy likes the buildup to last longer than just being bitten on the back of the neck—"

"Will you shut up?" North gritted out.

"She asked to hear my story about Lola."

"No. She didn't."

"Oh." Shaw rubbed his nose. "Then why am I telling it?"

"I don't know. Nobody fucking knows."

"Because Lola invited me inside!" A triumphant finger in the air, Shaw added, "And you should never go inside a stranger's house without being invited."

"Do you need him at the newsroom?" North asked. "He can be your coffee bitch. Or if the guys are horny, he can be their butt bitch. Or any kind of bitch, actually, as long as he's no longer under this roof and driving me out of my fucking mind."

"First of all, bitch is an offensive word. Unless it's been reclaimed? Has it been reclaimed, Belia?"

Belia stared at them.

"And second of all, you know I wrote seventeen pages of field notes on the ethology of the coffee bitch, so I'd be pretty good at that job. And third of all, it wouldn't be only the guys, North. Pegging is an empowering sexual experience that dozens of women every year—"

"Who the fuck are you, lady? And why the fuck haven't you gotten out of my house yet?"

"Belia Lopez. Channel Six News Team." She handed him a card.

"You already said that. If that's all you've got, then get the fuck out. Next time, I'll call the police on you for trespassing."

"As I said, I've been talking to your husband for a story that I'm working on. He suggested that you would like to comment on it."

"I wouldn't."

"I would," Shaw offered.

"And Tucker's not my husband. He's my ex-husband. Get your fucking facts straight."

"My apologies," she murmured coolly. She eyed them for a moment. The air conditioner kicked on again, stirring the muggy air. "I'd love to do a joint interview."

"Oh, we're really good at those," Shaw said. "One time the guy interviewing us got so excited he ran out of the room."

"He ran out of the room at minute twenty-nine of Dong Bait, subtitle, The Shaw Aldrich Story, sub-subtitle The Virgin Years."

"I meant you and your husband." Another cool smile. "Ex-husband."

North's laugh was jagged. "You're kidding."

"He's telling an exceptional story."

"He was always good at that. I believed the golf ones until I started finding other guys' underwear in our bed."

"He says he's been framed for the assault on Mr. Aldrich. He claims that there's a criminal syndicate in the city and that you, your father, and your agency, even the reclusive and fabulously wealthy Aldrich family are all tied up in it."

After a few slow, deep breaths, North said, "Get out of our house."

"My credentials are excellent. I'd handle your story fairly. If you're not familiar with my work, watch Channel Six tonight. You'll see my piece about the alleged cop killer, Darold Smith. I'm the only one who found where he'd been hiding, and we're doing an exclusive." Belia smiled. She had perfect, television teeth. "Watch tonight and see. I bet I'll find the gun he used before the police do."

"No."

"I'm doing this story with or without you."

"And you'll get a fucking slander suit slapped on you so hard you won't know your tits from your ass."

"Don't say tits," Shaw whispered.

"No, I don't think I will." The eagerness in her eyes sharpened. "I have at least one piece of evidence that corroborates the story."

"The story is bullshit. I watched my piece of shit husband try to murder Shaw. Shaw was in a cast for weeks, he still gets terrible headaches, he had internal bleeding, and my only regret is that I didn't cut that son of a bitch's throat when I had the chance."

"So you deny that members of a criminal organization influenced members of a jury at the request of you and your father?"

Nostrils flaring, North was silent for a moment. Then he said, "We're done."

"You want me on your side. I can help—"

"Get out."

With a tiny smirk, Belia drew her hair over her shoulder again. She cast Shaw an interested look, and then she sauntered toward the front door. She took her time opening it, and when she stepped outside, she turned on the porch. "Think about—"

North slammed the door so hard it rattled in its frame. A framed papyrus scroll, on which Shaw had written a prayer to Hestia, fell. It hit the floor, and glass shattered and sprayed across the dark-stained boards.

"God damn it," North shouted, kicking shards of glass.

"I'll clean it up."

"Why the fuck did you have to put that fucking piece of shit up in the first place?"

"I said I'll clean it up."

"God fucking damn it," North shouted, and then he snatched up the puppy and stalked toward the back door.

Chapter 3

NORTH LEFT THE PUPPY in the fenced yard and cut through the garage at the back of the lot. He was still holding that woman's card, and he thought about tearing it up. Instead, he tucked it into his wallet. So he wouldn't forget her name. On his way through the garage, he liberated the pack of American Spirits that he'd taped to the bottom of the GTO's driver's seat. Then, in the alley, he smoked down two and was halfway through the third when the rage washed out of him. For a while, he slumped against the cinderblock garage, eyes closed, the heat of the cigarette's ember crawling toward his fingers. When it burned him, he dropped it and toed it out. Mosquitos whined at his ear.

He cut through the garage again, replacing the pack of cigarettes on his way, and examined the backyard. One of the folding chairs lay on its side. The kettle grill leaked a few final wisps of smoke. The puppy was investigating the climbing roses that the last owner had planted along one side of the privacy fence. Under the twinkle of the fairy lights, the place looked like the aftermath of the Rapture—everything good snatched up and gone, and North McKinney left behind with all the shit.

He started with the grill. The burgers were briquettes by now, but the brats, although split and a little charred, had survived. He covered them with foil and set them in the kitchen. He packed up the folding chairs. He emptied the coolers, beer going on the deck, ice going into the grass. The pellets crunched and scraped against the plastic lining, shockingly cold when they brushed his hands.

When he looked up from dumping the last cooler, Shaw was leaning against the deck's rail. Today, Shaw had chosen a Hawaiian shirt printed with turquoise fronds and jean cut-offs. The clothes exposed the thin, sculpted lines of his body. He'd let his auburn hair down, and it fell past the clean slice of his jaw. Hazel eyes set in that impossibly beautiful face tracked North.

Standing below him, North said, "Asshole requesting permission to come aboard."

Shaw leaned over the rail and kissed him. He made a face. "You smell like smoke."

"Kids in the alley."

"You taste like smoke."

"Permission to come aboard?"

"I cleaned up the glass, so you can bring the puppy in."

They ate at the white gateleg table in the kitchen. The ceiling fan swung lazily overhead, helping to circulate the air conditioner's vain attempts at making the place cooler. North had his brats in buns he had meant to toast on the grill. Shaw ate his in lettuce wraps.

"I'm sorry I shouted at you," North said.

Shaw waved a limp piece of lettuce. "I know you weren't mad at me. I was more scared when you went on and on about how I ate all the pink Starbursts."

With the half-eaten brat, North smeared the coarse-grain mustard across his plate. "I think I need some time to cool down."

"Yeah, of course."

"By myself."

Shaw was quiet for a moment. He tore the scrap of lettuce into strips. He picked up each strip and snapped it in half.

"We talked about this," North said as gently as he could.

"Of course. I agree a hundred percent. You never had time when you could be yourself, not with Tucker, not with your dad, and I understand: you want time when you can do that, be yourself, and figure out how to be you, how to be independent and autonomous and self-actualized. I think that's fantastic. I think it's the best idea you've ever had. I'm totally signed on."

Sighing, North stood and carried his plate to the sink.

"What? I'm agreeing with you. I'm supporting you."

North watched the spray flick granules of mustard across the stainless steel. He turned the faucet off. Water dripped from his fingers.

"I fully and completely and a million-percent support you."

"Ok, Shaw. Do you want the living room or the bedroom?"

"What do you want?"

North had to fight the urge to pinch the bridge of his nose. "I'm asking you."

"But I want you to decide."

It was a fight waiting to happen, like the charge in the air before a lightning strike. North shook it off. "I'll take the living room. If you don't mind."

"No, that's great."

After the dishes had been loaded, North changed into shorts and settled onto the couch, the puppy curled up next to him, and flipped channels until he found a Cards game. They were playing the Brewers, and things didn't look great. On another night, North would have been swearing a streak and providing some input on the basic fucking essentials of baseball that Mike fucking Shildt apparently still needed help with. Tonight, though, he tried to turn his brain off and disappear into the rhythm of pitch and swing, the bubble of halide light, the scuff of red clay on the mound. At the back of his brain, hammering on the glass, were Tucker and his dad and Ronnie.

What made it all so fucking awful was that Belia wasn't wrong. North's father had approached Ronnie, who was involved in some sort of criminal operation, for help with a civil suit that a man had brought against North. David McKinney had done this without asking North what he wanted. He had done it without even telling North, until it was too late, what he was doing. But it had happened, and Ronnie had used the fact as blackmail, trying to coerce North and Shaw into helping him steal valuable intellectual property from Shaw's family's business. When North and Shaw had turned the tables and gotten Ronnie arrested, Ronnie had lost his mind. He had turned his attention to revenge, obsessed now with destroying North and Shaw, and Tucker had been his instrument. North still had nightmares about that moment in the Aldrichs' home, when Tucker had shoved Shaw off the landing, and for a moment, Shaw had hung in the air, the toes of his bunny slippers already drawn down by gravity. When those nightmares came, North woke with a scream in his throat, the sheets soaked through in cold sweat, and he spent the rest of those pre-dawn hours with the CZ in one hand, a round in the chamber.

Behind him, the door creaked. North settled into the couch, gaze locked on the TV. Another Bud Light commercial. The trimmed-down version of the one they'd used in the Super Bowl, the one based on that fantasy show Shaw had a hard-on for. Steps whispered against the boards behind him and into the kitchen. The steps came back. A cold Schlafly, their summer lager, already open and sweating, moved into his field of vision.

"I'm not interrupting," Shaw whispered, "but I thought one beer—just one—might help you relax."

North made a grateful noise and took the beer. He caught Shaw's fingers, kissed the tips, and released him. The steps padded away, and the bedroom door creaked shut.

Being alone wasn't new to North. He'd been alone, in different ways, for most of his life. Growing up. At school. Even when he'd been married, even when he'd had his husband in the same room. But having a time when he could be unguarded, when all the walls could come down, that was different. It wasn't even exactly the same as privacy, because they overlapped in strange places: there were ways he could be himself with Shaw, and there were places and times he needed privacy to drop his guard. To have all of it together, though—well, the word autonomous was a good one. He was trying, on the cusp of twenty-seven, to figure out who he was as an individual, without anyone else around to make him want to be something else. Some days, that sentence sounded so fucking pathetic it made him want to spend the rest of his life under the couch cushions, collecting fallen change. At least he'd be providing a service.

The protest of old hinges and shift in the air made him intensify his gaze on the TV. More of those soft steps—barefoot this time, because they had the slightly sticky sound of skin on the floorboards. But instead of heading into the kitchen, Shaw hovered in North's field of vision.

"Can I get you anything?" he whispered.

"No," North said in a normal voice.

Whisper: "Another beer?"

"Still working on this one."

Whisper: "A snack?"

"No, Shaw." He paused. "Thank you."

The barefoot steps moved away. The fridge opened, jars clinking in the door. The ice maker rumbled and gave off its popping noise that meant another load of cubes was about to be discharged. The clink of a plate. The soft-close drawers. Flatware. Unidentifiable sounds: crinkle-crackle, and something hitting the plate. More steps.

A plate of ridged potato chips and sour cream and onion dip floated into view.

"In case you get the nibbles," Shaw whispered.

North took the plate.

"I'm going back to my room."

"Thank you," North said, trying to keep the edge out of his voice.

"Unless you need anything."

"Shaw, we've been over this. A few times actually. I know you think I'm weird for wanting some time alone, but—"

"No, no, no." Whispered protests. "I think it's great. I think it's smart. You're totally right. I'm going back to my room right now."

Footsteps away. Footsteps back.

"Our room. I meant our room."

"Oh my God."

"I'm going to our room right now."

Seconds later, the door closed, and North picked up a chip. The sour cream and onion dip worked its magic. Between that and the beer, a knot between his shoulders loosened, even though the game was 2-2 now, and the Cardinals had rolled over for both runs like a rent boy at the end of the month.

Part of North's mind couldn't turn off, though. He was still working on the problem of Ronnie, still trying to figure out where Ronnie might be hiding, what he might try next. Finding Ronnie had been a dead end; North had tried all his usual haunts, had tried to shake down every piece of shit he could think of. For now, he had resigned himself to the fact that he wouldn't be catching up with Ronnie in person—not until Ronnie made a mistake.

The fact, though, was that last time, Ronnie had come close to succeeding. Next time, he might not make a mistake. The attack orchestrated through Tucker had been effective precisely because North hadn't expected it—Tucker had been paid for the attack, yes, but Tucker had simply thought he was helping Ronnie collect on a debt and, in the process, been getting his revenge on North and Shaw. The attack had worked because North had let his guard down around Tucker, which would never happen again. If Ronnie tried the same trick again—if next time, it wasn't a car bomb, or a hired gun waiting in the bedroom closet, or a knife in a crowded place—then North would be ready; he wasn't trusting anyone except Shaw from here on out.

The whisper of the door made North groan, although he tried to quash it. The clinging sound of bare skin against the humid boards announced Shaw's approach.

"Got a beer," North said. "Got a snack. All I need is some quiet."

But the steps came closer, and then Shaw was standing behind North, out of sight but registering as a presence of body heat and disturbed air flow and the smell of his body. Shaw lowered himself, head behind North's now, and warm hands settled on North's shoulders.

"You're stressed." He tugged on the tee. "That woman ruined your night. You keep watching your game, and I'm going to make you feel better."

North grunted.

"Off," Shaw said with a soft laugh, tugging on the tee again, and when North raised his arms, Shaw turned him out of the shirt. Then Shaw's hands were skating up North's chest, his mouth on North's neck. Goose bumps broke out across North's body when Shaw nipped at the sensitive spot between his shoulder blades.

"No fucking way," North said. "I wanted alone time, remember?"

"Pretend I'm not here."

But the little shit licked that spot again, the textured heat of his mouth making North hard enough that he had to adjust himself.

"Cut it out, Shaw."

But the warning had little force behind it. From behind him came the sound of a bottle being uncapped, and then something squirting out.

"If you're prepping yourself, you are in for some serious disappointment."

Shaw laughed again. "Jeez, I'm trying to be nice to you. Be quiet and have your alone time. Lean forward a little. Yeah, like that."

A moment later, Shaw's hands came to rest again on his shoulders. They were slick with oil already warm from his body heat, and his fingers glided across North's upper back, smoothing the oil into the skin, probing for tight muscles, caressing his arms. Because Shaw could be a dick, he spent a lot of time on that spot that drove North wild, and North had to adjust himself again—this time, he left his hand there. He was intensely aware of a drop of oil sliding down his spine, dampening his waistband when the elastic collected it.

Whatever other bullshit had come out of Shaw's New Age streak—crystals and spells to Greek broads and the time he'd tried to preserve a lock of North's hair (taken while North was asleep) in a magic amulet—he'd hit gold with massages. Sometimes, he dug deep, until the pleasure was painful in its own way—or maybe the pain was pleasurable. Tonight, he was gentle, stroking away tension, the warm, slick oil softening his touch. Sandalwood and frankincense curled up in North's chest like a fevered prayer. North made a noise that sounded embarrassingly gratified.

"I know," Shaw whispered with a tiny laugh. "We can stay like this if you want. Or you can lie down, and I can finish the rest of you."

North made himself find his voice, although it was a little scratchy when he finally did. "Breezi goes to the garage."

Those silken fingers kept moving. "Hm?"

"She's always tearing apart their cars because Nita hates the smell of engine grease. It keeps her out of Breezi's space."

"I'm insulted that you're thinking about our lesbian neighbors' garage right now."

"Plus she's got all those *Ladies with Power Tools* calendar pages stapled to the pegboard."

Shaw made an amused sound.

"Maybe I'll do that," North said, falling back into Shaw's touch. "I'll hang calendars of pinup boys and motorcycles. I've got those postcards you bought me from that modern art exhibit, the one with the twinks trying to lift their appletinis. Oh, and one of those singing fish. Maybe a stag's head."

"Don't even think about it."

"Breezi—"

"Breezi can get away with that because she's married."

"Christ, if I have to get married again to have some peace and quiet, then let's get married."

Time for a commercial. Michael Bublé was hawking sparkling water.

"Well?" North said.

"Well what?"

The sandalwood and frankincense had started a bonfire in North's chest. He worked his jaw. "What do you think about that?"

"About getting married?"

"No, Shaw, about hanging a singing bass on the wall."

Shaw's fingers slowed, but they began moving again almost immediately. "I think it's a great idea."

"No, you don't."

"Yes, I do."

North focused on the far wall. It was the picture of them on the quad. Christ knew who had taken it or why. But North remembered that evening, remembered how frightening it had felt to sling his arm around Shaw, even though they were both pretending they were just buddies. You go on pretending, he thought. You go on pretending and pretending.

Shaw's hands left his shoulders, and a moment later, Shaw came around the couch, kneeling between North's legs. With glistening fingers, he caught the double waistbands of North's shorts and trunks, and he tugged. "Let me show you how good of an idea I think it is."

"Shaw—"

"Please let me show you." Eyes downcast, he rubbed North's flagging erection through the poly-spandex blend. "I want to get married."

North fell back against the couch. Shaw had draped a towel there, he now realized, and he wondered how much of this had been planned.

"I want to get married to you," Shaw was whispering, the words directed to North's crotch. He tugged on the waistbands again, and when North didn't lift his hips, he simply shifted his grip and pulled down the front of the shorts, tucking the waistbands beneath North's balls. The combination of Shaw's persistence, the relatively cooler air, and the fact that Shaw was the most beautiful man North had ever known had a predictable effect on him. Shaw said, "Mmm," and leaned closer, giving kittenish licks to the head of North's dick, then long stripes from base to tip as it lengthened, and then taking it in his mouth. It took him a few tries to take North all the way to the root, and then he held himself there, staring up at North. His lips wrapped around North's cock. His hazel eyes dark with arousal. North surprised both of them by grabbing the back of Shaw's head and holding him there.

The flare of panic in Shaw's eyes was momentary and then gone.

"Squeeze my ankle if I hold you too long," North said roughly. "Squeeze it now so I know you understand."

Shaw squeezed his ankle.

North changed his grip, two-handed now, and began to move Shaw's head back and forth. Shaw gasped wetly for air, but North only gave him a few seconds before pulling him forward again. He kept a count in his head, varying the time, until spit and precome ran down Shaw's chin, and his lips were swollen, his eyes glassy as he gave himself over to this. Staring at him like that, North lost control. He pulled Shaw onto him again and unloaded, shaking as he clutched Shaw's head, counting each pulse the way he'd counted the seconds. Then, palm to Shaw's forehead, he pushed Shaw off and sagged against the couch.

"Holy fuck," Shaw was whispering, his voice raw. "Holy fuck. Holy fuck."

"Yeah," North muttered.

"But North, I mean—oh my God."

Elbowing up from his half-reclining position, North took him in again: flushed, face a mess, hair wild. "Are you ok? Christ, I cannot believe I did that. Did I hurt you?"

Shaw was touching his jock, where a stain showed that either he'd gotten off during the festivities or had, at the least, leaked like a faucet.

"Shaw?"

"Fucking hell, North, that was amazing. I mean, I'm going to be eating Jell-O for a week, but that was insane."

North tried for a smile. "Yeah."

Shaw stretched up, his body sinuous with muscle, and kissed North. He squeezed North's hand. "Let's shower together. I feel so close to you right now, and I don't want that to go away. Ever."

"You go on," North said. "I need to sit here for a minute."

"Ok. We'll cuddle."

North opened his mouth, but a knock at the door cut him off. The knock was frantic and hard, and it sent a flush of adrenaline through North, all the night's thoughts rushing back at him from their dark corners.

The knock stopped. Then it began again.

"Go get a gun," North whispered, pushing Shaw toward the bedroom. Standing, he stuffed himself back into his shorts. He took a step toward the door. "Who is it?"

"I need to see North McKinney." A man's voice. A young guy. "I need to see him right now. Right now. Right now. I need to see North McKinney right now."

Shaw was still standing there, so North whispered, "Gun," and Shaw darted for the bedroom.

North tried to remember if they'd locked the screen door and couldn't. He heard a step, glanced back, and saw Shaw in the bedroom doorway, naked except for the jock, holding his Springfield in both hands. He nodded.

When North opened the door, his first thought was relief: he could see the kid's hands, and they were empty. The kid paced on their small stoop—two steps and turn, two steps and turn—and he was mumbling to himself. His movements were jerky and erratic, hands flying up as though to catch something, then falling back with broken, fluttering motions. He smelled like BO and something slightly acrid—whatever was making him haul ass tonight. Brown skin. Dark hair. Wide eyes with hard, contracted pupils that didn't respond to the porch light or the flood of light from inside the house.

"What—" North began.

"Nik?" Shaw said behind him. "Nikshay? Nik?"

The boy's—Nik's—head swung around, and he fixed on Shaw. "You said if I need anything, he'd help. Borealis. North McKinney. You said if I needed—"

"Yeah, yes, sure. Nik, what—"

"I need you to find my friend."

Chapter 4

FROM THE KITCHEN, Shaw studied Nik, who was pacing in their living room, hands gesticulating for an invisible audience, the mumble of words unceasing. His hair had been cut into a tight fade and a faux hawk, but the fade had gotten shaggy, and the faux hawk drooped in the front, frizzy where humidity sent the individual strands curling. The peach-fuzz mustache still made him look like a kid, but his full lips were far too adult—and made Shaw think of his own mouth, minutes before. He wore a grubby white t-shirt, the five-for-ten-dollars kind that North stocked in his drawers, instead of the designer tee Shaw remembered. White-on-white Skechers, dingy, instead of the expensive Nikes.

"Who the fuck is that," North asked in an undertone, "and why is he in our fucking house?"

"Nikshay. He goes by Nik. I don't know his last name."

"I got that much already."

Nik spun, adjusting his t-shirt absently. It had slid across his shoulders as he paced, exposing a fresh scar, the skin pink and tight, on his collar bone. He was still talking. He'd lost an eyetooth over the last few months.

"Sweetheart," North said, cupping Shaw's face and turning it toward him, "he's breaking your heart for some reason, and I know this is hard for you, but you need to tell me what's going on."

"Right." Shaw sniffled, surprised to find his eyes were wet. "Right. Right. It's just, he was right there, and I was talking to him, and I knew I needed to help him, but I didn't, and now he's like this and—" It was the same problem, the same weakness, the thing that never got better: his mind ramping up, imagining every terrible possibility, and then imagining them again, and then imagining them again. Unregulated empathy, Dr. Farr called it. Crisp white sheets of thought, and Shaw's manic imagination scribbling across them in fat charcoal whorls. The nights Nik had slept with cardboard over him, to protect against the cold. No, worse than that. The nights Nik had let guys get rough with him, hurt him, for a place to sleep. No, worse. The night a john had knocked his tooth out, and Nik had still blown him for the cash on the dresser.

GREGORY ASHE

No, worse, worse, worse. The night the guy had liked putting out his cigarette—

"Stop it," North said, Shaw's face in his hands. "Or I'm calling Dr. Farr right now."

"No." Shaw drew a wet breath, coughed, and breathed more deeply. "I'm ok."

Considering him, North frowned. "No. You're not. Let's get you dressed. If Dr. Farr can't Facetime with you, we'll find someone—"

"He's the kid I met the night we went after Tony Gillman. Remember that? He was on the same street corner, and I talked to him for a few minutes. His parents are dead, and his uncle stole his inheritance, I think. Something like that. I did tell him that we'd try to help him, but he never came to the agency, and first I was recovering from, you know, Gillman, and then we got busy when we were hired to find Flip, and—and I forgot."

"Shaw, you met him once, right before a guy almost beat you to death. You don't know his last name. You don't even know if Nik is his real name. There's not a single person in this entire world who'd think you let that kid down."

Shaw's gaze slid back to Nik. The boy was leaning forward, inspecting the hearth, and a gold chain swung under his t-shirt. By some miracle, he'd kept the chain—and at what cost, Shaw wanted to ask. The nights he must have wanted to hock it so he could have something in his belly. No, worse. The nights he—

"No," North said. His voice was soft but firm. His fingers found Shaw's and laced their hands together. "No, Shaw. If you feel yourself sliding like that, you're going to grab me tight, aren't you?"

Exhaustion made standing feel like swimming, like Shaw was kicking just to tread water.

"Tell me you heard me."

Instead, Shaw clutched his hand once.

"Let's get you dressed," North said, a weary note mixing with something like resignation.

Apparently, that was literal, because North escorted him into the bedroom. He supervised while Shaw pulled on lightweight joggers and a tank, and then he grabbed a zip-up hoodie from the closet and tossed it at him.

"It's September.

"Put it on."

"It's a million degrees."

"Great. Put it on. You can take it off when you stop shivering."

When North turned toward a noise in the living room, Shaw scowled at his back.

28

"Make that face again," North said, still looking out at the living room, "and I'm going to give you ten on each cheek. That'll give you something to think about while you're standing around the rest of the night."

"I wasn't making a face."

North pointed to the mirror that hung on the closet door.

Shaw scrubbed the scowl off his face.

When Shaw had finished dressing, North took his hand, squeezed once, and stayed motionless until Shaw squeezed back. Then they went out into the living room again. Nik was still pacing, mumbling to himself, head down. He whirled around at the sound of their steps, and for a moment, those glassy eyes registered nothing. Then he cleared his throat and started walking again.

"If you stole something," North said, "I'm going to take it out of your hide with interest, so you'd better put it back."

"What's he going to steal? Your action figures?"

"Those are collectibles—" North managed to cut himself off somehow. Nik was still wandering the house, and North followed him with his eyes. He clapped his hands once, the sound cracking through the house. "Kid, sit your ass down."

"Do you check these?" Nik said, pointing at the ceiling. At the smoke detector, Shaw realized. "That's how they listen to you. Those, and the TV, and the microwave. Do you have a microwave?" He spun and charged into the kitchen.

They found him standing in front of the microwave, the door open, studying the glass tray. After a moment, he set it aside dismissively, laying it on the edge of the sink. He was trying to fit his head inside the microwave, apparently to inspect it, when he bumped the tray and it slid into the sink with a loud cracking noise.

"All right—" North began.

Shaw caught his shirt and shook his head.

"How the fuck am I supposed to make popcorn?" North pointed at the microwave. "How am I supposed to make nachos, Shaw? Nachos?"

Raising his voice to cut through Nik's mumbling, Shaw said, "Nik, they can't listen to us because I put selenite in all the walls. And in the basement. And in the attic. And I sewed a piece into the lining of North's jacket, even though he never said thank you."

"I didn't say thank you because I didn't ask you to do it and because you ruined the lining of that jacket. And because when I stumbled and ran into that wall, the edges on that fucking rock gave me a bone bruise that lasted six weeks."

"It's a crystal, not a rock. Nik, are you listening to me? They can't hear us because the resonant frequency of selenite is the exact same as the frequency they use for their transmitters—"

"Do not encourage him," North whispered.

"—so it makes all their listening devices useless."

Nik was still examining cheese spatters from North's last nacho endeavor. Shaw took his arm gently, and Nik started, his head cracking against the top of the microwave. He stumbled back, and Shaw released him. When he hit the counter, he slid along it until he'd cornered himself at the far end of the kitchen. Shaw raised both hands, palms out.

"Hey," Shaw said. "You're ok. You're safe here. Nobody's listening. Nobody can get in here."

"They'll get me when I leave. They take kids off the street."

"Who takes people off the street?"

"The government. They take you to their labs and they cut you open, and they put somebody else inside you, and when you come back, you're different, only nobody knows."

"I'm calling an ambulance," North said.

"No," Shaw said. Then, heat rushing into his face, he added, "Not yet. Please."

After a moment, North made a gesture for him to wrap it up.

"You look like you might be hungry, Nik. Do you want to sit down? Have something to eat?"

Strangely, the offer seemed to work, and Nik sat at the gateleg table. His leg bounced, his knee cracking against the white-painted wood every few moments. Shaw sat next to him, talking a constant stream, anything that popped into his head. Dark marks ringed Nik's eyes, and his head sagged from time to time, as though he couldn't keep himself upright much longer. His lids kept trying to close and then flying open, those hard pupils cutting wildly around the room as though someone might have tried to sneak up on him. North made up a plate: a brat, potato salad, a half-cob of roasted corn, lemonade. When he set down the plate, Shaw caught his hand and kissed it, and North turned his fingers to cradle the side of Shaw's face for a moment.

Nik watched them, and his bouncing leg slowed. It didn't stop, but it slowed. He wiped his face and then fiddled with his shirt, dragging it into place again, his fingers checking the fresh scar without him seeming to be aware of it. That pungent mix of BO and chemical stimulant was stronger in the small space of the kitchen.

"You're fucking. I knew you were fucking. I could smell it when I walked in. That's all right. That's all right. That's all right. That's all right. That's all—"

"Jesus," North whispered.

"Will you get my Xanax?"

North tweaked Shaw's ear and then headed out of the kitchen. When he came back, he was carrying the brown prescription vial, and he shook a pill out into his hand. He passed it to Shaw.

"Nik, you need some medicine." Shaw held out the pill. "You took something, and it's making your body work too hard. You've been going fast for a while now, right? Why don't we slow things down?"

Nik eyed the pill. His leg was bouncing faster.

"Go on. It's all right."

"They—"

"No," Shaw said. "You're safe here. Remember all that selenite? And you came here because you wanted help, right? So this is us helping. This is how it starts."

After a moment, Nik snatched the pill and dry-swallowed it. He got up and paced again, checking the windows, rattling the door handles, hands flailing as he explained something under his breath. But ten minutes later, he let Shaw lead him back to the table, and ten minutes after that, his leg had stopped bouncing, and he was holding a fork, picking at the food. The puppy, who had been lurking in the other room, finally decided it was safe to approach. He gave Nik's Skechers one sniff, but when Nik leaned forward to spear a piece of brat, the puppy scurried to North, who scooped him up and held him.

"Her name's Malorie," Nik said. "Malorie Walton."

The puppy yapped once. North shushed the little dog, stroking one hand over his head.

"What happened to Malorie?" Shaw asked.

"She's gone." Nik rolled the corn on the cob with his fork. "I can't think real good right now. They say she ran away, but she didn't run away. Something bad happened to her."

"Why do you think that?"

"I met her at the shelter. She was in a bad spot for a while. She was doing stuff for this guy. And she was using. But now she's got to think about the baby, so she cleaned up her life, and she has a real job, and she doesn't do what Jesse tells her to do anymore. She wouldn't run away. She was saving up to move out to California. She almost had enough money." He fumbled in his pocket and produced a strip of four photos featuring him and a girl. Malorie Walton had beaded braids, and although the photos were in black and white, Shaw could tell that her skin was darker than Nik's—closer to black than Nik's soft brown. She couldn't have been older than seventeen.

"How old is she?"

"Fifteen?"

The hair and makeup made her look older. "And you?"

"Sixteen last month."

Shaw was silent for a moment. "Do you think she could have moved without telling you?"

"No!" The fork clattered against the plate. "We were going to go together!"

"Ok."

"She wouldn't have left. She wouldn't have run off, wouldn't have…disappeared like this. We were going to meet up at the movies, but she never came. Something bad, something really bad, something—"

"How'd you find us?" North asked.

It took a moment for Nik to process the question. Then he picked up the fork and jabbed it at Shaw. "He told me."

"No, he told you about the agency. But that building burned down, and you showed up on our doorstep."

Nik bent over the plate. The fork skittered over the glass laminate. Lemonade sloshed onto the gateleg's top. He'd missed too many meals—or maybe whatever he was juiced on was eating away spare flesh—but he'd barely touched his food.

"The kid who showed up at the office," Shaw said. "Pari said a kid came into the office."

"I went there. You were gone." He raised his head, a defiant look focused on North. "You've got an ad in the *Riverfront Times*."

"Now the rest of it," North said.

"Make him go away," Nik said, grabbing Shaw's hand. Shaw fought the urge to pull back from the sudden, tight grip, slick with sweat. "Tell him to leave us alone. You gave me medicine. You're nice to me. I feel a lot better, but he's being a jerk, and I want him to get out."

"He said the same thing," North said, jerking his head at Shaw, "when I came home and interrupted his exorcism."

"The dog was possessed," Shaw explained. "He wouldn't stop barking."

"Because of that fucking gardening hat," North snapped. "And I'll tell you what I told him: stop fucking whining because I'm not going anywhere."

"Make him—"

"How the fuck did you find our home?"

"I went into your office! I told her I needed to use the bathroom, and then I went back to your office. Your desk is really messy. Someone puked on it."

North made a disgusted noise.

"Actually, that's homemade cat puke," Shaw said. "See, I have a theory that—"

"I need to talk to you," North growled, yanking on the hoodie so hard that Shaw came up from the seat. Shaw freed himself from Nik's grip and stumbled after North into their bedroom. North shut the door, set the puppy down, took out his phone, and placed a call on speaker. While it rang, he said, "This whole thing feels weird."

"He's on speed. Actually, probably meth."

"No duh. I'm talking about how he looks at—"

"What do you want, McKinney?" The voice from the phone belonged to Diamond Kelso, a detective in the Metropolitan Police's Juvenile Unit. They'd met her when she'd still been in uniform, and they'd collaborated with her—loosely—on a previous case involving a runaway. "I was in the bath."

"We have a kid who showed up here tonight. At our house. He's cranked—he's on something, anyway—and he's telling us his friend disappeared."

The silence on the other end of the call was broken by a few quiet splashes. "Ok."

"So I drive him to the station, and he fills out a missing person report, right?"

"That's about it."

"Diamond," Shaw broke in, "this girl, she's a kid. She's a black girl who went missing. And you know how it works: nobody's going to look for her. There's not going to be any media coverage. Nobody's going to be holding rallies or vigils."

More of that soft splashing, and then a gurgle, like water being let out of the tub. "That's about it."

"But that's not right. And—"

"And because I'm a black woman, I'm supposed to fix it?" Voice softening, she continued, "Look, Shaw, I get it. It's awful. Have the kid file a report. Text me what you know. I'll see what I can do."

"Thank you," Shaw said. "That would be great, Diamond. Thank you so much."

"Why can't you two be the nice kind of gay? Always making my life more difficult."

"I am the nice kind of gay," North said.

"No," Shaw said, "I am."

"I gave Mrs. Macumber a jump the other day. You wouldn't even get off your fat ass to answer the door."

"You only gave her a jump so you could spend fifteen minutes revving the GTO's engine because you know all the kids come out to watch and you like showing off. I, on the other hand, helped Mr. Selby with his gardening, which you know is hard for him, and he's a veteran so I get bonus points."

"You lopped the tops off half his mums with the weed eater. He was screaming for you to stop, and when you finally did, your exact words were, 'This thing is kind of hard to control.' I heard him crying later that day."

"Well, if you hadn't tried to act all trade with the lawn equipment and bought the mega-butch weed blaster 9000, I wouldn't have—"

"I got out of the bath for this," Diamond said, and the call disconnected. They stood there, and the screen timed out.

"She's not going to be able to do anything," Shaw said in a low voice.

"She's going to do whatever she can. You heard her. She's going to try."

"But she's not going to be able to do anything. She's overwhelmed with cases already. Kids disappear every day. Even if she wanted to help, she's got her own life, her own problems."

"Shaw, I know you feel connected to this kid. But I think you need to face some hard facts. He was juiced bad on something when he showed up. He lied to Pari and broke into our office so he could find out where we lived."

"Come on, that makes it sound way worse than what it was. The door wasn't locked. Probably."

"This story, his friend, and then all that bullshit about the smoke detectors? That's classic tweaker paranoia. He's spun or gacked out or coked to the gills, whatever you want to call it. We don't even know if his friend is actually missing."

"She is, North. He's on something—definitely not coke, because he couldn't afford that—but he's not wrong. Malorie is missing, and he is freaking out about it."

"Maybe he's right. Maybe not. His friend didn't show up to the movies. Big fucking deal. Stuff like that happens all the time. Maybe she shacked up with someone. Maybe she split. I know he said she didn't, but that doesn't mean he's right. Maybe she forgot, maybe she got a wild hair and went off with some other friends, maybe she found a new shelter." North rubbed his mouth, his lips set in a hard line. "That stuff about the government and—"

Shaw squeezed his eyes shut. For a moment, everything seemed dialed up: North's voice, the hiss of the air conditioning, the puppy's snuffling, the whooshing of the ceiling fan. He counted his breaths. He summoned his mantra, the new and improved one, two hundred and seventy-nine dollars if you also buy an astral easing session, redeemable weekdays only. When the welter faded, he let out a breath and opened his eyes.

"Right," Shaw said. "I get it. You're right. I know you're right. And I totally agree with you. But—but if Nik is telling the truth, if his friend was saving up to move, if she had turned her life around—" Shaw fumbled with the zipper, but it was stuck. "North, I told him we'd help him, and then I forgot about him."

"We can help him by getting him into a hospital and then into foster care."

Eyes closed tight again, Shaw tried. He really tried. But the tears leaked out. He whispered, "Yeah, ok."

"Shaw."

"If that's what you want. Ok. I mean, if that's what you think is best."

A note of frustration crept into North's voice. "Tell me what I'm missing."

"No, I agree."

"But you can't look at me."

His next breath was tremulous. Shaw fought to lock it down. No sobbing. No begging. No fits. Because relationships only worked if you made them work, and the way to make this one work was to put North first. North was what mattered. North was the only thing in his life that mattered, and Shaw wasn't about to lose him. Not again.

"Look," North said, "if you think we need to help him—"

"No, no, I'll do whatever you want. You're right. You're a way better judge of this kind of thing because I always let my emotions take over and I don't think about what I'm doing or saying, so tell me what you want to do, and I'll do it."

"What do you want?"

"I don't know. I mean, whatever you—"

"Will you stop saying that? I told you what I think."

"I'll just—I'll just tell him—I'll give him Eddie's name. Eddie's good right? He's a good detective, and he doesn't charge too much, and it'll be ok because Eddie can help him, and—"

North made a rumbling noise deep in his chest. "He's not going to Eddie."

"Eddie—"

"Look, we'll see what we can do."

Shaw blinked rapidly, dropping his gaze to the floor. "Thank you. Thank you so much, North."

"Is he staying here?"

"I mean, what do you—"

"I'm giving you another chance to look me in the eyes and respect me enough to tell me what you're really thinking, so answer the question: is Nik staying the night?"

"If you think—"

"Fine," North barked. After a moment of visible self-soothing, he said, "He's not moving in with us, Shaw."

"No, of course not."

"One night. We can't keep picking up strays."

"I know. I know."

"This whole thing is going to turn out to be some speed-freak fantasy. You owe me."

After some more blinking, Shaw trusted himself to say, "Good sex for a month."

"Fuck that. No PBS for a month. That's what I want."

"North, the new season of *Antiques*—no, no, no. That's fine. A whole month, though? North, come back, I was double checking."

While North conducted his usual routine, checking the windows and doors, setting all the locks, loading the last dishes into the dishwasher, Shaw perched on the couch in the living room. Nik's restless energy had slowed since the first Xanax, but he was still pacing, and he flinched every time North set a deadbolt or a board creaked.

"Nik," Shaw said.

He said something under his breath.

GREGORY ASHE

"Nik," Shaw tried again, more loudly.

The noise was a faint acknowledgment.

"You need to take a shower. Then you're going to sleep."

"Can't."

Shaw got to his feet and moved into Nik's path. When the boy tried to veer around him, Shaw put out an arm. Nik flinched and stepped back.

"Bathroom's over here," Shaw said. "You're going to feel a lot better after you're clean."

"I'm not staying up for this," North said.

"That's ok." Shaw herded Nik toward the hall bathroom. "I've got it under control."

North subvocalized something that might have been, "It sure fucking looks like it," and then he went back into the kitchen and returned to stand in the arched opening with a fresh beer.

Eventually, Shaw got Nik into the bathroom and ran the water for him. He left the boy to shower, and Nik's eyes followed him with disturbing intensity until Shaw shut the door. The fans whirred. The air conditioning whispered a cold breath across Shaw's bare feet. North read on his phone and worked on his beer while Shaw made up the guest room. Shaw came back from their bedroom with clean clothes, and he called out and rapped on the door and set them inside the bathroom. A few minutes later, the water stopped running, and Nik emerged in mesh shorts and a gray tee that was silk-screened with the words PROTAGONIST COFFEE.

"One more," Shaw said, holding out another Xanax.

"I can't," Nik said, his gaze roving the room, stopping on North for a long moment before skating back to Shaw, then away again. "Gotta—"

"Nik, if you take some more medicine, we'll see what we can do tomorrow about Malorie. You're safe here. Nothing's going to happen."

"Make him go away."

"He's not bothering anyone. He's reading about the sexual history of jackhammers and the first time Chester A. Arthur was impregnated."

"I'm not," North said without looking up. "It's the Cardinals, and in case anyone cares, they lost."

Nik's attention wavered between North and the guest room. "I don't want a door. I don't want you locking any doors."

"You can sleep on the couch. How's that?"

After more coaxing, Nik accepted the pill, and Shaw walked him around the living room until Nik slowed, his steps becoming stumbling. He got him settled on the couch and leaned over him to tuck in the blanket. As Shaw drew back, Nik turned his head, his mouth brushing Shaw's palm in what might have been a kiss. His eyes were large, the pupils closer to normal, and his breathing had slowed.

"If you need anything, we're in the room right over there."

36

Nik didn't respond. His doped gaze was unyielding, and Shaw looked away first. It was a relief to turn off the lights, and even more of a relief to shut his bedroom door.

After he and North had finished getting ready for bed, Shaw lay under North's arm, his back to North's chest. North's lips brushed the back of Shaw's neck, and he said, "That kid is going to be trouble."

"I know he's using, North, and he was definitely acting erratic tonight, but I don't think he's violent."

"That's not what I'm worried about."

Chapter 5

THE NIGHTMARE WAS DIFFERENT from the ones that had stalked North for the last months, and that novelty threaded a strange relief through his terror. In the dream, he was naked and trying to pull a door shut. Someone much stronger was trying to pull it open. When he woke, the sheets were damp with his sweat, tangled from his thrashing. A thin sediment of light settled on everything in the room, like silt washed in from the street. It painted the curve of Shaw's spine, the dimples of his ribs, the loose strands of auburn hair pasted to his neck. The dream lingered for a moment, an intensity of feeling attached to that overpowering force he had sensed on the other side of the door. Already his brain was racing, the kid in class who always put his hand up first, testing out answers: his dad, Tucker, Shaw. And then, peeling the soaked cotton from his legs, North told himself, that stupid reporter, you dumb fuck.

It was only then that he realized his phone was buzzing on the nightstand. He didn't recognize the number, but that was usual in his line of work. After a moment, he answered.

"North? It's…it's your father." A few strained breaths. "They've got me down at the city jail."

"What are you—what time is it?" North looked around for a clock. None, of course. They always used their phones. Buy a clock, dumbshit. Buy a twenty-dollar clock. "Hold on. Dad?"

"I need you to get a lawyer. I think the Ainslie kid, the cousin, I mean, I think he's a lawyer."

"What?" North rubbed his face. "Ben Ainslie does corporate work for, fuck, a shoe company, I think. What time is it?"

"North!"

"Lawyer, right. Ok. Jesus Christ, Dad. What is it?"

"Some bullshit about jury tampering."

"And they picked you up in the middle of the night? Fuck that. I'm going to have someone's badge for this fuckery."

"I've got to go."

"Don't talk to anyone."

"They're telling me I've got to go."

"Nobody, Dad. Not a word."

North scrolled through his phone, found Claude Isham, who went by Biff and who had handled Tucker's defense when he'd been charged with murder, and placed call after call until a groggily rageful "What?" cracked on the other end of the call. North explained the situation as best he could, and Isham agreed to meet him at the city jail.

By the time North disconnected, Shaw was sitting up, knees drawn to his chest.

"My dad—"

"I heard."

"I've got to—"

Shaw crawled across the bed and wrapped him in a hug. North squeezed him back, and then it was like something coming uncorked, too much to fit through a narrow opening, and he was shaking as he clutched Shaw to him tighter and tighter. Then it reached a point where North either tipped to one side and fell into the fear, or he tipped to the other and dealt with it later.

Shaw must have sensed it too because he kissed North's shoulder, kissed him on the mouth, and released him. "Let's get dressed. I know you called Biff, but I'm sure my dad can recommend—"

"You've got to stay here with Nik."

"North—"

"We can't leave him here alone."

"He's not going to steal anything, and even if he did, it doesn't matter. There's nothing here we can't replace except those high school football jerseys you wear when you think I'm not coming home for a while."

"You're staying with Nik, and I wasn't wearing them," North said, pushing up from the bed and stumbling toward the dresser. "I got them out one time, just to look at them, and I wanted to see if they still fit."

"I was standing in the doorway for ten minutes," Shaw said, turning on the lights, passing a pair of jeans and, when North couldn't do the button on the waistband because he was shaking so badly, fastening it for him. "You were staring at yourself in the mirror the whole time. I think you had a semi."

"I did not—" North started as his head popped through the neck of the tee he'd grabbed at random.

Shaw stopped him with another kiss. "Wallet, keys, phone, socks, take all the cash and the checkbook, boots are by the door. I'm going to grab you water and some of those protein bars in case you're stuck there for a while."

He was gone before North could object. North opened the safe, took out the stack of cash they kept on hand for emergencies, usually work related, and dug the checkbook out of his underwear drawer. He was lacing up the Redwings in the kitchen when Shaw set a drawstring bag on the table.

"I'd like to go with you," Shaw said, combing fingers through North's hair.

North shook his head. "I'll call if I need anything."

The look on Shaw's face was definitely unhappy, but he didn't say anything else. He kissed North once more, followed him to the door, and passed him the drawstring bag. North shot across the backyard toward the garage. Behind him, belatedly, the puppy began to bark.

He met Biff at the jail, and he sat in a molded-plastic chair while Biff, red-faced and dressed in a Duke t-shirt and track pants, made calls and talked to the young guy in the bond commissioner's office. The young guy kept checking his cornrows with one hand as he offered politely empty comments, and then Biff would go back to phone calls. The only other person in the room was a tiny old man in a shirt, tie, and pants worn the way they had in the '50s, a grease-stained paper bag between his feet making the waiting room smell like arepas.

When Biff pocketed his phone and made his way toward North, North shot out of the chair. "Well?"

"They're giving us the runaround. He's still being processed, supposedly, but they're giving me a song and dance about lost paperwork."

"That's bullshit."

"That's what they do when they're pissed. Don't give them the satisfaction. They'll finish processing him eventually—I'll light a fire under them."

"Then he bonds out and we take him home?"

"If the charge is on the bond schedule. If not, we wait for arraignment. From what you told me, we're going to have to wait for arraignment."

"When's that?"

"It's Sunday, technically, so tomorrow at the earliest, but if they're as pissed as I think, they'll find a way to stick it to us. It might not be until Tuesday or Wednesday."

"They can't do that. Twenty-four hours. They can only hold you twenty-four hours in Missouri without charging you."

"Busy weekend, transfer delays, processing delays, detainee is uncooperative, scheduling slip-up, and the perfectly understandable and ubiquitous paperwork mistakes." Biff ticked them off on his fingers. "The law says what they can do. Then there's what they really do. Why don't you go get us some coffee, and I'll make a few more calls?"

North kicked one of the chairs so hard that it spun across the floor on its wire frame. He marched out of the bond office, spotted a bank of payphones, and grabbed one of the receivers. He pounded it against the cradle one, two, three times, and then he let it fall. When he turned around, a woman was cradling a small boy against her shoulder, trying to shush him back to sleep. She met North's eyes and said, "Boy, someone's about to get his ass beat."

Eventually, the maze of ammonia-soaked hallways gave onto an empty sidewalk and the cool, crisp air of approaching autumn. Across the street stood City Hall, with its red roof and ornate, quasi-Victorian architecture. In the streetlights' flutter, the soot stains on the limestone blended into the shadows. North found a pack of American Spirits in the GTO, lit up, and called Jadon Reck.

The detective answered on the second ring. "North, what's wrong? Is it—"

"You motherfucking son of a bitch. You couldn't have told me? You're so fucking petty that you didn't even give me any warning? He's sick, you piece of shit. The stress of this, it's probably going to kill him. And if it does, you'd better believe I'm going to drive over to that shit heap you call a home and kick it down on top of you. Do you understand me? I'm going to—"

"Hey. Hey! What the hell are you talking about?"

"My dad." North bit out the words. "And don't give me any bullshit about how it was your professional obligation because I know—"

"Dumbass, will you shut up? I didn't have anything to do with whatever you're talking about. I work on the goddamn LGBT task force."

North took a few savage puffs. He ashed the cigarette. He dug his thumb into the corner of his eye.

"Your dad got arrested?" Jadon asked in a more controlled voice.

So North told him.

"I didn't know," Jadon said. "And it didn't have anything to do with my unit." A note of bitterness entered his words as he added, "They wouldn't have told me even if it did. They all think I'm too close with you guys already. I'll make some calls. Maybe I can get some answers."

"Yeah," North said. His whole body felt like an echo now.

"I never even heard a whisper about this, so whoever had it, they played it close to the vest. Any ideas who?" Rusty amusement. "Besides me, of course."

The ember of the cigarette glowed as North drew hard again. He exhaled, said, "Maybe," and punched End. His next call was to the reporter, whose card was still in his wallet.

Even at that ungodly hour, even woken, as she must have been, from sleep, she still had a voice like she was holding a mic and rehearsing with a teleprompter. "This is Belia Lopez."

"If you tipped off the cops because I wouldn't give you a fucking interview, I'm going to ruin your life. Do you understand me?"

From the other end of the call came the rustle of cloth, and then the subtle sounds of someone moving. When she spoke again, she was projecting more, trying to reach the dummies at the back of the room. "Mr. McKinney?"

"I swear to Christ, you get this one chance to tell me who gave you that information. If it's useful, if I can run him down, then I might overlook the fact that you put a dying man in a city jail cell. Might, Belia. That's the word you should focus on. So you'd better start talking, and it'd better be good, for your fucking sake."

"My sources are confidential—"

"Bullshit. Who gave you that fucking info?"

The words rang out along the empty morning street. A breeze wrapped a QT napkin around a light pole. Plane trees planted along the sidewalk shivered, their leaves making a sound like falling water.

"I don't know. It arrived at Channel Six in an unmarked envelope. A thumb drive with an audio recording."

"Someone left it in your office?"

"No. I don't know how it got into the building, but a girl in the mail room found it. I had to twist my boss's balls pretty hard to get the lead, but it's mine, and I'm running with it now."

"And you decided to go straight to the police."

"No."

"My dad—"

"Your father was arrested? When? Are you being charged as well?"

"You're a fucking vulture. And you just screwed yourself because I will never talk to you. If I decide to talk, I'll tell my story to every fucking newspaper and TV station and to fucking KMOX before I so much as spit on you. Do you hear me? You fucked with my dad, and that means you fucked with me, and I am going to make it my personal mission to ruin your fucking life."

"Mr. McKinney—"

"You have no fucking idea—"

"Mr. McKinney! I did not have anything to do with your father's arrest. I haven't spoken to the police, and I certainly wouldn't do what you're suggesting. Punishing someone for not speaking to me by making myself a police informant? It's not exactly the way to build a career."

The ember scorched North's fingers, and he swore. He flicked the cigarette down and crushed it out against the curb.

"Mr. McKinney—"

He disconnected and got in the GTO. Tossing the pack of American Spirits onto the seat, he considered his options. Tried to consider. But it was like watching a movie, and the camera panning left, no matter how hard he wanted to look right, his mind going back to Ronnie again and again. The disorientation from the night's events had made him hasty, and haste had made him overlook the obvious. Who wanted to get back at him? Ronnie. Who had an audio recording of his dad suggesting jury tampering? Ronnie.

North sent a message to Biff with a vague excuse about an emergency. Then he drove, taking I-64 to Big Bend, cutting down to Maplewood and the quiet two-story house where he had found Ronnie living. He didn't have his picks, so he wrapped an old t-shirt from the GTO around his arm, broke the half-lite window on the back door, and let himself into the kitchen. The place was empty. Nothing had changed. The same stale smell of grease. The same blue check wallpaper. The same oak cabinets. More dust, maybe. The smell of mold because the AC hadn't run all summer.

Back on the highway, he headed east to Kingshighway, turned at the exit, and went south. The Dublin Snug was located on Macklind, on the west side of the street. Dawn was a slash of gray on the opposite horizon, but the streetlights were still on, their pale cones of light blending by the millisecond with the coming morning. The Snug's windows were dark; it was a place for hard drinkers but not early risers, and it wouldn't open again until around noon, whenever the first bartender dragged his ass to work. A fiftyish guy in sweats jogged past with two Great Danes on matching leashes. When the slap of his Asics faded, North got out of the car and took the tire iron from the trunk.

The Snug didn't belong to Ronnie. It was one of Ronnie's hangouts, or it had been, before North had sent him to jail and before Ronnie had bonded out and disappeared. Before Ronnie had started coming after North, before Ronnie had decided to settle this one last debt.

North didn't bother with the front door. He followed the side of the building to the alley, squeezing past a stack of humidity-soft cardboard boxes, empty, where something scurried and made North swear under his breath. That hollowness in his chest felt twice as bad now, like his whole body was a drum, and the universe kept pounding on him to hear how it sounded.

Set into the brick wall at the back of the Snug, next to the dumpsters and a stack of broken pallets, was a steel security door. Something moved in the alley again. Rats. Trash, food waste, lots of hiding places. North set the tip of the iron between the door and the frame.

Fast, confident steps moved behind him. Cold metal touched the back of his skull as he started to turn.

"Uh uh," a man warned.

North held himself still. The barrel of the gun nudged him until the bricks bit into his forehead. His phone buzzed.

"Take it," the man said. "Slowly."

With two fingers, North drew the phone out of his pocket. He accepted the call—a blocked number, this time—and listened to the excited breathing on the other end. Gleeful. He could picture the smile.

"Do you see how easy that was?" Ronnie asked. "And I'm just getting started. You're going to beg for this by the time I'm through."

"Wait, we can—"

The muzzle lifted from his head for an instant and then came down again, hard, clubbing him. The blow drove his face into the bricks. More blows followed. North was distantly aware that he'd fallen. He tried, for the first few seconds, to crawl, slicing up his hands and arms on the alley's broken asphalt, shards of glass, and splintered wood. Then the blows stopped.

Steps moved away. Unhurried.

The asphalt was cool and wet with dew. The taste of blood and old tar patches filled North's mouth. He needed to get up. Something about his dad. The cats. He was supposed to let out the cats or his dad would be mad. Then the tar smell and the pitchiness of the asphalt took on depth, became vertical, and he was gone.

Chapter 6

ST. RITA'S OF Bevo Mill was a story-and-a-half brick building that sprawled across half a block. Its hipped roof was balding, with a few asphalt shingles caught in a dead boxwood. Behind their bars, several of the windows looked cracked, with cardboard taped into place. Where the institutional green paint had flaked away and exposed iron, trails of rust snaked down the concrete-block foundation.

Shaw looked up and down the street: the same brick buildings he'd noticed when he'd gotten here fifteen minutes ago, most of the storefronts boarded up, the only exceptions a pocket-sized convenience store with a flickering 24/7 sign and, farther down the block, a cell phone store with a sandwich board in front: GOVERNMENT PLANS AVAILABLE. Domestic sedans and trucks lined the street, all of them twenty and thirty years out of date, panels pitted and paint sloughing off. The Mercedes stood out like a sore thumb. So did the Lexus LX parked directly in front of the shelter.

"We can go inside," Nik said.

After almost twelve hours of sleep, Nik had spent most of the day apologizing. And eating. With his hair styled with North's American Crew gel, dressed in North's pink PRIDE IS HARD WORK tee, which featured a construction worker stick figure using power tools in sexually suggestive ways, and in a pair of North's jeans and a borrowed belt that he'd cinched all the way to the last hole, Nik looked like a kid swimming in his older brother's clothes. But at least he looked like a kid again, although the hard-edged wariness in his eyes surfaced from time to time when Shaw watched him closely.

"He'll be here."

"He's not answering your texts."

Shaw glanced at him, but all he said was "He answered. He just did it North fashion. How's your day? 'Good.' How are you feeling? 'Fine.' Let's talk about our relationship. 'It's good.' One time I spent four hours giving a prepared speech on the topic of safely exploring shibari, and the whole time he was cutting slices from this wedge of cheddar, and when I finished, he said, 'We're not doing that,' and he went outside and worked on his car and when he came back he was really sweaty and he smelled like car, you know, all that metal and oil, and he pushed me over the back of the sofa and said something like, 'Why do I need all that rope when I can do this?' And then he—this is where North usually interrupts me and says something like 'You can't tell this story in a church' or 'That guard is going to make us leave'—"

The throaty rumble of the GTO ran down the street, and a moment later, the car turned onto the street. He parked a few car lengths away and got out. Cuts covered his face, arms, and hands, and he moved stiffly.

"Holy shit," Shaw said and sprinted toward him.

"Ow, ow, ow, ow, ow," North said. "Christ, Shaw, he worked my ribs over. Baby, please."

"Sorry," Shaw said, relaxing the hug. "What happened?"

North told him.

"You went after Ronnie without me—"

"Please not now. And please not so loudly. I've got a headache like a motherfucker."

After a while, when North started to mutter and shift, Shaw released him. He stepped back to examine North, taking in the cuts and scrapes as he made North tell the story again more slowly.

"All right," Shaw said. "We have to find Ronnie."

"We," North emphasized the word, "aren't doing anything. He almost killed you once. He could have gotten me today. I'm going to handle this."

"North—"

"No, Shaw. You're staying out of it. And you're staying safe. That's final."

Looking down, Shaw straightened his button-up, a floral print of magnolia blossoms against dark green. The acid-washed jeans hung off his hips, and he'd stitched skulls into the rear pockets in purple thread. The Adidas kicks were ones North had picked for his birthday.

"Shaw?"

"Yes, ok. If that's what you want."

North grunted. "Why the fuck is he wearing my clothes?"

"Shaw said I could," Nik said with a note of defiance.

"He ate all of your cheese sticks too," Shaw said. "And two omelets. And he finished the ice cream sandwiches—"

"God damn it," North said. "I was saving those."

"Well, you weren't supposed to buy them in the first place because we agreed—"

"And they're not called cheese sticks, Shaw. String cheese. Cheese sticks sounds like something a serial killer would prep on Sundays and pack in his lunch all week."

"You literally asked me last week to chop up that block of cheese so you could take slices as a snack. With some grapes."

"Slices, Shaw. Not cheese sticks. Why is today the fucking worst?"

Without waiting for a reply, North stomped up the stairs to the shelter.

"He's fine," Shaw told Nik. "He's low on his B vitamins—"

"I surely fucking am not," North shouted back. "And I'm not taking those fucking voodoo pills Master Hermes sold you."

"—so I need to go back to crushing them up and slipping them into his ice cream—"

"Excuse me?" North said, stopping on the stairs. He turned.

"Um. I wasn't saying anything."

"Don't fucking touch my ice cream, Shaw. Those pills are going to give someone hoof-and-mouth disease, for fuck's sake."

"North, I wasn't saying anything. Maybe getting hit in the head affected your hearing. Maybe you've got tinnitus."

North's eyes narrowed, but he started up the stairs again.

"Close call," Shaw whispered to Nik.

Glaring after North, Nik laid a hand on Shaw's shoulder. "He shouldn't talk to you like that."

"Oh, that's just North."

"He's an asshole. You deserve someone better than an asshole."

Slipping out from under Nik's hand, Shaw tried for a smile and said, "Let's go inside."

They caught up to North in what looked like a combination reception area and lounge that took up most of the front of the building. Near the door stood a desk with a surprisingly nice computer, including a large, flatscreen monitor. A desk calendar, a clipboard with a sign-in log, and a mug holding a collection of blue translucent Bic pens completed the setup. The rest of the space had been given over to a motley collection of ancient couches and chairs, some of them arranged in groups, others facing a massive television. Rickety coffee tables held board games—Clue, Life, Chutes and Ladders—the boxes bent, flattened, and discolored. Monopoly money littered the floor like morning-after confetti.

North was speaking to a woman who looked like she was being dragged into her thirties against her will. She had a narrow face, probably too narrow for her hair cut; it made the French bob look like an ill-fitting helmet, which, in Shaw's opinion, was a waste of all those highlights. Her lipstick was matte, a purplish red that was probably called cherry or plum or cool raspberry. When she smiled, her veneers were blinding. She kept moving the Birkin bag up her arm as she said something to North. Shaw was certain the shoes were Jimmy Choos.

"—and most of our volunteers are the stringy kind, all vegans and soy lattes, arms you could thread a needle with. It's a nice change to have a red-blooded American male under the roof. And it doesn't hurt that he's handsome. A certain roughness. All those cuts and bruises. Do you box?"

"Not often," Shaw said.

North scowled at him. "She wasn't talking to you."

"I think she was. I'm handsome. And my blood is red. Well, except when it's still in my veins. Like there's this one big vein on my balls. And then my blood is blue. Well, purple. But you have to stretch the ball skin pretty tight to see—"

"She was talking about me, dumbass."

Shaw squinted. "I mean, you're American. She got part of it right. But you did order those cans of soymilk—"

"They came in the snack box. I didn't order them."

"I heard you try one in the kitchen, and you actually said out loud, to yourself, not knowing anybody else was listening, 'God damn, that's all right.' Like you were in a 1950s milk commercial. Only it would have had less swearing. Not in the milk. In the commercial, I mean. Because you do swear a lot, and—"

"Stop. Talking."

The woman slid her Birkin bag up her arm again. "And who are you?"

"My partner," North said. "Shaw Aldrich. Shaw, this is Ximena Linares. She runs the shelter."

"Runs, champions, makes sure the doors stay open and the lights on." She flashed the veneers again. "I know it's not much, but I'm doing what I can. Nik, sweetheart, you look like you're feeling better today."

"Hi, Ximena." Nik stood near the doorway, hands in his pockets, staring at the scuffed linoleum.

"Nik has had a few rough days. Are you going to stay with us tonight?"

"Maybe."

"You know the rules, sweetheart. Stay away from that stuff. I don't like having to turn you away."

"Yeah," Nik mumbled, a blush filling his face as he glanced at Shaw. "I don't—I mean, it's not all the time."

"He's an angel usually," Ximena said to North, in that jocularly indulgent tone that adults adopted when speaking about teens, especially when the teen was present, "until he has a new crush, and then it's off to the races, whatever he thinks will impress that boy."

"Xi," Nik said, his face growing redder.

"They're always trouble. Most of them want to mess around under the covers but still play it straight the rest of the time to keep their cred, and it's drugs or it's stealing or—" She laughed. "He has this adorable tattoo. Nik, show them."

Nik shook his head. He gave Shaw a pained look and dropped his gaze to the floor.

A black girl clip-clopped into the room on chunky wedges that looked too small for her feet. Her chemically straightened hair was the dollar-cuts version of Ximena's: a chunky bob on an already big head. Her eyebrows had reached category five, hedge-trimmer, and she'd applied her mascara poorly, perhaps in a hurry, the lashes clumping in places and thin in others.

"Now this one is pure trouble," Ximena said in that same tone. "Ryley, love, did you put on deodorant?"

The girl, Ryley, cast a worried glance around the room before nodding.

"Go fix your hair; you've got a million flyaways. You can borrow some of that serum from my office." An irritated note entered her voice. "And where are those earrings I gave you?"

Ryley's voice was husky, the words hurried, as though someone might cut her off. It wasn't hard to guess who. "I left them in the—"

"Go put them on. You got your ears pierced for a reason, didn't you?"

"But Xi, I—"

"And brush your teeth."

"I just wanted to—"

"Right now, child." As Ryley scurried off, Ximena said to North and Shaw, reverting to that eyerolling adult-to-adult indulgence, "I swear to God, one time that girl walked out of here with her skirt on backwards. She'd lose her head, you know?"

"Ms. Linares," North said.

With a trilling laugh, she slapped his chest lightly, seemingly oblivious to North's wince. "Ximena. We're not strangers."

"We wanted to ask you a few questions about Malorie Walton."

"That's what Nik said on the phone. I don't know why you're making such a fuss."

"What do you mean?" Shaw asked.

She flicked a glance at him and turned back to North. "Malorie isn't missing. She's off with a boy. Or she's off with a girl. Or she's sleeping one off. Or she left. She was always talking about leaving."

"Isn't that the same thing as missing?"

Another of those brush-off looks, then back to North. "I mean, there's missing and then there's gone, right?"

"When was the last time you saw Malorie?"

"I don't know. It must have been whenever she stayed at the shelter last."

"When was that?"

"I don't know."

"Four nights ago," Nik said from the doorway.

When North looked at Ximena, she said, "I told you I don't know."

"But you have records."

"We have a clipboard." Ximena picked it up and ran a turquoise nail down the list of names. "Let's see. Last night we had three Beyoncés, a Lady Gaga, and two Billies, which I guess is for Billie Eilish." She waved the clipboard at North, making a face when he plucked it out of her hand. "It's a shelter for at-risk teens. We don't ask for photo ID."

After flipping through several pages, North passed the clipboard to Shaw and raised an eyebrow. Shaw scanned the entries. He was only half listening when Nik said, "Malorie always signed her own name."

Even Ximena's sigh sounded indulgent.

"She did," Nik said. "She always put her own name."

"Several days' worth of entries are missing." Shaw flipped the pages in demonstration. "The last few days, in fact. Where are they?"

Ximena grimaced, but she smoothed the expression away a moment later. "They go missing. Someone drops the clipboard, and the pages fall out."

"But the older pages are still here. The missing ones didn't conveniently fall out."

This time, she let her glare linger. "Or a volunteer is an eager beaver and throws the old ones away. Or kids take them sometimes; they worry that someone is looking for them, and they think they have to hide their trail. Teenagers are very dramatic, if you haven't figured that out yet. My dad will kill me if he finds me. My ex said he'd cut up my face. My friend is missing." The tension in her face dissolved, and she rolled her eyes. "It's always something like that."

When Shaw glanced at Nik, the kid was rubbing his cheeks, on the verge of tears. "She is missing," he protested, but the words were directed toward the graying linoleum. "She said she was going to the clinic, then she was going to Jesse's, then she was going to pick up her pay. We were going to meet at the movies that night."

"Don't tell me Jamaal is still letting you in the back door." Ximena shook her head. "It's one thing for him to hook you up with a free popcorn and a drink, Nik, but if they catch him letting kids in the back, he's going to lose that job. Then where will he be? Right back here."

Nik's head came up, and he met Shaw's eyes. "Her locker."

"What?" Shaw asked.

"Her locker." Nik turned to Ximena. "Let's check her locker."

"They have lockers?" North frowned. "How does that work? I thought this was a night-only shelter."

"It is." Ximena glanced at the clock. "And I can't stand around all day. Ryley?" The name was a shout directed at the rear of the shelter. "Ryley, where are you? Kids are going to start showing up, and we have to finish getting ready. Ryley?"

"I'd like to see her locker," North said.

"Fine, but I can't stand around. Nik, is the door locked? All right, the lockers are back here. Ryley?"

When no answer came, she led them down a short hall. The shelter's lounge, with its ancient furniture and the stink of a resale shop, had been depressing, but now Shaw realized that the lounge was the shelter's equivalent of putting your best foot forward. Muddy shoeprints crisscrossed the hallway's linoleum, which was black with accumulated grime in the corners and, in many places, bubbling or peeling up entirely. The fluorescent panels flickered overhead, the ballast buzzing like a stirred-up hornets' nest. As they left the resale-shop smell behind, a new combination of odors took its place: the occasional whiff of something vinegary that made Shaw think of window cleaner; a chemical perfume that had probably been marketed as Summer Citrus or Orange Ka-Pow!; and everywhere, the smell of perpetually damp tile and polyester. When they passed one of the communal bathrooms (someone had removed the door), the plink-plink-plonk of a broken fixture met them; mold spotted a tangled shower curtain. Shaw found himself thinking of the Lexus parked in front.

The lockers were the kind Shaw had seen in every Hollywood movie set in a high school: full length, tan, banged to hell, their paint chipped. Several of the lockers were unsecured, while others had padlocks fastened through the handle. They were located between the communal bathrooms. Ximena pointed at the one they had passed and said, "Boys." Then she pointed at the one down the hall. "Girls. Enby and trans kids have to use biological sex. They sleep with biological sex too. It's not what they want, but sexual assault is a problem in every shelter, and putting them with their biological sex does help. A bit."

"Really?" Shaw asked. "I thought it was more complicated—"

"When they check in," she said over him, "they store all their stuff here. They can access it whenever they want, but they can't take it into the dorms." She waved at doors farther down the hall. "That's another rule. Nothing in the dorms. Nothing. You get caught, you're out on the street, and you don't get to come back. We used to say you could have one personal item, but some of these kids will fight about anything. They go in with the clothes on their back. That's it."

Nik's face had a teenager's mixture of annoyance and self-satisfied knowledge. North must have seen it too because he asked, "Strip search?"

"What?"

"Do you strip search them?"

"Of course not."

North made a noise that might have been amusement. He eyed the lockers. Shaw pointed to several of the handles, where scratches marred the locker panel. North nodded.

"You cut the locks off?" Shaw asked.

"Sometimes. If they don't come back. Or if I think they've got contraband. That's another hard-and-fast: drugs, booze, weapons, you're out, and you're not coming back."

"How long?" North asked.

"Never."

"No, how long do you wait before emptying their lockers?"

"It depends. If we need the space, I might do it the next night. If I know the kid, if they're here most nights—"

"If you like them," Nik muttered.

"Some people have earned additional consideration," Ximena said. "I don't think that's unreasonable."

"Is Malorie one of those people?" North asked.

"Yes. She's a special young lady; everyone who meets her says so."

"If you think doing drugs and hooking is special," Ryley said behind them.

Shaw glanced over his shoulder; he hadn't heard the girl approach. She stood a few yards off, leaning against the wall, one arm wrapped around her waist.

"Is that what Malorie does?" North asked.

"No," Nik said. "Check her locker. She wouldn't leave without her money. Check it right now."

Ryley looked at her feet, shifting her weight on the too-small wedges.

"Check it," Nik insisted. "You'll see how much money she has, and you'll know she wouldn't leave, and you'll know she's not doing what—what Ryley said."

"Ryley," Ximena said, "you know we leave that kind of thing outside." To North and Shaw, she said, "We tell them not to bring up what happens outside of the shelter. It's not productive. And," raising her voice slightly, perhaps for Ryley's benefit, "because everybody has a past."

"Which locker is Malorie's?" Shaw asked.

Ximena pointed. "As you can see, it's still—"

When Shaw tugged on the lock, the body came loose from the shackle.

"But it was still—" Ximena glanced from Shaw to North, tucking her hands into her armpits. The Birkin bag swung pendulously from her elbow. "You saw it. It was locked."

"No." North examined the lock, nodding when Shaw pointed to the tool marks on the shackle. "Someone forced it, and then they jimmied it back into place to look like it was untouched."

"Damn it." When North looked over, Shaw shook his head. "Should have used gloves."

Grunting, North worked the padlock free from the locker's handle. "We both should have thought of that. I have some in the GTO. Will you—"

"I'll get them," Nik said, flashing a smile that exposed his missing eyetooth. He snagged the keys from North and sprinted down the hallway. Ryley made a disgusted noise, following him with her eyes. They waited in silence for a few minutes until Nik jogged back. He held out the gloves to Shaw, who took them, peeled off a pair, and passed them to North.

Gloved up, North lifted the handle and opened the locker. The space inside was divided into three sections: a shelf near the top; a large middle section, with hooks on which were hung a nylon baseball jacket, a pink blouse, a navy miniskirt, and a lacy bra; and another shelf at the bottom, creating a cubby at the base of the locker where a flattened backpack had been stored.

But no money.

With childlike disappointment, Nik asked, "Where is it?"

Chapter 7

FOR A MOMENT, they all stared at the locker. Shaw felt a strange sense of expectation, as though if they all held still long enough, the money would reappear.

Ryley clip-clopped closer to the knot of bodies, obviously hoping for a peek inside the locker, and her movement broke the spell.

"Tell us about the money," Shaw said.

"She keeps her money in here," Nik said. "Ximena knows. She asked Ximena if it was ok. She had all her money here, and now it's gone."

"Nik, I didn't—" Ximena's shoulders curved inwards. "They know that we can't guarantee their belongings will be safe, and the lockers have been broken into before. I tell them—I mean, I certainly never promised—"

Sitting back on his heels, North grimaced. "How much are we talking?"

Nik mimed a stack. "A bunch of them that size."

"Ones? Fifties? Hundreds? That could be a little money or hell of a lot."

"Even if they were ones, it would be a lot for these kids." Ximena chewed her lip, and more of the lipstick came off on her veneers. "I want it on the record that I never told these kids their property was secure in these lockers. They were a convenience, and the users assumed all liability—"

"What fucking record?" North said under his breath. To Nik, he said, "Where'd she get that money?"

"The temp agency. I told you, she's temping."

"And hooking," Ryley put in. "She's still on a corner for Jesse. And she probably—"

"No, she isn't!" Nik shouted.

"—spent it all on drugs."

"She did not!"

"Everybody thinks she's this princess, walking on clouds, but she's mean. She's a bully, and she's dangerous. If she doesn't get what she wants, she goes crazy. She'll do anything to have her way, anything, and—"

"You don't like her because Xi likes her, and—"

"Shut up," Ximena screeched. "Shut up! Shut up!"

Ryley burst into tears.

"Get her out of here and calm her down," North said.

An arm around the girl, Ximena herded her down the hall, Ryley's wracking sobs echoing off the tile when they passed the opening to the bathroom. Then they turned, and the noise faded.

Shaw caught Nik's gaze. "Is she still using?"

"She told me she was clean. She said she was doing it for the baby."

"Tricking?"

"No." Nik bit his lip. He looked on the brink of tears as he shook his head. "No way."

"But you said she was going to see this guy, Jesse, and Ryley said that guy runs girls."

"Jesse is—he's a loser. You have to meet him to see. He's a wannabe. And Malorie doesn't do that anymore. She doesn't need to. She has a real job, and she's making money. We almost have enough. Had. We were going to leave."

"How many people knew about the money?" North asked.

Nik shrugged.

"Nik."

He wiped his eyes. "I don't know. I didn't tell anyone, and Malorie is always careful, but—I mean, there's not a lot of privacy here, and everybody's all up in each other's business. I bet Ryley took it."

"Why Ryley?"

"You heard her. Everybody loves Malorie except her, but she hates her because she's obsessed with Ximena. All Ryley wants is Xi's attention. Approval. We had kids like that in school, snitches who would tell the teacher everything so an adult would give them five seconds of their time. Ryley will do anything to get that from Xi."

"It's a night-only shelter, right?" Shaw asked. "During the day, who can get in here?"

Nik snuffled and wiped his nose on North's tee; North gave a tiny wince. "Anybody."

"They don't lock—"

"They do. But look at this place; it's a shit hole. There are all kinds of ways to get in here. Kids do it sometimes if they need a shower or somewhere they can hide, but you've got to be careful. If Xi catches you, you're out of the shelter permanently."

"So anybody could have come back during the day, forced the lock, and taken the money?"

"I guess."

"Did you open Malorie's locker?" North asked.

Nik's eyes got round. "What?"

"You're not in trouble if you did, but we need to know. You were worried about her. Maybe you wanted to see if she'd left anything."

"You think I stole the money?"

"I didn't say that."

"Fuck you. Fuck both of you. I wanted you to help me find her. Why would I do that if I stole her money?" He spun in the direction Ximena and Ryley had gone.

"Park your ass," North shouted, getting to his feet. "We're still asking you questions."

Nik spun back, so quickly that he caught Shaw by surprise, and got in North's face. "You can't tell me what to do. You got beat to shit today. You want to see what I can do to your ancient ass?"

"You little turd—"

"Nik, Nik, Nik." Shaw slid between them, a hand on Nik's chest, forcing them apart. Nik's heart was racing under Shaw's touch. His pupils were enlarged, and his hands were balled into fists. "Take a breath. A good, deep one. Ok. We're asking you questions because we want to find Malorie. If she's hurt, we want to find her as quickly as possible, right?"

Nik mumbled something.

"That's what we want, isn't it?" Shaw prompted.

"He shouldn't say things like that. I'd never do that."

"Did you ever get into Malorie's locker?"

"No."

"Do you know who did?"

"No."

"You said Malorie told you where she was going that day. Is there a chance Malorie would have come back, either between those appointments or after them, before she met you at the movies?"

Nik offered a sullen shrug.

"For fuck's sake," North muttered.

Shaw shot him a warning look, and North subsided, although the muscles in his jaw said he was clenching his teeth.

"Maybe," Nik said, the word falling to the linoleum.

"Ok."

"But she wouldn't have broken into her own locker, right? If she came back for her money, why wouldn't she take all her stuff, why wouldn't she use the combination to get into the locker?"

"Those are all good points," Shaw said, stroking Nik's arm.

North rolled his eyes. "Go away now. We need to talk."

"You can't tell me what to do. He can't tell me what to do. He can't—"

"Nik." Shaw squeezed his arm and nudged him toward the end of the hallway. "Go check on Ryley. See if Xi caught anybody inside the shelter when they weren't supposed to be here."

Nik directed a furious stare at North—one that was probably meant to be a stone-cold-killer look, but which fell more in the range of sulky, I-won't-pick-up-my-room teen—and slouched off down the hall. When he had turned the corner, North made a noise.

"Don't start," Shaw said.

"I told you he was going to be trouble."

"North."

"He's so in love with you he's already living halfway up your ass."

"Gross. And he's not in love with me. He's—"

"Crushing on you. Obsessed with you. Throwing bones every time you get within two feet of him."

"Real mature."

"I'm not joking. My jeans are big on him, but they're not that big."

"Ha ha."

"See for yourself; squeeze his shoulder next time you ask him to do something."

"I'm not—that wouldn't be—"

"You could probably use the ego boost after that old lady beat you up at Schnucks last week."

"She didn't beat me up. She took my coupons and pulled my hair, but that was only because I pushed her walker—wait, I didn't finish telling you the story. North! I got my coupons back! I just have a little bald patch now."

When Shaw caught up, North was trying—and failing—to hide the first smile Shaw had seen on his face since that morning. It was a tired face, bristling with blond stubble, dark spots under his eyes, not to mention cut and scraped from the tussle at the Snug earlier that day. North reached over, rubbed Shaw's nape, and drew him closer to kiss his temple.

"They were for twenty-five cents off cat food," Shaw whispered. "The wet food. In the cans."

"We don't have a cat."

"We might."

"We won't."

"But I could astrally project the essence of the cat food into another plane of existence. One where you're not scared of felines and we have a million cats together, and they're all named after the Bronte sisters. Emily Bronte 1. Emily Bronte 2. Emily Bronte-the-mean-one. Emily Bronte Tortoiseshell. Charlotte Bronte 1, Charlotte Bronte 2, Charlotte Bronte-lives-in-the-attic, Charlotte—"

"For the love of God, stop before I have to go back on Grindr and Scruff and Prowler."

They found Ximena and Nik in a commercial-scale kitchen, obviously designed to feed the shelter's large numbers every night. It was as bad as the rest of the house: the smell of rancid grease, mouse droppings along the baseboards, the afternoon sun picking out the streaks and spills and fingerprints on the stainless-steel countertops. Nik was pouting near the window, arms folded across his chest. Ximena was typing rapidly on her phone.

"Where's Ryley?" North asked.

"She was upset," Ximena said without looking up.

"That's an emotional state, not a place. Where the fuck is she?"

"Technically," Shaw said, "emotional states are places. Well, in a psychodynamic theory of the multiverse, which is actually a useful way to understand—"

"No, it isn't. Nik, where is she?"

Nik shrugged.

"For the love of fuck," North muttered.

Try as they might, they couldn't get anything else out of Ximena or Nik. Ximena had obviously gone into self-defense mode, probably suspecting some sort of lawsuit or criminal charge would be filed against her, and she refused to offer any more information. Nik stared blankly at North, a one-sided staring contest, while North's voice got louder and louder and his face got redder and redder, until Shaw finally sent him outside. Even then, Nik would only answer in curt, broken sentences, and his expression, when he looked at Shaw, was a mixture of pain and betrayal. The only victory, a small one, was that Ximena messaged them a picture of Malorie that she had taken on her phone.

When Shaw joined North outside, North was leaning against the GTO, hurriedly kicking something into the storm drain. The smell of cigarette smoke was strong.

"What are you doing?"

"Trash."

"That's not really an answer. And you shouldn't kick trash down those things. They get clogged and someone has to go down there."

"Fine. You're skinny enough; you go down there."

"Someone in a professional capacity."

North grunted.

"It wouldn't be right, me going down there. I'm not trained. I might actually make things worse."

"That didn't stop you when you offered to help Mr. Winns rewire his kitchen."

"He had no idea what he was doing."

"Neither did you!"

"Well, I had been recently immersed in the ectoplasmic exudation of Nikola Tesla, so I was pretty sure—"

"I didn't have power for a week, Shaw. In the summer. No AC. No cold beers. No ice cream, for the love of God. And that was after you almost burned down the duplex. I could have burned to death in my sleep."

"It was a tiny fire. Teeny tiny. They only had to send two fire engines."

Barely, just barely, North managed to lock down the smile before it fully surfaced. "What the fuck do we do now?"

"Now? You go home. You take Tylenol and ibuprofen. You put ice wherever it hurts, which is pretty much everywhere, so I should probably put you in my cryochamber—"

"Old refrigerator you stole from the curb."

"—or at the least draw you an ice bath."

"It's less of an ice bath and more of a soup when you use frozen vegetables. And I'm not doing any of that. I'm fine, Shaw. Let's work this case, figure out where this girl is crashing, and be done so we can go back to making money on real jobs with real clients who write real checks."

"What if we had a real job with a fake client who wrote a real check?"

North rubbed his face.

"Or a fake job with a real client and a fake check?"

"Here's what we're going to do. You're going to come closer, because I'm tired and sore and a little stiff, and I'm going to beat you up, because you obviously didn't meet enough bullies when you were a kid. Then, when I've got you properly socialized, we're going to start here. We don't know that Malorie went to any of those places that Nik told us about; she told him that's where she was going, but we don't know that she actually did. The only thing we know for certain is that she left the shelter Wednesday morning, and no one has seen her since. So, let's see if anyone saw what happened after she left."

"That's what I was going to suggest, but I like to let you figure things out on your own sometimes."

North grabbed him, still fast in spite of his aches, and wrestled Shaw against the car for a while, which turned into some light necking before Shaw pulled back and brushed his fingers along the edge of a scrape on North's forehead. "God," he whispered. "My heart about stopped when I saw you get out of the car."

North's voice was husky, rigid with an attempt at control. "I'm ok."

Shaw leaned forward, face in North's chest, smelling their soap, their dryer sheets, the fragility of the home and life they were building together.

"I'm ok." The words were barely more than a breath, and North's hand trembled as he stroked Shaw's hair. "Not any worse than a bad spill."

"Yeah." Shaw drew in several sharp breaths and dried his eyes on North's tee. "Right."

North tilted his head back and kissed him. It was gentle. It was a question, something North needed, and Shaw answered as best he could.

Someone shouted, "Gross."

Shaw broke the kiss and glanced around. Nik, standing on the shelter's stairs, watched them with his jaw dropped.

"He's inspecting me for ticks," Shaw called.

"No, I wasn't. I'm making out with him. When he holds still and stops giggling, that is."

Nik marched back inside, and the door slammed shut.

"Did he chub up a little?"

Shaw sighed. "A little."

"Christ, I'm never going to get those clothes back, am I?"

Swatting North's ass lightly, Shaw said, "Let's see if anyone spotted Malorie."

But most of the businesses were shuttered, obviously closed permanently, and the few that were open had no information to contribute. The man in the cell phone shop was a balding ginger who must have topped three hundred pounds, and although he tried to be pleasant, something was clearly bothering him, and his replies got snappier—and more and more breathless—as the conversation progressed. He hadn't seen anything—why couldn't they understand, he wanted to know, that he hadn't seen anything?

The owner of the convenience store was friendlier. Mr. Markovic, of Markovic Speedy Stop, seemed to enjoy chatting with them, his accent suggesting that he was part of the wave of Bosnian refugees who had come to the area in the 1990s. But he couldn't tell them anything—he knew many of the kids who went to the shelter, by sight if not by name, but mostly he wanted to complain about the problems they caused him—shoplifting, vandalism, harassing paying customers.

Outside, they had to stop because North was white-faced and sweating, and he stopped to sit on the narrow sill of the window. Shaw caught him by the shoulders when North hunched, a hand pressed to the side.

"I'm all right. Just hurts like a motherfucker."

"North—"

"No, give me five minutes, and then let's do this."

After five minutes, he let Shaw help him up, and they moved down the street again. The day was warm without being hot, closer to autumn than summer, but North was sweating like it was August. The smell of fried chicken drifted from the Lee's up the street.

They were halfway back to the shelter when Shaw stopped and pointed at a streetlight. A crumpled section of the black fiberglass pole showed traces of white paint. Shaw turned, imagining the vehicle's trajectory, and gestured at the skid marks on the pavement. "This looks fresh, right?"

North grunted. "Too high on the pole for a sedan. Had to be an SUV or a truck. Maybe a van. Damn, I'm losing it; how did we miss this when we walked past it the first time?"

"Because the pole looks normal from the other side. Now we're headed back to the shelter, and we're seeing the other side, where the impact happened. And we were looking for people to talk to, not for physical evidence. We probably looked right at the skid marks and didn't pay any attention."

Stiffly, North lowered himself to look at the marks. "They're definitely recent, but I can't tell how recent. Help me up."

Shaw gave him a hand, and North squeezed hard, once, in silent gratitude.

"Malorie leaves the shelter, and she's walking that way—"

"Why?"

"I don't know. The bus stop? Or maybe the clinic is in that direction? We can ask Nik."

North grunted.

"She's walking that way, and she makes it halfway down the block before—" Shaw frowned. "A car tries to hit her?"

"I don't think so. If I wanted to run somebody down, I wouldn't choose this street. Too many cars parked along the curb. Better to wait for her to get to an intersection or a street with no parking." North massaged his shoulder. "Maybe she sees an accident, and she tries to help the guy, but it's a Ted Bundy thing and he gets her in the truck. He was faking being hurt, and he subdues her and drives off."

Shaw hemmed. He moved toward the streetlight. More paint and fiberglass fragments had fallen around the base. He worked his way out in a spiral pattern, looking for anything else—broken glass from a headlight was the most obvious possibility, but he tried to keep his eyes open to anything that might be meaningful.

"Do you want me to help?" North asked, his voice strained.

"No. Stand there and look pretty."

"I'd look prettier if you ever let me use that beer-yeast shampoo."

Shaw stopped, staring at a slab of sidewalk.

"It's just skid marks, Shaw. We might be making something out of nothing."

"I found blood."

North swore under his breath and joined him.

Squatting, Shaw studied his find. The drop was fat and dark, blackberry colored against the pitted concrete. He rose and began a new spiral, but North interrupted him and said, "There." He was pointing a few yards down the block, where another dark spot marked the sidewalk.

"Someone was hurt and moving fast," Shaw said. "Maybe she got in the car. Then something bad happened, and she tried to run."

"Shaw, we know two things so far: somebody tried to brake and still hit the streetlight, and somebody was bleeding and moving fast. They might not even be connected. A kid might have been running with a bloody nose."

A few more steps led Shaw to a narrow alley between two brick buildings. Something was swimming in the dark waters of his subconscious. Like so many south-city alleys, this one was a cabinet of curiosities: overflowing dumpsters at either end, baking with the smell of hot garbage, of course; but also a couch standing on one end against the alley wall, its microfiber upholstery green with mildew; a stack of old tires, the rubber so broken down that it was hard to read DOUGLAS on the sidewalk; a hollow-core door laid over two foam coolers stamped HALIBUT - FROZEN, the big crystal doorknob refracting light across the pavement. The asphalt was pale here, patched in countless places, and the trail of blood led clearly between the brick walls. The drops were thicker and closer together. She was slowing down or bleeding more. Both, probably.

"She ran through here so they couldn't follow her. It's too narrow for a vehicle; that's why the dumpsters are at either end, because somebody has to push them out into the street every week for the garbage collectors."

North, his face drawn with pain, studied the scene in silence.

They followed the trail through the alley, past a wooden box painted with the phases of the moon, its tiny brass hinges snapped in half, its lid missing, used needles glinting in the sun. They followed the trail past a Take Five wrapper tangled in a clump of waist-high weeds that had somehow, impossibly, managed to thrive in the cramped alley.

When they emerged onto the next street, they found more of the commercial section of Bevo, a jumble of warehouses and businesses: a gas station that had obviously been closed for years; a dialysis center that backed up to a warehouse for a roofing business; another warehouse that belonged to a glazer.

The trail of blood led them out into the street, and Shaw tried to calculate a timeline. Malorie had left the shelter in the morning—they'd need an exact time. But whatever had happened with the skid marks and the blood, it must have happened later. Other kids would have been leaving the shelter that morning around the same time, and nobody had seen anything. His best guess was that Malorie had left and come back to the shelter, probably in the late afternoon or early evening—before the shelter opened for the night, but after businesses in this area had closed for the day, when a girl could be shot and stumble down the middle of the street without anyone seeing her.

North caught his arm as a truck whipped past, throwing up a cloud of exhaust and hot air.

"Big boys look both ways before they cross the street," he murmured.

Shaw kissed his cheek.

When the street was empty, Shaw trotted out, following the drip trail. He made it almost a hundred yards before the trail ended abruptly. He stared at the pavement in disbelief.

"Where did she go?"

"I don't know," North said, "but we're getting back on the sidewalk—this street is too narrow for people to go around, and the light's about to change. Come on."

He let North tug him up between two parked cars and up onto the sidewalk, almost falling into a storm drain when he didn't watch his step. Then he turned back to the street. The blood trail ended completely.

"She might have done what we did," North said, "and gone back on the sidewalk."

"But she would have left a trail cutting across the street."

"Maybe whoever was in the truck or van caught up to her here."

"It would take longer to go around the block."

"She'd been hurt pretty bad."

"But it doesn't look like she tried to run. Even if they caught up to her, wouldn't she have gone left or right, tried to put some of the parked cars between her and whoever was chasing her?"

"I don't know, Shaw. Maybe it was a friend. She called someone while she ran, and she climbed in the car."

"Unless they were already in the car, parked just down the block, there's no way—"

North's hand rested on the back of his neck, squeezed, and then his thumb massaged a knot of tension. "Take a breath."

Shaw took a breath. Down the street, a tarp snapped in the breeze; it was stowed in the back of one of those ubiquitous white Fords, F-150s, base models, that most big contractors and construction companies seemed to prefer. A handful of them were parked on this street, and more were parked in the warehouse lots, all of them ten years old, all with racks in their beds, all with the kind of day-to-day gear that would be a pain to unload and not worth stealing: buckets, tie-downs, coolers open and turned upside down to dry overnight. Tarps.

The sun glinted amber off the windows on the four-plex opposite. It gave the trucks and cars parked along the street a nimbus that softened old paint and dings and split upholstery. Shaw took another breath, tasting a hint of cigarette smoke and the warmth of North's body, sweat and salt at the end of a bad day. Not clean sweat, not even work sweat from a hard day on a job site, not—

"Oh my God," he whispered.

"What?"

"She used a tarp," Shaw said, his gaze moving from the final drop of blood in the center of the street, across the asphalt, and stopping at the storm drain on which they stood. "She knew someone was following her. Could follow her, I mean, because of the blood. The street's narrow. One of those roofing trucks was parked here. She grabbed a tarp, spread it out, crawled across it, and pulled it down the storm drain after her. I bet it's still—"

North caught his wrist in a grip like iron when Shaw started to crouch. "North—"

"No. Get your phone and stand over there."

"But I'm the one who—"

"I said no, Shaw."

Heat rushed into Shaw's face.

"If it's bad," North said in a gentler tone, "I don't want you carrying it around inside your head."

It took a moment for Shaw to nod, the movement robotic, but North didn't release him until he moved across the verge and onto the grass on the other side of the walk. Grunting, North lowered himself to hands and knees. He peered through the wide, low opening in the gutter. After a moment, he swore, fished out his phone, and shone the flashlight into the relative darkness of the drain.

"Mother of God," he said quietly.

"North?"

North started taking pictures, reaching as far into the drain as he could. "It's her. Call it in."

Chapter 8

THE HOMICIDE DETECTIVES SEPARATED them and kept them sitting in the evening sun until North's headache had taken on an optical quality, a dancing ring of light that moved with him wherever he turned his head. Questions. Then more questions. Then the same questions again. The asshole's name was Monzyk, and his partner was Contalonis. Monzyk, purple nosed, his blond hair thinning, hammered at them like he'd caught them with the gun in their hands. Contalonis, watery eyed and drooping in his sack suit, was supposed to be playing good cop, but it was obvious he'd only skimmed the script.

A crowd had gathered—residents of the street, a girl in a polyester polo and short shorts from the bar and grill, a guy in a Carhartt shirt and jeans who kept tucking his ball cap under one arm, then moving it across his heart, then back under one arm like he thought they were about to start the Pledge of Allegiance. People from the shelter had come. Ryley clip-clopped between a pair of old women in curlers, her face unreadable as she stared at the nylon privacy screen that the police had used to cordon off the scene. Nik drifted through the crowd too, lifting something—a gold chain around his neck—to his lips from time to time, saying something under his breath.

Somebody important arrived in a black Town Car, and Monzyk and Contalonis hurried off to suck ass and give each other congratulatory hand jobs. North gave them a ten-count, got to his feet, and began moving. Casually. Slowly. Purposefully. He kept his gaze from meeting any of the uniformed officers who were dicking around. He reached Shaw, who was staring at the ground, plucking blades of grass and shredding them. His breathing was too rapid.

"Come on," he said, grunting as he hoisted Shaw to his feet. The headache doubled, and North's vision swam as the ring of light flared. For a moment, nausea overwhelmed him, he clenched his throat against the upsurge of vomit. "Shaw, baby, I really need you right now."

The words must have meant something because Shaw emerged from the labyrinth he had built for himself, all the tortuous and torturous paths he laid out and crisscrossed. He got to his feet, checked North's eyes, and said, "You need to see a doctor. A real doctor."

"I need to get out of here before Douchebag and Doofus remember they're trying to long-dick us. As soon as they get fitted with their new French ticklers, they're going to be back at it, and we've got work to do."

"What's a—"

"Hey!"

The shout came from a peach-fuzz kid in uniform.

"Come on," North said again, but when he took a step, the nausea rose up again. Shaw grabbed him, steadied him, and half-carried him toward the crowd.

"Hey, you!"

"Faster," Shaw whispered.

Cold sweat soaked North. His legs trembled.

Then Nik was there, the kid emerging from the crowd, his face tear-soaked and blotchy. "Is it her? Is it her?"

"Help me," Shaw said crisply.

The words seemed to shock Nik into action, and he took North's other arm, and they were swallowed up by the throng of bodies. Nik guided them between a pair of apartment buildings, where the heat shimmered in the narrow space between the brick walls. A bearded guy, shirtless and in cargo shorts and flip-flops, was barbequing at the back of the lot, and he watched them as they did their three-legged-race past him. The smell of seared meat did it, and North doubled over and did some massive upchucking on the cracked concrete walk.

"They're going to come after us," Nik said in a low voice, bouncing on his toes. He was crying again. "It was her, wasn't it? It was Malorie."

"It was her," North said between heaves. "Pictures."

"North, can you—oh gosh, that is a lot." Shaw's hand rubbed his back.

"I'm ok." North wiped his mouth. "I'm ok."

"You are definitely not ok, but can you do another hundred yards for me?"

"I'm ok," North mumbled as they set off again. He leaned heavily on Shaw, aware that he was making it harder for all of them, no matter how much Nik tried to take some of his weight. "I'm totally ok."

He stopped to puke again in a patch of drooping honeysuckle before they made it through a gap in a privacy fence, across an overgrown yard, and out a side gate. He was dimly aware they they'd cut through the shelter's backyard. The GTO wasn't ten yards off.

"No way you're driving. We'll pick it up tomorrow."

"Somebody—" North steadied himself. "Boost it."

"Fine. We'll leave the Mercedes—"

"No." Licking his lips, he shook his head. "Totally fine."

"I can drive," Nik said, wiping his eyes. He coughed to clear his throat.

"No!"

"Nik, you're upset," Shaw said. "You should—"

"Please. I can't go back to the shelter; I'm going crazy thinking about her, and it'll be worse if I'm sitting in there, where she used to—where she and I—"

North realized he was starting to tip over.

"Merciful Buddha," Shaw said, bracing North with one hand, fishing out his keys with the other. "Nik, follow me. North, I'm not trying to give you a fiver, I just need to get your keys out of your pocket."

In a surprisingly short amount of time, North found himself sprawled in the GTO's passenger seat, the Morrokide cool under his cheek, the dusk like a balm to his eyes. That ring of light was still following him, but if he kept his head back and breathed right, he didn't need to puke.

"The closest hospital—" Shaw was saying.

"No," North groaned.

"The clinic," Nik said.

"He needs a—"

"Dr. Egg is a real doctor. And you can talk to her about Malorie. And then we go ask Jesse if she came by, and we can talk to the people at the temp agency."

"North isn't in any condition to—"

"Clinic," North said.

"I really don't think—"

"Clinic," he managed to say a little more forcefully. The effort thunderclapped inside his head, and he sagged back against the seat.

"You are definitely going into the cryochamber when we get home," Shaw muttered as he started the GTO.

"Nik," North croaked, "save me."

Chapter 9

THE CLINIC WAS ANOTHER of the low, redbrick buildings that constituted the Bevo neighborhood. It was detached, and the lot needed some serious yard work—or maybe just a dose of Agent Orange. On the ride over, the AC and the chance to sit helped, and when Shaw parked, North was able to stand and hobble inside with nothing more than Shaw's hand on his arm to steady him.

The waiting room was what North, after a lifetime of being poor, had come to expect from this kind of place: outdated magazines with torn covers, grubby toys, peeling wallpaper in neutral colors and patterns meant to hide dirt. The perfume insert from a *Vogue* magazine gave off the overpowering scent of gardenias, which mixed with the smells of instant coffee, unwashed bodies, and accumulated skin oils ingrained in every surface. The clock on the wall said it was almost seven, which North had a hard time believing. Next to the clock, a poster showed a blonde in a maxi dress strolling along a beach, which apparently had something to do with erectile dysfunction.

The reception window had a name plate that said MISS DEB, and behind it sat a shapeless older woman. She wore an Easter-egg-green polyester top, and her face was flushed behind enormous glasses on a fake-pearl chain. North would have bet his next mortgage payment that she cut her own hair. When she pressed something, her voice emerged from a tinny-sounding speaker: "Yes?"

"I think he has a concussion," Shaw said. "He was hit in the head at least once, his pupils are dilated, and he's been vomiting."

"I do not have a fucking concussion."

"He's also been swearing a lot, using obscene phrases, making indecent advances on my virtue, and objectifying me for his own sexual gratification."

Miss Deb stared at them.

"Those are symptoms of a concussion too," Shaw told her.

"They surely fucking aren't," North said.

"Do you have an appointment?" Miss Deb asked.

North looked around the empty room. "Are you kidding me? We've got to talk to the doctor. Tell her it's about a murdered girl."

Miss Deb laughed nervously, eyes wide and rolling. "Well, yes, I see, but do you have an appointment?"

"What the actual—"

"It's ok," Shaw said, patting him. "I can make a reverse transtemporal agenda reification."

"No, you can't." North yanked his arm away; a wave of nausea made him immediately regret it. "And there's nobody else here, so why the hell would we need—"

"Actually, I can. I watched this eight-millimeter movie on Swedish chronometrics and C potency versus D potency—" He interrupted himself with a laugh. "Oh my God, North, D potency. Do you get it?"

"You're never going to have D potency again in your goddamn life—"

"Don't talk to him like that," Nik shouted.

"It's fine." Shaw smiled at Nik. "The super interesting part is that because of its interdimensional lapse, Sweden has a matriarchal aura; it's totally free of alpha-male aggression and the toxic patterns—"

"What is this?" North demanded. "Are you punishing me? Are you angry? Swedish chronometrics and interdimensional dick potency, is that some kind of code about the whole alpha-butch thing? Because I got pistol whipped today, and I feel like shit, and I'm having a really fucking hard time understanding what the hell is going on."

"Don't—" Nik started.

With a softer smile, Shaw ducked his head. He put a hand out to silence Nik. After a moment, he shrugged and said, "Sorry. Yeah. If you want the truth, I was kind of…stretching things, I guess. I wanted to make you feel better."

North grunted.

"The whole truth—" Shaw began.

North groaned.

"—is that I honestly can't remember if that film said the interdimensional lapse was in Denmark or Sweden."

A few deep breaths. A hand pressed to his temple, where the headache had kicked into overdrive. Somehow, he managed to keep his voice even: "Why does it fucking matter?"

"Well, it probably matters to the people in Denmark. Or Sweden, I guess."

North had to stand very still for a while.

"Excuse me." Miss Deb's nervous laughter broke free again. "But if you don't have an appointment—"

The sound of a door opening came from the other side of the reception window, and a woman snapped, "Deb, what in the world is going on? Do we need to have another conversation about chitchat?"

"No, Dr. Eggenberg, but—"

"Did you finish reconciling the purchase orders?"

"I was—"

"What did you do instead?"

A honking guffaw escaped Miss Deb, but her eyes were rolling faster than ever. "Some of the children had—"

"Since I told you to reconcile the purchase orders, what were you supposed to do?"

"Reconcile—"

"And is it unreasonable that I should expect you to have done the only thing I asked you to do?"

Snatching tissues from a box, Miss Deb shook her head, more laughter bursting out in staccato that she was obviously trying desperately to rein in. Nerves, not amusement. Nerves frayed to the point of snapping. "No, no, Dr. Eggenberg—"

"Dr. Egg," Nik shouted in the direction of the voice, "it's me, Nik. We need to talk to you about Malorie. Someone killed her."

A woman moved into view on the other side of the reception window. In profile, she was striking: the sharp contrast of red-gold hair and cream skin, a hint of freckles. The illusion only lasted an instant. As she turned, the rest of the picture assembled. Her eyes were too far apart and expressionless. Her mouth was thin lipped. An overall fishiness in her face was reinforced by the way she guppied her lips.

"Nikshay," she said. "I've asked you not to call me that. Whatever you—"

"It's Malorie. Someone killed her, and we're trying to figure out who did it, and she was coming here—"

"All right." Dr. Egg's words were clipped. She considered North for a moment. "What's wrong with him?"

"Nothing," North said.

"Well, a concussion," Shaw said, "but there's also his mulishness, his obstinacy, strong-willedness—"

"That's not a fucking word."

"—determination, grit, moxie—"

"I am not a 1920s flapper."

"I think you were in a past life, though. That one time you had that feather boa, I know you were only joking, but it came to you very naturally—"

"Shut. Up."

"—and you do drink a lot of gin. Well, a lot of beer. But gin too. Sometimes. Maybe it has to do with the moon. Do you think the moon was in Virgo when you were born? I need to—"

"I don't have time for this," Dr. Egg said.

"Please." Nik took a step forward. Grief had laid his face bare, and he rubbed his eyes as he asked again, "Please?"

She directed a look at Miss Deb. "Put them in an exam room. Now, if it isn't too much trouble."

Dr. Egg disappeared behind a door that, North guessed, led to her office. Miss Deb let them in at the waiting room door. She was still trembling with the laughs that ripped free every few minutes, but she looked on the verge of tears. After settling them in an exam room down the hall, she pulled the door shut firmly, and her steps hurried away.

"Christ," North said, "I would not want to be her. Did you hear how that woman talks to her?"

"That's interesting," Shaw said, strolling around the room. "Because you used a lot of those same expressions the last time you got mad at me. You were all 'Did you send that invoice certified mail?' and I was all 'Well, certified mail reinforces government hegemony over snail, e-, and psychic mail,' and you were all 'I fucking told you to send it certified,' and I was all 'I did something even better. I telepathically transmitted the invoice to an ethereal telegraph machine in the Alexander Graham Bell Museum in Nova Scotia, and as soon as they find a ghost who knows Morse code, they'll transcribe the message and mail it to the client,' and you were all—"

"I cannot do this."

"Yes, exactly! And then you kicked that box of surveillance equipment, and I thought I heard something break, and you gave me a look and took it outside, and when you came back, I asked if anything broke, and you said you didn't know what I was talking about, and I haven't seen that box again."

North opened his mouth to reply, but a wave of nausea crested. Cold sweat broke out all over him. He struggled with the need to puke. After a moment, it subsided, and Shaw was there, helping him up onto the exam table. It was partially upright, the back section raised at an angle so that North could recline against it. The paper crinkled under him. Shaw fiddled with something, and a stirrup came into view.

"Not on your fucking life," North said.

"Your leg will be more comfortable—"

"I will break your damn hand if you try to get me into that thing."

The smile was a ghost that wisped away into a—mostly real, North thought—expression of concern. "Relax," Shaw said quietly.

"Something weird," North said. He took out his phone, unlocked it on his second, fumbling try, and accessed the pictures. He displayed them for Shaw, careful to keep Nik from noticing, as he went through photo after photo of Malorie Walton, dead in a storm drain. The girl had been dressed for a night out—her good clothes, the kind a teenager might wear to impress her friends: a white tube top, fashionably ripped jeans, strappy silver sandals.

"What's that?" Shaw asked.

North went back a picture. It showed the tarp tangled around one leg, and then Malorie's sandals. One had slipped halfway off her foot. Shaw pinched the screen to zoom, and then North saw it: a paper rectangle caught between her heel and the insole.

"It looks like a receipt," North said.

"Can I try something?"

North passed over the phone, and Shaw tapped and swiped, adjusting color and saturation and contrast, until at the top of the paper, red letters became clear.

"Big Murphy," North read.

Shaw gave him a disgusted look.

"It's the concussion," North mumbled. "My vision is fine."

"Big Muddy," Shaw said. "What the hell is the Big Muddy?"

They glanced at Nik, and the boy shook his head.

"What was Malorie wearing when she left the shelter Wednesday?" Shaw asked.

"This stupid Gucci t-shirt that she thinks is tough," Nik said. "Um, shorts, I think."

"Not a white top and jeans?"

Nik shook his head.

"So she changed clothes at some point," North said.

"She had that outfit in the locker at the shelter," Nik said. "She liked those clothes."

"Which means she definitely went back at some point," Shaw said.

The conclusion didn't tell them anything else, though, so North tried to search on his phone for the Big Muddy. Staring at the screen made the room tilt after a few minutes, and the heaves hit him. Shaw stroked his hair and plucked away the phone, and North closed his eyes. He relaxed by inches. When sleep came, it happened all of a sudden, and for a moment he was at the tree line of that vast, uncharted wilderness. The booger woods. His dad had told him stories about the booger woods when he'd been a kid. The booger woods, the place you don't want to go alone. Told those stories until North's mom had said to stop. But now they were here again, and North was here too, on the verge of stepping into a dark forest of half-formed dreams and fears, everything that had been building in his subconscious since the early-morning call about his dad.

He woke and opened his eyes. He must have only slept for a few minutes because Nik and Shaw were sitting in tubular chairs, talking quietly while Shaw either read Nik's palm or was preparing to spit there, the old swimming pool joke. North tried to look through the pictures of Malorie again, but after a few minutes, his head began to throb. He shifted his weight. The exam table was hard under him; the vinyl had split in several places, and the foam padding protruded in stiff triangles. He let his gaze wander, trying to keep himself alert. Along one wall ran a counter and cabinets. On top of the counter, someone had piled clipboards and charts and reams of paper, which partially obscured the glass jars at the back that held swabs and cotton balls and tongue depressors. An ancient poster on the other wall showed a man's arm, the sleeve of a black suit, maybe a tux. The hand held a silver tray with a plate of food. In cheery script, the poster informed him, YOU CAN'T GET AIDS FROM FOOD SERVICE.

"That seems pretty optimistic," Shaw interrupted his palm reading, "considering some of the wait staff you banged it out with when we were in college."

The corner of North's mouth twitched, but he managed to get away with only saying, "That sounds an awful lot like slut shaming."

"No, I—"

"Gross," Nik said, giving North the hairy eyeball. "He really is a slut."

"That's not a word—"

"He used it."

"But—"

"Go on, Shaw. Explain to him how it's different."

The door opened, and Shaw whispered, "Thank you, Samantabhadra of the Lotus Sutra."

Dr. Egg stepped into the room. She eyed Nik, then Shaw, and North last. Stepping over to the exam table, she pulled on a pair of disposable gloves and said, "Turn your head toward me."

"Make him take off his shirt."

"For Christ's sake," North muttered as cool hands tilted his head.

"No talking," Dr. Egg said.

"There's all this fur down there." Shaw's tone was aggrieved. "Sometimes it gets in my mouth."

"Didn't you hear her?"

"I meant you," Dr. Egg snapped.

"She meant you," Nik said.

North tried to swallow the growl building in his throat.

"It was pretty obvious she meant you," Shaw offered quietly.

"I'm fine," North said.

"He was puking and almost passing out."

"I went to the urgent care. They checked me out. I was fine all day."

"But then you went running around," Shaw said, "overdoing it. Would that make the concussion worse, Doctor?"

"I wasn't running around—"

"What don't you understand," Dr. Egg said, "about be quiet? Yes, overexertion would certainly have made the symptoms worse, even if he was feeling 'back to normal.' No more talking from anyone."

The doctor checked his vision and hearing, his balance and coordination, his reflexes. She asked him questions. North tried to tell her to get it over with, but another whirlpool of nausea dragged him down, and as he puked into a plastic basin, he figured he'd lost the battle before it had even started.

"Tylenol today," Dr. Egg said, opening a drawer and taking out a foil-wrapped packet. She tore the packaging and passed the tablets to North. "Ibuprofen tomorrow. And these," another foil-wrapped packet, "as long as you need them, but if the nausea doesn't subside or the other symptoms get worse, you need to go to a hospital."

"What's this?"

"Dimenhydrinate," Shaw said.

"And what the fuck is that?"

"Over-the-counter anti-nausea medication. Dramamine."

North swallowed the pills with water from a paper cup. Nobody told him to get down from the exam table, so he leaned back and tried not to sigh in relief.

Snapping off the gloves, Dr. Egg said, "What's this about Malorie?"

"She's dead." Nik trembled as he added, "Somebody killed her."

She directed a questioning look at North and Shaw.

Shaw nodded, and North said, "We found her. Just a few hours ago, actually."

"Am I supposed to be flattered or worried that you came straight here?"

North and Shaw kept their silence. Nik scooted to the edge of his seat and said, "We need to know if Malorie came to her appointment on Wednesday."

"Nik, you know that doctor-patient confidentiality—"

"She's dead," North said.

"That privilege still applies in some cases."

"In certain limited cases," Shaw said. "When it might damage someone else who's still alive. Is that what you're worried about?"

Dr. Egg sat on a rolling stool. Her lips guppied silently. Then she said, "Not necessarily. I don't suppose it's going to harm anyone to tell you that yes, Malorie came for her appointment on Wednesday. I believe it was early afternoon."

"Do you remember all your patients that clearly?" North asked.

"I have an excellent memory."

"That's not an answer."

Those too-wide eyes fixed on him. "Who are you?"

"North McKinney. This is my partner, Shaw Aldrich. We're private investigators."

"Someone hired you to look into Malorie's death? Who? How? You said you found her a few hours ago."

"Client confidentiality," North said with a hard smile.

"How did Malorie seem?" Shaw asked.

"Was she scared?" Nik shrank back when North looked at him, but he asked, "Did she seem worried?"

"Be quiet," North said.

"You can't—"

"Nik," Shaw said, "let us do this. If you think we're missing something, then tell us, but otherwise let us handle it."

Nik tried to hold Shaw's gaze, but he looked away first, a blush climbing his cheeks.

"To answer your question," Dr. Egg said into the silence, "she seemed like Malorie."

"What was she like?" Shaw asked.

"She was a hard girl." When Nik brought up his head, Dr. Egg waved a hand at him. "Not unpleasant. The opposite, actually. She could be quite charming. But she knew what she wanted, and she did what she had to do to get it. She was resilient, but she was also…well, I believe she had acquired some maladaptive habits. She'd had a hard life. That came through pretty clearly sometimes."

"What do you mean?"

Dr. Egg smoothed away a lock of red-gold hair. "Substance abuse."

"She didn't use drugs," Nik said. "She was clean. She got clean for the baby."

"If it would be easier to wait in the hall," Shaw said, touching Nik's arm.

Nik jerked away, his eyes full of tears as he stared at Shaw.

"Malorie was upfront with me about her drug use." Dr. Egg's voice was clinical. "Marijuana primarily. Occasionally methamphetamines. Even more rarely, crack cocaine."

"She didn't use."

"Did she seem worried?" Shaw asked. "About her own health, I mean, or the baby?"

"I explained the dangers to both of them. Malorie was convinced that her use was minimal and wouldn't affect either of them."

"What about more generally?" North forced himself to sit upright. "Nik asked you earlier, did she seem upset? Afraid? Worried about something else?"

"Not at all. She said something about going to the movies."

Nik let out a hitching sob, and then he started to cry. When North looked at Shaw, Shaw took Nik's arm and helped the boy to his feet. Nik was bawling into Shaw's side as Shaw walked him out of the room, and as they left, the boy was mumbling, "She wouldn't, she didn't, she was clean."

The door shut behind them. The room had a staticky silence, and North found it strangely difficult to meet the doctor's eyes. Maybe it had been the professional dynamic of the exam. Maybe it was the lack of affect in her eyes and face and voice.

"How was she dressed?" North asked.

Dr. Egg frowned.

"A white top? Jeans?"

"No, I don't think so. Why?"

"She changed clothes at some point. We're trying to figure out when. Tell me about the Big Muddy." He didn't know where the question had come from; the headache aura—which ringed the lights, which made her white lab coat incandescent and glinted off the steel nib of the pen—made it impossible to track his own thoughts. North tried not to imagine what Shaw would attribute it to.

But the question didn't land. Fish eyes narrowed slightly as Dr. Egg asked, "What's the Big Muddy?"

"You've never heard of it?"

"No. Should I have?"

"Do you know who she was sleeping with? Who she was seeing? Where else might she have been going on Wednesday?"

"Mr. McKinney, I don't know what's prompting these questions or why you think I might know the answers, but you're under some sort of misunderstanding where it comes to me and Malorie. I've seen Malorie through the course of her pregnancy. I know some of her bad habits—recreational drugs, unsafe sex. She had frequent new partners, and she didn't always use protection. She did receive a course of antibiotics to treat chlamydia, which we caught early. But who she slept with and where are outside my expertise."

A hiss of white noise had started in North's head. Gravity was dragging him down on the exam table. But he said, "You don't seem particularly torn up about Malorie's death."

"No. I suppose I don't. Malorie was a patient. She wasn't my daughter or my sister or my friend. And in this line of work, in a place like this, I see a lot of tragic things. A young woman murdered—"

"And her baby."

Dr. Egg frowned. "And her baby, well, if I fell to pieces every time something like that happened, I'd never be able to do my job."

North nodded, and the nod turned into his head drooping. He struggled to drag himself upright.

Her fish eyes were glistening and bright. "The dimenhydrinate will make you drowsy. I recommend that you go straight home to bed and, as I said, seek follow-up care as necessary."

She walked him to reception, where Nik was pressing tissues against his face while Shaw rubbed his back. Shaw took North's arm across his shoulder again, and they said goodnight as Dr. Egg let them out into the September night. The heat had evaporated, and the breeze was brisk and brought a mineral scent. In the blurred vision from the headache, the streetlights burned like alien torches.

A good night's sleep, North thought, the words trickling like sand between his fingers. A good night's sleep in the booger woods. He slept in the car, slept again in his bed after Shaw had helped him stumble inside, and woke to a dream of Ronnie peering at him through a weir of knotted branches. The headache was gone, but the exhaustion hung on him, threatening to drag him back down. Someone was watching him, he realized. Just a shadowy outline through the cracked door, the glitter of an eye in the weak ambient light.

Shaw gave a hiccoughing sob, and North turned.

"I'm—I'm—I'm sorry," Shaw whispered, making a visible effort to bring himself under control. "I didn't want to wake you up. Go back to sleep. Your head."

Shaw Aldrich, North thought, who never got scars, who never toughened up, who the world kept hurting over and over again, and who hurt himself with all his imaginings more than the world ever could. North pulled him into his arms. For a moment, Shaw was tense, all wire and coils. Then he said, "She fought so hard, and she ran, and she was smart, and she wanted to save her baby. And she died alone in that—in that pit, and nobody cared."

Stroking Shaw's hair, North shushed him while Shaw cried into his chest. He said the only thing he knew would help: "Nik cares. We care. And we'll find who did it. We can do that much. That's a promise—we'll find them."

Shaw raised his head. His eyes were wet and red from weeping, but they held a question that went bone deep. More than a question. A need.

North nodded and brushed his hair across his forehead.

For a while, Shaw cried again, but the weeping was a normal grief now instead of that place inside his head that North had come to think of as the labyrinth. Then the crying ended, and Shaw's breathing evened out, and he slept.

When North looked up again, the shadow in the doorway was gone.

Chapter 10

"TELL ME AGAIN," North said, "why she still has anything to do with this prick?"

Overnight, a storm had moved in. The rain had broken for the moment, but the sky was dark and colorless. The decaying brick bungalow in front of them sat on one of the many sloped lots in South City, with a crumbling retaining wall that had shifted and fallen in places across the sidewalk. The low-slope roof had scabs of three-tab shingles peeling back, and the grass was overgrown, tangled with weeds. A gang of kids formed a tight knot a few houses down; the nervous energy of their bodies said that somebody—an unpleasant neighbor, an unlucky dog, a passing car—was going to have trouble.

Nik was wearing another pair of North's jeans and another of North's tees—this one featured a crane that was supposed to look like a wireframe engineer's sketch. He shook his head. "Malorie said he was all right."

"He was her pimp," North said.

Shaw was checking a patch sewn onto the sleeve of his field jacket, which he was wearing over a pink tank and translucent Lululemon pants and, thank God for small miracles, pink Nikes, which were better than the geta or the clogs or those bed-of-nail torture shoes he thought were toughening him up. Nik had checked out the Lululemons at least ten times since Shaw came out of their bedroom that morning, obviously clocking the bulge in front. Shaw hadn't noticed; he seemed more worried that his RAINBOW HOMO BRIGADE patch was going to fall off. "I think the preferred term is manager."

"Managing sex workers by beating the shit out of them. I think they teach that class at Olin."

Shaw made a disgusted noise, but a moment later, when the patch came off and he stared at it in his hand, North realized the reaction hadn't been meant for him. He decided this was a good time to get out of the car.

North was halfway around the GTO when a Sunkist can in front of him flew into the air. A popping noise came from a few houses down, and then shrieks of laughter. The boys were disappearing around the side of the house, air rifle raised in victory, while the can was still rolling along the sidewalk.

"Get your asses back here," North shouted.

"They were just having fun," Nik said.

"Fun? Almost putting my eye out, that's fun? Fuck, I hate kids. I fucking hate them."

"He's like this when he's gassy," Shaw said in an undertone, "so I like to—"

Whatever he saw on North's face made him stop. North resumed his march toward the house, and Shaw and Nik trailed him to the steps. It was mid-morning, and on the other side of the door, the house was silent. North knocked. He kept at it for almost a minute.

Nothing.

When he looked over his shoulder, Shaw was licking the back of the patch.

"For fuck's sake."

"North, give it back! It fell off, and maybe it's like stamp glue, you have to lick it—"

"It's not. It's hot glue. I know because you accidentally-but-kind-of-on-purpose hot glued your balls to the chair. You kept calling it 'extreme crafting,' which apparently means naked crafting, and then you'd giggle so hard you'd lie down on the table. Then you decided you needed to test the hot glue's adhesive qualities as it cooled. And that's how, fifteen minutes later, I had to use ice and a putty knife to get your balls loose."

"My test worked, North. I learned it was still sticky. That was a sacrifice for science."

"Yeah, well, science didn't have to spend his Saturday night on his knees, your junk in his face, and when he wanted a little compensation get told, quote, 'I'm still a little tender down there.' Why the fuck isn't this asshole answering his door?"

North hammered on the door again.

"I wouldn't have minded," Nik said, dark eyes flashing as he tried to catch North's gaze. North ignored him. "If I had a boyfriend, I'd be happy to do things like that for him."

"Good fucking luck," North muttered.

"What was that?" Shaw asked.

"Nothing."

"Can I have my patch back, please? Maybe Jesse has some glue."

"No. If I give it back, you're going to refuse to put it in your jacket pockets. You'll stick it in your waistband because those goddamn Lululemons don't have pockets. And then you'll lose it. And then I'm going to spend my Monday night crawling around a pimp's living room trying to find proof that you served in the Rainbow Homo Brigade during the Flamer Wars."

"I was a rear admiral."

"Brigades don't have—" North swallowed the noise building in his throat. Aside from the bruises and the day-after stiffness, he felt much better, but his head still felt fragile. He didn't want to set it off again.

"I'll hold it for you." Nik put his hand out. "I've got pockets. I'll hold the patch for you."

"Kid," North said, slapping the patch against Nik's chest and then releasing it so Nik had to scramble to catch it, "be my guest."

Nik gave Shaw several hopeful looks, obviously expecting acknowledgment.

Shaw had pulled back the waistband on the Lululemons and was apparently giving himself a lump inspection.

"Right now?" North said.

"I got a tickle," Shaw said defensively.

North knocked again and said, "Maybe I'll leave the parking brake off."

"What?" Nik said.

"Don't engage," Shaw said as he resumed his inspection. Nik was trying to get a peek without being caught.

"I'll leave the parking brake off, and I'll park on a hill. Right by a lake. And the car will roll down the hill, nice and easy. I'll have my windows down. I'll go right under. No struggle."

"He's dramatic," Shaw said, doing some below-the-equator scratching and adjusting. "It all started when he stole the show as Crumpet—"

"Do not fucking start with that shit."

The door flew open. The guy standing there was white, wiry, and had greasy strands of hair falling in front of his face. There wasn't anything remarkable about him—he looked like run-of-the-mill tweaker trash—but he had the smirk and the eyes and a kind of cockiness in his body that said he was one of those guys who got ass all the time, and you'd never be able to say why. He was wearing what a guy like him probably called a wifebeater and a pair of too-large jeans that sagged below his cheeks.

"What the hell, man? Do you know what time it is?"

"Almost ten in the fucking morning. You Jesse?"

"Who's—"

"Me, dumbshit. I'm asking. My name's North McKinney. I'm a private investigator, and I want to talk to you about Malorie Walton. If, that is, Beavis and Butthead can shut the fuck up for five minutes."

"I'm Butthead," Shaw whispered to Nik. "You're Beavis."

"You're her pussy-boy friend, right?" Jesse said, directing the words past North to Nik. "What the fuck is this about?"

"It's about you moving out of the fucking way so I can come inside and ask you some questions," North said. "Now, before you ruin my oh-so-pleasant fucking morning."

"He was thinking about drowning us," Shaw said brightly. "All of us. In his car."

Jesse's confusion resolved itself in what was probably his default course of action. He began to shut the door as he said, "Fuck off, man."

Wedging one of the Redwings between the door and the frame, North said, "No, man. I can't fuck off, man. You know why, man? Because my other option is finding a steep hill and a deep lake. So here's what we're going to do. You're going to park your ass and talk to me about Malorie. Because if you don't, I'm going to call Jadon Reck. Jadon is a detective with the Metropolitan Police. So if you don't open the door, sit your ass down, and answer every fucking question to my ultimate fucking satisfaction about who killed Malorie and why, Jadon is going to knock this fucking door off its fucking hinges with an entry ram. Then he'll haul your ass downtown, and you'll answer the questions anyway, while I tell everybody who will listen that you're a narc and you love squealing."

Jesse's eyes were wide, his mouth hanging open, spittle spanning upper and lower teeth. "What do you mean—what do you mean? That thing about Malorie, what do you—"

"Someone killed her," North said. "Now, are you going to—"

Face screwing up, Jesse started to cry. He stumbled back into the house, wailing.

"Nice," Nik said.

"Yeah? The fucker shouldn't have been so fucking obstinate. He—" North cut off when Shaw squeezed his shoulder. He shook himself, pushed the door open the rest of the way, and stepped into the house.

Behind him, Nik said, "Jesse's actually all right, even if he does say stupid stuff. Nobody should be mean to him like that."

Shaw's sigh suggested that even he might have a limit to his patience.

Inside, the house was even worse than the exterior had suggested. They stood in a small living room with only a blue microsuede couch and a flatscreen TV balanced on top of a cardboard box. Arby's wrappers covered the floor; a flattened Velveeta cheese pouch had ants trapped in the streaks of yellow goop; empty Shasta cola two-liters lay everywhere. The bottles made hollow plastic clunks when North's boot sent them rolling across the room. He headed toward the kitchen, where the sound of crying continued, passing through the invisible cloud of weed and Manwich that suggested the two primary substances being consumed in the house.

The kitchen was a narrow room, galley style, with a large window over the sink and a large sliding glass door. The tile was navy blue and ran across the floor and halfway up the walls. The appliances were stainless steel painted white, chipped in countless places. Jesse was hugging a white girl, his face pressed into her shoulder while she made a limp effort to stir the scrambled eggs on the stove. She was plump, and she wore a floral-print jumpsuit. A belt

GREGORY ASHE

as wide as North's hand rode high on her waist. On second thought, North reconsidered: not white, pink. Her skin was rosy, every exposed inch of it. Her hair was on the carrot side of orange.

"Sweetie," she kept saying in a saccharine tone, stroking Jesse's back while poking at the scrambled eggs. "Aww, sweetcakes, what's wrong? Tell me all about it."

He snuffled a reply into one fleshy shoulder.

The girl rubbed his back. "Do you want some eggs? I bet some eggs will fix you right up. And then you have a nice smoke, and you'll feel right as rain." Whatever Jesse mumbled, she must have understood because she laughed, "Of course we'll get you some of those cookies. We'll fix you right up, and you won't even think about those nasty guys coming around again. Hey, who are you?"

"Hay is for horses," North said. "Who the fuck are you?"

"North would know," Shaw said. "About the hay, I mean. He was a baby cow—whoops, I mean, he was a baby calf—"

"Jess, sweetcakes, there are some guys here." She gave another noodle-armed poke at the frying pan. "One of them is scary and one of them is pretty. Oh, and Malorie's friend's here too."

"I'm scary," Shaw said.

"Fuck that." North put his hands on his hips and gave him a look. "I'm scary. You're pretty."

"I think she meant you. Pretty, I mean. A lot of it's in your face—your jaw, your cheekbones, your nose. Even your hair, although I wish you'd let me use that balm—"

"No, thanks, I don't need your old come mixed with the still-beating heart of a mermaid or whatever the fuck it is."

"First of all, plenty of studies have shown that semen—"

Jesse rounded on them. "Why can't you leave me alone?"

"What about them eggs—"

"God damn it." He spun back and struck the woman on the cheek. She let out a cry and released the spoon, which clattered as it fell between the burners. "Why can't you shut your mouth for five seconds?"

Hand to her cheek, she was crying as she said, "Jesse, you said you like the eggs, you said—"

Jesse raised his hand again, but North caught his arm and twisted it behind his back. When Jesse let out a cry and tried to tear free, North tightened his grip, ratcheting the arm up until Jesse's wrist was almost between his shoulder blades. He screamed.

"Stop it, stop it, you're killing him!" the carrot-haired girl shouted.

"Get out," North said. "We're going to have a conversation. Isn't that right, Jesse?"

82

Jesse thrashed his head in acknowledgment. "Get out, get out, get the fuck out!"

The girl scurried out of the room. On the burner, the eggs caked to the spoon were smoking against the hot element. Nik reached over and turned off the stove. Then he wrapped his arms around himself, shoulders curved in.

"We're going out there," North said, giving Jesse another shake, "and we're going to sit down and have a civilized conversation."

"My breakfast," Jesse whimpered.

When North tugged on his wrist again, he squealed and nodded.

In the living room, Jesse sat on the couch, North standing in front of him. Nik leaned against a window. Shaw toed through the garbage.

"A lot of these foods have guar gum in them," Shaw said, shaking his head. "At the rate you're eating them, you're probably half guar yourself."

Jesse sniffled and adjusted the chains around his neck. He massaged his arms and threw dirty looks at North. "What's guar gum?"

"He doesn't know," North said. "He's going to make something up."

"I do too know. A guar is a human-sized lizard that kind of looks like a T-rex, if you shrank it down until, well, it was human-sized. And their gums are used as a naturally high source of collagen—"

"No, they're not. None of that is true; put it in the big book of bullshit shawiana. What did you do to Malorie?"

"Nothing," Shaw said. "I was with you the whole time."

"Not you, dumbass."

"Nothing!" Jesse shifted on the seat as though about to rise, but when North made a noise, he shrank back down. "Nothing, man. I don't even know—I mean, you just showed up, and you yelled at me and said she was dead, and man, I loved her."

From the hallway came a wounded scoffing noise.

"Yeah," North said. "You loved her so much you had to pimp her out. True love. I'm pimping Shaw out tonight."

"You are? That's wonderful. I bought this latex bodysuit—"

"I didn't—man, you don't know anything." Jesse folded his arms and looked at Nik. "Who are these clowns?"

"They found Malorie," Nik said. "Someone killed her. And you were mad she wasn't working for you, and you were mad she wouldn't tell you who the baby's daddy was, and you were mad she wouldn't sleep in your crib."

"You little faggot!"

As Jesse came out of the seat, North was ready for him. He shoved Jesse back down and raised a fist. He didn't even have to land the blow; Jesse curled up like a stomped spider.

"Start talking," North said.

"Look, it wasn't like that. She did stuff, I guess. With guys. She'd get money sometimes. But it's not like I made her. Sometimes she'd have trouble and she'd call me, and I'd show up with, you know, my piece. But I never made that girl do anything she didn't want to. Nobody did."

"That's not true," Nik said.

"Nik, not right now," Shaw whispered.

"What about last Wednesday? Did she come over?"

"What day is today?" Jesse asked.

"She came on Wednesday." The voice came from the hallway. A moment later, the girl slunk into view, a hand pressed to her cheek. "I got my nails done, and when I came back, that bitch was here."

"What time?"

"Three. Four. No, three, because I was going to watch my show." The girl's voice grew pitchy. "She was smoking my weed."

"She didn't smoke anymore," Nik said. "She didn't."

"What was she wearing?" Shaw asked.

"I don't know," Jesse said.

"That dumb Gucci t-shirt," the girl said. "Skanky shorts."

"Cinnamon, get your ass back into the bedroom."

"That's not your real name, is it?" Shaw asked.

The pink girl turned even pinker. "I'm an artist. That's my stage name. Jesse's got friends who are producers; he's going to get me into the business."

North barely managed to turn the laugh into a snort. "What business?"

She blinked and fiddled with the high-riding belt. "All of it. You know, recording, live performances, dance, probably movies, I guess."

"Right. Good luck with that."

"You don't think I can do it because I'm big, but there are lots of guys who like big girls."

"That wasn't my first concern."

"My first concern—" Shaw began.

"Nobody asked you."

"—is your stage name. Obviously Cinnamon has some great things going for it, but have you considered Tawny?"

"Tawny was Jesse's last ho. He got her a job performing too. I think she has a record coming out next month."

North's eyebrows went up at that, but Shaw spoke first: "Ok, not Tawny. What about Butterscotch?"

Cinnamon made a face.

"Fulvous?"

"Isn't that a—" Jesse made a circle above his crotch. "—lady part?"

Shaw frowned. "Is there a word for the color of mushy apples when they're starting to turn brown?"

"I'm going to put the brakes on this particular shit-brain train," North said. "Do you have any idea who she might have been seeing either romantically or sexually?"

Jesse shook his head. "She didn't tell me no names. The guys, she was the one who found them."

"What about places she liked to take these guys?"

"Their cars. Sometimes a motel, but the guys always picked. It's not like she was a pro, man. She just wanted some cash on the side."

"Ask him about his cut," Nik said.

"Bitch—"

"No, he's right," North said. "How much were you charging for protection?"

The roll of the eyes was surprisingly endearing on Jesse, for some reason. "Man, we were in love."

Cinnamon huffed.

"I did it to take care of her."

"That's so sweet," Shaw said. "North, you could learn a thing or two about pimping me out. Last time, when you made me do tongue stuff with that furry guy so we could sneak into that apartment, you weren't a good pimp at all."

"In the first fucking place, it was a Corgi. And in the second, I didn't make you do anything. You lay on the floor, giggling and letting it lick the inside of your mouth. Which reminds me to never fucking kiss you again."

Jesse raised a hand. "Then I put that baby in her—"

"You did not," Nik said. "She never would have had a baby with you."

"—and she took off. Broke my heart."

"But you still saw her?" North said.

"Well, yeah."

"Why?"

"We were—"

"Quit fucking telling me about being in love."

"She liked to smoke his weed," Cinnamon announced. Her arms were folded under her ample bosom, and her pink face had moved into the red zone. "She'd come over and make him think he was going to get some, smoke all our weed, and then leave. She wasn't even a performer. Jesse said she couldn't dance or sing or anything, and when he offered to hook her up, she laughed at him."

"Bitch, shut up." But Jesse ducked his head, and a blush burned in his face.

"All right." North glanced at Shaw. "Tell us about Wednesday."

"I don't know, man. If Cinnamon said she came, then she came."

"But you don't remember anything?"

Jesse shrugged.

"Had Malorie seemed upset recently?" Shaw asked. "Worried? Afraid? Different in any way?"

After a moment, Jesse shook his head. "She was just Malorie."

"What about a place called the Big Muddy?"

"Uh, um, no man."

"Isn't that the place—" Cinnamon said.

"Bitch, shut your fucking mouth!"

"What place?" North said.

"You know what, man?" Jesse shot to his feet, and North shoved him back. "Get the fuck out." Jesse tried again, and North forced him onto the couch again. "Get the fuck out of my crib, motherfucker!"

When Jesse got up the third time, he took a swing. The blow caught North in the belly; it wasn't a very good punch, and it didn't do more than make North grunt. He clubbed Jesse on the side of the head, and Jesse staggered and went down on one knee.

"Get out!' Cinnamon screamed. She had produced a boxy little pistol, and she was waving it as she screamed, "Get out, get out, don't touch him, get the fuck out!"

"Oh my God," Nik shouted. "Oh my God."

"Does that jumpsuit have pockets?" Shaw asked.

"Get the fuck out!"

"Jesus Christ," North said, raising both hands slowly. "We're going."

"Oh my God," Nik was saying.

"Shut him up," North said.

"I didn't think they made jumpsuits with pockets," Shaw said.

"Oh my God!"

"Nik, I'm trying to have a conversation—"

"We're going," North said, snagging Shaw's arm and backing toward the door.

"Don't come back," Cinnamon said in a trembly voice. Her eyes were blank with adrenaline and fear. "I'll—I'll shoot your dicks off if you come back."

Jesse was still on one knee, groaning and rubbing the side of his head.

"Here we go," North said. It was a struggle to keep his voice even as he shoved Nik through the doorway first, then Shaw. He backed out, hands still raised. "We're gone."

As soon as he reached the bottom of the stairs, North caught Shaw's arm and barked, "Run, dumbshits."

Chapter 11

H&H EMPLOYMENT Solutions was their last stop in following Malorie's route the day she had died. The temp agency occupied a suite in a brick maze of an office complex. It was an older building, the brick a dark red, black in places so that it looked burnt. The design had probably been meant to convey openness and spaciousness, with every suite accessed by an exterior corridor, and with plazas and courtyards and breezeways that made the whole thing a bitch to navigate. The place had obviously seen better years; the sidewalks were cracked, the courtyards were overgrown, and Hot Pocket microwave sleeves and clamshell foam takeout containers and Captain D's bags piled in the corners. In a few places, security gates stood open, and a printed eight-and-a-half by eleven sign said, DO NOT LET GEESE PAST THE GATES – SAUNDRA, I SEE YOU.

Shaw kept a close eye on North instead of on Saundra. The blond man's color had gone down on the drive to the temp agency, but halfway there North had reached under the driver's seat, as though groping for something, and then sat upright suddenly and pulled his hand back. He kept reaching out and squeezing Shaw's shoulder. When he did it the next time, Shaw took his hand and laced their fingers together, and North let out a soft noise that Shaw didn't think he was even aware of.

"PDAs are gross," Nik said.

"Be quiet," North said.

"Can't you guys just be cool about things?"

"I can," Shaw said. "North can't."

"Bull-fucking-shit. In college, when we hit it off with the rugby club guys, and everything was going well, you were the one who blew our cool."

"I don't think—"

"You literally invited them to our place to watch all your old VHS tapes of *Power Rangers*."

"I thought they'd enjoy them. Rugby, like *Power Rangers*, arises out of a cult of traditional masculine—"

"Some of those guys actually thought I was normal before you did that. I was actually making new friends for once."

"They didn't all think it was weird," Shaw told Nik. "Some of them showed up for the watch party."

"One of them showed up," North said. "Kurtley fucking Peterson. And he only showed up because he wanted to plow you."

"Which was very flattering. He had an enormous wiener."

North choked, spat, and said in a strangled voice, "It wasn't enormous."

"It was really big."

"It wasn't that big."

"Oh my God, shut up and kiss already," Nik said as he walked faster, leaving them behind.

North and Shaw walked a few more paces.

"Sometimes Nik has good ideas," Shaw suggested.

So North kissed him. A few times, his arms tightening around Shaw, his breathing clipped and struggling.

"It's ok," Shaw said, brushing his fingers over the short hair above North's ear.

For another moment, North squeezed his eyes shut. Then he opened them, released Shaw, and started walking. "Of course it's ok," he called without looking back. "And his cock was average plus at best."

Nik was waiting at a glass door ahead of them, making faces that suggested adult men in their twenties who kissed were perhaps the single grossest thing in the universe.

"How does a girl who's underage and a runaway get a job with a temp agency?" North asked.

Glancing at the door, Nik shrugged.

"What does that mean?"

"I don't want to get Alex in trouble."

"Fine," North said, yanking open the door. "I'll ask her myself."

Shaw hadn't ever worked for a temp agency, but he'd been to others—usually trying to run down a guy who had skipped alimony or a girl who'd been taking cash out of the till. They were all the same. Versions of the Platonic ideal of a temp agency, he guessed. High-traffic carpeting. Stackable chairs with scratched plastic seats. Cubicle dividers, particle-board desks, and the tired eyes of long-timers who had seen the churn of too many temps.

In H&H Employment Solutions, the generic template for a temp agency was accented by the smell of Wite-Out, the gurgle of the water cooler, and a back-of-the-throat taste that Shaw realized was pencil shavings. A floppy-haired boy was dustbusting the hell out of the carpet, the vacuum's tiny motor whining enthusiastically as he cleaned up the spill from a sharpener. Aside from Floppy, the front office was empty.

"I need to speak to Alex—" North glanced at Nik.

Nik pretended not to notice.

"Nik," Shaw said.

Rolling his eyes, Nik said, "Hussein."

The dustbuster was still whining.

"Hello?" North shouted.

Shaw squeezed his arm and moved to stand in front of the floppy-haired boy. The boy looked up with a start and smiled. He had a gap between his front teeth, and he was cute in a round-cheeked, chipmunkish way. He clicked the dustbuster off and got to his feet.

"Hi, sorry. Had a little accident, and I didn't hear you come in."

"Alex Hussein," North said from behind him.

The boy startled and turned. "Oh. There are a lot of you. Are you looking for—"

"For the third time," North said, in the same tone he'd used when Shaw had not responded promptly to his requests to *take out the fucking trash that you just piled rancid chicken in*, "Alex Hussein."

"Ms. Hussein doesn't handle first-round interviews. I can get you started with an application, and I'll take your resumes and then a valid form of ID, and if you have—"

"She'll want to talk to us," Shaw said, offering a Borealis business card. "Could you give this to her, please?"

"Well, we don't contract from other agencies. If these Borealis guys are trying to hire you out—"

"Get your ass in there right fucking now," North said in a half shout, "and tell her we want to talk to her about Malorie Walton being murdered."

Floppy's eyes filled with tears, and he began to cry as he said, "Malorie's dead?"

Shaw gave North a look as he pulled Floppy into a hug. The boy sobbed as Shaw rubbed his back. North had the decency to turn red and look away.

"Dick," Nik muttered.

North glared at him, but the red in his face deepened.

It took two cups of water from the cooler and a few more hugs before Floppy toddled off into the maze of cubicles.

"Not one fucking word," North said under his breath.

"I want you to say I'm sorry to that poor boy in three creative ways."

"No."

"And then I want you to grow out your hair like his. As an apology."

"Sure. I'll just tell them to give me the Doris Day bangs. Then I'll throw on some blue eyeshadow, shove a few peacock feathers up my asshole, and hit the town."

"That would be lovely—"

"I'm not doing any of that," North snapped.

Floppy came back a moment later, drying his eyes again, and motioned for them to follow. He led them past cubicles and toward an office at the back of the suite. He pushed the door open and motioned them inside.

Voices met them. An argument.

A man's voice: "—don't care what you say, I'm not going to let that bitch ruin a good thing—"

The conversation cut off as they entered the room.

Shaw's first impression was that he'd wandered into a boudoir. On second glance, he realized that Alex Hussein's decorating scheme for her office was Outgrown Teenage Princess with a soupçon of an Arabian Nights bachelorette party: pink silk veils were strung across the room, pink throw pillows filled the chairs, faux Impressionist prints hung on the walls in faux-tarnished, faux-silver frames. On a white veneer etagere, dozens of crystal cats posed and licked their paws and chased balls of yarn and checked their collars. One of them, Shaw thought, was riding a rocket ship and having an unladylike amount of fun. Blue LED bulbs provided the only light, and they gave everything an underwater feel.

Two people occupied the room. A woman sat behind a white desk with gold-spindle legs. She had sleek dark hair pulled into a ponytail, and her makeup was an archaeologist's dream: strata on top of strata, starting with her smoky eyes and going down, down, down. Her nails were adorned with sequin decals, and she wore lots of jewelry—if even half of the silver and stones were real, she was going to make a mugger very happy one day.

The man sat in a chair against the wall, leaning forward, his posture combative. It was hard to tell, because he was sitting, but Shaw thought that he was short. He was built like a bodybuilder, with gold and silver chains woven through his chest hair and a Gucci t-shirt straining over his biceps. He obviously skipped leg days, though, and acne scars pocked his face.

For a moment, they all stared at each other in silence.

"Well?" the woman demanded. "Pete said you've got a girl for me."

"I'm North McKinney, and this is—"

"What can she do?"

"Excuse me?"

"Your friend. What does she know how to do?"

"Oh my God," Shaw said with a breathless trill of excitement. "Everything."

"He's not my—he's not—what the fuck?"

"Typing," Shaw said, elbowing North aside, "and filing, and shorthand, oh, I can take dictation, and when Mr. Stormwent needs something to eat, I can run down to the lunch counter. I'll get along with all the gals in the secretarial pool, and—"

"Who the fuck is Mr. Stormwent?"

"He's my new boss. It's like *50 Shades of Gray* meets *Mad Men* meets *The Devil Wears Prada* meets—"

"Stop talking."

"Alex is teasing you," Nik said from behind them. "This is how she starts when we bring somebody new from the shelter."

Alex rolled her eyes, her face relaxing, and held up the business card that Shaw had given Floppy. "Nik, love, you know we don't talk about that."

"Kick them out," the man said. "You want me to throw their asses out? I'll do it."

"That's enough, Farid." She looked at the business card again. "You're Mr. McKinney, which must make you Mr. Aldrich."

"Miss Aldrich is fine, too, if Mr. Stormwent prefers—"

"We need to talk to you about Malorie," North cut in. He looked at Farid. "Alone would be good."

"My brother," Alex said. "We're inseparable."

"Start being separable."

"That's it," Farid said, getting to his feet. "Your punk ass is coming with me, and if you think about causing trouble—"

"Farid, give us a minute."

Under his olive skin, Farid blushed. For a moment, he puffed up, shoulders and chest out, his gaze moving from North to Shaw as he looked for a challenge.

"Farid!"

His head dropped. He slunk out of the room, and Nik shut the door behind him.

They sat, and Alex turned the Borealis business card in her hand, and then she put the card down and examined her nails.

"Malorie's dead, Alex," Nik said quietly. "I don't know if Pete told you."

"He told me." She picked at one of the sequin decals, frowning. "Sorry, kid. Looks like you need a new fag hag."

Nik's eyes flooded with tears, and Shaw reached over to rub his back. For a moment, Nik buried his face in his hands, his body still. Then he launched out of the seat and ran out the door. With a sigh, North leaned over and pushed it closed.

"This is a good schtick," he said, "the callus bitch thing, but we're still going to ask you some questions."

"So ask."

"You can't run us off like you did your brother and Nik."

"So ask me already. I'm sitting here, aren't I?"

"Did you already know Malorie was dead?"

"Pete told me."

"Before that." North was studying her openly. "You don't seem surprised. You don't seem upset. You played a joke, actually. A bad one, but still a joke."

She glanced up. The smoky eyes seemed a mile deep. "I'm coping," she said. "Look at my coping mechanism."

"Miss Hussein—"

"Just Alex. Look, I don't know what you want me to tell you. I didn't know that girl except to get her jobs every once in a while. I didn't know who she ran around with. I didn't know where she liked to go. I can't tell you anything about her. She was a kid, and she got killed. Sure, that's sad, but it happens every day. The world's going to keep spinning whether I cry for her or not, and I've got a business to run."

"I can tell," North said, glancing around the pink confection of the room.

"What does that mean?"

"Alex," Shaw said, "maybe you could tell us about meeting Malorie, any details that stood out while she worked for you, anything the contracted employers might have mentioned."

"Like I said, I didn't know that girl. Nik brought her around. He brings a lot of the girls from the shelter. He's got this thing; he wants to help everybody. I told him one time, 'Kid, nobody's going to help you but you, so you need to start looking out for yourself.' But he's dumb. He sucks a few cocks, and he does some crank, and then he hates himself and thinks he can make up for it by helping these girls. And let me tell you, these girls can take care of themselves way better than he can. You ever met a chauvinist homo?"

"Yes," Shaw said, "once."

"So help me God," North muttered.

"Malorie was fifteen," Shaw said. "She was homeless, most likely a runaway. How were you able to hire her?"

Alex blinked smoky eyes at him. "I didn't know that, Officer. She had all the documentation and paperwork when she came to see me."

"Really?" North said. "Let's see it. And I'm sure you'll have the work certificate that Missouri requires fifteen-year-olds to get from their school."

More of those wide-eyed blinks. "It must have been misplaced. It's so hard to get good help."

"And you in a temp agency," North said flatly. "What a shame."

"If you have a pattern of hiring underage and undocumented workers—" Shaw began.

"Let me stop you right there," Alex said. With one nail, she flicked the Borealis card across the desk toward them. "If you think you can threaten me, you're wrong. If you think you can scare me with the labor board, you're wrong. I run a legitimate business. I make sure these kids bring me the right paperwork. If one or two slips through the cracks, I'll take a slap on the wrist, but I'm not going to roll over for you. If you think you can come in here, with your big, swinging-dick routine, and get what you want because I'm a woman and I'm going to crumble, you're wrong. I've been dealing with sexist pigs my whole life; you two are the *Tom and Jerry* show compared to them."

"I'm Jerry," Shaw whispered.

"You're Jer—" North started to say. "God damn it, you're not supposed to want to be Jerry."

"Is that all?" Alex asked. "Because I am busy."

"Where did you send Malorie to work?"

"I'm sorry, our contracts are confidential."

"Did she you ever send her to work at the Big Muddy?"

Alex smiled tightly.

"Are you familiar with the Big Muddy?" North said.

"What's that?"

"Were you aware that Malorie was doing sex work?" Shaw asked.

"Most of those girls are. Hey, that's fine. A job's a job. I ought to know, right?" She tee-heed at that.

"Do you know who Malorie's sexual partners might have been?"

"How would I know that?"

"Do you know?" Shaw pressed.

"No, of course not."

"Do you know where she might have been going?"

"How would I—oh, get that look off your face. No, I don't know."

"Do your employees take a drug test?"

"Only when I send them to specific places. Malorie didn't want to go to any of those; a couple of times I smelled grass on her, and I know those kids, especially the ones like your boy, get into harder stuff. I didn't press her on it." With excruciating care to compensate for her long nails, Alex tapped a key on the computer. "Oh, look at that. I've got an appointment. Sorry, boys; our time is at an end."

"When did you last see Malorie?" North asked.

"How should I know?"

"You could check your records. See when she was scheduled to work."

"I could." She drew her hand back from the keyboard and inspected her nails again.

"All right," North said. "We'll go back to the homicide detectives, and we'll say, 'Yeah, we did that legwork like you wanted us to, and you know what? H & H, the temp place, they're shady as shit. You should start there. Tear that place apart.' And they will. They'll be here with a warrant. They'll go to every client where you placed Malorie. They won't even have to try; they'll drag your business through the mud in the normal course of the investigation."

Alex watched them. The undersea lighting gave her a corpselike pallor. "I can't tell you where I placed her. Some of the places I work with prefer privacy; it would ruin me."

North shrugged.

Chewing her lip, Alex tapped the keyboard a few more times. "Her last job was the Friday before last. It was the end of a payroll period, and she said she was done."

"She was done?"

"She didn't want to work here anymore. She had enough money to get out of town. I swear to God, I don't know where she was going, but that's what she told me."

"And her last paycheck?"

Alex's nails clicked on the desk. "We paid her cash. Some of the girls, it's easier that way."

"Easier for who?" North asked.

"Look, I'm doing these kids a favor. You'd rather have them out there taking cocks up the shitter or whatever these weirdos want to do to them? They get a little cash, they're in a safe environment, they're learning the ropes. I'm helping them start a career. Life skills, you know?"

"You're a saint."

"Did Malorie come here on Wednesday?"

"Is that the day she—" Alex made a noise that suggested being killed.

Shaw nodded. "We think so."

"She picked up her pay. Came right before I left, good thing for her. I keep some cash in the safe."

"What time was that?"

"Probably around five. A little after."

"And?"

"And nothing. I paid up through the last job, and she left. That's all. Look, I've got stuff to do, and I told you everything. I swear to God, I didn't know that girl except to give her a job, so I can't help you."

"What was she wearing?" North asked.

Alex frowned. "Why does it matter?"

"Answer the question."

"I don't know."

"You don't remember anything?"

With a frustrated noise, Alex rolled her eyes. "Let's see. She was sitting in that chair, one leg over the other, kind of bouncing them like she was impatient. She hadn't shaved in a couple of days. So she was either wearing shorts or a skirt."

"Not jeans."

"Definitely not. Now you've got to go; I have things to do."

They left.

At the front of the suite, Floppy was gone, and so was Nik.

"He's like a puppy," North said as they pushed their way out into the storm-cool September day. "He'll find his way home on his own."

Shaw gave him a look.

Sighing, North rolled his head on his neck. Then he made a frustrated noise, grabbed Shaw's arm, and started walking. For a while, they navigated the maze of corridors and passageways and stairs. Finally they emerged, by chance more than anything, at the rear of the office complex, where an uneven asphalt lot and a handful of loading docks provided more functional access. The clouds churned overhead, and a breeze raced along, threatening to pull Shaw's hair from its bun. The sound of crying drifted from somewhere nearby.

They found Nik and Floppy behind a white panel van. Nik had his arms around Floppy, and Floppy was sobbing into Nik's—technically North's—shirt. Nik was saying something in a low, reassuring voice, the words interspersed with kisses to Floppy's cheek and ear. Floppy noticed them first, pulling away from Nik and sucking in a wet breath.

A fire burned in Nik's face as he looked at them—at Shaw, in particular—and then looked away. In the too-large jeans, there was no missing his erection.

"All right," North said. "Get him off really quickly, hand stuff only, and then we're going."

He grunted when Shaw elbowed him. "Nik," Shaw said, "we need to keep moving. Do you want to—"

"Yeah." He glanced at Floppy.

The boy must have caught the look in his peripheral vision; his gaze remained rooted on the ground, and he was wiping his cheek, but he nodded.

"Bye, Pete."

Floppy—Pete—nodded again.

As Shaw turned, a hand caught the back of his tank and dragged him sideways. He stumbled and then crashed into the van. Farid stood there, his compact body set for a fight, a knife glittering in one hand. North was bringing up his fists.

"Hey," Shaw said. "Calm down. Everybody slow down."

"Get lost," Farid said. "Both of you. Don't come around here again."

North still looked like he was thinking about a punch.

"No," Shaw said quietly. "North, don't you dare."

"No more questions," Farid said. "Hear me?"

"We hear you. North, we hear him, right?"

Farid spat, the spittle spraying across the Redwings. "And you don't come around here again."

"We're leaving," Shaw said. He pushed off from the van, caught North's arm, the muscles corded and trembling. "We're leaving right now."

For a moment, North resisted. Then he let Shaw tug him away from Farid, the knife hovering between them. Nik trotted after them as they headed for the car.

Chapter 12

IT WAS DARK WHEN North left the City Justice Center. He pushed through the doors, walking quickly, his mind already halfway down the block toward the garage where he had stashed the GTO.

"Mr. McKinney."

The voice belonged to a tall man who sat on a bench near the door, folding a copy of the *Times,* an umbrella propped up next to him. He wore a trench coat over a blue suit of summer-weight wool. Italian cut. Well tailored. His eyes were almost the same color as the wool. North had been in college, finals week junior year, when he'd seen a piece of shit in a 370Z driving too fast—late for a final, maybe. The guy had hit a cat that was trying to sprint across the road. North remembered the sound of the impact, a thunk that he'd felt in his belly. He remembered the sound of the 370Z accelerating as the guy sped away. And he remembered the cat's dead eyes, empty and blue. The smile this man offered was empty too.

"A moment, if you would."

For a moment, North considered ignoring him. After a pointless day trying to find another lead on Malorie, he'd left Shaw and Nik at the office when Biff had called him to the city jail. But the visit with his dad had been shit, his dad combative to North's every suggestion, North's frustration made worse by Biff's apparent unconcern. The lawyer had finagled the meeting, but then he had spent the time answering emails on his phone and scattering anodyne reassurances that they'd make bail at the arraignment the next day—Wednesday at the latest. The question of bail—and, hidden within it, the question of Biff's fee—was a clusterfuck exploding in slow motion, but North couldn't focus on it. His brain kept rebooting, and the same image kept coming up: his dad under the washed-out iridescence of the fluorescent tubes, looking more jaundiced than ever in the baggy yellow shirt and trousers, cannula askew, wispy hair sticking up.

"It's about a mutual friend." The hesitation was so slight that North might have imagined it. "Your uncle."

North turned on his heel.

The man raised both hands, the empty smile a little bigger now. "Mr. McKinney, I'm on your side. Whatever you're thinking about doing, take a deep breath and reconsider it. I could be a very good friend. I am a very bad enemy."

The storm still hadn't moved out, and although it wasn't raining, the air was misty. North wiped his face and found it wet. He stared at his fingers. He dried them on his shirt.

"Fuck off," he said.

"Mr.—"

"What don't you get about fuck off? I've had enough deals and enough favors and enough two-bit players who think they're the shit."

Rising, the man nodded. He lowered his hands slowly, tucked the paper under one arm, and collected his umbrella. "At least let me explain the situation for you. Give you the lay of the land. I imagine you have some questions."

Down the block, a street sweeper chugged along, the whir of the brush broken up by the harsh, high-pressure jets of water. The clouds roiled overhead. All the stars were drowned.

"You probably wondered, for example," the man said slowly, that paper-doll smile unrolling again, "why he waited until now to…create this situation for you."

"Can you walk and talk at the same time? Guys like you, sometimes that's asking too much."

"I'll try to keep up." He held out his free hand. "Vinnikov."

North started down the block.

The man's laugh was soft as he caught up.

"Well?" North kept his gaze straight ahead.

"You understand that your uncle—"

"He's not my fucking uncle. Quit calling him that."

"Ronnie is—was—part of a cooperative. A group of people who assist each other. Some of these people have more…sway than others."

"Somebody told him not to use the blackmail." North tried to force himself to focus, to think, but it was hard. He'd fallen into what he thought was a kiddie pool and now found himself swimming with a shark. Or sharks. "Because blackmail stops being useful once you go public with it."

"And it was in our best interest to keep two very competent and, therefore, useful people in a position where they might be willing to do us favors, instead of the debacle that is currently unfolding."

"Yeah, it must be really embarrassing that you can't pull my strings anymore."

Vinnikov laughed softly again. "Unfortunately, Ronnie has become…unstable. Increasingly erratic, in fact. There was a time when this was an asset. People are wary around unpredictable agents. Now it has become a liability. It's been my experience that the best way to maintain a stable business is to remove liabilities."

The parking garage loomed on their left, leaking the smell of colder air, brushed concrete, and gasoline. Every other breath, it mixed with the clean, misty drizzle, turning North's stomach. Tires squealed. Higher up in the garage, a door slammed like a shotgun going off.

"I'm turning in here," North said. "If you're smart, you'll keep walking."

"Mr. McKinney, we can solve each other's problems."

"I don't need any help, thanks."

This time, the smile wasn't a paper doll's. It wasn't empty. It had a bitingly hot, wry amusement. It made North feel five years old, asking his parents what animals chicken nuggets used to be, and his dad laughing until North, not knowing what else to do, tried to climb under the table. He thought of the bail, the mounting fees, the legal web that, even with his experience, he knew he'd need experts to help him unravel.

Instead of responding to the silent challenge, though, North only said, "You can take care of your own problem."

"I can't, actually. The situation is more complicated than that. Fluid, but the situation is always fluid. Consider it a question of territories. If I remove Ronnie, other people, interested parties, might think that I'm trying to expand. They might consider me a threat. They might misinterpret."

"But you do want his territory. You wouldn't be here offering me a deal if you didn't."

"Of course."

"And if I get rid of him?"

"You have a history of personal grievances. Ronnie was out of line in deploying the blackmail. I would make sure there were no reprisals."

"And you'd step into that vacuum without anyone knowing you had a hand in getting rid of him."

He had pale, thin lips. They quirked. Dead-cat eyes fixed North as he pressed a card into his hand. "My first impression of you was that you are a smart man who knows a good deal when he sees one."

A voice came from within the parking garage. A woman. The echoes distorted the words, and then she emerged, a phone in one hand, tugging on the jacket of her black suit. "Tell Marlene that if she can't have the Hawkins Foundation sewn up by Friday, she can find another firm. No, I'm not going to tell her, Gregory. That's your job. That's why you're a partner."

She passed them, heels clicking, and the storm winds swallowed the rest of her words.

"There's something about first impressions," North said, turning into the garage. "My first impression was to tell you to fuck off. I'm going to go with that."

Chapter 13

NORTH WENT TO THE office first, where Truck and Pari were watching the news on a small TV that Pari had added to the reception area. Belia Lopez, the reporter who had interrupted North and Shaw's party, was giving an update on the suspected cop killer, Darold Smith. Since Smith was in the wind, the story mostly consisted of recaps. Belia emphasized her own role locating Smith's crib first, and she ended by explaining that the police were also looking for the weapon Smith had allegedly used to kill a police officer before he vanished.

"Where are they?" North asked.

"Pantynose is such a twat," Truck said, pulling hir long, curly hair into a ponytail.

"Excuse me?" Pari said.

"Darold. That's his name, Pantynose, because one time—"

"No, I don't want to know."

Truck grinned. "He's an idiot; he always ditches his shit in the same place. I bet I could take a fifteen-minute drive and find that gun."

"Where are they?" North asked again.

"They went home, and the puppy is staying with me and Truck tonight," Pari said absently, her attention still fixed on Truck. "I don't like you talking about things like that. You're supposed to be an upstanding citizen. You're a private detective now, and pretty soon, you're going to be a partner here."

"Like fuck," North said loudly.

Neither of them reacted, so he let himself out before he had to hear anything else.

When North got home, he parked in the garage and then walked down the alley and back up the block, checking for anything that looked out of place. The garage door was up at Breezi and Nita's place, and the faint clang of metal, underscored by rhythmic swearing, said Breezi was hard at work. He turned toward his and Shaw's house and went in through the front door.

Big Brother was on his TV, and Nik was on his couch. In another of his tees. And in his gym shorts. Free balling it.

"Why are you here?"

Nik glared at him and then turned his attention back to the television.

In the kitchen, Shaw was making nachos.

"Don't you fucking dare," North said.

Shaw paused, spoon still stuck in the abomination he was about to put on the chips. "Oh, hi. Welcome home."

"Throw that away."

Giving the glop a stir, Shaw said, "North—"

"Throw it away. Right fucking now."

"But I had to soak the cashews, and the sauerkraut was extra vinegary, and—no!"

North tossed the spoon in the sink and dropped the container into the trash. He opened the fridge, pulled out the bag of pre-shredded cheddar, extra sharp, and began dumping it on the chips. Arms folded across his chest, Shaw watched, throwing the occasional glance at the trash can.

"Go for it," North said, eyeing the nachos and then giving another liberal shake of the cheese. "See what happens."

With a sigh, Shaw rubbed his back. "You're in a mood."

"Because that kid's on my couch, watching my TV—"

"Ok, ok, ok. I know we said it wouldn't be permanent, but—"

"—free balling it in my shorts—"

"—we went back to the shelter to ask Ximena and Ryley about the Big Muddy, and neither of them said they'd heard of it. It turned into a big fight, actually, and then Ximena kept saying maybe Nik needed to stay somewhere else for a while, and Nik blew up the way teenagers do, said he'd never wanted to stay there in the first place, he was better off on his own, he could find his own place. I mean, you could have ripped it from a CW script."

"Were they lying?"

"No, I think the fight was real. But the good news is that I googled the Big Muddy and got a hit—a truck stop about fifteen miles past Columbia. I thought we could go out there tomorrow."

North grunted as he stuck the baking sheet with the nachos into the oven and set the broiler. He opened the fridge and began moving jars of condiments around. Glass clinked against glass. Plastic bottles tipped over and thumped against the fridge's liner. The sauerkraut left over from Shaw's vegan cheese was overpowering, and North's eyes watered. "Where is that nacho cheese dip?"

"North, they already have cheese on them. Lots of cheese. A whole cow's worth of cheese."

"I know. I want to dip them in cheese sauce."

"But you know it's not even real cheese, right?" A note of panic had entered Shaw's voice. "I mean, maybe I could make you some vegan nacho cheese sauce. There's so much sauerkraut—"

"Did you throw it away?"

"Um, well, you see——"

"You know what? This is what I wanted. I had this shit day with…with everything. And I wanted to come home and find my boyfriend playing houseboy for a street kid who's taking over my life and then I wanted to go dumpster diving to rescue my fucking cheese sauce that I paid for with my money and kept in my fridge in my house. That's what I wanted, Shaw."

"Shut up!" Nik shouted from the living room.

North turned and took a step.

Catching his arm, Shaw whispered, "I didn't throw it away. Nik was starving, and the only thing he'd eat was nacho cheese dogs, and we had the leftover hot dogs from the barbecue. I used the last of it. I'm sorry. I'll buy you a jar. Ten jars. A pallet!"

"He did that on purpose. He knew I was going to want some, and he ate it all so I couldn't have some." Something in Shaw's eyes made North hear how that sentence sounded from a less…emotional point of view. He took a breath and added, "Ok. You know what? I'm going to——"

"Shaw, where are my nachos?" Nik called from the living room.

"Oh, fuck no."

Shaw's fingers tightened. "North, please——"

"And I'm thirsty!"

"Then get off your fucking ass and get your own fucking glass of water!" North shouted toward the front of the house.

"He's a kid who lost everything," Shaw whispered, fingers pincer tight. "He hasn't had any control, hasn't had any say about anything. Now he does, and he's trying to figure out boundaries."

"Great. He wants boundaries? I'll lay them out perfectly fucking clearly."

"North."

It was the way he said it, expecting better, that made North twist out of his grip, level a frustrated look at him, and accept a few butterfly kisses. He rolled his eyes to make his position clear.

"Thank you," Shaw whispered and kissed him again.

"Gross," Nik said from the doorway. "All you guys do is kiss."

"Sometimes I hit people who annoy me," North said.

"How'd that go yesterday?" Nik said with a smirk as he filled a glass with water.

"Let's try it again. We'll see if I do any better——"

"My nachos are burning," Nik said, pointing to the oven.

"God damn it," North said, snatching an oven mitt. He retrieved the nachos—toasty brown, but not burnt—and by the time he looked around, Nik was gone.

"No," Shaw said as he caught North's wrist. "Let them cool so I don't have to hear about the roof of your mouth for the next two days. Tell me what happened."

North told him.

"You can't trust this guy, Vinnikov," Shaw said when he finished.

"I know that."

"He's going to come back, North. He wants you to do something, and these guys don't take no for an answer."

North pulled one of the toasty-yet-still-gooey-and-therefore-perfect nachos from the sheet and ate it. Around a mouthful of chip and cheese, he said, "Maybe."

"He was giving you two options. One, you get rid of Ronnie, he helps you get your dad out of prison—and then has you under his thumb forever, the same way Ronnie wanted to. Or two, you don't help him, and he—he makes things worse."

North's chewing slowed. Vinnikov hadn't said anything like that, but as North replayed the conversation, he realized the threat had been implied. Something about removing liabilities. He crunched into another chip.

"It'll be ok," Shaw said, smoothing hair away from North's forehead. "We'll figure it out."

For the next few minutes, both men were silent. North ate nachos. Shaw prepared another tray of chips, and when he glanced at the trash, North made a serious growling noise.

"Fine," Shaw said, but there was laughter in his eyes, and if North were being honest, the whole thing had made him feel a lot better. When he'd finished prepping the nachos, he pulled out his phone and started to read.

"Shaw, I can't figure out the remote," Nik called.

Shaw rolled his eyes.

"Daddy," North simpered, "your boy needs you."

"I hate you."

North gave him a lazy bird and ate another nacho as Shaw set his phone on the counter and headed into the living room.

It was an accident. North wasn't trying to snoop. He was carrying the empty baking sheet to the sink when he saw the article on Shaw's phone, the headline still displayed: *Seven Signs He's Not Ready to Take the Plunge (Even Though He Says He Is)*.

"I'm going to take over the guest room for a couple of hours," North said when Shaw came back. He was washing the baking sheet, and he was proud of himself for not looking over when Shaw picked up the phone. "I'm wrecked. My head is killing me, and everything with my dad—I think I want a little time to unwind. By myself."

"Ok," Shaw said.

"I know you want to be supportive and comforting, but I need to turn off for a little while."

"Uh huh."

"Hey."

"No, I get it."

North let the hot water run over his hands, carrying soapy bubbles away. He said, "Are we going to do this every time?"

"North, I think it's a great idea that you want to, you know, have time to ourselves, and have these rich, independent inner lives, and become autonomous, self-actualized people while we build a relationship together."

"Sure you do. That's why you're using the same voice as when you read the list of ingredients in my Star-Spangled-Banner flavor yogurt. Tell me you don't want to do it so we can at least talk about why."

"No, I want to. It makes total sense. Considering, you know, everything." He shoved the fresh tray of nachos in the oven, set the broiler again, and faced North with his arms folded. "It's just that Nik has all his stuff in the guest room."

"Right. That's the only problem here."

"And he's watching his show."

"The rerun of *Big Brother* that has to be, what? Fifteen years old?"

"I guess I could stay in the kitchen, and you could have our bedroom."

North closed his eyes, imagining. I just needed my penis pump. I'll be so quiet, I just have to check on my collection of sex-education LPs. Pretend I'm not here, I'm just going to embroider my buffalo robe.

"Or Nik could hang out in the garage," Shaw said. "He was telling me today that he wants to know more about cars, and he really likes the GTO."

"He's going to murder me in my sleep. You realize that, right? It's a whole *Single White Female* thing."

"First of all, that movie was a fifty-year setback for feminism because of the way it demonized gynosocial friendship—"

"He's not going anywhere near my fucking car." North ran a hand through his hair. "I'll go to the basement."

"No, look, I'll go into the bedroom, and you can stay here—"

North shook his head. He kissed Shaw on the cheek and headed for the stairs.

The basement was unfinished, but the concrete foundation had been sealed, and they'd stored some extra furniture from North's house down here, including a couch. The washer and dryer sat along one wall. In the back corner, North had set up his weights and a bench. He considered the couch for a moment, but instead, he straddled the bench and lay back. Light gleamed on the barbell above him. The basement smell reminded him of the parking garage, Vinnikov: the damp chill of the concrete, the tang of steel. Then he caught a whiff of Downy and grinned at himself, pressing the heels of his hands into his eyes.

Who was North fucking McKinney when he was all by himself?

Who fucking cared?

He'd left an intermediate amount of weight on the bar, and he did two sets. By the end of the second, his chest and arms and back were pleasantly warm, and a flush lit up his face. He reset the bar, took out his phone, and pulled up an episode of Golden Kamuy. He was close to finishing the first season, not that he had much time to watch anymore, and this episode was tense. Ienaga Kano had Shiraisihi and Ushiyama in a basement torture chamber. She was trying to kill Asirpa. North rolled onto his side, enjoying the show, enjoying the limber warmth in his body, enjoying, in a weird way, even the smell of the bar on his hands on the relative discomfort of the bench.

Footsteps on the stairs. Soft, whispery footsteps.

North silenced a groan. Best-case scenario? Nik was going to murder him and wear his skin.

"Don't look up," Shaw whispered. "I'm not even here. But you didn't drink anything with your nachos, and you had a hard day, and I thought maybe you'd want a beer."

North turned up the volume on his phone.

"I'm going to put it right here."

The bottle clinked on the concrete next to the bench.

"It's already open."

Sugimoto was doing something, but North felt like he had double vision. Or maybe that was the inevitable aneurysm building.

"Is your show good?"

"Shaw." The name was dragged out of him.

"Right, right, right. I'm gone."

The stairs creaked. Overhead, Nik said something like, "Can you show me how to do yoga?"

He's yours if you can catch him, North thought. And good fucking luck.

Something had changed, and he couldn't focus on the episode now. He stopped it. He drank some beer—the Schlafly white pumpkin ale, which was fucking fantastic. After a while, he read. *Bleacher Report. STLToday. Redbird Rants.* He was digging into a breakdown of the series against the Brewers, with a solid explanation of why the Cards had lost that Saturday game, when a bare foot scuffed the linoleum at the top of the stairs, and then one of the treads squeaked.

North laid his phone on his chest.

"I am so, so sorry."

North let his hands hang off the bench. He could feel blood pooling in them, pulled by gravity, the pulse in his fingertips.

"I just had to get this laundry started. We should have done it this weekend, but—"

"I'll do it."

"Oh, no, this is your alone time, and—"

"It's not very fucking alone, is it? Leave the basket, Shaw. I'll do it."

"I could get it started—"

"No." North softened his voice. "I promise I'll do it."

The plastic basket clicked against the concrete.

Steps.

Nik's voice upstairs: "I tried one of those stretches you showed me, and I think I pulled my hamstring. Could you take a look?"

Treads protesting. Bare feet whispering to a stop at the bottom of the stairs.

"Oh my gosh, North, I just realized something."

North stared up at the barbell, the shine of light, the oil from his skin streaking the steel. Two hundred and fifteen pounds. If it fell on his neck right then, he'd be dead, and this would be over.

"I was doing numerology with your name, and do you know what? North is five plus six plus nine plus two plus eight. And that equals?"

It would probably be fast. Maybe, North thought, I wouldn't even feel anything.

"Thirty," Shaw said with the tone of someone agreeing. "And thirty, three plus zero, is three. And three is the number of domesticity."

North rubbed at a smear on the bar. Domestic homicide, he thought. Maybe.

"I thought you'd find that interesting," Shaw said, "because you offered to do the laundry, and that's a domestic chore, and then I found out that in that particular system of numerology, your name means domestic, which means you're really channeling your best energy right now."

"Shaw, for the love of God."

"I thought you'd want to know that!"

"Great. Now I know."

"I'm going right back upstairs."

"Sure."

"I am!" Clothing rustled. Shaw was tugging at the hem of his tank, North guessed. Or pulling down one leg of the Lululemon pants. "Unless, you know, you wanted to talk about something."

"About what?"

"Oh, anything."

Leave it, North told himself. Let it go.

Instead, he sat up and said, "Ok. Let's talk about that article you were reading on your phone."

"You can't—I wasn't—" Color was bright in the sharp triangle of Shaw's features. "What article?"

"Seven ways to tell your boyfriend to fuck off because you don't want to marry him."

"North, what?"

"Go upstairs, Shaw."

"First of all, I'm a little upset you were searching my phone—"

"I wasn't searching your phone. You left it face up with the article displayed. I wasn't even trying to read it. If you don't want to get married, you don't have to lie to me to spare my feelings."

Shaw rubbed his mouth. "I do want to get married! I want to get married to you!"

"Ok."

"I—"

"No, I can't do this right now. This is why I wanted some time to myself. Go play with your puppy."

"The puppy is with Truck and Pari."

"You know what I meant."

North lay down again, grabbed his phone, and tapped blindly through a labyrinth of baseball pages. The sound of bare feet on concrete moved around the basement, but he refused to look up. A moment later, Shaw straddled him. Naked.

"No," North said and held his phone higher.

Shaw grabbed his free hand, guiding it toward his crotch.

North yanked free. "I said no."

Bending, Shaw ran his hands up North's arms. He kissed one biceps. Then the other. He was hardening, his dick poking into North's belly, as he whispered. "You've been working out."

"Needed to be strong enough to get rid of ancient twinks who won't leave me the hell alone." And to emphasize the point, North shoved Shaw off him.

Shaw stumbled, caught himself, and started laughing. He padded away. North watched his taut ass in his peripheral vision, pretending to read again. Shaw had long, lean legs, and the muscles popped when he stretched up on tiptoe to reach something on the shelf above the washing machine.

When he came back, he said, "Do you know what McKinney is? In numerology, I mean?"

North scrolled blindly. Sue me, he thought to the universe. Sue me if it's hard to concentrate when a great dick is inches from my face.

"Four plus three plus two plus nine plus five plus five plus five plus seven. That's forty. And forty is four and zero. Which is four." It was impossible to miss the grin in Shaw's voice. "And four is the numerological sign for asshole."

He grabbed Shaw before Shaw could run, dragging him forward, delivering a few clumsy slaps to Shaw's ass before Shaw lay on top of him, and somehow then they were kissing. Then North remembered the article on the phone, and he shoved Shaw back. It didn't accomplish much; Shaw was still sitting on him, naked, and now they were both hard.

The buckle jingled as Shaw worked his belt open.

"Uh uh," North said, but he didn't stop those busy hands as they worked his waistband open, then the zipper. "Go mop the floors or something."

"North." Shaw brushed back his shirt to kiss low on North's belly, then lower, his nose buried in the thick patch of blond hair between North's legs, then lower, his tongue poking out for an instant to slide along the shaft of North's dick. "I was reading that because, well, of you."

Abandoning the phone, North looked up at his boyfriend who was currently alternating between tugging him out of his clothes and giving tiny licks to his cock. "Right. Because I said the M word."

"No. Well, yes. But because—I thought maybe you said that because of what happened this summer. Feeling rushed because we almost died. I don't want you to feel rushed."

"I don't feel rushed. Do you?"

Shaw's hazel eyes were wet, and he blinked once and shook his head. The cap on a bottle snapped. Then one of Shaw's hands was between North's legs, nudging them apart, cold wetness and gentle, back-and-forth probing. Shaw's other hand stroked North's thigh; the muscles in his quad were tensed. His muscles everywhere were tensed.

"Relax," Shaw whispered.

It was harder than that. But then Shaw's mouth was on him, and then it wasn't quite so hard, and the first finger slipped inside, curling until North grunted and his vision swam.

When Shaw pulled off, saliva running from the corner of his mouth, he smirked. "Hold on to the bar and be quiet."

North reached up, wrapping his hands around the steel. The knurled pattern felt magnified under his palm. Everything felt magnified. He was doubly aware of the television upstairs, of the teenager who might come looking for them at any moment.

Then Shaw entered him, and for the first few heartbeats, it was almost too much. North's hand tightened around the bar until his knuckles popped out. His breathing hitched. Shaw rubbed his legs, making soothing noises, helping North breathe through it. They hadn't done this lately, not this way, and North was remembering now why sometimes he asked for it, why sometimes this way felt right.

"Good," Shaw whispered. "So good. Don't make any noise, right?"

He rocked his hips.

North managed a strangled noise.

"North? Was that a yes?"

"Fuck. Yes. Fuck me."

Shaw's face was intent, but his eyes held the hint of a smirk as he rolled his hips again, grabbing North's legs behind the knees, angling the joining of their bodies until North made a punched-out noise. The bar rolled under his hands as he struggled to hold on, steel scraping against steel in the rack.

He was doing pretty well, restricting himself to grunts, until Shaw put a hand on him. Then, in a matter of minutes, his vision tunneled whitely. The orgasm screamed through him, and he started to talk.

"Yeah, fuck me. Fuck me. Stick that fucking dick in me. You're mine, do you hear me? You're mine. I'm—uh. I'm not letting you go. I'm—I'm going to lie. I'm going to go off of the pill without telling you, and you're going to fuck a baby into me, and then it won't matter how many fucking articles you read, you're not getting away."

It was the kind of crazy talk that could only be excused on the apex of coming. North didn't know where it came from, didn't know why he said it, only knew that one minute the words were coming out of his mouth, and the next minute, the orgasm came down with the roar and whiteout of a thunderstorm. Even through the flood of hormones, though, he could hear the ragged, helpless note in Shaw's voice as he screamed, "Oh fuck," and pounded into North with a new intensity. A moment later, as the storm wall of the orgasm turned, North was aware of Shaw climaxing inside him. His eyes refocused: Shaw's jaw hanging open, his eyes huge, a vein throbbing in his forehead. He realized he had never seen Shaw like this, never been fucked like this.

Then Shaw slumped, catching himself one-handed on the bar, gasping like he'd finished a marathon.

Chuckling, North pulled him down so they lay chest to chest, North's load cooling between them. North stroked his back as Shaw's racing heart slowed. But Shaw was still shivering, moving in fits and starts. When he pulled out, North made a noise of discomfort, and Shaw tried to sit up.

"I'm fine," North whispered, wrapping arms around Shaw to keep him in place. "You really went to town, though. That did something for you, huh? Thinking about putting a baby in me?"

Shaw groaned and turned his face into North's chest. He mumbled a string of semi-coherent denials.

With another quiet laugh, North stroked his spine until Shaw had finished.

"Oh my God," Shaw finally said, peeling a sticky cheek away from North's chest to look up at him. "You cannot tell anyone about this."

"Because I'm the one who went around telling everyone about the new butt plug he bought."

"It was articulated! People need to know!"

North kissed his forehead. Then he frowned. "Why do you keep lube with the laundry supplies?"

"The erotic component of laundry, all that fluffing—"

"Because of the workout bench?"

"Yes, obviously."

From the top of the stairs came a voice charged with the kind of disgust only adolescents can generate: "If you two are finished putting babies in each other, could one of you please tell me where the bowls are so I can have some ice cream?"

Chapter 14

THE BIG MUDDY WAS a truck stop west of Columbia. It had what looked like a full acre of fuel pumps under a shiny new canopy (trucks please use separate entrance), as well as a sprawling building—timber veneer, picture windows, a look that suggested rustic hospitality and good country manners while, at the same time, promising wifi and satellite television. The flashing sign near the road said THE BIG MUDDY – CHEAP GAS – HOT SHOWERS – CLEAN ROOMS – DINA'S GRUB.

"They didn't mention the booby joint," North said, pointing at the back of the lot, where a separate building stood. It shared the timber veneer, but it lacked windows and signage, and at a casual glance might have suggested storage or offices.

"Maybe it's a surprise," Shaw said.

North grunted.

"People like surprises, North. You were so happy when I surprised you with that cactus girdle that you had to have a private moment to calm down."

"I had to have a private moment to pull all those fucking cactus spines out of my ass. I don't know why you thought a fucking cactus girdle was a good idea, but those goddamn needles could have gone in my junk, Shaw."

"But you were definitely surprised."

"Yes, fuck, I was surprised. I would have been surprised if you'd put a road flare up my bung hole too. No, don't get that look, I was not suggesting that." North let the rented Ford roll to a stop at the edge of the lot. The concrete pavement looked fresh. The curbs were sharp. The grass along the verge was thick and well-tended before giving way to untamed prairie. The brown ribbon of the Mississippi unspooled to the north and east, glinting where the sun struck it like flint.

The late morning was beautiful—warm and bright. The storm had moved on, and they'd hit that thin strip of gorgeous weather balanced between the heat of summer and the chill of autumn. Perfect weather for the gray sharkskin suit Shaw had decided to wear. The t-shirt he wore under the jacket said MY

CITRINE IS SMARTER THAN YOUR HONOR STUDENT. The pink ostrich-skin loafers made sure everyone knew he was only joking.

Best of all, it was only the two of them; after a pitched battle in the living room, Nik had finally collapsed onto the couch, staring at an episode of *Voltron*, ignoring them when they said goodbye. Well, Shaw had said goodbye. North had said something about not being such a perfect stereotype of a teenage prick.

"How'd she get out here," North asked, "and wind up back in St. Louis, dead, a few hours later?"

"She got a ride with whoever killed her."

"Maybe."

"Or maybe she didn't come out here," Shaw said. "The timeline is tight; it's a two-hour drive, one way. She didn't leave the shelter until eight, and she still made it to the appointment with Dr. Egg, to Jesse's, and to the temp agency before they closed. It's possible, but it would have been close."

"So she picked up that receipt on her heel some other way."

"I think that's more likely."

"From the floor of the car, the same one that hit that light post, right by where we found the blood trail."

Shaw nodded.

"Which still ties her back to this place," North said. His phone buzzed, and he glanced at it before silencing it and putting it in a pocket. "Fuck this, we're going to have to go inside."

"Monzyk or Contalonis?" Shaw asked.

"The dick bag." North clarified, "Monzyk."

"They're doing their jobs, North."

"They're threatening to throw us in jail with a list of charges starting with interfering with a police investigation. I'd be worried if I thought they could find their own asses with both hands."

"They're homicide detectives, and we found a murdered girl in a storm drain. Then we ran away from the scene, and—" Shaw pulled out his phone. Jadon's name flashed on the screen. "Hold on."

"Don't you dare take that call."

Shaw put it on speaker. "Hi, Jadon."

"Shaw, I need you to come into the station today." His voice shifted as he spoke away from the phone: "Monzyk, back off. I'm taking care of it."

"Oh," North said. "You're taking care of it."

The silence was almost as bad as a sigh. Then Jadon said, "Hello, North."

"Bye, Jadon."

"Shaw, these guys need to talk to you. To both of you. You walked away from a murder scene before they'd even processed you out. That's a big deal. Now you're dodging their calls, and when they showed up at your house this morning, some kid read them every bad word in the dictionary."

"I knew I liked Nik," North said.

Shaw frowned. "On the drive out here, you talked for forty-five minutes about how the only legitimate excuse for Nik acting the way he did was to be suffering from ingrown ass hairs."

"Ok, yes, I thought he was a little shit. I still do. But I like him a little bit more now."

"Out where?" Jadon said.

Reaching for the disconnect button, North said, "Mind your own business."

"This isn't a game, all right? Monzyk and Contalonis are pissed, and they're not exactly easygoing to start with. Where are you? Maybe we can all meet somewhere and deescalate this."

"Are we suspects?" Shaw asked.

North and Jadon snorted at exactly the same time.

"That was everything," Shaw whispered.

"No, it wasn't," North said.

Jadon, sounding even more tired than usual, said, "Of course you aren't suspects. But you two weren't real popular around the station to begin with, and this kind of thing, well, it's not helping."

"Can you tell us anything about Malorie?" Shaw asked. "Do they have a time of death? Ballistics?"

"This isn't *CSI: Miami*. Sorry. I'm tired, and I've had these two riding me all day—"

"Another gem from the Jadon Reck bedroom collection," North said.

"—to get you two in for an interview."

"They don't have anything?" Shaw asked. "Jay, please, anything would help."

After a moment, Jadon heaved an explosive breath. "Shaw, could you not do that?"

"I'm sorry, Jay. I am. But it's important."

"Damn it." The silence had the quality of a struggle to it, and then Jadon said, "The medical examiner hasn't finished, but the time of death estimate is consistent with her disappearing on Wednesday."

"Cause of death?"

"They recovered a bullet. A nine-millimeter."

"Great, the most common ammo in the US," North said. "Did they lift any prints off it?"

"No, and now that I've answered your questions, the fair thing to do is for you to come in, make a statement, and answer any questions the detectives have."

"Too bad." North reached for the button again.

"What if Shaw met with them, and I—"

"No. He's busy. And quit trying to steal my man."

Despite Shaw's best efforts, North disconnected the call.

Shaw eyed him.

"What?"

"Maybe if you said it with a big, blond perm."

"Jesus Christ."

"Bouffant. A bouffant perm."

"Never mind. I don't want to marry you anymore."

"And you had two-inch-long nails painted scarlet. Oh. And a dog on the porch. And a banjo was playing in the background."

"I'm getting out of the car now."

"Quit trying to steal my man, Jebediah!"

North slammed the door, but not very hard. He shouted through the glass, "And it's Jedidiah, you mental defective."

He looked like he was trying hard not to smile when Shaw caught up to him under the fuel pump canopy.

Inside, the truck stop was like all the others Shaw had visited. The convenience store area in front smelled like cola, probably because of the thirty-six-flavor fountain drink station, and also like overcooked roller dogs. The dogs in question looked leathery, blistered and splitting in places from too much time on the grill. Neon signs marked the coolers along the back wall: SODA – WATER – BEER – PARTY TIME. Next to PARTY TIME were taped sun-bleached Four Loko advertisements, which based on the guys snowboarding and the girls in bikinis, could get you simultaneously smashed and wired and laid at a Colorado resort, if only you had a time machine. A heavyset man in a Canadian tuxedo was eyeing the Four Loko girls' faded breasts. His trucker hat said ROADKILL? I CALL IT MEALS ON WHEELS.

North caught Shaw's arm. "Leave it."

"He needs to know that those animals have souls, and it's not funny to make jokes about—"

But North was already towing him away.

On either side of the convenience store were dining options: one side had a KFC/Taco Bell combination, where a lone girl, the scalp at her part purple with cheap dye, was waiting on a line of restless customers; the other side was Dina's, which seemed to offer country-style meals. North got distracted— probably having amorous thoughts about a plate of onion rings—and Shaw almost made it.

"I'm just going to tell him about reincarnation and moksha and why taking pleasure in running down innocent animals—no, stop, he's that way."

A hallway connected the convenience store with an arcade. Pinball machines and hunting games predominated, although there was one racing pod and a couple of old-fashioned ones. GRANNY SLAYER sounded promising, Shaw thought. The low-wattage bulbs left the room dim, to accentuate the flashing lights of the games.

Next, they passed the showers—individual rooms that could be rented. The hiss of the spray made a blanket of white noise that muffled the Brooks and Dunn tracks that were playing on repeat at a deafening volume everywhere else in the truck stop. One of the shower doors opened, and a middle-aged guy in nothing but a towel stared at them. He was good looking in a rough way, a classic dad bod, his scruff salt and pepper. He raised one eyebrow at Shaw and whistled.

"Oh, thank you," Shaw said, "but I'm actually getting married. Well, not right now. Well, actually, maybe right now. I don't know when because North hasn't set a date. Or if he has, he hasn't told me. Technically, I guess I might be eloping, and maybe this whole thing has been a setup, and it's entirely possible that I'm about to walk into a surprise wedding—"

"Sure," North said. "Classic surprise wedding setup: a murdered girl, a kid who won't stay out of my fucking dresser, this shithole in the middle of Bumfuck, Nowhere."

"—and while I appreciate being sexually objectified by a stranger in a towel as much as the next guy—"

The door slammed shut.

"That was kind of rude, don't you think?"

"He's got the right idea. We need more doors in our house."

"I know you're joking, but doors are actually the seventh-most common cause of trapped negative energy—"

Shaw cut off when they turned to follow a corridor that ran perpendicular to the showers. The next door said JOSEPH "BIG JOE" SCARAMUZZO – COME ON IN! Shouting on the other side of the door made Shaw believe that now might not be the best time to try this open-door policy.

"—if you hadn't gotten so fucking greedy," a coarse voice bellowed. "You've called me four times about this; quit fucking calling already. If I'd seen them, you'd know about it." The silence suggested listening. "Don't tell me how to run my business, cunt. Jesus, if you send me those fucking pictures again, I'm going to lose my mind. I told you: if they show up, I'll handle it."

North caught Shaw's upper arm and hurried him along the hallway. North's mouth was compressed into a thin line, his lips white. He didn't look back, but his whole body, all his energy, were attuned in the direction of the office they'd passed. Shaw had to quicken his pace to keep up.

On the wall, a series of plaques culminated in the employee of the year for 2018. The photo was of a big man in a Bass Pro hat and plaid shirt; under the photo, "BIG JOE" was engraved in the wood. North must have seen it too because he muttered, "Fucker made himself employee of the year."

Behind them, a door opened, and voices spilled out into the hallway.

"—what I pay you for." That was the same man who had been on the phone—Big Joe, Shaw guessed. "I don't pay you to sit around and listen to my phone calls."

Five yards ahead, the corridor connected with the rear of the convenience store. They were practically running now, and North made surprisingly little noise in the Redwings. His hand was iron around Shaw's arm. Over the pulse of blood in his ears, Shaw thought he heard steps behind them.

Then they reached the convenience store, and North cut right, dragging Shaw with him. They were in the clothing section, off-brand jeans, flannel button-ups, hoodies that said I DIDN'T LOSE MY LURE. IT'S INSIDE THAT CRAPPIE RIGHT THERE. A meth-skinny woman was whipping through the t-shirts on a display rack, apparently convinced that one of the shirts—which all said WE GOT DIRTY AT THE BIG MUDDY—was going to be infinitely superior to the others. The hangers shrilled against the metal bar, sending a frisson down Shaw's spine.

The exit felt like it was a hundred miles away. Shaw let North tow him through acre after acre of junk—coffee mugs, crystal figurines, desk ornaments, electric griddles you could plug into a car's cigarette lighter, movies that weren't quite pornos but that featured lots of girls washing lots of cars and wearing very few clothes. Then North bumped the crash bar with his hip, and they stepped out into the smell of motor oil, diesel, and mango—which Shaw realized, a moment later, was coming from a kid's vape.

"Fuck, fuck, fuck," North said as they reached the rented Ford.

The day was mild, but the heat trapped in the car felt suffocating to Shaw. Sweat broke out across his forehead and back. He popped the door open again, and cooler air rushed in. After a moment, he shrugged out of the sharkskin jacket. In doing so, he twisted at the waist and caught a look backward, over his shoulder. That was the only reason he saw the big man approaching their car.

"North."

"For fuck's sake. Someone we talked to yesterday must have told them we were coming. We've got to make a list of everybody we mentioned the Big Muddy to."

Shaw thought he recognized the man headed toward them. His heart beat a little faster. "North."

North was still watching the truck stop, fingers drumming on the steering wheel. "Good news, we're definitely on the right track. Bad news, these fuckers have pictures of us."

"Um, North?"

"What?" He turned, blinked, and said, "What the fuck are you doing here?"

"I was about to ask you the same thing," Emery Hazard said.

Chapter 15

EMERY HAZARD WAS A big man with dark hair and straw-colored eyes who North would admit—to himself, if nobody else—he found a little spooky. He wore a plain blue tee, dark jeans, and boots that looked surprisingly practical. He carried more muscle than North, which was annoying, and he might have been taller, although North was pretty sure he wasn't. Or at least not by much. Right then, the former police detective, now a private investigator out of a shithole town called Wahredua, was not supposed to be here.

"We're here because we're trying to find a murderer," Shaw said, trying to get out of the car—probably with the very, very, very stupid idea of hugging Hazard. "And you're here, I bet, because of our psychic entanglement, and you knew we needed help, and of course, you add the best friends thing on top of that, and—"

"No," Hazard said. Those cool, amber eyes found North again, weighing, calculating, assessing. "Well?"

"I asked first," North said, catching Shaw's tee.

That must have drawn Hazard's attention; his gaze moved to the tee, and he said, "Citrine is a type of crystal. A quartz, I believe."

"Oh, right, well, it also supercharges your creativity and your intelligence, and—North, I think I'm caught on something, and I'm trying to get out of the car so I can give Emery a squeeze—"

"Huh," North said, yanking him back into his seat. "I don't see anything."

"No, I'm definitely caught on something."

"Maybe a witch cast a spell on you. What kind of crystal would you need for that?"

"Probably larvikite, but it would have to be infused with reiki energy, and—"

"For Christ's sake, let go of him," Hazard said. Then, as though unable to help himself: "And there's no such thing as witches. Or magic crystals. Or intelligent crystals, although I suppose it's possible that a crystalline structure might be involved in quantum computing, in which case—"

"God, I forgot how annoying you are," North said, releasing Shaw.

"—that system would definitely be smarter than an honor roll child, but—oof."

The *oof* marked the exact moment Shaw collided with him, wrapping himself around Hazard's waist. Hazard rocked back, arms outstretched like he wanted everyone to know this wasn't his idea. The hug went on and on. After a moment, Hazard pushed on Shaw's shoulder.

"You might as well hug him now," North said. "He's not going to let you go until you do."

The hug was brief and, to judge from the look on Hazard's face, physically painful.

"All right, Shaw," North said. "Personal space."

Shaw released Hazard. "North's always telling me about personal space. Once, he said I had to stop trying to climb into a Bible lady's minivan, but I was only doing that because she said a mean thing about homos and then told us she let Jesus take the wheel, and I wanted to see where he was sitting. And once he said I couldn't take off a Bible lady's sweater—different Bible lady—because even though North told me she was only grumpy because her bra was pinching her tits harder than a freshman after homecoming, and I said we don't say tits, and I only wanted to check her bra to make sure it wasn't creating a medical complication, North said that was an invasion of personal space. Oh! And one time he told me I was kissing a banana pepper too much and that the banana pepper needed personal space, but I think he was just jealous because his banana pepper wasn't getting any attention, if you know what I mean, and—"

"Get in the back," North said, with a sigh, casting another glance at the Big Muddy. So far, all the activity seemed normal, which meant that in spite of their stupidity in strolling around inside, nobody seemed to have spotted them. Yet. "This is going to take a while. For the love of Christ, Shaw, not you."

Redirected, Shaw got in the front seat, and Hazard got in the back.

"Well?" North said.

"I'm working," Hazard said.

"Oh, I thought you were on your way to Disney World."

"Really? Why?"

North pinched the bridge of his nose.

"What happened to your face?"

"I got a new kind of facial."

"What's it called? I've never heard of any kind of facial that results in so much bruising."

"Don't worry about him," Shaw said to Hazard. "He's grumpy because we almost got caught. He was almost this grumpy when we were chasing that roller-skate curly-fry bandit and she kept getting away because she was way, way faster, and sometimes North starts breathing hard when he runs—"

"You were ass-up in a fucking dumpster, Shaw. Because a Sonic drive-in girl put you there. If you're going to tell the fucking story, tell it right."

"That was only because it was a new moon in Aries, and the fact that I'm an Aquarius made it even worse, even though we're fearless and resilient and independent—"

"Says the guy who asked me to hold his hand while he made wheat grass juice last week."

"—and also the most beautiful—wait, what sign are you?"

Hazard's eyes flitted to North. "He knows astrology is all bunk, right?"

"Sure. He knows it's hogwash. Balderdash. Malarkey. The old applesauce hokey-pokey."

Faint red lines had appeared in Hazard's pale cheeks.

"I bet you're a Taurus," Shaw said. "You're stable, you're low key, you and I always have so much fun, even when we don't go out and do anything."

"What are you talking about? What is he talking about?"

"Hooey," North suggested, relaxing against the car door to better enjoy the show.

"Like one of the best times we ever had together," Shaw waved his hands for emphasis, leaning over the back seat, halfway to crawling into Hazard's lap, "was when we hung out at your office together. Remember? You were sad, and I made you tea, and then you drank my tea, and then you were better. Oh! And Taureans are also incredibly disciplined and strong willed, and they have phenomenal sexual stamina, which makes sense because physically, I mean, with your glutes and hamstrings and quads, your whole derriere, actually—"

"Ok," North said.

"What the fuck?" Hazard said.

"That's probably enough best-friending. What kind of job are you working?"

"An embezzler. A woman who worked at one of those payday-loan stores. She's on the run, but she's been texting a friend, and I think the friend is going to lead me back to her." Hazard's gaze refocused on Shaw. "Was he telling the truth? Are you really looking for a murderer? Or was that more of his...nonsense?"

"I was telling the truth," Shaw said proudly.

North nodded and checked the truck stop again.

"You came out of there pretty fast," Hazard said. "And your body language was tense. You hadn't caught a lead; you weren't excited, and you sat in your car watching the truck stop instead of moving on to your next action item."

"I came for the murderer," North said, "but I stayed for the cheese dog."

"You shouldn't eat those," Shaw began.

"The nitrates alone," Hazard began.

Both men cut off. Shaw beamed at Hazard. Hazard glared—suspiciously, North thought, as though he suspected a prank—back.

"We're, like, swoon-worthy level best friends," Shaw said.

"No. We aren't." Those amber eyes narrowed again. "You were grabbing his arm. You kept looking back. You were scared. You're driving this piece of shit. So, you're afraid someone is going to recognize your personal vehicle. But you aren't sure, otherwise you would have driven off."

"Actually, out here, a day like this, it's the perfect time to work on my farmer's tan," North said. "I might sit here all day."

"And eat a cheese dog," Hazard said flatly.

"North, you really can't do that because, well, you're so fair, and you get pink, and then you get that lobster color, and you know I have psychic trauma from shellfish, and then sometimes I have to put lotion on you, and yeah, it's fun, especially when you get all nakedy and you want me to make my hand super tight so you can—"

"Shaw, for the love of God." North directed a meaningful look at the back seat.

It took a moment. Then Shaw nodded. To Hazard, he said, "I'm sorry."

One of Hazard's eyebrows went up.

"You're very fair too." Shaw stretched over the back seat to pat Hazard's hand.

Hazard pulled his hand away. He looked like he was three seconds away from kicking open the door and running for his life.

"Mother of Christ," North muttered. "Ok, yes, we think someone tipped them off that we're coming." In a few sentences, North laid out the facts of the case. "So for the moment, we're sitting here, trying to figure out our next step. Hey, maybe that's an option—how would you feel about being a subcontractor on this job? It's dangerous, and it'll mean long hours and hard work, but the plus side is you're not going to get paid a dime."

"Why would that be a plus?"

"Is he serious?" North asked. "When he says stuff like that, does he genuinely not get it?"

"When he says things in that tone," Shaw told Hazard, "you should probably give him a pity laugh. I do it all the time. I'll be thinking about the ancient aliens who helped the Mayans build their pyramids, and then I hear that tone, and I laugh just so he'll let it go and I can get back to work. Otherwise it's a whole thing. He prides himself on his sense of humor, so if I don't laugh it becomes an ego issue, which then means it's a performance issue, which— holy shit, North, I can't feel my whole leg."

North shook out his fist. "You are a jerk."

"I was trying to help Emery—"

"No, you are a real jerk. You like my jokes. That one time, back when I—"

"For fuck's sake!" Hazard shouted. "Is this what you do all day? Go back and forth like this? Shut up for five seconds, please. If I had to put up with this from John, I would literally kill myself. Jesus Christ, Son of God, shut up."

"He can't hear you right now," Shaw whispered, massaging his leg. "He's driving that Bible lady's minivan."

North couldn't help himself; that one got him, and then Shaw was laughing too, and the way Hazard watched them, with a mixture of horror and rage and helplessness, only made them laugh harder. Shaw ended up turned all around, his head hanging down into the footwell, and North was sprawled against the door wiping his eyes.

"Fuck both of you," Hazard said, sliding toward the door.

"Come on," North said. "We'll cut out the dumbshit act."

"Act?" Shaw said.

"Look, you've been watching this place. This is your neck of the woods. What's going on in there? What's the story?"

The fringe of flush in Hazard's cheeks hadn't faded, and he held himself stiffly, but after a moment he said, "I don't know. I mean, I've heard of the Big Muddy, and people talk. But this isn't Wahredua, and I don't work out this way often enough to know what's going on."

"But you've heard things," Shaw said.

"What do people say when they talk about this place?" North asked.

Hazard shook his head. "It's hearsay." When North rolled his eyes, Hazard grimaced, but some of the tension went out of his body. "I've heard about drugs. And you always hear stories about strip clubs."

"Why haven't Barney Fife and the other locals—"

"Is that Jesse?" Shaw said.

North craned his head to look back at the truck stop. A white guy with stringy hair, a dirty A-shirt, and sagging jeans stood at one of the truck stop's side entrances. The woman next to him wore a black bustier, a floral pink skirt that barely reached her knees, and fishnet stockings. Her hair was on the wrong side of carrot colored.

"And Cinnamon," North said.

The man who stepped out of the Big Muddy and shook Jesse's hand had to be Big Joe—he matched the man they'd seen in the employee-of-the-month plaque, down to the Bass Pro Shop hat. In life, he was bigger than he had looked in the picture, and his jeans rode too high and too tight, giving him a muffin top. When he removed the hat, his thinning hair flapped in the breeze, and he smoothed it into place with stubby fingers.

Big Joe and Jesse shook hands, and when Big Joe dropped his hand, Jesse, seemingly without thinking about it, touched a bulge in his front pocket.

"Cash," Hazard said.

"Fun Dip," North said.

"His grandmother's diaphragm," Shaw said.

"What the actual fuck, Shaw?" North said. "That's gross. And creepy. And seriously gross, like, borderline disgusting."

"It's obviously cash," Hazard said.

"This is so much fun," Shaw said.

Jesse said something to Cinnamon, who bent and kissed him on the cheek. Jesse's body language said he didn't appreciate the gesture, and he strutted off toward a beater Impala. Cinnamon and Big Joe talked, and then Big Joe pointed across the lot.

"Cinnamon's big break," North said. "She finally got that recording contract."

"No," Hazard said. "He hired her to be a stripper."

"That's a sexist assumption. Maybe he hired her to pier the foundation."

"It's not an assumption, and it's not sexist. It's an inference based on multiple data points. Point 1, the woman, subpoint 1A, body type, sub-subpoint 1Ai visual estimate of muscle mass percentage—"

"Please, God, make this stop," North muttered.

"No, let him finish," Shaw said. "I want to hear when he gets to subpoint 1F, footwear, sub-subpoint 1Fiii, kitten heels."

"If anything," Hazard said, "footwear would be sub-subpoint 2C—"

North let out a small scream. "Enough. Whatever he hired her to do, I don't think it's stripping. She's getting into that SUV."

Cinnamon disappeared into the rear passenger door, and the black Ford Explorer rolled away. The windows were tinted, but North could make out the man driving: he was black, and he had a blocky head with his hair shaved. From what North could see, he looked to be of average height and build.

"Shit," Hazard said. "That's Shane Kirby."

"Who's Shane Kirby?" Shaw asked.

"A crazy motherfucker. According to him, ex-military, Special Forces, although I haven't been able to confirm that. He gets around in these parts. People eat up his bullshit, the whole soldier thing. For all I know, he's nothing but a piece of shit who owns a ghillie suit and a good rifle, but whatever he is, he's dangerous—I've heard about people getting hurt, people disappearing, but nobody's willing to finger this guy, which means he's throwing a serious scare."

"I'd be willing to finger him," Shaw said.

"Stop. Talking," North said.

"Well, I would. It would be a sting operation."

"How would it be a sting operation?" Hazard asked.

North rubbed his forehead. "Can you please not encourage him?"

"I'd be doing a public service," Shaw said.

"In what sense—" Hazard began.

"Do you not realize that he feeds off this?" North asked. "Are you really that clueless?"

"God damn," Hazard muttered. He pulled on the handle and elbowed the door open. "She's moving."

A tinselly blonde in yoga pants was trotting across the concrete pad, heading for a white Honda Civic.

"There's a place, the Peach Grove, not far from here. On a back road. Supposedly, it's a motel, but…" He shrugged. "Everybody says Big Joe owns it, but there's nothing on paper. Nothing I could find, anyway. I spent a weekend looking just for kicks."

"Sounds like a ball," North said.

"John-Henry is a lucky guy," Shaw said with aggravating sincerity.

"I called my dorm room in college the peach grove."

"That's sexist," Shaw said. "You should have called it the pork pen. Oh! And you could call your car the wiener wagon."

"I'd say good luck," Hazard said as he levered himself out of the car, "but I think you two are beyond that."

"Fuck you," North called cheerily as Hazard slammed the door.

"That was nice of him," Shaw said.

"No, it wasn't."

"He said we didn't even need luck anymore. We're beyond that."

"He didn't mean—" North stopped himself. "You know what? One day I'm going to catch you, and then this whole charade is going to be over."

"What charade?" Shaw asked, with a slightly too innocent expression.

"No more talking," North said, hunkering down. "We need a plan."

Chapter 16

"WHY DO I have to wear jeans?" Shaw tugged on the denim, stretching his legs in the rented Ford's footwell. "They're so stiff and uncomfortable."

"Quit complaining; this was your idea."

"It's like they don't have any elastane at all. What percentage do you think is spider silk?"

North considered his boyfriend, who in a rugby shirt, crisp blue jeans, and white Adidas sneakers, could have passed for straight.

"Is my ass provocative enough?" Shaw asked.

"Until he opens his mouth," North muttered.

"What?"

"I said, what ass?"

They had spent the day watching the Big Muddy, making jaunts back to Columbia to borrow cars from a car-share service. The idea was that, at a busy stop like the Big Muddy, no one would notice the cars that lingered a little longer—families sharing a meal, maybe, or men taking advantage of the booby joint before heading home to dear wifey. As far as North could tell, their plan had worked; no one had approached them. On the other hand, they had seen nothing that put them any closer to figuring out what was going on. Big Joe had made an appearance once. Shaw had spotted him through the windows of Dina's, the small restaurant attached to the stop, where Big Joe had been glad-handing men—exclusively men. Shane Kirby had come back in the Explorer, sans Cinnamon, only to disappear into the truck stop and not emerge again. Kirby's return had been enough to keep North from risking a trip into the booby joint. He wasn't ready for a confrontation, not until he knew more.

"In case your pot-addled brain has forgotten," North said, "repeat after me: this is recon."

"This is recon." Shaw held up bunny ears, which he probably thought was the equivalent of Scout's honor—or, more likely, was the secret pledge of fealty to some sort of dark, cosmic, leporine power. "I'm going to march right in there and tell them I want to put my private parts on a girl's private parts."

"On? How do you think the straights—no, never mind. Shaw, I seriously think I should be the one to do this."

"No, you always get to do sexy disguises. Last week you got to be sexy riverboat captain and sexy septic tank unclogger. I can do this. I'm going to say 'in.' I want to stick it in, um, a lady's—wait, should I say lady?"

"That settles it. I'm going in."

"No, no, no, no, no." And before North could object further, Shaw launched himself out of the car and headed across the gravel lot.

The Peach Grove had once been a gambrel-roofed barn, but over the years, additions had been put on, until the original structure was a front for the one-story maze that spread out behind it. The barn itself was still red with white trim, and a veranda with pressure-treated support posts held Adirondack chairs and a porch swing. The newer construction had vinyl siding that looked like it had been scavenged from a war zone, chipped and broken and covered in mildew. Privacy film had been applied to the inside of the windows, but sloppily, so that light leaked out where the film didn't reach the frame. It gave the whole building a restless, Twilight Zone energy, as though a million eyes could snap open at any moment, full of bright, hungry light.

Too much time with Shaw, North told himself. Too much time with rabbit space gods and goat cults and that time he made his stuffed animals go through puberty.

The minutes ticked past. North checked his phone. He tried to make himself wait, tried to tell himself checking every fifteen seconds wasn't helping. It was night, and a few moths and late-summer flies danced in the pillars of yellow light along the veranda. At least a dozen other cars and trucks occupied the lot. Was that good or bad? What kind of questions would they ask? Had it been too long? Should Shaw have emerged again, claiming sexual dysfunction or a stomachache or a forgotten appointment with his coven? North checked his phone again, and a minute had passed, which seemed utterly fucking impossible.

When the text from Shaw came, the phone's buzz startled North, and his heart lurched into a pounding sprint.

Left-hand door, the text said.

What the fuck does that mean?

Oh sorry my left. And then almost immediately, *HURRY!!!*

North slid out of the Ford. He shut the door quietly and jogged into the waist-high grass that lined the gravel lot; the stalks whispered against his legs, a trade-off for the crunch of gravel underfoot. He had no idea what *my left* meant, but he decided to go right. He passed the veranda, the empty Adirondacks, the spinning insects in the yellow light. He moved along the newer construction. Under the first window, he heard a man grunting rhythmically. Under the next, a guy was saying, "This has never happened to me before." Under the next, a slap, loud, and then a woman's cry that didn't sound like make believe. A heat like a rash went through North, and he went faster.

He followed the side of the building, and ten feet down, a door stood open. Only a crack, sure, but a door. North opened it another inch, and then he swore, yanked it open, and slipped inside. He pulled Shaw into a one-armed hug while he glanced around.

The floors were plywood, and sawdust had been thrown down, presumably to soak up jizz and puke and then be swept away. A bubblegum air freshener couldn't cover up the sweat, sex, and smoke—cigarillos, with that hint of something like ammonia, and marijuana. Music played somewhere, a thudding bass. Relentless. The heat was too high, and the cotton tee clung and bunched under North's arms.

"What the fuck happened," he asked in a growl, giving Shaw a shake for good measure, "to recon?"

"It's not my fault," Shaw whispered. "I didn't do anything, and then all of a sudden I had the perfect opportunity to do some extra exploring, and I found this door, and I texted you, only you didn't understand what I meant by left, so—"

"I know perfectly fucking well what left means!" It was a whisper, but only barely. "I didn't understand why you were wandering around and risking getting caught. If that girl talks—"

"Oh, she won't tell anyone."

North narrowed his eyes. "Why? What did you do?"

"I told you, it's not my fault. I did it just like we talked about: I went inside, I told them I wanted a redhead on the off chance they'd put me with Cinnamon, only they didn't put me with Cinnamon. I didn't even get a redhead."

The indignant note in his voice, combined with the surreal sequence of the night's events, threatened to tip North into laughter. "And redheads are your favorite."

"Well, no, but I did ask for one. I got a blonde, only the dye job was so bad, and it looked fake. And she was wearing rayon, which you know I have chafing issues with—"

"Wait, you had her keep her clothes on?"

"Of course! I'm a virgin. Well, a straight virgin. I'm still pure."

North scanned the hallway, but they were still alone. "This from the guy who once told me he watched straight porn because, quote, 'They do great work with the sets and lighting.'"

"They do! And sometimes the cinematography, the ball shots—"

"Mother of God. Get on with it."

"Sometimes I bet the girls feel that way because the guys go on and on—"

"Shaw!"

"Ok, ok. So this girl was scratching herself, and she kind of smelled like that tropical body oil that stained my jock, but also kind of like puke, and a little bit like mouthwash. And I told her I needed to go slow, on account of the delicate flower of my chastity—"

"Jesus Christ."

"Yes, exactly, the holy blossom between my legs that I saved to be plucked by our Lord—"

"I'm done. You can go back and get straight-deflowered, but I'm going home."

North had to let Shaw wrestle him for a few moments, dragging him away from the door, Shaw trying incredibly hard not to giggle—and failing.

"Finally this guy came in and gave her a shot," Shaw said when North finally surrendered, "and she got dopey. She started yanking on my zipper, but I told her I wanted to go slow, on account of my holy maidenhead. And then she wanted me to touch, you know, her business area, so I said I wanted to go really slow, and then I said maybe we should try meditation and guided breathing—"

"Guys get normal boyfriends all the time. They go on Grindr or Prowler or Scruff and they find normal, regular guys. Maybe I should try. What could it hurt?"

"—and she fell asleep! And stop being mean to me because now we have a chance to look around this place."

"Did she have track marks?"

Shaw nodded. "I think it was heroin. The look on her face? I've seen it before."

"It probably was. A lot of girls in the business get hooked on it, sometimes not by choice. Some places keep them on a leash that way. Some places keep them from making a fuss with it."

Shaw paled, and North stroked the coppery patch of hair and whispered, "Sorry, I shouldn't have said that."

"No." Shaw shook his head. "I knew. But I hate knowing. I hate that the world is that way." He must have seen something on North's face because he hurried to add, "I won't fall apart, I promise."

North thought about pressing the issue, sending Shaw back to the car; whatever was in this place, he didn't want it taking up eternal shelf space in Shaw's head. But the look on Shaw's face told him he didn't have a choice. North glanced at the front of the building, where the music seemed louder, and started in the opposite direction. The walls were drywall under a thin coat of paint—so thin that, in places, uneven tape and mud showed through. Every few steps, the plywood flexed underfoot, threatening to buckle. The music faded until it was nothing more than a droning pulse point North felt at the base of his skull. They passed an open door, where a pregnant girl in a white teddy strutted halfheartedly and rubbed her belly. Another cracked door showed them two girls scissoring robotically while a man watched; he had to be in his early twenties, good looking, clean cut, groping a substantial erection through cargo shorts.

"How does a place like this stay in operation?" Shaw whispered as they kept moving.

"Good question," North said. He wasn't sure he wanted to know the answer, but he added, "They have to have some sort of semi-legal façade—Hazard said they were a motel."

"But nobody who walks through the front door would believe that. No cop that ever came to check on this place would believe that."

"No," North said.

After a moment, Shaw said, "Oh."

North reached over and squeezed his hand.

They found the reinforced door at the back of the addition. The builders had made no attempt to hide it or to disguise it. The other doors they had passed had been flimsy, hollow-core designs. Many had been hung imperfectly and, as a result, did not close completely. In contrast, this door was steel, with a hasp and padlock securing it.

North stared at the door for a moment, and then he looked at Shaw. "I want you to go back to the car."

Shaking his head, Shaw swallowed.

"Shaw—"

"Can you open it? Or do you want me to try?"

The steel was matte. Their reflections, such as they were, were dark and amorphous.

"North?"

"I can open it. Find me something solid."

North examined the hasp and padlock, which was a knock-off brand he could have picked up at Walmart for a couple of dollars. It wasn't designed to keep people out; it was meant to keep someone in. When Shaw came back, he was carrying a small red fire extinguisher. He held it up.

"That'll work." North put two fingers through the lock's shackle, forcing the base down until the shackle no longer had any slack. Then, gripping the extinguisher near the base, he hammered against the side of the lock. Metal chimed, and in the quiet of this part of the building, it sounded as loud as an alarm. On the fifth blow, the shackle came loose, and the padlock opened.

North worked it free from the hasp and set it on the floor next to the fire extinguisher. He gave Shaw one last look, asking without asking, but Shaw refused to concede. With a sigh, North turned the handle and pushed.

The room was a cinderblock box, and it smelled like urine and closed-up bodies. A wedge of light spilled through the doorway, widening as North entered: soiled mattresses on the concrete slab; a yellow plastic bucket; a hose snaked around a spigot.

"Cinnamon?" Shaw said, pushing past North. "Are you here? North, where is she?"

"Wherever she is, she's not here. We need to—" North began.

But something made him turn. A sound. The creak of plywood under new weight.

He saw the fire extinguisher coming right before it connected. Then red flared in his vision. Then black.

Chapter 17

THE BLOWS WENT ON for a long time. Shaw only got a good look at the first man, the one Hazard had called Shane Kirby, with his blocky head and shaved hair. Even Kirby couldn't hold his attention, though; Shaw had been focused on North, who had fallen to the ground and wasn't moving. Then Kirby had gotten in the first blow—something red, maybe the extinguisher—and then Shaw had been falling, trying to protect himself, curling up, arms around his head. Lots of kicking. The toes of boots finding spots that made Shaw scream and try to crawl free. But they had hurt him other ways too—what might have been hoses and weights wrapped in towels and once, a broom handle that had snapped. Not their hands. He understood, at a primitive level. The way some guys whacked a dog's nose with a newspaper. This wasn't a fight; it was a punishment.

When they started with the ropes, Shaw barely had the presence of mind to remember the old tricks. He was on a train, part of his brain told him. He was leaving the station. Old tracks, bad suspension, a bumpy start. But the horizon grayed out nicely, and he figured he was well on his way. But he remembered. Enough. Make yourself as big as possible. Hold your breath. Hands in fists. Wrists apart. Pull away from the knots. *Escapology for Kids: Amaze Your Friends! Astound Your Family!* And the Houdini-esque figure in a union suit, rippling with muscle, bowed under a million chains but not broken. Not yet.

Next, his head was bouncing on corrugated steel. A van, part of his brain told him muzzily. He smelled cigarillos again, but distantly—probably because his nostrils were crusted almost completely shut. North lay next to him, eyes closed, unmoving, arms tied behind his back. A circle of dark red marked North's temple, the beginning of a bruise. Why hadn't he woken up yet? Shaw's brain lit up, the labyrinth glowing with a thousand incandescent paths: broken orbital socket, optic nerve neuropathy, traumatic brain injury, subdural hematoma—put on the brakes, put on the brakes, you can't help North if you're scared-lost inside your own head, so put on the brakes—

They hit a pothole, and Shaw's head cracked against the steel floor, and he was on the train again.

Cold. Wet. The side of his face, his arm, soaking through the new 501s. Blood—that was the same part of his brain that had suggested *van*, but a moment later, Shaw realized the texture was wrong—too slippery, too thick, too dense. Mud. A murmur. Water rippling close by.

"Quit fucking around and roll them in."

"Did I ask you?"

"Like a couple of kittens. They won't even wake up."

"Jed, shut the fuck up. I got a plan. You don't got a plan. You don't got nothing but a fat-tittied wife who won't give your dumb ass the fucking time of day."

"The Beadle brothers are a couple of pussies. The only time Bo Beadle ever threw a punch was when the other guy was already down."

Steps moved behind Shaw, the sound of sand and loose stones, and at the last moment, Shaw remembered to push against his ropes so they appeared tight. Someone tugged on the bindings. He moaned—his joints, especially his elbows, were hinged with fire, and he couldn't hold back the noise. Whoever was behind him, and he suspected it was Kirby, gave a satisfied grunt and stood. More steps, more of the soft crunch of sand and pebbles clicking.

"That's what I want, ain't it? I want a peckerwood dog, bottom of the pack, the kind that stays on the edge until the dust settles and then goes in for the kill. That kind, he finds a couple of faggots already down for the count, he's going to have some fun, and then nobody comes back looking for where we stepped in the shit. Now, I told you, I got a plan, ain't I?"

Sullen silence. Then: "You can't talk about Vera Ann that way or I got to do something about it."

Kirby—it had to be Kirby—burst out laughing. "Fuck you, and fuck that big-titty hog. Call Bo and tell him you seen these faggots playing some fag rope games on his stretch of Spinner Creek."

The other man made a muffled protest as their steps moved away.

An engine started. Grass hissed and crunched under tires. An old suspension protested on the uneven ground. The sounds faded until Shaw could hear only the creek and his own breathing.

Struggling to his knees, he said, "North."

North opened his eyes, although one was partially swollen shut. "I'm awake."

"Thank God. I thought—" Relief exposed, for a moment, how deep the fear had gone, and Shaw struggled to hold himself on the precipice.

He might have lost that struggle and broken down completely except North closed his eyes again, rocked on the sand, and humped his body a few inches toward Shaw. The movement was so bizarre that Shaw burst out laughing, the sound stringy and uneven.

"What are you doing?" he asked.

"I'm trying to get closer to you. I had a pocketknife, if these shitbirds didn't take it." He grunted and humped a few more inches of sand. "Even if they did, we might be able to—fuck. Aww, Jesus. That rock got me right in the nads."

For another moment, Shaw watched as North squirmed sideways through the sand. Then Shaw made a sacrifice: no matter how fun it was to watch North, it wouldn't be worth it if the Beadle brothers, whoever they were, caught up with them. He set to work on his own ropes.

The old escapology tricks had worked the way they were supposed to, giving him valuable slack around his wrists and chest. He worked the rope in a circular motion around his hands until the ends brushed his fingers. He tugged, hoping that they'd tied a bad knot that would fall apart. No luck. He followed one end of the rope up until he found the knot itself, and then he began pushing and pulling. It was uncomfortable, and after a few minutes of trying, his fingers were raw. But then he felt the end slide through a loop, and after that, it was easy.

Thirty seconds later, he was shrugging out of the coils of ropes.

North was still wriggling on the sand, grunting. He was about three feet away. "I think I'm in position," he said. "I had the knife in my front right pocket, so you'll need to get up high enough to reach. And don't even think about the magic-fingers routine, Shaw, because we are on a tight fucking schedule." North spat sand and shook his head. "Fuck this. I can't see a fucking thing. This sand is a bitch."

"Oh, here, let me get that." Shaw bent over and wiped the sand from North's face.

Blinking, North stared up at him. "How the fuck did you—" Even in the moonlight, the flush was visible in his cheeks. "You motherfucker. I am going to murder you. How long?"

"Just right now, but that's not the point—"

"Shaw, for the love of God, get me out of these fucking ropes."

Shaw squatted to work on the knot at North's wrists. As soon as he was free, North got to his knees and caught Shaw's face in both hands, turning his head up. The bruise darkening around North's eye looked bad, and the eye itself had a nasty looking nova of broken blood vessels.

"I was worried about you," Shaw whispered. "I am worried."

North kissed him. Then, wincing, he rubbed his forehead. "That son of a bitch got me good. I don't know if I can—"

In the distance, drawing nearer, small engines buzzed.

"Four-wheelers, ATVs, some shit like that," North muttered. He tried to stand and sank back down again. "Shit, help me up."

Shaw got him on his feet, but it was a challenge. For all North's bitching about Shaw's lack of time at a weight bench, Shaw knew he was stronger than he looked. North, however, was both bigger and heavier than he was, and Shaw was shouldering a lot more of North's weight than he expected.

"We can't run like this," North said. He was rubbing his head again. "If we can hide…"

But he didn't finish the sentence, and the engines—two of them, at least—were coming closer. Shaw glanced around. He didn't know what time it was, but the stars and the moon gave a surprising amount of light in the open countryside. Their side of the creek had sparse vegetation: along the bank itself, a few cottonwoods and willows grew in staggered increments; where the sandy bank ended, waist-high grass began. Shaw could see where Kirby and the other man had walked in the grass, because the stalks were trampled; their trail was even easier to read on the sand.

The other side of the creek, though, had thicker stands of trees and brush. Thick enough to hide them. For a while.

"We're going to go swimming," Shaw said, hauling North upright when North stumbled. "We're going the creek. They can't follow in their four-wheelers. Maybe they'll give up looking for us."

"They won't," North said. "Kirby picked these guys and this spot for a reason, because they're sadistic, territorial shit-dribbles from an incestuous gene pool. If they can catch us—and they're going to try—they won't let us go. Oh shit, I'm going to throw up. Get the rope."

North hinged at the waist, puking onto the sand between his boots. Shaw stumbled back up the beach. He grabbed both lengths of rope and hurried back. Hands on knees, North was struggling to stay upright.

He wiped his mouth and said, "You follow running water. Down, I mean. Follow it down. Hit a road."

"Ok," Shaw said, "but first, we're getting over to those trees. That'll buy us some time."

"Unless—" North had to stop and press a hand to his head. "Ford the creek. They'll know a place. Maybe a bridge."

"Shit," Shaw whispered. "Shit, shit, shit." He tried to think. What do you do when someone's trying to hunt you down and murder you in the middle of nowhere? Shaw had no idea. He knew cities, he knew suburbs, he knew skyscrapers and how to get past secretaries and clerks and mail jockeys who thought they were big stuff.

Then it hit him: "Easter bunny."

North groaned.

"That guy with the Easter bunny fetish," Shaw said, "and he was attacking all those mall workers, and so you went around all day in a bunny costume, and one time I caught you on that bench and you smelled like smoke, and you said some of the other Easter bunnies were smoking cigarettes, which is a bad message for kids."

"Oh shit. Shaw."

The whine of the engines was definitely louder.

Shaw spoke more quickly. "We used the bunny suit to make that fake set of bunny prints down the alley, and the guy walked right past us because he was following them."

North wobbled. If he had heard or understood, he gave no sign of it.

Shaw squeezed his arm and said, "I'll be right back."

He jogged downstream twenty yards and dropped one of the lengths of rope at the water's edge. Then he tied the other into a bundle and pitched it across the creek. The creek wasn't wide, but for a moment, it looked like the rope was going to fall short. It landed in a tangle of brush, the weight dragging the branches down to skim the water. Good enough.

Shaw shucked the Adidas and his socks. He shoved the socks into the shoes, tied the laces, and slung them around his neck. Then he stepped into the creek. The water was cold—it was September, and it was the middle of the night, and the shock made him wince. But he waded deeper, until he gauged he was far enough from the shore, and reversed course to head upstream toward North. He padded up to where the water met the sand, careful to keep from leaving fresh prints on dry land, and beckoned.

"Come on, a few steps over here and then I'll help you."

North staggered toward him. When he reached the water, he let out an explosive gasp, clutching Shaw's shoulder to steady himself. Shaw knelt in the shallows and fumbled with North's laces. "Foot up," he encouraged in a whisper. "That's right. Hold it like that for me."

First boot off. First sock off.

The engines sounded like a swarm of angry bees now. When one of the four-wheelers crested a swell in the ground, headlights splashed off the creek.

"Other foot, other foot," Shaw whispered.

"I'm going to chuck."

"That's ok, that's ok, barf all over me if you have to, but other foot. Other foot, baby, come on."

Shaw yanked the second boot and sock off, tied the laces, and pulled North into the water. That was almost the end of both of them; North stumbled, and only luck kept Shaw from falling and taking both of them into the water. With North's boots around his neck—heavy pieces of shit, especially compared to the sneakers—Shaw guided North deeper into the creek. Then he turned, North half-draped across him, and waded upstream again.

They were settling into an undercut curve of the bank, where an old cottonwood's roots provided a shelf of dirt and grass, when the four-wheelers came into sight. Two of them.

The creek pulled at Shaw and North. The current wasn't strong, but it was there, and the water was colder than Shaw had first thought. North was shaking next to him, and Shaw pulled North's face into his shoulder, arms wrapped around his waist, and whispered, "Just float. I got you. You don't have to do anything but float."

The sudden addition of weight as North gave in to the head wound and the current made Shaw grunt and lurch a half step. The creek's murmur barely covered the soft splash.

Down the bank, the men had dismounted from the four-wheelers. They were wearing boots, jeans, plaid shirts, and ski masks. One of them had a knife on his belt that was almost as long as Shaw's forearm. That one pointed at the tangle of coils Shaw had left by the water's edge. The other shone a flashlight across the water. It took the shitheels almost five minutes to spot the second bundle that had caught up in the brambles on the opposite bank. The sound of the water made it hard for Shaw to catch their conversation; most of what he heard was swears and complaints.

For a few minutes more, they tromped up and down the bank, shining lights on the sand. They followed North's trail to the water's edge, and one of them played a light upstream. Shaw clutched North tighter. He considered pulling him down into the water, and fuck dry footwear. But the light skipped past their hiding place. The light gave the creek ruffles, crests, troughs, a skin of sparks riding the water. The taste in Shaw's mouth was mud and crawfish and blood. Then the light went out, and the current dragged darkness down on them.

A moment later, the engines roared to life, and the sound moved away.

Shivering, Shaw held North against the current and counted to sixty. He kissed North's temple. "North, love, we've got to move."

Nodding groggily, North tried to stand, but he needed Shaw's help out of the water.

Shaw rolled up their pants and dried their feet with his polo. He put the shirt back on, and then he got them both back into socks and shoes. North helped by rolling onto his side and puking again halfway through the process.

"Ok," North said when Shaw helped him up again. "Ok. I can do this."

But *I can do this* meant, apparently, he could stagger along, leaning on Shaw so heavily that Shaw's shoulder and back started screaming at him before they'd made it a mile. They followed North's original plan, tracing the creek's course as much as possible—along the sandy bank, winding over low bluffs, pushing their way through white pines that scratched their hands and faces and left them sticky with sap.

When they reached a blackberry patch that stretched as far as Shaw could see, with no way around it, he wanted to give up.

"I've got to rest for a minute."

North nodded dully, eyes already half closed.

As Shaw caught his breath, he stretched his shoulder and back as best he could, twisting at the waist to try to pop a knot in his spine. That was why he saw the flashlights behind them.

"Down," he whispered, dragging North on top of him. "Down."

North grunted as he landed. Shaw bit back a swear. Blackberry thorns dug into the tender flesh on the back of his arm. The voices moved closer.

"You seen the rope," one of the men said querulously.

"I seen an old rope. That's all you seen too."

"They said they were playing them fag games around here."

"And I say it was a fucking joke, making us look like peckerwoods."

On the bank opposite, the lights stopped. The wave of relief through Shaw was as cold and as clear as creek water; in the darkness, he had been sure the men were right behind them. The voices carried across the Spinner's rippling murmur.

"Somebody was on this piece of land. Our land. And that means something, don't it?"

"Fuck off. You get a boner thinking about them fags, that's what it is. I'm going home."

"Fuck you."

"Fuck you."

The lights swiveled. For a moment, they formed a white vee across the water, and then they crossed, an X, and then they were headed in separate directions. When darkness flowed into place again, Shaw squeezed North's arm.

"Up, buster." He went for a lie: "We've got to get through these bushes, and then it's only a little farther."

It was hard to tell in the moonlight, but North looked gray as he stumbled through the bushes, clinging onto Shaw.

The blackberries were the worst part; Shaw emerged scratched ten ways to hell, and North didn't look much better. But the ground rolled smoothly downhill after that, and they hit a truss bridge, the beams rusting through their Army green paint. Shaw helped North up the embankment. More thistles. Loose gravel crunching on the shoulder. A skink that had been crushed flat recently—it still looked fresh. Shaw looked both ways, did a mental coin toss, and turned right.

Headlights flared to life, and Shaw froze. He thought about running, but North couldn't run. He thought about pushing North down the hill and running in the other direction, hoping he could lure them away. But the truth was, he wasn't sure he could run either. Exhaustion paralyzed him.

The vehicle came towards them and turned sharply, cutting across the asphalt. With the lights now at an angle, Shaw recognized the Honda hood ornament.

"No fucking way," North muttered. "This is not how I go down, not by some motherfucker in a soccer mom minivan."

The window buzzed down, and Emery Hazard said, "Get in."

Chapter 18

HAZARD HAD IBUPROFEN, Tylenol, and cans of lukewarm Pepsi. North took the pills with as much of the soda as he could stomach. Then he lay on the bench seat at the back of the minivan, drawing his legs up to fit.

"I didn't even know they still made Pepsi," Shaw said. He was already talking faster. "I figured once people tasted Coke, you know, real Coca Cola, they wouldn't ever go back to Pepsi again, and then the Pepsi empire would collapse, and then there wouldn't be any more Pepsi."

"John likes Pepsi," Hazard said.

"Oh, right, but I mean, he's probably never had Coke before, has he? Is that another can? I'm going to try a little bit more just to be sure—"

"Cut him off after two," North called up to them.

"He's a grown man," Hazard said.

"All right, you can listen to his conspiracy theory about the nineteenth century, the decline of the wimple, and the rise of the bonnet."

"Wimples were more common in the Middle Ages," Hazard said, "so I'm not sure—"

"That's what Big Bonnet wants you to think," Shaw announced too loudly. North rubbed the side of his head that hadn't almost been smashed in. "But Paracletan's *Secret History of the Wimple* reveals the vigorous, dynamic role of the wimple until it was crushed by the bonnet industry's thugs." A slurping noise competed with the sound of the minivan's tires. "Why do you think Blue Bonnet was the bestselling margarine spread of the twentieth century?"

"I'd have to see comparable margarine sales—" Hazard cut himself off. His voice sounded louder, as though he were pitching it back to North. "After two, you said?"

North held up two fingers.

"Give me those," Hazard said.

"No, wait, please—North!"

"My head," North said.

"North," Shaw whispered, "make him give them back."

"How did you know where to find us?" North asked. "Hell, how did you know we were in trouble, for that matter?"

"The woman I was following went back to the Big Muddy. She's waiting for something, although I don't know what. A phone call, I'd guess. I was in the lot when Kirby tore out of there with his ass on fire."

"How'd Kirby and the others know we were inside the Peach Grove?" Shaw asked.

"You took too long," Hazard said. "They went to turn you out, so another guy could have a go at that girl, and you were gone. That's my guess, anyway. When I saw Kirby move, it wasn't much of a jump from A to B, and I figured you two had fucked up somehow."

"Excuse me?" North said.

"And you knew we were in trouble because of our psychic entanglement," Shaw said, his voice jittery with sugar and caffeine. "And our best-friendedness and that erotic dream I had where you were yelling at me about the history of iodine, in which a yardstick featured prominently, and—"

"Can you take us back to our car? Take me back, actually. Do your country boy thing and tie Shaw in a sack and drop him in a river."

"Rude," Shaw said, "and first of all, we can't go back to our car because it's parked at the Peach Grove, so I think Emery will have to park somewhere else, and then he can get our car because no one will be looking for him, and I'll tag along, exactly one hundred paces behind him, and I'll match every footstep, and I'll position myself so that his outline covers mine, and then no one will know that two people are walking along the road."

"Unless someone looks at a slight angle," North said.

"Unless someone looks—" Hazard cut off. It took him a moment; it seemed like he was recovering his mental footing. "Your car's gone, so it's a moot point."

"What do you mean, gone?"

"What do most people mean?"

"God, do you realize I actually thought it was a bad thing when they canned your ass? At least you solved cases. But I forgot about this whole interpersonal experience."

"I'll have to drive you back to St. Louis."

"No shit, Sherlock."

"That's a compliment," Shaw informed Hazard. "He says it when someone made a good deduction or solved a difficult mystery."

"I think you're joking," Hazard said, hands flexing around the steering wheel, "but it's surprisingly hard to tell. It doesn't sound like a compliment."

"It's not," North said.

They drove for a while in silence, and North slipped in and out of a place of dreams. Lying down, combined with the one-two of Tylenol and ibuprofen, and the dark, and the blessed quiet, meant that when he surfaced from the dreams, he felt much better. The dreams themselves, though, were thorny—briar mazes, with the sound of footsteps, the sound of running water, the sweep of light, the booger woods—

He jerked halfway upright as a semi passed in the opposite direction. The brilliance from its headlights ebbed, and then the interior of the minivan was dark again. North thought he smelled animal crackers. Then he realized Shaw was sitting in the middle seats, reaching back to hold his hand.

"Are you sitting in a booster seat?" he asked, wondering if this was still part of the dream.

"He's sitting in my daughter's car seat, which was not designed for an adult, and he's eating my daughter's animal crackers."

"Oh no, I think a mischievous leprechaun left these animal crackers, because I found them behind the seat, and I don't think anybody knew they were there. And I'm pretty sure whoever designed this car seat accessed the Akashic records and knew, without even knowing, how to design it to fit me, because it's surprisingly comfortable."

"Yes, Shaw," North said, closing his eyes again, "they designed that car seat for you. They had a twink past his expiration date in mind."

When he opened his eyes again, they had reached St. Louis's suburbs. Hazard and Shaw were talking in the front seats.

"—put North in that hyperbaric chamber, or maybe a chamomile-infused oxygen tent—"

"No, he needs rest, more Tylenol and ibuprofen, and possibly a CT scan, although that's for a doctor to decide."

"Actually, alternative medicine—"

"There's no such thing as alternative medicine. That's like saying, 'alternative bridge building.' It doesn't exist."

"I took a course on how to build dream bridges so I could spy on people's dreams. That's a kind of alternative bridge building."

"Drop me off here," North said. "I'll walk the rest of the way."

"Is he doing this on purpose?" Hazard asked; he had a faintly persecuted note under what sounded like genuine bewilderment. "I can't tell."

"I've been asking myself that for eight fucking years. Let me know if you figure it out." North propped himself up. "Do all country boys drive minivans? Or did they make you leave your balls behind when you left the city?"

"Not everyone needs to prove their masculinity by driving something that appeals to the fourteen-and-younger crowd."

"And toxic masculinity," Shaw prompted. "Tell him about that."

"No," Hazard snapped.

"Maybe we could stop for something to eat," Shaw said. "There's a great vegan barbeque place—"

"Fuck no," North said.

"No goddamn way," Hazard said at the same time.

"It's not even barbeque, Shaw."

"A barbeque by definition involves meat," Hazard said. "Why is he smiling?"

"Because," North said, squirming on the too-small bench, "he got exactly what he wanted. Again."

"Did you know that Emery and John-Henry had a bad Fourth of July too?" Shaw asked. "Emery said he didn't want to talk about it, but his aura has all this black lightning in it, and then I thought I saw a cockatoo, and so it was probably really, really bad."

"They can join the club. We'll make jackets: *Shittiest Fourth of July Ever.*"

"Why would we want jackets for that?" Hazard asked.

"This is why I asked to be dropped off five miles ago." North rubbed his head, which was feeling much better. "Wait a minute. You said you followed Kirby?"

"Yes."

"To the Peach Grove?"

"I didn't drive into the lot, but yes."

"And then you followed them when they dumped us on those psychopaths' land?"

"The Beadle brothers. Yes, they genuinely are psychopaths. They don't live anywhere close to Wahredua, but I've still heard about them. They make the Ozark Volunteers look like a tea-room wait staff."

"But you couldn't have known they were going to leave us there. What if they'd decided to shoot us? Or bury us alive?"

"I was willing to take that chance."

The tires hissed against the pavement. They passed a car dealership lit up with spotlights, which triggered North's headache like a fork to the eye.

In a slightly defensive tone, Hazard continued, "I assumed you would escape and follow the creek until it debouched in Spinner Lake. That's why I waited at the bridge. I was correct."

"John-Henry is going to murder you in your sleep one night. He's going to use a pillow. And you know what? I'm going to tell him, next time I see him, that when that happens, to call me. I'll help him cover it up."

Hazard's silence had a worried quality.

"Don't mind him," Shaw said, "he's grumpy because he doesn't feel well and because sometimes he doesn't know what big words mean." Turning, he shouted at full volume toward the back of the car, "Debouch is something some guys do before, you know, doing the roly-poly. You have this bulb full of water, and you stick the nozzle—"

"I know what fucking debouch means. I was the one who fucking graduated college."

"You both yell a lot," Hazard said.

"It's his hearing," Shaw said. "At first it was his vision, but now it's his hearing. Well, it's both."

"It's neither!" North had to take several deep breaths to stave off an aneurysm. "Hazard, what the fuck is going on back there?" He explained what they had seen: the girl who had been drugged, the sex work, and the locked room at the back. "How the fuck haven't the police shut them down?"

They turned onto the street of gingerbread brick houses, and North decided Shaw must have given Hazard their new address while he'd been sleeping. The minivan slowed. It was after three in the morning, North saw on the dashboard clock. The stillness of the street seemed oppressive.

"I'm not sure about the Peach Grove," Hazard said slowly. "It might be multiple variables. Yes, Shaw saw that girl having some sort of drug administered, but that doesn't mean it wasn't voluntary. Or at least, partially voluntary. The line becomes blurred, or nonexistent, in cases of dependency. And girls who will conduct sex work under those conditions aren't necessarily being kept against their will. It's reasonable to assume they'd lie to the police in exchange for consistent access to whatever they needed."

"Give me a break. I'm not arguing about the girls, but the guys running that place weren't even trying to hide the kind of operation they've got going on. And that locked room. That's another level, some seriously scary shit."

"It is," Hazard said as he rolled to a stop. "And your question about the police, about why they haven't done anything, is worrisome. I think you're right; there's no way the police don't know what's happening there." His voice took on a dry note as he pressed something, and the side door opened. "After all, the two of you figured it out."

Chapter 19

"NIK'S ASLEEP," Shaw whispered as he pulled the door to the guest room shut.

"Thank God." North tried to turn himself out of his tee, but something twinged in his shoulder, and his head gave a massive throb. "Fuck."

Shaw was there, peeling the shirt off him, gentle, always gentle. His hands were cool on North's shoulders as he guided North into their bedroom. When North sat, he helped with the rest of the clothes.

"Do you want a shower?"

"I honestly don't think I can fucking stand right now."

"Ok. Do you want water? More meds?"

North shook his head and patted the bed.

Shaw stripped, turned off the lights, and climbed up next to him. He smelled like a day's worth of sweat and something else, a silty, freshwater dampness. He burrowed under North's arm, head on North's chest, and the last thing North remembered was wanting to ask Shaw about his hair product, could he put a little in before bed because he liked how it smelled.

Dreams. Trackless miles of sand. The creek's babble was louder than it ever had been in life, thunderous, swallowing every other noise. The horizon, the rim of a chalice of ink and stars beyond the booger woods. He couldn't move. Couldn't raise himself. Blood in his mouth, slick. Sand in his mouth, grit. Shaw a few feet away. It might as well have been miles. And the coyotes were coming, only they sounded like small engines, howling as they came for an easy meal.

North sat up, heart hammering in his chest. The bedding was soaked with his sweat. Shaw had rolled away from him at some point in the night, and he lay at the edge of the mattress. With shaky hands, North wiped his face, pushed his hair back, and fought for a moment that felt like an eternity with the need to bawl. When it passed, he pulled the sheet and blanket over Shaw, grabbed his phone, and padded out of the room. He was vaguely aware that he was naked and that Nik might stumble upon him; he told himself fuck it, the kid had seen cocks before.

Sprawled on the couch, the air wicking along his body where sweat still clung to him, he indulged for a moment in the pleasure of being naked and cool after the choking tangle of his dreams. He tried Bleacher Report. He scrolled blindly through Redbird Rants. And then, without really thinking about it, he found himself staring at the twenty-one most beautiful villages in the UK. He picked out flights and a rental car to get to Portmeirion, Wales. Then, an itinerary for Portree, on the Isle of Skye. Then Cerne Abbas. That was in Dorsetshire. Then he googled what a shire was.

The creak of hinges alerted him, and he turned into the cushions to dry his eyes. A moment later, a hand was stroking his hair. North cleared his throat; he wasn't up for anything more.

"Bad dreams?" Shaw asked quietly.

"Bad enough."

"I'll change the sheets, and then you need to come back to bed."

"I can't sleep."

"You can't sleep if you're out here on your phone looking at—what is a shire?"

"It's a county. In England, I guess."

"I know, I was reading your search—never mind. Come on. Pee, drink some water, and by then I'll have the bed changed."

"I was thinking we should go on a trip."

Strain tightened Shaw's voice this time. "North, I want to go to bed."

"So go to bed."

"With you. You need sleep. If your head is hurting, I'll get you the ibuprofen—"

"You can get these wedding visas. Or something like that. We could get away from this shit for a while. A destination wedding. That's what they call them."

Something had ratcheted Shaw's voice down even more when he said, "Tonight's not the night—"

"It most definitely is." North turned to look over his shoulder; Shaw stood behind the couch, holding himself stiffly, doubtless a mass of aches and bruises after the beating he'd taken. "I want to talk about this. You know what? You were right. I'm freaking the fuck out because the man I love most in the world was almost killed. Twice. One of those times was tonight. And I—I just want to get the fuck out of here. We'll call the cops, we'll call the FBI, and we'll tell them everything. Jadon will make sure nobody sweeps it under the rug. So let's go. Pack a bag. Get your grandmother's wedding dress out of the coffin or wherever you keep it. And let's go."

"I said tonight is not the night." The words were a whiplash. It was a tone North wasn't sure he'd ever heard from Shaw before, but it was strangely familiar. It took his brain a half second to catch up with his sympathetic nervous system, with the sudden launch into fight-or-flight mode. Tucker. He'd heard this tone from Tucker. "What do you not understand about that? I'm exhausted. We're both exhausted. We had the shit beaten out of us, and I was in that van, my head bouncing on that fucking floor, imagining every horrible thing that might have happened to you, and then I wasn't allowed to feel any of it because I had to get us out of there, I had to carry you, and I thought something serious had happened to your brain, and then I wake up and you're gone, you're fucking gone, and when I find you, when I try to get you back to bed, you start up with this shit about—"

He cut off. His ragged breathing ran through the room. North, though, felt a remembered calm. An old friend back for a visit—back to stay, maybe. He closed the browser on his phone. He had gone into a familiar mode. Retreat, withdraw, mitigate, placate. Oil on fucking troubled waters.

"Sorry," he said.

"No, I'm sorry." But Shaw's face was tight and red, his eyebrows drawn together. "You're right. I see what you mean. If you want to get out of town, if you want us to do a destination wedding, I totally support—"

"Let's not talk about it." It was like a spidey sense, this old awareness of thin ice, the microcalculations to avoid, repair, escape. "No, me, I'm sorry. I should have realized you were worried about me. And I shouldn't have pushed—this. Let me put a towel down, and we'll go to bed."

Silence. The house breathing, when neither of them seemed to be. Finally, Shaw said, "I said I'd change the sheets."

"I know." North stood. He squeezed Shaw's hand. "You're tired, though. They worked you over like hell, and you haven't complained once. I don't want you changing the bed. A towel will be fine. And I'm going to put some of that emu oil stuff on you before you fall asleep again, ok? Otherwise you'll be stiff as hell tomorrow."

Shaw wavered. Something lingered in his face, the sooty print after a fire had burned itself out. With Tucker, North thought like a man doing a field study, it took so much longer to reach this point.

"Come on," North said gently. "I ruined your night. Let me make it better."

This time, that was all it took. This time.

Shaw stretched out, and North worked the emu oil into his back and shoulders, arms and legs, everywhere that a touch drew out pleased groans indicating that, yes, these spots hurt too. He fell asleep as North was finishing. North washed his hands and pulled on a pair of jeans, and the old routine was a comfort: sneakers, sockless, slip outside, the September night so humid that it was like velvet on his bare shoulders and chest. In the alley, he smoked half a pack of American Spirits and watched the smoke fuse with the amber light of the sodium lamps. He jolted when his phone buzzed, and he frowned at the unknown number. Past four in the morning. He answered.

A man's voice, too young to have learned to be clinical, all nervy self-importance: "Mr. McKinney? It's your father. He's here at Barnes-Jewish; he's been stabbed."

Chapter 20

IN HINDSIGHT, NORTH should have woken Shaw, but instead he settled for grabbing keys, wallet, and the filthy tee from the bedroom floor. He made the drive in nine minutes; it should have been fourteen.

The garage was blessedly dark and cool, with the smell of motor oil and urine and the squeak of rubber—tires, sneaker soles. The hospital met him with a wall of light that made him squint; it started the drums at the back of his head. Inside the hospital itself, a flood of fluorescent banks, bleach, floor polish, and the whir of machinery out of sight crashed over him. After learning his dad was still in surgery, North paced the waiting room. The man who found him wore a corrections officer's uniform—blue polo, khakis, kiddie badge. He was white, young, jowls and paunch in a way that suggested Mom's good cooking. He kept trying to look serious.

"It's not clear exactly what happened because the attack took place in the showers—"

"What the fuck was he doing alone in the showers?"

"Mr. McKinney—"

"What the fuck is your job if it isn't keeping my dad safe?"

"Your tone—"

"You don't like my tone? Then you're going to fucking hate this."

That was when North took a swing, but his shoulder bitched at him, and the CO stumbled out of reach.

"Hey!" Scared as fuck, but still trying for serious, the jowly kid grabbed at his sidearm. "Hey, you can't—"

The issue of *Good Housekeeping* caught him in the face, the spine striking dead on, and the kid yelped and forgot about the pistol so he could rub his nose.

"What's going on in here?"

The voice came from a nurse, a black guy with frosted tips who had to be pushing forty.

"This man is under arrest—"

"Like shit I am," North said. "Get the fuck out of here, and tell your boss to get ready for an epic fucking lawsuit."

The CO looked to the nurse in appeal, but the other man, stone faced, gave him nothing. After a moment, he turned and left, his steps hitched in what was probably meant to be a swagger. The nurse leaned against the door to let him past, but his gaze never left North's.

When the CO was out of sight, the nurse said, "You know he's going to snitch."

North pinched the bridge of his nose and nodded.

"Your dad made it through surgery. They're moving him to the PACU right now. The doctor's going to want to talk to you, and then you'd better get your butt out of here before that kid's balls drop and he comes back."

"Can I see him?"

"He's not awake yet."

"I said see him."

The nurse sighed. "Wait here for the doctor."

The doctor was a heavyset Asian woman with bird-bright eyes. She kept adjusting her scrubs, her gaze flitting back to North before she gave the top another tug. She was immensely pleased with herself. She wasn't smiling when she told him how bad the stab wounds had been—both of them—but she was glowing. A full-body smile, North thought. He couldn't even say anything because it never touched her lips.

"—lucky they brought him here; not a lot of people make it through something like that."

Translation: say *thank you.*

"Thank you."

After a while, the surgeon left him. Probably sprinting to hack out somebody's liver or cut out a few yards of small intestine, North thought. He couldn't find the nurse who had interrupted his argument with the CO, and none of the other nurses would take him to see his dad. He got the same chorus of responses: he's resting, we'll let you know when he can have visitors, why don't you take a seat. Sitting wasn't an option. He tried, and thirty seconds later, he bounced out of the chair. His heart was going a mile a minute. He paced, and pacing turned into rambling, and the oatmeal-colored hallways and the repeating intersections, the identical doors and the nurses' stations, they became filmstrip loops, spliced and run through the projector again and again, until he felt like he could detect the faint flicker of a bad bulb. Reality unreeling at twenty-four frames per second. Or maybe, he thought, that was just the fluorescents. Or the aftereffects of getting his gourd cracked twice in two days.

He stopped in the emergency department's waiting room. A man was screaming somewhere out of sight. A pair of white girls with lots of tattoos huddled together, their own concerns swallowed up in fear at the sounds the man was making. A Latino guy was hugging a black woman, who kept looking around for the source of the screams. A black man rocked on a motorized scooter, one leg bandaged, the bandages red with blood, head down like he didn't want to look up and see what was going on. North leaned against the wall, listening to the pitch and yaw of the screams. Like the zero-gravity flights he'd read about. His stomach kept dropping out. He wondered if the nurses would tell him what had happened to the man. Professional interest, he could explain. See, I've got this guy, Ronnie.

When the screams stopped, he started wandering again. He ended up in the interfaith chapel. The lights were turned down. His impression of the place was a smell like brass polish, dusty cushions, a whisper of recirculated air. The Holy Spirit, he thought, dropping into a chair. Move in me. He folded his arms along the back of the chair in front of him and let his head rest on his arms. As his eyes adjusted to the gloom, he could make out a children's coloring book that had fallen under the seats. Barn animals. Very interfaith. After a while, the silence took on its own noise, a rushing sound that reminded him of the creek.

On his way out, he stopped at a plastic display case full of pamphlets. A box of bulk-order tissues was conveniently in place in case you needed to dry your eyes with the sanctified equivalent of sandpaper. So much wisdom printed and folded and tucked away. LETTING GO, said one. HOW TO CARRY ON. Another, YOUR PAST, YOUR FUTURE: LEARNING TO HEAL. He thought of Tucker, of Shaw, and the rawness of his throat as he flicked butt after butt across the alley, the embers still burning sometimes like falling stars. If the private dick thing doesn't work out, go into pamphlets, North old boy. Plenty of money in pamphlets. SO YOU'RE FUCKED UP: WHAT'S NEXT?

He made his way back to the waiting room and found the nurse again, who grudgingly agreed to let North look in on his dad. This was all starting to feel the same. His mom dying years ago. His dad dying slowly. The smell of plastic and shit like cling wrap on North's skin. All these cubbyholes for human beings. He barely recognized the man mummified in bandages and tubes and masks. The shape of the head, maybe. The wispy hair. Someone needed to comb his hair. But seeing him helped. Something in North had been stuck. A two-pole switch jammed in the middle. And now this, seeing him, flipped the switch. Lights on. Blazing. He felt like he was seeing clearly for the first time in years.

"Someone needs to comb his hair," he said as the nurse led him to the waiting room.

"We're going to take good care of him."

"If you need a comb, I'll get one."

The look on the nurse's face was practiced, a kind of control. North recognized it from batshit interviews, from listening to Pari's complaints, from dealing with Shaw. On his lunch break, or whatever counted as lunch break on an overnight shift, this guy would be telling the gals about the nut who wouldn't let up about the comb. All he said, though, was "We've got combs."

North nodded and walked out to stand on the sidewalk fronting Kingshighway. Four lanes. A grassy median. Another four lanes. The brocade of lights through Forest Park. On this side, the smell of car exhaust, the whine of sirens, the ankle-deep hot air that floated in off the street and made it feel like summer instead of September. On that side, the prairie grasses, the lakes, the darkness flooding the low-lying ground like water meadows. Then the trees. North patted himself with shaking hands, but he'd lost the smokes. The trees, he thought. The booger woods.

The first call was to Pari. "What's wrong?" she asked, her voice thick with sleep but the words focused. "Are you and Shaw all right?"

He told her.

"Truck and Zion and I will take turns," she said. "Nobody's going to get to your dad in there."

"They won't let you sit around like an armed guard."

"We'll figure something out. I can always have sick aunties."

The next call rang eight times before a man answered, but he sounded perfectly alert. "Mr. McKinney, it's late."

"I'll do it."

Vinnikov's voice had a smile in it. "Excellent. I'll find out where he's hiding, and we can proceed from there."

Chapter 21

SHAW TRIED TO FOCUS on Jesse's house, on the job, as they headed up the walk. It was late morning. It was a beautiful September day: the sky blue and puffy with cumulus clouds, verging on warm but with a breeze. He had on a flannel shirt, blue-gray with a grandad collar, and spandex bike shorts. After being dumped in the middle of nowhere, he'd decided that practical footwear was currently a prerequisite; hence the toe shoes. That morning, it had been easier to think about clothes, about being practical—like the inflatable wedge he now carried under one arm—than about everything else.

The call to the detectives investigating Malorie's death had been bad enough. Shaw had contacted them first thing that morning; Monzyk had shouted Shaw down as soon as he understood who Shaw was, and Contalonis hadn't been much better. They hadn't wanted to hear about the Peach Grove or the Big Muddy. They'd wanted Shaw and North to come in for interviews—although that was partially conjecture on Shaw's part, because most of the time the two detectives just swore themselves blue.

The fight with North, though, had been even worse. Awful. Mostly because it hadn't ever made its way to the surface. Shaw had been panicked to wake and find North gone and not answering his phone. Then Pari had called, suspecting that Shaw hadn't heard about North's dad. Then North had arrived home sometime after sunrise and answered questions in monosyllables or broken fragments and finally terminated the conversation with "I don't feel like talking right now." Then he'd gotten in the shower, and Shaw had gone into the basement, taken an edible, shoved his head into the dryer, muffling himself with the clothes still in the drum, and screamed for a solid five minutes.

When screaming didn't help anymore, Shaw called the rental car agency and reported the car stolen, which actually seemed to make the agent happy—probably because of the exorbitant fee. After the rental car agency, Shaw had gone outside to work on his potion cauldron, which was mostly an excuse to look busy while North got ready—and, more importantly, an excuse to avoid North in their small house.

When they reached Jesse's stoop, North gestured with two fingers, and Shaw broke off. He headed around the back of the house. The sound of North's knocking followed him.

The side of the bungalow had once featured flowerbeds, now overgrown with weeds. A concrete pad with rusting rebar suggested where an air conditioning unit had once sat—stolen, sold, who knew? The windows were old glass, thin, some of them cracked. At the back of the structure, the fascia was pulling away from the roof, and the gutter hung out over empty air. It suggested, to Shaw anyway, a waterslide—one with an abrupt, and perhaps fatal, ending.

The back of the house was even worse. Heaps of black, contractor-style garbage bags lined a chain-link fence. Ancient patio furniture bled rust. The stainless-steel grill looked like it had probably once cost a lot of money, but it was missing a propane tank, and hoses dangled underneath like the beast had been gutted. What Shaw cared about, though, was the back door: the paint cracked and peeling at the base, the half lite curtained with what looked like calico, a knob with its brass finish flaking off.

At the front of the house, North knocked again.

Shaw squatted to examine the locks. The deadbolt wasn't set, which was stupid on Jesse's part, but which made Shaw's life enormously easier. He could have tried his set of common keys, bumped the lock, or—worst case—picked it, but Jesse had cut his work down to a fraction. Shaw waited until North knocked again, the pounding sound going on and on and drowning out lesser noises, and he heard Jesse yell something. Heavy footsteps moved toward the front of the house. When North knocked again, Shaw leaned into the fiberglass. It shifted, and he slid the inflatable wedge between the frame and the door. It took him a few yanks to work the wedge up to where it was near the latch. Then he grabbed the bulb and began to pump.

Sold in hardware stores as a leveling tool, the inflatable wedge had another—and to Shaw's way of seeing—more useful function. Once the wedge reached a certain size, it displaced the door, and the latch popped free. Quieter than bump keys, faster than picking, and perfect for this kind of situation.

"—told you I'm not talking to you," Jesse was saying.

Shaw stepped into the kitchen. The smell of Manwich was stronger than he remembered, ketchupy, vinegary, and it was hard to tell where the Manwich ended and the BO funk began. A pan on the stove held crumbled gray meat that was fuzzed with something white. A blunt that had hardly been smoked had been ground out in a teacup printed with Yorkies, and Shaw decided to liberate the blunt and store it in a pocket of the bike shorts.

When he reached the living room, Jesse had the front door on a chain, and he was holding the same boxy little pistol that Cinnamon had pulled on them last time. Jesse's attention was focused on North. North kept smacking the door.

"Bruh, what the fuck don't you understand? I've got a fucking gun. I will fucking waste you if you don't fucking leave me alone. I will—"

Jesse cut off with a short, high-pitched noise when Shaw hit him in the kidney. A yelp, Shaw decided. He stumbled forward, face smacking the door. North had already reached through the opening; now he caught Jessie's hand and twisted, applying pressure until the pistol fell to the floor.

This time, Jesse screamed, "My finger, oh my God, my finger!"

He was rebounding from the door when Shaw kicked him in the back of the knee. Jesse hit the floor hard, the boards creaking under his weight. Shaw kicked him in the head. This time, the only noise was Jesse's head clipping the boards.

Shaw took the door off the chain, and North stepped inside. He wrinkled his nose. "Did he piss himself?"

"It's hard to tell," Shaw said. "Manwich."

They got Jesse into a wooden chair from the kitchen, and North produced a roll of duct tape, which they used to secure his wrists and ankles. With a noise of disgust, North examined the gun.

"Nine-millimeter," he said. He went out to the car and came back gloved up. Then he broke down the pistol and bagged the parts. "Same caliber used on Malorie."

Jesse moaned.

North moved deeper into the house. A door opened and closed. Jesse made some more unhappy noises; the print from the ball of Shaw's foot was turning red along his temple.

When North came back, he had a wad of bills and a shoebox: weed in baggies, edibles in baggies, a bong shaped like a giant penis, and several pre-rolled joints and blunts. North passed Shaw the box and said, "You did a good job."

As Shaw pocketed everything but the bong, he tried for a smile. "So I get a treat?"

Cocking his head, North was silent for a moment. "I'm sorry about last night. This morning. Shit, all of it, I guess."

"It's ok."

"It's not. I was out of my mind. How are you?"

"The emu oil helped, and I did some yoga while you were in the shower." Shaw touched his temple. "How are you?"

"Headache. A normal one—not like last night; it's fine. Shaw, I am sorry. Talking about running away, fuck, I know we can't do that. And pressuring you—"

"You weren't pressuring me. I want, um, what you said, what we were talking about. I want that too."

Jesse rolled his head to the side and spat. Blood mixed with saliva on the floor.

"You don't have to keep saying stuff like that," North said.

"I mean it. I do."

"Right."

"I really do. But last night was awful, that's all. I wasn't thinking clearly."

Sliding in the seat, Jesse looked like he might fall out of the chair. North hauled him upright by the wife beater and gave him a shake.

"Oh shit," mumbled Jesse.

"Fine," North said, his gaze fixed on the man in the chair now, although the words were clearly meant for Shaw. "Great. I'm so glad we're on the same fucking page."

Shaw opened his mouth.

"Like always," North said.

"What does that mean?"

"My head," Jesse whispered.

"I'm trying to tell you last night was fucked up." North ran a hand through his hair; blond bristles stuck up hedgehog style. "All of it. I shouldn't have— whatever. And when I heard about my dad, I should have woken you up, told you. So can you let me apologize, because apologizing is fucking awful and I want to get it over with?"

"You don't have to apologize," Shaw said. "You don't have anything to apologize for."

North took several deep breaths. "Fine," he said again. "Great."

"I—"

"Fucking fantastic."

"I don't understand what is going on," Shaw said.

"Nothing. Shithead, wake the fuck up!"

Jesse was trying to slide out of the seat again.

"Knock it off," North said.

A garbled phrase, something like "Brain damage," was the only response.

"I'll give you brain damage if you don't sit your ass in that chair right. I'm going to count to five."

By three, Jesse was sitting upright. A tiny trickle of blood leaked from one nostril, and it had crusted along his upper lip. His nose was puffy. A red line across his forehead showed where it had connected with the door. He made another soft noise.

"Here's the deal," North said. "I'm going to ask you some questions, and you're going to answer them."

Jesse shook his head, but he spoke clearly enough. "What? You're going to call your cop buddy if I don't talk? Man, you don't know the kind of shit you're swimming in."

"Not my cop buddy, no. We're not going to involve the cops now. You lied to me, Jesse. You told me you didn't know anything about the Big Muddy. And then I saw you there, saw you selling Cinnamon to that fat fuck Big Joe, and you know what I said when I saw you? The first thing I said was 'Now there's a lying motherfucker who owes me some answers.'"

"Actually, the first thing he said was 'Is that Jesse?' Oh! I think maybe I said that. And North said—"

"Bruh, I didn't—whatever you—I mean, I'm not saying anything." Too late, he added, "So fuck you."

"I think I can convince you," North said.

"You don't scare me." The flat delivery was more convincing than the bluster that Jesse had suddenly abandoned. "You have no idea what you're dealing with. Those guys, the things they do, it's nightmare stuff. You and your boyfriend can beat the shit out of me, but man, you got nothing on them."

"North can be pretty scary," Shaw said. "One time, I walked in on him when he was singing a song about a cookie cat, and he turned really red, and he made this high-pitched noise, and I thought maybe he'd seen a spider, so I asked if he'd seen a spider, and he said, 'Close the goddamn door,' and I said if there was a spider in the room, I probably shouldn't close the door, and he said, 'For the love of Christ, shut the fucking door,' and—"

"I'd just gotten out of the shower, and this dumbass walked in like he owned the place."

"I was curious. I wanted to know about a magic cat that was also a cookie."

"I was buck-ass naked, and they were giving this family of four a tour of the student apartments. June Cleaver was staring at my wang."

"That doesn't sound scary," Jesse said through his sniffles.

"You should have seen Mrs. Cleaver," Shaw said. "White as a ghost and clutching her pearls."

"You guys are so weird. Big Joe, his guys, they don't stand around talking about, I don't know, whatever you're talking about. They're serious. They mean business."

"What kind of business?" North asked.

Jesse ducked his head.

"The kind of business," Shaw said, "where you show up with girls, and they give you cash?"

"No—"

"Don't fucking lie to me," North shouted; Jesse flinched. "We saw that deal go down."

"He pays me to—" But Jesse remembered at the last moment, and his jaw clamped shut.

"Here's what he does: he pays you to bring him girls, and then the girls go away, right? They think they're going off to be singers or movie stars, and because you don't ever see them again, you never think about it again."

"Some of those girls," Shaw yanked Jesse's head back by the hair, "they get sold forty, fifty times a day for sex. How would you like that?"

"That's a great question, Shaw," North said. "I bet Jesse didn't know that Big Joe will pay for boys too. Jesse, how do you feel about spreading those cheeks fifty times a day?"

"I bet that's making you a little jittery," Shaw said, "but it's normal to feel anxious if anal isn't something you're familiar with. Remember the male G-spot. The P-spot. Remember that. Oh, and don't tighten up. I mean, if he wants you to, then yeah, definitely tighten up. But not, you know, at the beginning. Unless he wants that too. Some guys like it to be a struggle."

"Look at that," North said. "He's got the shakes."

"It's the knees. Guys who think they're straight, their knees go all crumbly when they hear about rear entry mechanics."

"Powdery, I'd have said."

"Oh, dusty. No, no, no—chalky."

"Friable."

"North! That's not fair. That's a really good one, and I wanted it."

"You could have used it. I gave you plenty of chances."

"I was working my way up. You always go in hard and fast. Oh, kind of like these guys are going to do to Jesse—"

"Stop it!" Jesse's eyes filled with tears. "He pays me to find him dancers, that's all."

"How'd you meet him?"

"I used to truck. In-state stuff. You can get good shit at the Big Muddy, everybody knows that."

"And that escalated into selling him girls. Nice."

"They go dance for him! A lot of them move out west because they all think they're gonna be movie stars."

"Bullshit. You know what he does to those girls. You do it to them anyway because you're a greedy motherfucker and because you don't care. What happened with Malorie? Did you take her out there, and she changed her mind? Did she figure out something was wrong?"

"I didn't do anything to Malorie."

"Did she know some of the girls who disappeared? Is that why you had to kill her?"

"I didn't touch her. I didn't—"

"Call the Big Muddy," Shaw said. "I'm tired of listening to him."

As North took out his phone, Jesse began to sob. Through his tears, he managed to say, "I didn't—I didn't—I didn't—"

"The fuck you didn't," North said as he pretended to place a call.

"I was with Cinnamon! We were here the whole day. Malorie came, she left, that's all." Another sob racked Jesse. Bloody snot leaked from his nose. His eyes were already red and puffy. "They go out to be dancers. That's all. He pays me to bring him dancers. Oh God, please don't let anything bad happen to them."

"Don't cry. What the fuck do you have to cry about? You're here, jerking off into your sloppy joes or whatever the fuck a piece of shit like you does all day. Why the fuck are you crying? Cinnamon wasn't there, dumbshit. We looked. She was already gone. So whatever they're doing, they're not keeping local girls in the area. They send them off to Chicago or Nashville or KC. Those girls, you sent them off into God knows what, so they're the ones who should be crying." North slapped him. It was open-handed, a cracking blow that sounded like a gunshot in the small room, and it knocked Jesse's head to the side.

The skinny guy's chest heaved, but his sobs had stopped.

"You've got nothing I want," North told him.

"So if you're lucky," Shaw said, "you'll get to spend the next ten to twenty years getting passed around in prison. And if you're not lucky, we're taking a drive out to the Big Muddy."

"Cinnamon—" Jesse said thickly.

North made a disgusted noise. "Cinnamon? Cinnamon can't tell us jack shit because you sold her out. You've got nobody to back up your story, fuckwad, and it's your own fault. Christ, look at you, you disgusting piece of shit. I'll be lucky if I can get Joe to give me five hundred bucks for your white trash ass."

"She's got a van." Jesse squirmed in the seat to look at North. "I've seen her out there. She takes the van out to the Peach Grove, and they load it up. White van. I've seen her putting them in there, girls and guys. I've seen the goddamn van."

Shaw remembered a white van. When he met North's eyes, North gave a tiny nod.

"Who?" Shaw said.

"This towel-head chick. She and her brother have a place. A business. Malorie used to work for her; I think her name's Alex."

Chapter 22

NORTH HID JESSE'S BROKEN-down gun in the GTO's trunk—in case the cops needed it down the road for a ballistics test, although how they'd deal with chain of custody was a problem for another day. Then they drove to H&H Employment Solutions. The white van was still parked behind the office complex. On a Wednesday, around lunch time, the lot only had a smattering of cars. Shaw guessed that even at its busiest, it never got more than half full— this part of the city, and an old office complex like this, they weren't exactly thriving.

"It's a Dodge Ram," North said. "Second generation."

"Good work," Shaw said in what he thought was his most commendatory tone. "Probably a 1947 model."

"No, it's somewhere between '79 and '93. Probably closer to '93."

"Well done; I was testing you. Anything else you want to add?"

"These people are cheap pieces of shit who don't keep their things nice. Look at all the rust."

"Anything else?"

"I've had four hours of sleep, Shaw. Tops. I've had two different people try to crack my skull. I had to spend what felt like an eternity around Emery Hazard. Can we do this another time?"

"All right."

"I'll grab a slim jim."

"It's white. That's what you forgot to notice."

"I didn't forget—nope, I'm not doing this. Not today."

"That's why I'm the practical one. You and your arcane knowledge and your flights of fancy. Good thing I'm here to keep you grounded, deal with the day-to-day stuff."

"You." North rubbed a spot between his eyebrows. "You're the practical one."

"Obviously."

"The grounded one."

Shaw nodded.

"You, the one who spent an ungodly sum on those bullshit supplements from Master Hermes because you were convinced you had contracted an animals-only STD through 'a quantum sexual echo of a past life not bestiality,' as you told that poor veterinarian."

"STI. Disease is a stigmatizing word."

"You had some hair on your shoulders. It happens once you age—fucking ungracefully, I might add—out of twinkdom."

"I don't think—"

"They were dog probiotics. They still had the PetSmart label."

"No, he wouldn't have—"

"Glossier coat in seven days."

"Thank you for noticing. My coat has been extra glossy lately, and—North, wait, do you want help getting the slim jim?"

Shaw sat on a parking stop and watched as North came back with the slim jim held discretely against his leg. He kept scowling at Shaw, big, ugly faces that he obviously intended to be threatening. After the night before and the stilted tension of the morning, it was like someone uncoiling a spring in Shaw's chest.

Five minutes later, he said, "I thought you just put the slim jim in and wiggled it around until it made a noise and then pulled out."

"It's not—"

"Kind of like how you do sex."

North went still. He craned his head, and only his head, to stare at Shaw. "What?"

"Actually, now that I think about it, nothing."

"Do you have complaints?"

"No, obviously. I mean, I'm the one who makes the noise."

"Be quiet now."

Shaw mimed zipping his lips.

North went back to work. Stopped again. Turned. "It's not like every door is exactly the same. Sometimes things are in different places. You have to line things up when you put it in—" His face turned surprisingly red all of a sudden.

Shaw was a more spiritually evolved being, so he managed not to laugh.

"Go away," North said in a deadly voice.

"I'll scout the perimeter."

"Do that. See if you can walk into traffic."

"North!"

North gave him the bird and went back to work.

Shaw did a loop of the parking lot. He found bird droppings in the shape of North's head, and he found a Shasta can, and he found the cellophane wrapper from what he thought had probably been a pack of cigarettes, and he found a pink inflatable pool floatie that had been hacked to ribbons. When he got back, North was looking at something on his phone.

"Go away some more," North said without looking up.

Shaw went around to the other side of the van. He tried the door. Then he tried the rear doors. They were locked.

"This stuff is messed up, right?" North said, his words carrying to Shaw even with the van between them.

"It's pretty bad."

The slim jim made some scraping noises, and North swore softly. Silence. The wind picked up a flattened mac and cheese box, and the cardboard skated over the asphalt on one edge.

"Shaw, I'm trying to figure things out."

"It's ok. If we can't get the door open—"

"No, I mean us. Me, actually. I do not want…repeat, I guess, the way things were with Tucker. The way I was. And it's not you; I know you're not Tucker, and you don't act like him, and you don't treat me like him. But I'm still me, and all the ways I learned to act in a relationship, they're still there, and I—I don't want to do those things. With Tucker, especially at the end, every day was thin ice. I was constantly trying to anticipate, predict, guess. What did he want? What would make him happy? What would bring out the smile, the guy I had liked in college, instead of the one who shouted and broke things and—shit, you know. And with you sometimes, lately, I have no idea what you—" He cut off with a heavy breath. "I'm trying to say, that's one of the reasons I want time alone. That's a big part of what I'm trying to figure out. How to be in a—fuck—in a healthy relationship."

Shaw thought about the nights North wanted the Cardinals, a few beers, and a bag of chips. The nights North wanted to read that poetry collection, Richie Hofmann, and listen to The Cure. The nights he wanted to stretch out in nothing but his boxers, a bowl of popcorn balanced on his chest, and watch anime until his eyes bled. He had thought it was North learning to be North, without his dad or Tucker or the Chouteau bros or the guys on the job site expecting him to be something else. And now, his eyes wet, Shaw realized that was true—but that North had been trying to figure out so much more as well.

"Well, dumbshit?"

"Yeah," Shaw said. "I mean, I'm not exactly an expert on relationships. Maybe sometimes we could try to figure that stuff out together."

North's answer was soft: "Yeah. Ok."

Music blared down the block. Guitars, deep voices, *gritos mexicanos*. Ranchera music. It was so loud that Shaw's ears hurt, and he couldn't even tell where the music was coming from. He poked his head around the van.

North made a face. "I can't hear anything."

At least, that's what Shaw thought he said.

Pointing at the other side of the van, North said, "Keep a lookout."

Maybe. Maybe that's what he said.

Shaw decided it wouldn't hurt to keep a lookout, with the music making it impossible to hear anyone approaching, so he ducked around the van again.

It took him two seconds to process the guy: bodybuilder, gold chains, chest hair. Alex's brother, Farid, was ten feet away; he pulled up short when he saw Shaw. Shaw turned to head around the van for North, but Farid sprinted forward. He caught Shaw by the arms and slammed him into the van. Up close, he smelled like baby oil, garlic, and chickpeas.

"What the fuck are you doing to my van?"

North made an irritated noise from the other side of the vehicle, and Shaw realized that North couldn't see him, had no idea what was going on.

Farid slammed Shaw into the van again. "Well? Huh?"

The impact ignited the aches and bruises that still peppered Shaw's body. Shaw walled away the pain and focused on Farid. The acne scars were more visible up close. A Versace t-shirt today, too small, tight where it cuffed massive biceps. That same aura, like he thought he was bigger than he was; unnecessary, in the current moment, since he was plenty big enough to beat Shaw to death before North realized something was wrong.

"Your nipples," Shaw shouted over the music.

Farid's face blanked with surprise. Then red mottled his olive skin. "What the fuck did you—"

"They're pointy. Are they an erogenous zone for you? Because a lot of guys neglect—"

"What kind of fag shit are you talking about?"

"Oh, it's not faggy. Well, I don't think. I'd ask North, but he can't hear me. Even straight guys like their nipples played with every once in a while. In fact, straight guys could learn a lot from gay guys. Not only the nips and the P-spot stuff, but footwear, facial peels, how to give a useful weather report. I need a meteorologist who will tell me how to do my hair."

Farid looked lost, so he settled for slamming Shaw against the van again.

North's shout definitely sounded irritated this time.

"Cut it out with the soft boi bullshit," Farid said. "You don't fool me."

"That's good," Shaw said, "because honesty is the most important part of a relationship, which is why I feel really bad that I'm not always honest with North about what I want. But I made him a promise, see, and oh my God, you have no idea how good it feels to tell someone—"

This time, when Shaw's head hit the van, the world went a little scrambly for a moment.

He heard himself talking from a distance. "Did you know there's an inverse correlation between masculine aggression and nipple piercing? People have done studies. Well, I've done studies. Well, I just like to pull on nipple rings, I guess, so it's more of a dilettante situation."

"What in the hell—"

Shaw grabbed Farid's nipple and twisted. Shock detonated in the bodybuilder's face, and he released Shaw. Shaw took advantage of the opening

GREGORY ASHE

to bring his knee up. As Farid was falling, Shaw drove his elbow into Farid's head. The bodybuilder's eyes went blank and then rolled halfway closed.

The music cut off.

Shaw's breathing was suddenly loud and ragged.

On the other side of the van, something clicked, and North crowed with triumph. "Look at that! Look at fucking that! I got it, Shaw. I had to look up the door panel diagram for this fucking model, but look at fucking that!"

Shaw made a winded noise that he hoped came close to congratulatory. He squatted, dug through Farid's pockets, and came up with a wallet, a keyring, a phone, and a bottle of pills. He staggered a little when he stood.

"That's why persistence is a virtue, Shaw. You can't give up when things don't work out right away. Like last weekend, what we were trying—"

"To get me off hands free," Shaw said, wiping his face.

"Jesus Christ. I'm just saying, persistence. You don't give up. And that's something you could learn if—"

Shaw used the keys to unlock the passenger door. Across from him, North stood with the driver's door open.

"What the fuck?"

"Farid." Shaw jingled the keys. "He let me borrow these."

The disbelief on North's face was priceless.

"What were you saying about persistence?" Shaw asked.

"Fucking unbelievable," North muttered as he climbed into the van and began to search.

Chapter 23

THEY FOUND NOTHING, so they taped Farid's feet and wrists and left him in the back of the van. He was making lots of unhappy noises; North figured the leg-day-skipping-fuck would be fine.

"I bet if a forensic team ripped that piece of shit apart," North said, "they'd find hairs, fibers, fingerprints."

"But we're not a forensic team."

"I know, fuck nugget. I'm speaking hypothetically."

"What exactly is a fuck nugget? Is it that little bit of come that dries inside—"

"Stop talking."

"You're the one who—"

"No, stop."

Shaw was grinning, and North was grinning too, although he kept trying to glower.

"Farid has a lot of cash," Shaw said, tossing a wallet to North. "And a new phone, and expensive clothes, and these." A bottle of pills followed.

North started with the pills. "Judging by that dipshit's appearance, he's got a thing for gym candy. Illegal. Maybe those detectives could use them to pull a warrant." He looked at the wallet. Lots of cash—almost five hundred dollars. A gym membership card. A driver's license. A Schnucks savers card. An insurance card. A dental insurance card. A picture of himself, naked, with a boner. "Fucking twat. Ok, lots of cash, and he throws wood from looking at himself. It doesn't necessarily mean anything. He and his sister own a business; maybe they're just doing well."

"A temp agency in Bevo? There's no way they're doing this well."

"Fuck," North finally said. "Alex?"

Nodding, Shaw led the way into the building. As they worked their way through the maze of exterior corridors and courtyards and goose shit, he said over his shoulder, "Kirby wasn't driving a van."

"That doesn't mean anything."

"It means Jesse's tip—"

"Jesse told us he saw girls being loaded into Alex's white van out at the Big Muddy."

"But we didn't see Cinnamon in a van."

North tried not to, but he knew that his silence had a bristling quality to it.

"As the practical one," Shaw said into the dead air, "it's my obligation to point out certain unpleasant realities, like—oh sweet Mary, North, my ass!"

The pinch had gone through the bike shorts as though the spandex weren't there.

North tried—with equal lack of success—not to look unbearably satisfied with himself for the rest of the walk.

Inside the H&H Employment Solutions suite, the floppy-haired boy—Pete—was merrily sharpening pencils behind his desk. Maybe that was all the poor kid did all day. The dustiness of pencil shavings mixed with the smell of toner and the distant hum and rattle of a Xerox machine. From a CD player on Floppy's desk, Enya was singing to them out of the '90s.

"Hi," Floppy said with what sounded like gratingly genuine enthusiasm. "How can I—"

"I need to update my resume," Shaw said. "Last time I was here, Alex asked, 'What can she do?' and I told her about the typing pool and, um, get Mr. Stormworth's lunch—"

"Stormwent," North said.

"What?"

"Last time, you told her you'd go to the lunch counter to get Mr. Stormwent's lunch."

Shaw shook his head slowly. "I don't think so. I don't even know anybody named Mr. Stormwent. Honestly, it sounds kind of made up."

"Of course it sounds made up—" North struggled to rein it in, but more burst out: "It's not like Stormworth sounds any better—"

"Ms. Hussein is very busy for the rest of the day," Floppy told them.

"Too bad." North grabbed Shaw's arm and steered him into the maze of cubicles. He held the other hand out. "Stay there, Floppy Pete. We know the way."

"Floppy Pete sounds like a medical condition. Like you'd need a specially engineered stent or prop or splint. A wiener stabilizer."

"Do you remember the book *Part-Time Dog?*"

"I don't think so."

"It's a kids' book."

"Oh. That's why. I was only allowed to read books written by warlocks or about warlocks. Or about their unholy conjoinings with the Beast, I guess, but that was kind of a gray area."

North tried not to close his eyes. He tried to keep walking. Five, four, three—

"It was my own rule," Shaw said.

"Of course it fucking was," North muttered. In a louder voice, he said, "*Part-Time Dog* is about a dog that spends his mornings in one house, his afternoons with another family, on and on like that."

"Kind of like us and the puppy and Truck and Pari."

"What if we tried something like that?"

"Well, we already are, sort of, like I said with—"

"No, with you. What if you spent some of the time, say, three hundred days a year, with Hazard? Your best friend. And the other sixty-five, mostly weekends and holidays, you came back to me."

"That's so sweet of you," Shaw said, "but I think in terms of your sexual needs, it wouldn't work."

North yanked open the door to Alex's office and shoved Shaw inside. "My sexual needs will be fine, thanks."

"I don't know," Shaw said. "Remember last week when you really, really wanted to—well, you kept calling it 'make love,' and you were blushing when you said it, but I was busy embroidering my mandala with the hair from that sacred ox, and you were practically begging—"

"It wasn't sacred. It wasn't even an ox!" North took a breath. "It was a stuffed cow you bought at Grant's Farm, and I definitely wasn't begging—"

"You kept saying, 'Please, baby, please, I will be so good to you.'" Shaw turned to face Alex, who was frozen in the act of spritzing herself with something that smelled like attar of rose. "I have the same atomizer," Shaw told her. Then, "He'd never be able to cope without me. And I'm the practical one, so I have to think ahead about these kinds of things."

"He's not practical," North told Alex.

"That's one of the things Mr. Stormwent values most about me."

North knew he was making a noise; he couldn't seem to stop it. "Sure, all right, he's the practical one. This is the same guy who went to a custom candle store and made me a twenty-hour soy three-wick that smelled like cow shit."

"Blessed Byre!" Shaw said. "I forgot I was going to market that!"

"What are you doing in here?" Alex demanded.

For a moment, North had the same question. The pink silk veils. The crystal cats. The LED bulbs that today were tuned to a low, warm yellow like candlelight so that shadows bloomed in the corners.

"Well," Shaw said, "we wanted to talk to you about your part in human trafficking."

Alex froze. Then she set down the atomizer unsteadily, the glass base clunking against the desk. "I'm calling the police."

"You should probably call a lawyer," North said. "But the police are a good start. We'll tell them about how we ran into your brother while he was trying to clean out the back of that panel van you've got in the back lot. We'll tell them about how he got combative, tried to hurt my partner."

"Don't worry," Shaw told Alex. "I'm very resilient."

"And when things escalated, well." North took out the bottle of steroids and tossed them onto the desk. "That was sitting right out in the open. And I bet the police will be even more interested in the blood and hair we found Farid trying to eliminate from the van. I bet they're going to have a lot of questions, especially once they spray luminol all over that van. I bet it lights up like Shaw's old bedroom under a blacklight."

"You can't!" Under the olive tone to her skin, Alex paled. "That's impossible, we—"

She froze again. Her breathing sounded labored.

"I've got an eyewitness who will put you at the Big Muddy loading girls into that van," North said in a low voice. "So go ahead and call the police."

"What do you want? Money?" She turned stiffly in the chair, reaching for her purse.

"Don't touch that," North said. "Keep your hands where I can see them."

"But to answer the question," Shaw said, "I do want money. There's this new strain of cannabis that's supposed to let you eat ghosts—"

"No," North said, "that's Pac-Man."

Alex's eyes pingponged between them. She looked on the verge of tears. "I don't know what you want. Is it—" Her fingers strayed to the buttons on her blouse. "Sex?"

"Gross," Shaw said. "Sorry, not to be rude, it's not you. That's gross on general principle. Sticking, you know my thing, onto, the, um, other thing."

"Onto," North breathed.

Alex's eyes locked onto North.

More loudly, he said, "Uh, no, that's a pass. What we want is to know why you killed Malorie Walton."

"I didn't."

"All right," North said, pulling out his phone, "Detective Reck—"

"No, no, please." Alex ran her spangled nails across the desk. "Look, I'll tell you, but you can't call them. Please. I didn't—I didn't do anything wrong."

North glanced at Shaw.

"You've got five minutes," Shaw said with a shrug.

For a moment, Alex's hands stopped moving. "It's not sex work. And they're not slaves."

"Not exactly a high bar to clear. Go on."

"Look, I do staffing, right? Employment solutions. Well, there are lots of businesses, manufacturing especially, where—I mean, the profit margin is razor thin, and if they can cut back on wages, that can make a huge difference." Her eyes came up, dark and defiant. "I'm not doing anything wrong, ok?"

"You're just using people for cheap, underpaid labor," North said, "possibly while they're being coerced or trapped in a system that's basically the equivalent of slavery."

"And you're a capitalist pig," Shaw said.

"I'm taking care of my parents." Alex wrung her hands. Some of the silver star decals fell from her nails. "I'm taking care of them. That's my responsibility. They came over here before I was born, and my mom doesn't speak any English, and my dad worked as a janitor at Mehlville, and they've got nothing. So Farid and I, we take care of them, but Farid's worthless—" Heat blazed in her voice and died out again. "—so I've got to do everything. It's not what you said."

"It sure sounds like trafficking," North said. "Do these people have documentation? Do they pay taxes? Are they on any official paperwork? Have you seen where they live, where they come from? Of course you don't; the last time we were here, you were so proud of helping underage, undocumented teenagers get jobs. You practically dislocated your shoulder patting yourself on the back."

"They're not—it's not—they're not doing sex work!"

"Most trafficking isn't sex work," Shaw said. "Start at the beginning, how it all got started."

Alex licked pink lips. "I had a client. They're out of business now, so don't bother asking me who. They needed people to shrink wrap and box shipments. I couldn't get anybody, anybody. Farid said he knew someone; he'd met them, um, at a gentleman's club. He'd gone to school at Mizzou for a couple years; that's why he was in that part of the state."

"A titty bar," North clarified for Shaw.

"Oh. I thought she meant like one of those Oxford dons kind of things."

"He took me out to the Big Muddy. I met Joe. He said there were lots of country people who wanted a job. Farid and I brought them in, they did the work. The next time, we did it again. Like that." Her eyes challenged North. "I paid them myself. Cash. They weren't slaves."

North sneered. "Yeah? And what happened when they got back to Joe? Jesus Christ, woman."

"I didn't do anything wrong! People want jobs. And I—I have to take care of—"

"Save it," North said.

Shaw leaned forward. "Tell us about Malorie."

"What? I don't know anything about Malorie. The day she came by for her pay, the day you said she got killed, I was here that whole day—you can check with Pete or Farid. And I went home to my parents after. I've got alibis!"

"Your alibi is your brother or your parents or an employee? Pretty weak. What was Farid doing all day? Maybe he picked up Malorie in his car and tried to take her out to the Big Muddy, but things didn't go the way he wanted. Maybe she tried to run, and he couldn't let her get away, so he shot her in the back."

"We never did that! We never took girls out there. We run a business, a legitimate business—"

"This is a fucking waste of time," North told Shaw.

Shaw nodded. "Better call your best buddy in the whole world—"

"No, wait! Wait, wait, wait!" Alex tried to steady her hands on the desk, but she was shaking, and her nails chittered against the white veneer. "Ximena."

"What about her?"

"She's—she's a greedy bitch. She is! She's always stealing from that shelter. How do you think she drives that kind of car, wears those clothes, always has whatever she wants? And do you think she has to support her parents? No. She's totally selfish, but she puts on this whole act like she's a saint because she runs a nonprofit, but she's a stealing, lying, greedy bitch. That's what she is."

"How do you know Ximena?"

"It's not that big of a neighborhood." After a moment, Alex mumbled, "She sends those kids here, and I give her a little something. That's why I could cut things off with Joe; I don't work with him anymore because Ximena sends me the kids."

"And?" North asked.

"And it's a shelter, right? And Malorie was staying there? And kids disappear all the time? I mean, nobody would even ask any questions because that's the whole point of a shelter—they're only there for a while. Look, I know she steals from the nonprofit. But if you're looking for someone who might be—" She looked sick. "—selling those kids, or whatever, wouldn't it be her?"

"You say you know she steals," Shaw said. "How do you know?"

Alex rolled her eyes, a trapped animal looking for a way out.

"Answer the fucking question," North advised.

"We've got a thing. Not just the kickbacks for when she sends kids my way. She—she's got contracts with us. She hires temps. Only there aren't any temps. She pays us out of the nonprofit's budget, and then she shows up and collects the pay in cash. Sometimes she's got ten or fifteen temps 'working' in one week. The bitch is robbing that place blind."

"And you're getting some off the top, aren't you?" Shaw asked.

Alex waffled and then pressed forward. "Look, kids show up at that shelter, they disappear, and nobody even blinks. What you said, about someone wanting to take Malorie out there and Malorie putting up a fight? That sounds pretty real to me. Malorie was a fighter. And Ximena could do that. Shoot Malorie, I mean. She acts like she's those kids' mom, but she's cold. She's ice."

North looked at Shaw, and Shaw nodded.

"Get me those contracts," North said. "The ones you and Ximena have been using to embezzle. The originals. And then you might want to go down and see if your brother needs help."

Chapter 24

NIK WAS WAITING FOR them outside St. Rita's. He was wearing a tee that Shaw had given North—tea leaves and the words *One Green Sereni-tea, Please!*—a pair of North's gym shorts, the drawstrings pulled tight to keep them from sagging, and North's relatively new Nikes.

"Is that fucker wearing my thong, too?" North growled.

"No, your thong is in the wash."

"I don't have a fucking thong. I was being sarcastic."

"Really? Then whose thong did I spend all that time scrubbing?"

North directed a glare at his probably-soon-to-be-ex-this-time-for-good boyfriend. Shaw was too busy looking puzzled to notice.

"Nice kicks," North said when they got close enough.

Nik gave him a look of pure scorn and then turned his attention to Shaw. "You guys have been, like, totally AWOL. Did you find something? Is that why you asked me to meet you here?"

It was early afternoon. North's headache had stabilized, probably helped by the fact that Shaw had forced him to stop for a prepackaged, refrigerated sandwich at the Bevo Beverages and Kwik-Mart. North had rounded out the surprisingly not-disgusting ham and Swiss with a full-sized bag of Doritos, Spicy Nacho, and more ibuprofen. He felt almost human again. Had felt. Until Nik.

Shaw sketched out the course of their investigation, with Nik nodding and cooing and touching Shaw's arm.

When Shaw told them about being beaten and dragged out into the country by Joe's men, Nik started pawing at Shaw again. "Take his shirt off," North suggested. "So you can see better."

"At least I care," Nik said. "He got hurt. He shouldn't be out working."

"I got my fucking head caved in," North said—judging by Shaw's shocked expression, perhaps a little too loudly.

"Don't worry about him," Shaw said. "The spirit of that pig he ate is giving him wicked energy."

"You ate two cheesy dogs. What do you think those are made of?"

"Dreams," Shaw said haughtily, lifting his chin.

Nik directed some more very-serious-teen-boy scowling at North while stroking Shaw's arm. Finally he managed to stop scowling long enough to say, "So, you probably need somebody to check things out at this truck stop—what was it called? The Big Muddy? I could do that."

"Knock yourself out," North said.

"I can drive," Nik said, the words directed at Shaw but a defiant glance spared for North.

"Maybe," Shaw said. "Right now, we need to get inside the shelter and take a look around."

Nik rocked back on his heels, considering them again. "What? Why?"

"Because we fucking told you so," North said.

"Fuck you," Nik said. "You're always yelling at me like I'm supposed to be scared, but I'm not scared of you. I—"

"Nik," Shaw said, "we need to check a few things inside the shelter."

"Ximena—"

"Before we talk to Ximena."

Nik rubbed his chin. "Is she going to get into trouble?"

"We don't know."

"Did she—" Nik voice threatened to crack. "Did she do that to Malorie?"

"We don't know that either. If you could show us how to get in, that'll be enough. You could go back to the house—"

"No." Nik knuckled at his eyes for a moment and then nodded. "It's around back."

A couple of days had brought no improvements to the shelter. It still had the same balding hipped roof, the same barred windows, the same institutional green paint flaking away, the same rust trails snaking down the bare concrete of the foundation. Weeds grew knee-high in the backyard. Nik trampled a path through them to one of the basement windows. He squatted and pointed out where the bars were set in the concrete, and North grunted. The concrete was pitted and gouged, and when Nik pulled on the bars, the whole grille came free from the foundation. He set it aside. He used a QT gift card to loid the latch between the sashes of the horizontal slider, and then he used the heel of his hand to hammer one of the sashes sideways. It skidded and stuck, and then, a moment later, the way was open.

"Nice job," Shaw said.

Nik flashed him a huge smile that changed to a glower when he remembered North. Lying on his belly, he scooted backward until he was almost entirely through the window. Then he let go and fell the rest of the way into the relative darkness.

"If that runt makes a face at me one more time," North said.

"Stop it. He's dealing with a lot right now."

"He's trying to take over my life. I'll be lucky if he doesn't poison me or smother me in my sleep."

"You're being dramatic today. It's the spirit of that wicked pig."

"He's wearing my new kicks!"

Shaw apparently didn't have an answer to this because he wormed his way through the window and dropped out of sight. North followed—it was a squeeze, especially for his shoulders.

"That looked tight," Nik said when the Redwings hit the concrete.

"It's a basement slider. It wasn't exactly designed for grown-ass men."

"Yeah, your ass was definitely part of the problem."

"Ok," North said, rounding on the kid. "Let's have a little talk about respect—"

Shushing him, Shaw caught his arm and pulled him away. "Go on, Nik."

The basement was dark, with the smell of mildew and air that is cool year-round. Nik navigated the shadows without any difficulty, leading them to a flight of rickety stairs and up into the shelter's kitchen. A blast of window cleaner, artificial citrus, and mildew hit them. Nik reached for a switch and turned on the lights; ancient ballast whined in the fluorescent panels. North slapped them off again.

"What—" Nik began.

"Be quiet," North whispered.

Nik rolled his eyes. At a normal volume, he said, "Nobody's here."

Something thunked at the other end of the shelter. Nik's eyes widened.

"Yeah, smartass," North whispered, "so keep it the fuck down."

"But—" Whatever Nik saw on North's face stopped him.

Elbowing the kid out of his way, North proceeded toward the sound. Behind him, Shaw was whispering something consoling—probably something about his moon flow. North passed the first communal bathroom. Water dripped steadily, and the heavy, humid air gave the impression of perpetual damp. He passed the lockers, where they had begun their search for Malorie. He passed the second communal bathroom. A door marked STORAGE stood ajar. Someone had forced it, and in doing so, the deadbolt had torn out a chunk of the frame. North guessed the eight-pound sledgehammer leaning against the wall had something to do with it.

Movement came from the other side of the door, and the yellow light of an incandescent bulb. Someone was breathing heavily. It was hard to tell from only breathing, but North thought it was a woman. Something about the sound suggested a woman's voice. He motioned for Shaw and Nik to stop, stood to one side of the door, and said, "Whoever's in there, come out nice and slow."

The breathing caught. When it resumed, it had a hyperventilated quality.

"Don't do anything dumb," North suggested.

The door flew open, and the relative brightness of the incandescent bulb blinded North for a moment. A figure shot past him. He caught an arm—soft, round, woman's, his brain told him—and her momentum dragged him a few steps before he planted himself. Then he yanked, and she stumbled back, lost her balance, and landed on her ass.

"Hi, Ryley," Shaw said. "What are you doing here? Wait, don't tell me. I bet you're looking for those earrings you lost."

Chapter 25

"START TALKING," Ximena said as she let herself in through the front door. "Why did I have to walk out of the esthetician's? It took me three weeks to get that appointment."

Today she was in a black shift dress, ruched at the breasts and hips. Her lips were green, with a purple tinge that must have been a second layer of gloss or lipstick or whatever—North had no idea, but he decided to call the color combination poisonberry. He judged, by how Shaw's eyes went to the handbag, that it was expensive; Shaw's gaze lingered longer on the metallic leather platform sandals with the crystal studded heels. North wondered if they were talking thousands of dollars or tens of thousands of dollars. She could have bought two-dollar flip-flops and gotten her toes broken just as easily.

"Well?" She looked around. "How did you get in here, anyway? Did you break in?"

"Ryley found your earrings," Shaw said—with a note of pride, North noted, as though he had helped. "Well, her earrings. The ones you gave her."

Ryley was wearing leopard-print shorts and a McDonald's McFlurry tee— the combo looked like they were meant either for the gym or for pajamas. The slides on her feet had once been white but were now scuffed and stained. No makeup today. And she hadn't straightened her hair. She was wearing the earrings, though—black circles with yellow smiley faces. She kept her head down and didn't make a noise, which had been the sum of her behavior after being caught.

"She was stealing from the shelter," North said. He pointed to the computer, which had been removed from the registration desk and set next to the front door. A second computer stood alongside it, still in a Dell box—that was what North had heard fall in the storage room. The common area's TV was unplugged, although it seemed that Ryley had been waiting for someone else to arrive to help her move it. "She started with the high-ticket items."

"That's ridiculous." Ximena took a few clipped steps and stopped, brushing back strands of fine, dark hair. "Ryley wouldn't steal."

Ryley contracted tighter, her body forming a ball.

"What were you doing, Ryley?" Ximena demanded. "What's going on?"

"I told you what's going on," North said. "I want you to talk to her. Convince her to talk to us. Otherwise, I'm calling the police."

"Talk to you? About what?"

"About when she took Malorie's money, for one thing."

"I didn't take it," Ryley shouted, raising her head from her knees long enough to fix North with a teary glare. "I didn't take anything. They're lying, Xi, they're lying about me."

"The kids know how to come and go," North said. "That's a fact. This place has more than one way inside—Nik showed us one, and Ryley obviously knew another. That's a fact. Malorie kept her savings here. That's a fact. Those savings disappeared. That's a fact. And somebody killed Malorie. That's a fact. So, what I'm trying to do is fill in the blank spaces between all those facts, and this shit, Ryley raiding this place like it's her personal piggy bank, well, that fills in a lot of blank spaces."

"I didn't take Malorie's money. I didn't take anything!" Inspiration must have struck because Ryley's head came up again, and she said, "I was rearranging things."

North snorted.

Ryley started to cry.

"Let's give Ximena and Ryley some time to talk," Shaw said, "and we'll see what the police—"

"No," Ximena said, shaking the French bob into place. Her narrow face was tight with anger. "I'm not doing any of that. I believe Ryley."

"You do?" Shaw asked.

"Fine." North drew out his phone. "I'll call the police myself—"

"No," Ximena said. "You won't. If you do, I'll tell them I allowed Ryley to stay. I asked her to rearrange."

Some of the mixture of frustration and confusion must have bled into North's face because Nik looked at him, laughed abruptly, and said, "Oh my God, he looks so stupid."

Shaw shushed him.

"Lady," North said, "that whole filling-in-the-blanks things I told you about? You're next on my list. Either you start cooperating—"

"She's a child," Ximena said. "She made a mistake. I'm not going to let you turn her life inside out because you like bullying women and children."

"Let's all take a breath," Shaw said.

"You want to see bullying?" North extracted the sheaf of contracts that Alex had given him. "Here we fucking go. Latrina Eyman." He slapped a page onto the registration desk. "Rossie Ketelsen. Al Wojcik. Leo Hager. Manny Zeitner. Brent Caines. You want me to keep going?"

Ximena adjusted the expensive-looking bag on her shoulder. She smiled. The veneers made North think of bone under those poisonberry lips.

"How stupid are you?" she asked.

"It varies," Shaw said.

"Moderately," North said.

"Do you have any idea how much trouble you're in? Do you have any idea what kind of grief I can cause for you? You admitted, in front of two witnesses, that you broke into this shelter. You're harassing this girl. You're harassing me. You're threatening me." She splayed matching poisonberry nails against the bag, as though fighting the urge to clutch it. Or, perhaps, the animal part of North thought, showing her claws. "I read about the two of you, about the woman who shot her husband, about the boy who died on those train tracks. People die around you, and you walk away from it all. But people aren't going to believe those stories forever. People are going to start asking questions eventually. So either you leave right now, and you never come back, and you never bother me or my kids again—"

"Xi," Nik said, "they're trying to help with Malorie."

"—or I call the police, and you get taken in for breaking and entering, burglary, assault, and anything else my lawyer can dream up."

"I call bullshit," North said. "I've got a stack of faked contracts right here. I know you're embezzling. I know about the deals you worked out with Alex. And I think it goes a lot deeper than that. I think you like nice things. I think you think you deserve them. And embezzling from a shelter, that's not going to make you much money. Neither is getting a kickback when you send underage kids to work for Alex and her brother. No, you want the big score. You know what I think happens?"

"I don't have to listen to this." Ximena turned and headed for the door. "I'm calling the police."

Shaw slid into her path.

"I think you started selling kids to Big Joe. They're already runaways, aren't they? They're already missing. So who's going to notice?"

"Get out of my way," Ximena snapped. She pulled the bag up her arm.

"How much does he give you for each one?"

"Move," Ximena shouted.

"Did Malorie put up a fight? She knew too much. Is that why you had to plug her in the back when she ran?"

With a scream, Ximena launched herself at Shaw. She rained down slaps, which Shaw tried to ward off with his arms, and then she grabbed his hair. She didn't get a good grip, which probably saved Shaw's scalp, but it distracted him long enough for her to barrel into him and knock him off his feet. She stepped over him and wobbled toward the door, trying to run on the crystal heels.

When North caught the strap of her bag, she spun, and she had a pistol in one hand.

He reacted without thinking: he yanked on the strap in his hand, jerking her off balance. The hand with the gun flew up as she tried to steady herself.

The pistol was aimed at the ceiling when she depressed the trigger. Plaster rained down. The boom of the shot in the tiny space was deafening. Nik was shouting something. Someone was screaming. North still held the strap of her bag, which he released now and transferred his hand to her shoulder. He shoved, and she stumbled into the door. Her head cracked against the wood, and her eyes went wide, the gun pointed out to the side now. North grabbed her hand and twisted until she screamed, and then he twisted more until she released the pistol. He took it and stepped back.

His ears were ringing. Specks of plaster were still drifting down. North realized he was sucking air like he'd sprinted a mile, and black spots swam in his vision.

"Drop the bag! Drop the fucking bag!"

She let it fall.

"Get on the fucking couch."

Her narrow face was so white she looked like she might puke or pass out, but she tottered over to the couch and sat, knees together, a proper lady. She was cradling the hand that had held the gun. Part of North's brain ran backward, trying to remember if he'd felt bones break.

Without taking his eyes from her, he said, "Shaw?"

"All right." A moment later, Shaw was standing next to him, fixing his hair in its bun again. "That's why I shaved my head the first time, remember?"

"Yeah, well, don't fucking try that stunt again."

"I have a nice skull shape. Everybody says so."

"I'm serious. Don't even fucking think it."

Shaw touched the small of North's back, and all of a sudden North was aware of the tension in his body, every muscle locked tight with the need to fight. He took a slower, deeper breath, his body relaxing by degrees. The urge to laugh—huge, lunatic guffaws—rolled over him, and he fought it. His second urge was to pull Shaw to him, check every inch of him, touch that coppery spot of hair. It was harder to fight that one, and he only succeeded because the flat of Shaw's hand was pressed against him, and that connection was enough.

He forced his voice as close to normal as possible when he said, "And you don't have a nice skull or whatever the fuck you said. You've got all sorts of weird bumps and ridges on your skull. You could be a phrenologist's life work."

"I want to go," Ximena said, still holding one hand with the other, like she was cupping a dead bird. "Just let me go and this can be over. I don't understand what's going on, and I want to leave."

"A phlebotomist is a sadist who specializes in needles," Shaw explained to her. "Although I'll admit that I'm a little bit lost too. Sometimes North's references are hard to follow."

"Phrenologist, dumbass. Not phlebotomist. And you want to talk about obscure references? Who asked for a Hermes Trismegistus birthday cake and then added, 'The flavor, not the decorations'? What the fuck does that mean?"

"Where's Nik?" Shaw asked. "And Ryley?"

"Fuck," North muttered. "Check if they're still here. And don't think I didn't notice that you changed the subject because even you don't know what a Hermes Trismegistus-flavored cake would taste like."

"Quicksilver," Shaw said with a shrug as he jogged off. "And papyrus."

"Please," Ximena whispered.

"Stop talking. And drop the act. You pulled a gun on me; playing wounded dove isn't going to work."

Shaw came back for the tail end of that. "Is wounded dove that thing we did where I asked you to tie my arms behind my back so my shoulder blades—"

"Shaw, baby, you are fucking killing my vibe."

"Oh. Sorry."

"Nik?"

"They're gone; the back door is open. I think I saw Ryley take off, and I guess Nik went after her, but everything went kind of upside-downy when I fell."

"When this bitch tried to rip your hair out and trample you."

"Don't say bitch."

"Start talking," North said, still holding the gun on Ximena. "All of it. How long you've been dealing with Joe, how long you've been trafficking kids, all the way back to the beginning."

Her thin face was still set in injured innocence. "I don't know what you're talking about. I don't know who Joe is or what any of the rest of that means."

"Shaw, call the cops."

"Yes, call them. They'll see an injured woman being threatened by two men who broke into a shelter for runaway teens."

"The gun has your prints on it."

"I have a concealed carry permit. I found you robbing the place, and you disarmed me."

"Why'd I call the police, then?"

"You knew I'd report the break-in, and you decided to try to control the story."

"For fuck's sake," North said, "nobody's going to believe that."

But then he thought of Monzyk and Contalonis, the two homicide detectives licking their chops at any excuse to jam up North and Shaw for a few days. At the least, it would be payback for leaving the scene and avoiding their calls.

"So, go on, please," Ximena said, an avid cast to her features as she leaned forward. "Call them."

"Is that a Hermes bag?" Shaw asked. He picked it up by the bottom, inspecting it and, in the process, spilling the contents: an alligator-skin wallet, a tube of lipstick, a compact mirror, a pearlescent silver bottle. The bottle

GREGORY ASHE

shattered when it hit the linoleum, and a fruity, floral perfume splashed across the floor. The fragrance was cloying in the closed room.

"You idiot," Ximena snapped, half rising before she remembered the gun. "That was La Mer!"

"Oops," Shaw said. "But you didn't answer my question: is this a Hermes bag?"

"Put it down! That's mine, that's my personal property!"

"Huh. North, do you know anything about handbags?"

"Oh sure. In a past life, I was a natural-born witch whose only power was divining if high-end handbags were authentic or not."

Ximena stared at him.

Shaw stared at him.

North ran a hand through his hair and said, "I'm the one with the gun, if you'd all kindly remember that fact?"

"God," Shaw whispered, "I love you so much."

North rolled his eyes, but he didn't miss the fact that Ximena's gaze was locked on the bag. Shaw carried it over to the registration desk and began opening drawers.

"What are you doing?" Ximena asked. "Stop that. Stop whatever you're doing."

"North, I'm going to ask you because you're a natural-born witch—" Shaw began.

"Was. Past life."

"Right. Well, do you know anything about the construction of these bags?"

"Give me that." Ximena waved a hand, as though perhaps they had simply overlooked her. "That's mine."

"What's interesting is that—" Shaw cocked a hip up onto the desk, opened a drawer, and rummaged around. He came up with a pair of scissors. "—the quality of workmanship varies widely between brands. You might pay five thousand dollars, ten thousand dollars, and get a bag that's got the same shoddy stitching as something you'd get off the clearance at Kmart."

"Is Kmart even still open?" North asked.

"You can't do this," Ximena said, "you can't do this."

"The one by our house is closed." Shaw set the scissors inside the bag and then began snipping. To Ximena, he said, "That's the one where North got a handy when he was sixteen from an old man."

"He wasn't old. For fuck's sake, you make it sound so creepy."

"You said old."

"I said older. He was eighteen. He was hot. He had a tattoo of a dragon on his arm, and he had these amazing emo bangs."

"No, you're ruining it—" But Ximena stopped shouting to stare at him.

Shaw stopped snipping to stare at him.

176

"Again," North said, "I'm the one with the fucking gun."

"Anyway," Shaw said, reaching inside the bag. He yanked, fabric tore, and he pulled out a handful of lining. "That stuff ripped like tissue paper. Maybe it is tissue paper!"

"Stop, stop, stop, stop, stop!" Ximena's eyes went from the gun to the bag to the gun to the bag.

"I'm going to deconstruct this whole thing and then use the scraps to make a hat. No, a brassiere. No, a hat. No, cock sock." Shaw sighed. "No, it's definitely going to be a hat. The muse has spoken."

"That's mine, that's my property, that's my personal property—"

"And then I'm going to take those Miu Miu sandals and make, hmm, earrings out of them. Oh! And a cock ring."

"No," Ximena wailed.

"That's about where I'm at too," North said, wagging the gun. "So do us both a favor and start talking."

"I didn't do anything. I swear to God! What you said, about Malorie, I didn't do anything. I was at the shelter, and then I went home, and I didn't come back until right before we opened again. I watched her walk out of here that morning, and that's the last time I ever saw her."

"Convenient," North said. "And I guess nobody can prove you're telling the truth?"

Ximena made a snuffling noise and looked at the bag again. After a moment, she shook her head. "The other part—the stuff with Alex—that's true. But it's just money. Big companies give a lot of money; right now, everybody wants to look inclusive, so they support 'diverse causes,' and then they forget about us. It's not hurting anybody."

"Yeah, the black mold, the bed bugs, the cheap food you feed them— that's not hurting anybody. Shaw, take her heels."

When Shaw rose from the desk, Ximena shrieked and tried to pull her feet up under her. "No, no, no! I'm telling you what you want to know. I'm telling you everything. I never met anybody named Big Joe. I don't even know what the Big Muddy is. I don't do anything to these kids except give them a place to sleep and send them to Alex for work. I like nice things, that's all. That's not a crime."

"Embezzlement, tax fraud, contributing to the delinquency of a minor. Those are crimes."

"Like that eighteen-year-old who made love to North with his hand, and in the process gave North his first sexual experience at the admittedly somewhat late age of sixteen, and in the admittedly less than ideal setting of the Kmart stockroom by the baler, probably while they were hiding under the Martha Stewart nightgown collection."

North counted to five. "Are you done?"

"Made for high-powered women by a high-powered woman."

GREGORY ASHE

He counted to five again. "Now?"

"When you say he had good bangs, was that part of the fantasy, or—"

"Look," North said, rounding on Ximena, "you're not giving us shit, so I think we're going with plan B. Shaw, those earrings you were talking about making, how dangly are they?"

"Pretty dangly. But the part I'm really excited about is the cock ring I'm going to make out of those heels. Imagine a guillotine crossed with a noose. But for your penis."

"Jesus Christ," North muttered.

"And it's bedazzled."

"Of course it is. Well, that nightmare isn't going to manifest itself. You'd better take her heels."

Ximena was trying to climb higher onto the couch. "It was Freddie!"

Shaw stopped his approach. North gestured with the pistol.

"She—she did something with Malorie. Freddie. Dr. Eggenberg, I mean. She did something to Malorie. She's the one you should talk to."

"Easy to say," Shaw said with a shrug. "Do those straps have a buckle, or do they—"

"I've got a picture." The drip-drip from the communal bathroom measured the seconds. When neither Shaw nor North spoke, Ximena continued, "I was going through the lockers. Sometimes—sometimes the kids have something valuable. And they're just going to pawn it to get drugs, so I…" She trailed off and shrugged. "Besides, they know the risks when they leave stuff here."

"You're a real piece of shit," North said. "Congratulations."

"Tell us about the picture," Shaw said.

"It was in Malorie's locker."

"You found it when you took the money."

Ximena shook her head. "That wasn't me. I swear to God. I found the picture a couple of weeks ago. I thought—well, you'll see." She made to rise and then sank back. "Can I get up?"

"Slowly," North said.

"Not too slowly," Shaw said. In a tone he obviously considered explanatory, he added, "Gravity."

They followed Ximena back to a small office. The door hung slightly ajar, and she studied it for a moment before shaking her head and whispering, "Ryley."

North said, "Now you're going to tell us, 'It was right here, I swear,' but it's conveniently gone."

With a shrug, Ximena proceeded into the office. A nice, modern desktop computer. A particleboard desk. The smell of paper and a musty, closed-up space. She opened the desk's center drawer, pushed things around, and pulled out a four-by-six. After a final look, she passed it to North, saying, "It doesn't

178

have—I mean, there's nothing obvious, but it's medical, and Malorie only ever goes to her clinic. It has to be her, right? I thought maybe I could use it to get...something out of her."

It wasn't clear which her Ximena meant, but North thought it was safe to assume both Dr. Freddie Eggenberg and Malorie. The picture showed what looked like a mock-up of a doctor's office—everything boiled down and concentrated: cabinets, a plasticky fern, an anatomical chart, and an exam chair. The exam chair dominated the scene. Whether it was genuinely an antique or had simply been designed to look like one, North couldn't tell, but the scuffed stainless steel and the white enamel gave it a surgical feel, as well as like something out of a horror film. Malorie sat in the chair.

She was naked, and she had been posed in the stirrups so that her dilated sex and the swell of her pregnant belly were the focus of the shot. Her hands were behind the headrest of the exam chair—the suggestion, at least, was that she was restrained. Her head was raised, as though she were struggling to sit up, perhaps to get free. Eyes wide. Mouth a pink O. Screaming, maybe. Begging, maybe. Whatever the viewer wanted.

"Fuck me," North breathed.

"I think," Shaw said quietly, "we need to talk to Freddie."

Chapter 26

THERE WAS NO SIGN of Nik when they left the shelter, and without any idea of where he might have gone—or where Ryley might have led him—they were forced to leave without him. Home first, to get the guns they kept in safes bolted to the floor under the bed. Shaw's was a Springfield XD9. North's was a CZ 75B. They sat on the bed, thumbing cartridges into the magazines, while the puppy climbed on North, occasionally yipping at Shaw in case Shaw forgot that his presence was, at best, tolerated.

"It was porn," North said.

"She was wearing makeup," Shaw said. "The lighting was more than fluorescent panels. The setting of that photo could have been a stage; it definitely wasn't at the clinic."

North grunted. They finished loading the magazines, and then North took the puppy outside to store the guns in the car safe they kept in the GTO. When he came back in, the puppy cradled in one arm and licking his neck like a maniac, North said, "It might have been porn."

Shaw nodded. He understood; his first impression of the picture had been porn. But there had been something else, something genuine, that suggested— what? He wasn't sure he wanted to follow that thread. Instead, he asked, "Ximena's gun?"

"Disassembled. I hid both of them in the garage, hers and Jesse's. It's another nine-millimeter, in case you're wondering. We're getting quite a collection."

They drove past Freddie's work, and Shaw took pictures of the building, her car (the registration was available on the county government's website), and of a patient entering the clinic. They found her home address in a white-page lookup, and they drove there next. It was a Sunset Hills mini-mansion, with a wrought-iron fence, white stucco, and huge, tinted windows. More pictures. Shaw even hopped the fence and took pictures around back. Then they went to their office.

Shaw had let North pick the location, after his home had burned down, and North had chosen an aging strip mall in Benton Park. The Pestalozzi Street

Shopping Plaza (ALDI COMING SOON!!!) was situated on a quiet road, and they had a landlord who only contacted them when the rent was due and ignored any requests for maintenance. There were some downsides: the office was possibly haunted by a french-fry ghost in pursuit of justice, the ceiling fan was definitely possessed, the shag carpeting was mustard colored, and the walls alternated between concrete blocks painted a dandruff color and ancient faux-wood paneling. The only good part about the whole place was the manifestation in the hallway (which North insisted was a water stain) of Our Lady of the Pestalozzi Street Shopping Plaza (ALDI COMING SOON!!!).

Pari was filing her nails and checking on the countertop oven she had added to her desk, where she was apparently baking banana bread. The smell complemented the psychic resonance of the murdered french fries.

North got a GPS tracker from their supply closet. The tracker had a magnetic, waterproof case that allowed it to be attached to a vehicle and continue transmitting, regardless of weather. Shaw started up his MacBook and opened a TOR browser. He turned on his VPN, and then he created a new email account. He took a picture of the photograph Ximena had given them, and then he uploaded it to his computer and attached it to his email. He attached the other pictures they had taken, entered an email address he had found for Freddie on the clinic's website, and composed a simple message: *Someone has been very naughty. Let's talk at your special spot. Otherwise, I'll send the really interesting pictures to the police.* He scheduled the email to send in an hour and shut down the laptop.

"Yeah?" North said.

Shaw nodded.

They drove back to Freddie's clinic. Shaw kept lookout while North crawled under the doctor's maroon Volvo station wagon. An Asian woman passed on the sidewalk, jogging with a stroller in a sweatsuit that seemed too heavy for the warm September day. She didn't glance over, and Shaw didn't have to resort to his explanation that his butch boyfriend was fiddling around with his undercarriage.

"Done," North said as he crawled out from under the Volvo.

As they jogged back to the GTO, Shaw said, "What is an undercarriage?"

North snorted. "What?"

"I wanted you to fiddle around with my undercarriage. Is it just the underneath part? I mean, is that literally what it is?"

"Keep wearing shorts that disappear up your ass crack, and you're going to find out. Maybe I'll show you tonight."

Shaw rolled his eyes.

"Are you directing traffic with that thing?" North asked.

Shaw gave him the finger and did some readjusting, but the tiny spandex shorts weren't exactly accommodating.

They drove two blocks over and parked in the lot of a 7-Eleven, and North watched the tracker on an app on his phone. They sat with the windows down, the air smelling like asphalt and the GTO's Morrokide and American Crew hair gel, which didn't help with the spandex-shorts situation. A few cars buzzed up and down the street, but this section of the city was poor, without major commercial or business interests to draw in outsiders; the traffic was minimal. The most interesting thing was an ancient Volkswagen that looked kind of like someone had turned a tuna can into a hearse. It puttered along at about fifteen miles an hour. The kid driving it was probably sitting on a stack of phonebooks, and he couldn't have looked more pleased with himself.

Twenty minutes later, Shaw said, "The email should have gone through by now."

Twenty-three minutes after that, North had to pee, and he trotted inside. He came back with a cherry Slurpee for himself and a vanilla Coke for Shaw.

Seven minutes after that, the tracker started to move. North got the guns from the safe, and they followed.

"The bitch is flying," North said.

"Don't say bitch."

North squeezed him so hard through the spandex that Shaw yelped. Bonerization was instantaneous.

"Dummy," Shaw shouted, massaging himself—perhaps a bit too enthusiastically, he realized in hindsight, considering the light in North's eyes. "What if I'd spilled my Coke?"

"On my seats? In my car? I would have taken it out of your ass."

They drove a parallel course, following side roads in the same general direction as the tracker. Freddie—if it was Freddie driving, which Shaw knew was the most likely possibility but not the only one—was heading south, out of the city and into the county. Eventually, their options for alternate routes became limited, and North cut over to the road the tracker was following, although he stayed a couple of miles back and out of sight.

Houses began to mix with empty fields. Then they dropped down onto a flood plain. Ahead of them ran a line of tall trees—oaks, willows, and cottonwoods skirted by clumps of honeysuckle and milkweed. Sun glinting on muddy brown water explained the vegetation.

"Is that the Meramec?" Shaw asked.

"According to the GPS." North made a face. "This countryside-nature bullshit can fucking sit on it. Why the fuck can't these assholes keep their shit inside the city limits?"

"That was a profound question."

More squeezing. More yelping. Instant bonerization, but, thank God, no spilled Coke.

The road curved to follow the river, but the tracker had stopped. Shaw pointed, and North swore and pumped the brakes, easing the GTO onto the shoulder. A gravel drive, overgrown and almost invisible, turned off ahead of them. They got out of the car, checked their guns, followed the gravel down toward the river.

The building was one of those inexplicable phenomena that happened in rural areas. There seemed to be no logical reason for its placement here, on the banks of the river, where flooding must have been a regular risk. It had no clear signage from the main road, and Shaw could think of no reason why someone might have decided that this was the ideal location to operate a business. But it was clearly a business—at least, part of it was.

The structure was cinderblock with bubbling gray paint. The cloudy domes of skylights peeked up from the flat roof. It was obviously divided in half and intended to serve two separate businesses: the front of the building was symmetrical, with matching rolling doors of corrugated steel, matching fire doors, and matching glass-block accents. A molded plastic sign on the right said Kroyer Auto Body, but the sign was dusty and speckled with bird droppings. On the left, there was no indication who occupied it. The Volvo was nowhere to be seen.

"The drive-in door," North said, nodding at the roll-up.

"Duh."

"What did you say to me?"

Shaw grinned, but the expression dropped away almost immediately. The Springfield felt heavy in his hand; he hadn't carried in a while, except for regular practice at the range, and the weight made him feel off balance. If North felt anything similar, he didn't show it—the CZ looked like an extension of him, the same loose-limbed assurance extending beyond his fingertips and into the steel. They headed toward the left-hand fire door. The gravel crunched underfoot, the warm dustiness of the stone mingling with the smell of the river. For a moment, the memory of night, the creek, the darkness weighed down on Shaw. He took another breath and flexed his fingers around the pebbled polymer grip. Someone had shot Malorie Walton in the back. The smell of the river threatened to choke him. Someone had shot her in the back. Someone she had trusted enough to get in their car.

"North."

The Redwings crunched to a halt.

Shaw shook his head. "Not the front door."

After a moment, North dried his hands on his jeans and nodded.

They cut back up the hill, fighting a path through the brush until they could skid and slide down a rocky slope to the rear of the building. Matching steel doors opened onto a narrow concrete apron, where trash suggested how the space had been used: a few ancient cigarette butts; a broken crate; a pink and black can, the aluminum twisted, from an energy drink (cotton candy flavor). In that moment, it seemed like the taste equivalent of an aneurysm.

North picked the lock on the closest door in thirty seconds, but when he reached for the handle, Shaw stopped him. North glanced up. No questions—or rather, just the one that he didn't need to put into words. Shaw waited.

Next door, in the half of the building that belonged to Kroyer Auto Body, a pounding noise began. It was the sound of something heavy hitting something metallic, and it went on and on—almost frantic at first, and then taking on a steady, rapid rhythm. It ended as abruptly as it began.

North exhaled.

Shaw shook his head.

When the pounding began again, with that same frenetic energy, Shaw whispered, "Now."

North tested the handle. It turned slightly. Shaw felt the silent three-count, like their bodies shared a metronome. He knew it, the moment North's would pull. Then it all happened fast.

North depressed the handle and yanked. The steel door flew open, and North sprinted inside. Shaw followed. Neither of them had real training for this, but they both knew how it worked: every guy had a corner, take care of your corner. Something high-pitched, the sonic equivalent of a contrail, was making its way through Shaw's brain.

It was a hallway. No corners for Shaw to cover. Nothing but high-traffic carpet worn through to the backing in places. Holes in the drywall. Keep moving, his brain said. Keep running.

"Hands up," North was shouting, voice sharp with adrenaline, "hands up, put your fucking hands up!"

Dr. Freddie Eggenberg stood at the other end of the hall, and she turned at the sound of North's voice. She was wearing a blue windbreaker with an ominous bulge, tan slacks, and black flats. Her mouth was guppying like crazy as she held her hands in the air. Then one hand dipped, the gesture so faint that another Shaw, a younger Shaw, wouldn't have been sure it had been a movement at all.

"I wouldn't do that," North said, voice still stripped down with the rush of it all. He gestured with the gun again. After a moment, Freddie straightened both arms again and let out a breath, nodding slowly. Together, North and Shaw moved down the hall until they were only a pair of yards away from Freddie. Then North said, "Shaw."

Shaw found the pistol in the windbreaker pocket and stuck it in his waistband. Then he searched her more thoroughly, ignoring the way she shifted in distaste, but found nothing except her car keys. No pepper spray on the ring. No pocket knife. Maybe she had a cyanide capsule in a fake tooth like those movies North made him watch sometimes, the ones with all the busty ladies who did the pommel-horse tricks.

He moved back to North's side. This pistol was a Glock, and when he checked the chamber, he saw the shiny brass of a nine-millimeter cartridge. He displayed it for North, who swore under his breath, and then released the slide. The sound of the metal snapping home seemed too loud for the narrow hallway.

Freddie watched all of this, her face unreadable. A flush stained her fair cheeks and made her freckles more noticeable. She cleared her throat. "May I lower my hands?"

"Slowly," North said.

She did. Then she watched them.

"This might be a good time," North said, the pistol level, "to do some fucking explaining."

"All right," she said. "Go ahead."

"Bitch—"

"Don't say bitch," Shaw whispered.

"—you've got no idea how much trouble you're in."

"Am I?" Freddie's eyes were cool, ice blue, almost the exact same shade as North's. "What I see is assault with a deadly weapon, breaking and entering, trespassing, blackmail or extortion—I'm not sure which one actually applies."

"Blackmail," Shaw said.

"What are you doing?" North asked.

"She's struggling." To Freddie, Shaw said, "Extortion is an umbrella term. Blackmail is a specific crime covered that falls unto that larger category. It's a felony." Back to North, Shaw said, "There. Do you see how happy that made her?"

"Happy? She's looking at us like she wants that gun back so she can kill both of us and then top herself just to be done with this conversation."

"She's ecstatic," Shaw said. "She's grinning ear to ear. She made this dumb mistake, doing whatever that weird porny thing is with the picture, and then an even bigger, dumber mistake by trying to traffic Malorie and ending up killing her, and then she got stupid and followed the instructions in that email by coming straight here."

"Hey," Freddie said. "I didn't—"

"She's not grinning, Shaw. Do you know what a grin is? Do you understand basic human facial expressions? I don't even know why I'm asking because I know you don't. That's why you jumped on that guy at the gym. And she wasn't following the instructions in that email. She's stupid, but she's not so stupid that she'd do what a blackmailer told her. She came here because she assumed we already knew about this place, and she set a trap to kill us."

"Hey, I didn't do any—"

"I thought that guy at the gym was having a heart attack! I was trying to save his life!"

"Gas, Shaw. The guy had bad gas, and you're lucky you didn't break a rib giving him CPR or whatever you thought you were doing."

Shaw stabbed a finger in North's direction and barked scornfully: "Ha! Ha!"

"Hey, I don't know what you're talking about," Freddie shouted.

"Ha! You're wrong," Shaw said.

"Get that out of my face," North said, slapping Shaw's hand away.

"He didn't have bad gas; he had the shits. He was trying not to shit himself. Which is way more serious. And he was doing squats, so his face was already weird."

"Ok, well, that's a difference of degree not—"

"Pay attention to me!" Freddie's scream echoed in the narrow corridor.

"Yikes," Shaw said.

North nodded. "Uh huh."

"Can you imagine dating someone like that? Always so desperate for attention. Always yammering on and on. Always having to get the last word in."

"I can't even fucking imagine," North said in an underbreath.

"I'm leaving," Freddie said. She pranced a few steps toward the front of the building and froze again when North gestured with the CZ. "You can't— you can't keep me here! I'm a doctor. I help people, I—"

"You traffic kids. You killed Malorie Walton. You—"

"I didn't do that!" Freddie wiped her cheeks, which were dry but blotchier than ever. "I don't do that. What you're saying, I don't do that."

"Sure," Shaw said. "The med-porn fetish, the pregnancy kink, those are hobbies."

The rhythmic thumping from the auto body shop picked up again.

Freddie's lips were making those little guppy movements again.

"Tell you what," North said. "Let's call it a draw. We'll get the police down here, and we'll let them charge us, and we'll let them charge you, and they'll tear this place apart. Then we'll see what happens when the dust settles."

"No!" Freddie wiped her cheeks again. The movement continued down her body, her hands running over the windbreaker in what Shaw thought was an unfriendly display of how much she missed the Glock. When she reached the bottom of the jacket, though, she made a distressed noise and said, "Fine. Fine. Just—no police, all right?"

"No promises," North said, "on account of you lying in wait to kill us."

"I think she's thinking about killing us right now," Shaw said.

"Oh, she definitely wants to kill us right now," North said. "Good thing I told you to get her gun."

"You didn't tell me! That was pure initiative. My initiative. You were feeling macho because of how you came through the door, and your balls were probably churning out a million times the toxic level of testosterone, and all you did was kind of move your head like this and say, 'Shaw,' like you were my sexy lieutenant and after lights out you were going to come into the barracks and discipline my ass for messing up the training exercise—oh, wait, you also said, 'I wouldn't do that,' which is exactly what the lieutenant would say when he caught the private touching himself in the group showers, and—"

"Never mind," North said. "Give her the gun back; a bullet to the head would actually be fine if it got me the fuck out of this mess."

Freddie's eyes brightened, and she stared at Shaw.

"He's not being serious," Shaw said. "This is a treat. He loves this kind of thing."

"Masochist through and through. Start talking, Dr. Egg."

Freddie's lips quivered again. Then she gestured behind them and said, "It'll be easier to show you."

With a savage noise, North gestured for her to move.

Freddie went through the door first; although the hallway-facing side of the door looked like a standard interior model, as soon as she opened it, North saw that it had been padded heavily on the opposite side. As he followed her through the doorway, he saw why: the walls were soundproofed. He was standing in a homemade soundstage. It wasn't perfect—he could still hear the muffled pounding from the auto body shop—but he imagined that when the guys next door weren't pounding the hell out of an old Ford panel, the stage worked pretty well.

The majority of the space had been given over to a three-walled set: the doctor's office featured in the picture Ximena had given them, with its laminate cabinets, anatomical chart, and elevated exam chair. The stainless steel and enamel glowed under the overhead lights that Freddie had turned on. The stirrups were elevated and extended.

"We saw the picture," North said.

Freddie nodded.

"Let me guess," North said. "You had extra stirrups lying around the house, and you figured why not."

Freddie's laugh was surprisingly sharp and amused. "Actually, something along those lines. It probably won't surprise you that I had a vanilla childhood; a white suburban girl who went on to be a white suburban med student. When I started volunteering, I realized that depravity runs deeper in most people than I had realized—deeper than most of us are willing to admit. I kept volunteering. And then I started the clinic. I kept seeing the same girl, the same story, with a different face each time. I kept getting emergency calls to motels where girls had been used so many times and so hard that they wouldn't stop bleeding." She turned out the windbreaker's pockets, picking lint from the corners. "I called the police the first time, and the next day, a man came to my office. He told me—" Her face looked cheesy green under the overhead lights. "He told me what would happen to me if I ever called the police again. 'The same thing,' he said, 'only we won't call nobody, and we'll give freebies to anyone that wants to keep going.'" Her fingers trembled as she scraped lint from the fabric. "So," she said with a shaky laugh, "I kept answering the calls, but I didn't go to the police again."

"That sounds awful," Shaw said quietly.

"Let me guess," North said. "One of these guys was Big Joe. He'd bring girls into the city, and when a john got too rough, he'd call you to patch the girl up."

Freddie nodded.

"It doesn't sound like an explanation, though," North said. "It sounds like a sob story."

"Do you know how much it costs to operate a clinic like mine? Not talking about support staff or even my salary. Let's say the facilities. Hell, let's say just the rent. That building costs me almost four thousand dollars a month. Do you think I'm getting four thousand dollars a month from the girls who come in because their boyfriends knocked their faces in, or because they tried Plan B and they're not sure it worked, or because they've got an infection and they've been trying to treat it with hydrogen peroxide or toothpaste or whatever their mother or sister or girlfriend told them would make it go away? I got tired of it. And I got tired of being poor. People I'd gone to school with, people who I did better than in every class, on every exam, those people own lake houses and boats and go to Paris for their anniversaries. It wasn't fair. I was helping people."

"Yeah, I bet that was a big shock when the get-rich-quick scheme of a free clinic didn't pan out."

"You were facing a difficult reality," Shaw said. "You'd given a lot of your life trying to make the world a better place. It's natural to feel frustrated, to feel exhausted, to want something better. That's human."

"That's fucking selfish. Get a different job. Go be a fucking corporate rat in one of those doctor-in-a-box operations. I'm tired of the sob story; tell me about Malorie."

Freddie shoved the pockets back inside the jacket and yanked on the hem, straightening it. "People don't want to give their hard-earned money to help take care of the poor. They don't want to give to charity. They don't want to pay taxes. But they're all willing to pay for something—whatever their secret little fantasy is. Whatever they can't get on their own, they're willing to pay for that."

"Kink," Shaw said. "Fetish."

"Pregnant girls. Underage pregnant girls. Underage pregnant girls in a medical setting."

North spat. "Underage pregnant girls in a medical setting, chained up, being hurt."

"I never hurt any of those girls! And they weren't locked up; that was for show. I—" Renewed pounding from next door, extra loud in spite of all the soundproofing, made Freddie jump, and then she wiped her face and said,

"Good God, really? Now?" She blew out a breath. "Those girls got paid—and paid well—for anything they did. I didn't pimp them out. I didn't hurt them. I didn't make them do anything they weren't comfortable with. It was safe, it was consensual, and in other parts of the country, it would have been perfectly legal."

"Except that they were underage. Except that they trusted you as their physician. Except that they didn't have anyone besides you to make sure they were safe and that no one was taking advantage of them."

"North," Shaw said, squeezing his arm.

"No, this is bullshit. She can talk circles about how hard life is, how unfair it is that she's driving a Volvo instead of a Mercedes, about how she was doing this to help these girls—"

"I was helping them! Where do you think Malorie got that money? She was going to start a new life. She was going to move and take care of the baby, and I made that possible for her."

"You coerced those girls into making porn. You used them. And when you were tired of them, or when they weren't making enough money, you sold them off. Is that what happened? Malorie didn't want to go, and so you had to shoot her to keep her from telling everyone else?"

"I didn't hurt Malorie! I didn't hurt anyone!"

"You were waiting for us to walk through that door so you could empty that fucking Glock into us!"

"I've been threatened." She turned on Shaw, hands up. "The men who run these businesses, they're dangerous. They don't like competition. That man came into my clinic and told me what he'd do to me, and I thought they'd figured it out, I thought they knew what I was doing. I was protecting myself."

"Freddie," Shaw said, "if you're hiding something—"

"Of course she's hiding something. She killed that girl and stuffed her down a storm drain."

"I didn't hurt Malorie! I was at the clinic that day. I never left. You can check with Deb—she'll tell you."

"Why the fuck—"

North cut off when Shaw squeezed his arm again. Drawing out his phone, Shaw said, "Let's see about that."

He placed the call, and it rang several times before a woman answered, "Bevo Community Health."

Shaw nodded at Freddie.

"Deb, this is Dr. Eggenberg."

"Oh, thank God. Dr. Eggenberg, how's your brother? Was the accident serious—"

"Deb, I need you to look at my agenda from—"

"Last Wednesday," Shaw whispered. "September 11."

Freddie repeated the date.

"Well," Deb said, "I suppose I can see. All right. Here it is. Your first appointment was at eleven. You saw—"

"Did I have any openings in my day? Did I leave for any reason?"

"You had a full day—every appointment slot was booked."

"Lunch?"

"You don't take a lunch." Deb's voice took on a worried note. "Dr. Eggenberg, are you sure you're all right?"

"When was my last appointment, please?"

"Well, it says seven, but I think you stayed late. You do, sometimes. I know you don't like me to know, but I do."

Shaw disconnected the call; he didn't look at North, but he knew what the other man was thinking. If Deb was telling the truth—and if Freddie hadn't slipped out some other way—then Freddie Eggenberg had a solid alibi for the day Malorie was killed.

"We'll be in touch," North said, and he jerked his head at Shaw, and they left.

Chapter 27

THEY ADDED THE DOCTOR'S nine-millimeter to the disassembled collection in the garage. After that, though, things got worse.

Monzyk and Contalonis didn't want to hear any of it.

"Sure," Monzyk said over the phone, pausing for great, chomping bites. He probably wanted to sound casual, like he was really enjoying the meal, but what came across was the savage mechanics of mastication. North imagined yellowing incisors tearing into rubbery gray curds of ground beef. "Come in and we'll take a statement."

Contalonis yelled into the receiver, "Or we'll come to you. Service with a smile."

"Yeah, fuckwad, we'll come to you. Where the fuck are you so we can finish the conversation we started a couple of days ago?"

North disconnected. He tried the FBI. He tried the St. Louis office. He tried the KC office. He tried the publicly available numbers. He tried a number he'd cadged off a special agent he'd fingered in a gay bar—to Shaw's disappointment, not literally. The voices varied—some female, some male, some gruff, some quaintly friendly, as though the FBI were operating a country diner, and would you like a slice of pie with your bullshit? At first, the answers stayed the same: noncommittal responses and then a transfer, a lengthy wait on hold, Beethoven thundering in his ears. Then the voices became progressively more homogenous: white, male, clipped. Instead of answers, he got questions.

After what might have been the fourteenth time of explaining the situation to a bodiless voice, North got the Friday night special: don't call us, we'll call you. He screamed in frustration, which caused the puppy to leap down from his lap and begin barking wildly at Shaw.

Shaw gathered the puppy into his arms, stroking his furry head, which only caused the puppy to bark more ferociously. Then there was a yelp. It took North a moment to process the fact that Shaw had made the sound. He was shaking out his finger as he set the puppy down.

"Your child bit me!"

"Bad puppy."

The puppy slunk over to the sofa, whining, head down until it almost touched his paws.

"Jesus," North muttered, leaning over to scoop him up. He gave the puppy a few pets and mumbled something reassuring—mostly "There, that's better," although he wasn't paying much attention. In his head, he was replaying the conversations, the dead-ends, the frustration looping back on itself in a feedback system that was getting him righteously pissed.

Someone cleared his throat.

North looked up.

Shaw was standing there, holding out a finger.

"What?" North said.

"Your child bit me, and I'm over here bleeding to death, and who's getting all the attention and love and comfort?"

"You're not bleeding to death."

"I might have rabies."

"No, you've both had your rabies shots."

"His teeth could have transmitted flesh-eating bacteria."

"Shaw, for the love of fuck, I am having a day here, ok?"

"You're having a day? I'm the one who almost had his finger amputated by that—that mutt. That cur. That mongrel. And then he gets rewarded for his bad behavior! You're reinforcing him. You're training him to be an attack dog."

It was like shifting gears, easing into well-worn second. North wasn't oblivious. He was self-aware—enough, anyway—to know what Shaw was doing. But that didn't mean it didn't work. It had worked well in college, after North had bombed a calc exam. It had worked when he'd gotten turned down for a loan to start up Borealis. And, the fuck of all fuckery, it was working now.

Setting the puppy on the floor, North stood. He grabbed Shaw's arm and hustled him into the kitchen. "Stay."

"That doesn't work on me. It doesn't work on either of us."

Over his shoulder, North shouted, "It fucking better."

He retrieved the first aid kit from the bathroom. When he came back, Shaw was still in the kitchen chair, which meant Shaw was taking it easy on him. North set the kit on the table, opened it, and began sorting through the contents. He set out antiseptic wipes, Betadine, and, after a moment's consideration, a Goofy bandage. Shaw made a distressed noise.

"Too bad," North said. "You get to pick when you're not driving me up a fucking wall. Attack dog? You want to talk about attack dogs? Where's your attack dog who's been biting my head off all week?"

"Nik isn't my attack dog. He's protective. And he feels a lot of loyalty to me. Probably some hero worship. I'm an excellent example of the well-adjusted gay male."

"Well adjusted."

"I don't see why that's funny."

"It might have something to do with the therapist bills—jumping shitstacks, Shaw!"

Shaw held up the blond hairs he had ripped from North's arm and, with a smile, let them fall. "Oops."

"What the fuck has gotten into you?"

Shaw was grinning and trying not to. North was on the verge of slipping himself, so he focused on the task at hand. He balled up the wipes he had used. He smoothed Betadine over the tiny—at this point, almost invisible—puncture wounds. When he picked up the Goofy bandage, Shaw made that same troubled noise again. North rolled his eyes, but he returned the bandage to the kit and chose Toodles instead. Shaw gave an oh-so-fucking-magnanimous nod, and North applied the bandage.

"I know you're frustrated," Shaw said quietly, smoothing North's hair across his forehead. "But we've made a lot of progress. This is a roadblock, not the end of the road."

North grunted and began packing up the kit again.

"So, what are we going to do?" Shaw asked.

"How the fuck should I know?"

"Because you figured it out while your brain was turned off. Like you did when you figured out you had filled in the wrong row of bubbles on that calc exam and you weren't, to borrow your words, the complete fucking idiot you thought you were."

North rolled his eyes.

"Well?"

"We know they're moving girls through the Big Muddy. We know some of them are coming into the city for labor. We know girls in the city are being taken to the truck stop. But we don't know what happens to those girls when they're taken. We didn't see Cinnamon at the Peach Grove, and those guys got an itch in their fannies when we started poking around."

"So we're going to poke around their fannies and see if we can scratch that itch."

"A lot of private investigators work alone. They do fine."

"I was using your language, North. Obviously I meant go to the truck stop and not, you know, lady parts."

"Some of them are successful," North said as he finished packing up the first aid kit. "Some of them are probably even happy."

Chapter 28

BY THE TIME THEY made the drive, it was late evening. The darkness bloomed against the rented Ford's windows (rented under North's name, after what happened to the last one), a blue haze deepening to violet. The truck stop was a cube of frigid halide light that belied the flashing red letters of the sign—THE BIG MUDDY – CHEAP GAS – HOT SHOWERS – CLEAN ROOMS – DINA'S GRUB—and the country charm of the log veneer. North parked the Ford on one side of the lot. Rows of tractor-trailers suggested men who planned to spend the night at the Big Muddy, either in their truck or in one of the rooms. Perhaps at the Peach Grove. But some families, hard pressed or frugal or both, had obviously adopted the same plan. A few stalls down from North and Shaw, a harried-looking young man was trying to wrangle two boys under five, which mostly consisted of shouted suggestions about how much fun it would be to sleep in the back of the minivan.

"I should have a vasectomy," North said. "You should have a vasectomy too. Just in case."

Shaw felt his face heat, but he went for the joke and immediately fumbled it. "I thought you wanted me to, uh, um…"

"Fuck a baby into me?" North's smirk glowed in the darkness.

"Is it hot in here?"

"No. Is that what you were talking about? When I said I wanted you to unload inside me? Fill me up with your babies?"

"I think this shirt might be a nylon blend." Shaw plucked at it, craning his head, anything to avoid looking at North. "My pits are getting swampy."

North chuckled, a dark sound. And then, while Shaw was still trying to find the shirt's label, a hand closed over him, and he heard himself, heard the desperation. North chuckled again and left his hand there.

A case of life-threatening blue balls aside, nothing happened as the hours dragged past. North suggested they sleep in shifts, and Shaw wanted to ask how long they'd try this—a day? A week? A month? And they didn't have any idea when Big Joe might try to move girls again.

"I don't know," North said, speaking into the silence to answer the questions before Shaw could finish forming them. "But I don't know what else to do."

Shaw found his hand in the night shadows and squeezed it.

"Get some sleep," North said.

He tried, but the Big Muddy was busy around the clock. Part of the problem was the lights; the interior of the Ford lay in a shadowy half-darkness, but the intensity of the halides persisted at the edge of Shaw's vision. It was like having the light on in another room and not being able to get up and turn it off. The noise, though, was the bigger issue. Small things: a can of Skoal rolling on its side, the plastic rattling against the cement. Big things: the wind in the prairie grass, the whistle of air brakes. A sardine-can Toyota on balding tires pulled into the stall immediately next to them, blasting thrasher metal at the approximate volume of a jet taking off. The driver was a white girl with a skin-colored eyepatch, and the smell of her vape—caramelized sugar, and a dry woodiness that made Shaw think of tobacco—filtered into the Ford.

He must have dozed, though, because then North's hand was on his shoulder, rousing him.

"Wha—"

"Something's going down. Kirby loaded some girls into a van, and—shit, here we go."

North started the Ford and eased out of the parking stall. He hung back, letting the van leave the lot first, and then he accelerated. Shaw's mind was still rebooting, the mental equivalent of an old color-block test pattern, but his gut told him something was wrong. His gut told him this was too convenient, too easy, their first night even trying to catch—

Blue police lights whirled to life ahead of them, followed by sirens a moment later, and a patrol car swerved to block the access road ahead of them. North swore; in the rearview mirror, another set of lights flared to life. And then a third.

"Fuck, fuck, fuck," North shouted. "Fuck!"

"It was a trap," Shaw said. "They saw us—they must have seen us—and they set a trap."

One of the cruisers had parked behind them, boxing them in, and a portly officer was climbing out of the vehicle.

"Hands on the dash," North said as he buzzed down their windows.

Shaw fumbled with his phone.

"Shaw, put your hands on the fucking dash. Do not give them an excuse."

"I know, I know, I—there." Shaw set his phone on the dash and then splayed his hands across the molded plastic.

North opened his mouth, but a high-pitched, singsong voice cut him off. "Look at those hands. Nice job, boys. Very nice job. Keep those hands right where I can see them, how about that?" Movement in Shaw's peripheral vision, and North tensed. Then the Ford died, and the keys jingled as the cop extracted them.

"Officer, my name is Shaw Aldrich, and the man driving this car is North McKinney—"

"Son, when I want you to speak—"

"—and this encounter is currently being broadcast live to my friends—"

"Mother fu—"

"—who are listening to me as I tell them that North and I will not resist arrest and are in good health—"

A hand reached into Shaw's field of vision, grabbed the phone, and tapped the glass until the stream stopped. That cop, the one on Shaw's side of the car, was breathing hard when he finished. On the other side of the car, the one with the high-pitched voice was swearing under his breath. He finally snapped, "Watch them," and moved back toward his cruiser.

The wind seemed louder in the grass now. The only other sound was the cop by Shaw's window, still breathing hard. Adrenaline from an encounter with men who might be armed and dangerous? Fear because this was his first stop, and he didn't want to fuck it up? Shaw had no way of knowing, but an animal part of him thought he recognized the emotion under that near-hyperventilation: excitement. Dark, violent excitement.

Through the rolled-down windows, the high-pitched man's voice carried in bursts.

"—can't do that now...I understand, but...Facebook bullshit—"

Steps slapped the asphalt. The beam from a flashlight spun across them, dazzling Shaw.

"All right, boys," the singsong voice told them from behind the light. "We'll do it this way. Get out of the car nice and slow. You're under arrest."

Chapter 29

"I WANT MY lawyer," North said. It was the seventh time; he was keeping track. "I want to call my lawyer."

The cop who was walking him down the hall stared straight ahead. He was the portly one, the one who had done all the talking in his high-pitched voice. His name tag said Aldo. A white guy, he had the requisite soup strainer and a high-and-tight that was mostly gray. His buddy looked Latino, and he was wearing a uniform but no name tag. He'd been the one to turn off Shaw's stream. He'd already knocked Shaw around a few times, steering him into walls, into door jambs. North was playing a game in his head where he knocked out the guy's teeth, one by one, with the muzzle of his CZ.

They had been cuffed. They had been searched. They had been relieved of their personal possessions.

But, North's brain said. But I've still got my belt. I've still got my boots and my laces. They take those away for a reason. Nobody wants an accident.

They had been driven in the back of Aldo's cruiser to the station, a single-story gray building with harsh floodlights perched high on the walls, illuminating flowerbeds weed-choked with cigarette butts and cellophane strips and styrofoam particles. Inside was worse. The fluorescents were on their way out, flickering and humming. The community safety posters were faded —WE ARE TOTALLY INVOLVED, said one, featuring a black man and an Asian woman standing in front of a suburban home, expressions warning you not to try anything funny. But the smell was what got North: grape-scented disinfectant, urine, and reheated food.

The cell was a double: a stainless-steel toilet and sink combination; wall-mounted stainless-steel bunks; a rack-and-pinion barred door with chipped paint the color of old milk. Aldo shoved North when he passed through the door, and North stumbled before catching himself, his knee fetching up against the bunk. By the time he'd turned around, Aldo's buddy had forced Shaw through the door. He must have tacked on something nasty at the end, something that made Shaw wince, but North hadn't seen what it was.

"What the fuck are you going to charge us with?" North shouted, approaching the cell door as Aldo rolled it shut. "Driving on a public fucking road? How long do you think it's going to take for a judge to laugh you out of court? And then I'm coming for your fucking badge, you fucking overgrown twat."

"Jesus," Aldo said, and it took North a moment to realize that Aldo wasn't swearing—he was bastardizing his buddy's name. "What do you think we're looking at here?"

Jesus flicked his chin.

"I think," Aldo puffed up his chest, "we're looking at breaking and entering to start. Burglary, that's for damn sure. We heard all about your performance at the Peach Grove. Add to that anything else the county prosecutor might cogitate upon. He's a mean old dog, so you never know."

"I want my lawyer!"

"Sure, son. Sure. We'll get you that phone call the next day. You take a night to cool off. Let this place work on you a while."

"You're in so much fucking shit, you won't know where to start digging yourself out when I'm through with you."

Aldo smiled. "We had a guy in here once. A real holy-roller type. Liked to read us our sins straight out of the Good Book, figuring, I guess, the way the Lord said it ought to be good enough for us. I was on duty that night, and that man hurt himself something terrible. Didn't have much of a face left when morning came, the damage he done to himself. Real religious. Calling, 'Jesus, Jesus, Jesus.' All night." His grin widened. "Jesus, Jesus, Jesus."

Jesus was smiling too now, a huge, empty expression that didn't touch his hollow eyes.

North opened his mouth; he shut it again when Shaw touched his arm.

With a peacock strut, Aldo moved off away from the cell. Jesus lingered a moment, the smile melting away until his face was empty of everything except eagerness. Then he left too, and they were alone.

"Shit," North said, kicking the bars. They rang out under the steel toe of the Redwings. "Shit, goddamn, fuck."

"It's ok."

"It's not ok, Shaw. We're going to get the fucking hillbilly midnight special if we don't get out of here." He began taking off the Redwings.

"What are you doing?"

When the Redwings were off, North began working the laces free from the eyelets.

"North?"

"Making a garrote so I can murder these fuckers if they try anything. I'll give you my belt; use the buckle, and try to get them in the face."

"North."

"Or the balls, I guess. They're going to be expecting the face, so when they put their arms up, get them in the balls with the buckle. After that, remember, eyes, nose, ears. Don't hold back."

Hands settled on his shoulders. Shaw's fingers tightened, released, slid along the ridge of bone to rub away tension. He kissed the side of North's head. "North, take a breath. We're going to be ok."

"We're going to be ok if we keep our heads on a swivel and don't let those fuckers catch us. That door looks ancient; maybe we can—"

The slow massage continued as Shaw spoke over him. "What if that's what they want? What if their plan is to come in here and start roughing us up because they want you to try something? They left you your boots and belt for a reason, North. We'll be dead, and our prints will be all over improvised weapons. What if they want us to try to escape? What if they're waiting for us to make a move?"

North's hands slowed. He finished tugging the laces free. He hesitated, and then he began tying them together. "I'm not letting anything happen to you."

"Oh Lord."

"Yeah, you can complain about toxic masculinity all you want tomorrow. Right now, we need to make it through tonight. The whole department can't be in on this shit, so I'm guessing it's Aldo and Jesus, maybe a third guy tops. This place is deserted; that's the only reason they can get away with this bullshit. Tomorrow, someone else will have to come in, and we'll get the fuck out of here."

The wall-mounted bunk clanged softly as Shaw settled onto it. His fingers hooked North's belt loop and tugged, and North sat down heavily. The bunk boomed under his weight. Shaw looped an arm around North's chest and pressed him down, and all of a sudden, North found himself lying on the bunk, his head in Shaw's lap, closing his eyes against the new angle of light from the corridor.

"You haven't slept in days," Shaw said, carding his hair. "Not really, anyway. And you're carrying around so much, taking care of your dad, taking care of me."

"For the most part, you take pretty good care of yourself."

Shaw hummed and sifted North's hair some more.

"I said for the most part."

Shaw laughed under his breath.

"When you did all those whippets and were so buzzed that you asked Davy Kaste to waltz with you, that's an example of you not knowing how to take care of yourself."

"It would have been fine except he kept trying to lead."

"Of course he kept trying to lead; he had about a hundred pounds of muscle on you, plus he was president of the Young Republican Douche Canoes and the I'm Saving My Ball Juice for Jesus clubs."

"He had a perky butt."

North tried not to say something; it came out under his breath.

"What was that?" Shaw said.

"Nothing."

"You think his butt was mediocre?"

"Shaw, best case scenario tonight, Jesus comes in here to toss our salads. Can we not do this right now?"

"You don't have to be jealous. I like your butt too. Davy had, you know, that whole bubble thing going on. That's all."

"Jesus fucking Christ."

Laughing, Shaw pulled him back down. He stroked North's hair again and said, "Get some rest; I'll keep watch."

"Help me take my belt off."

"I appreciate the sentiment, and if Jesus doesn't perform his services, I'd be happy to make your ass into a chef's salad—"

"Toss our salads, for fuck's sake."

"—but do you really think now is the right time?"

"For a weapon, fucko."

"I don't want—" But when North started to sit up, Shaw said, "Fine, fine, fine." As he helped North remove the belt, he said, "Holy Buddha, do you realize how particular you are about things? You could learn a thing or two from me about being easygoing. Go with the flow. Accept what the universe brings you."

North was going to bring up the episode of Shaw ordering and rejecting fourteen different versions of what he kept calling "Good Witch garters," but it felt so good to lie there, Shaw's hand in his hair, and then he had slipped into deep waters.

He woke when Jesus brought them food: cardboard trays, plastic forks, straggly cannelloni that had been microwaved until steam had burst through the plastic in places. The red sauce—North couldn't bring himself to call it tomato sauce—looked slightly plasticized.

"Don't eat it," he told Shaw. "In case they put something in it."

"That's the least of my worries." Making a face, Shaw stowed the trays on the empty bunk and returned to pull North's head into his lap again. He was humming something. Britney. "Stronger." North closed his eyes and leaned against him to feel the notes reverberating in Shaw's chest. The shadows of the bars spread and branched. He walked the border of the booger woods and woke and slept in fits, distantly aware of Shaw rubbing his chest in smooth, slow circles.

The next time North woke, it was to the sound of steps. Heavy steps. Two sets. No, three. He sat up and slid his feet into the laceless Redwings. Shaw's hand was steady between his shoulder blades. No clock, but it had to be sometime in the small hours of the morning. Sleep and lingering exhaustion made North feel mildly drunk.

"—I said I got it," Aldo whined. "But I don't know why you're mad at me. It's not my fault; I didn't tell them."

"Stop talking," said an unfamiliar voice; North guessed it wasn't Jesus.

Aldo was first, the cock-of-the-walk strut absent now as he scurried to the cell door. Jesus was second. Shane Kirby was third. The self-described sniper still looked like an ordinary guy; tonight, he wore Doc Martens, jeans, and a green plaid shirt. His eyes, though, were what held North's attention. He examined them with a thousand-yard stare—through them, beyond them. North didn't know if Kirby truly had been Special Forces or a sniper, but he knew right then that Kirby was a killer.

"What's going on?" North asked.

"Good news," Aldo said, keys jingling as he sorted through them. "Your lucky number came up, and you're getting a transfer."

"Like fuck."

"Sonny," Aldo inserted the key and looked up, his smile strained and buckling at the edges, "you don't have much say in the matter."

"Face the wall," Kirby said. "Hands behind your back."

"Who the fuck are you?" North said. "You're not police. You're nobody. We're not going anywhere with you."

Kirby didn't answer, but something hooked one corner of his mouth—a snarl that hadn't fully materialized.

North spat, and the spittle caught Kirby in the face: across the nose, one eye, the upper lip.

"You're somebody's dog," North said. "Get the fuck along, little doggie."

Aldo's shoulders curved, and he tried to make himself smaller as he stared into the middle distance, obviously unwilling to look directly at Kirby. "Uh, Mr. Kirby, sir, Jesus and I will take care of that right now. We'll get them ready to go, and we'll make sure they know good and well they can't—"

Kirby wiped his face and studied the spittle on his hand. Then he wiped his fingers on his jeans. They were Wranglers, North guessed. Walmart. His heart was pounding in his chest, adrenaline wiring him, a live voltage that slowed the world down. North could still see the little bubbles of sputum that Kirby had missed on the side of his nose.

"We'll get them right now, Mr. Kirby, you'll see—"

When Aldo racked the door back, North leaped. The punch caught Aldo right on the jaw, and Aldo turned to rubber. Even through the haze of battle hormones, it was funny—the way he staggered, wobbled, legs turning under him. North hit him again, a hard shove that sent Aldo back into Jesus. Aldo's head hit Jesus in the mouth, and the crack sounded like broken teeth. Jesus let out a wordless cry, blood running down his chin as he shoved Aldo to the side. The little peacock went down in a heap.

North grabbed the door and rolled it shut, but before it could close and the automatic lock could set itself, something yanked the door in the opposite direction. Kirby heaved, and he was surprisingly strong for a guy who looked like a shmuck off the street.

"Shaw," North gritted out.

Before he could say more, Jesus was there, reaching between the bars to club at North's head. North dodged the first blow and then he sacrificed his grip and released the door with one hand. He caught Jesus's arm and twisted, using the leverage provided by the bars to force the limb up and back until he heard it snap. Jesus screamed. North put on a little body English, thinking of Aldo saying, "Jesus, Jesus, Jesus," and Jesus kept screaming.

But even while he was still screaming, the Latino man turned in toward the cell door, his free hand coming up, and North saw the can of pepper spray a moment too late. He bellowed as his whole face caught fire: skin, eyes, nose, mouth. His reaction was instinctive, to get away, to put out the fire. He released the door and stumbled back, rucking up his shirt to wipe his face.

Kirby grunted, and the door squealed open on its rack, and North realized his mistake.

Then the door's squealing stopped, and Kirby swore.

"Get that off of there," he said.

Jesus was still screaming about his arm. North was trying to breathe, but snot and swelling in his throat was making it frighteningly difficult.

"No," Shaw said.

"If you make me cut it off, it's going to be worse for you."

Shaw didn't respond. After a moment, though, he called out, "North, two steps back."

North stepped back twice. His butt collided with something solid that gave a shivery metallic noise. He turned, groped blindly at the sink until the water was running, and began washing his face.

"All right," Kirby said. "We can do it this way."

North blew his nose and dried his face with a clean section of his shirt. He blinked. The world was wavy, and his face still burned, but he could make out the dark shape of someone crouched by the bars. Two someones. Kirby and Shaw.

From down the hall—in the main area of the station, North guessed—came a man's voice: "Hello?"

Another man's voice rang out a moment later: "Who's a guy gotta plow to get some service around here?"

A wild laugh escaped Shaw, and then North recognized the voices. Monzyk and Contalonis. Fucking Monzyk and Contalonis.

The shadow that was Kirby stood and turned toward the voices. For a moment, his posture was considering, as though he were trying to decide if he wanted to deal with these fresh inconveniences. Then he turned and loped in the other direction.

Jesus had somehow extracted himself from the bars, and his screams had subsided to ragged breathing. Aldo lay at the base of the wall, unmoving.

"We're in here," North shouted.

Chapter 30

NORTH RUBBED HIS THROBBING eyes and instantly regretted it. The interview room blurred, a smear of particleboard and chrome, the smell of body odor and carpet cleaner. Opposite, Monzyk was a plum-colored blob. The homicide detective had only gotten angrier throughout the interview, and North figured some sort of arterial event was approaching.

"And you tied a belt around the bars, preventing the cell door from moving in either direction, because..."

"It was an artistic statement." Shaw's hair had come free from its bun, and he kept having to brush it out of his face. "Accessories engineered to suspend, elevate, raise, or hang articles of clothing are part of a fascist regime. Big Belt, for example, has been behind all the major wars of the twentieth century. Do you know who owns Raytheon, the RAND corporation, and JPL? Custom Beaver Belts. They want you to think they're a little mom-and-pop operation out of Fargo, but—"

"My goddamn back," Contalonis grunted as he got up from the chair. He stretched, a hand pressed to the lumbar region, and made a relieved noise. "Kid—"

"I'm actually not a kid," Shaw said. "I'm a striking young man. The world is my oyster, and I am full of great expectations. Oh. Wait, I need to ask North who has the great expectations."

"Me," North said.

Shaw had apparently mastered the spousal art of disagreeing through slight changes to breathing. North tried to fight the temptation, lost, and rubbed his eyes again. It only made things worse.

When Monzyk and Contalonis had found them in the cell, Jesus with a broken arm, Aldo knocked unconscious, North bleary-eyed with pepper spray, and Shaw clutching the belt that he had used to tie the bars of the cell door to the fixed bars of the cell wall, they had asked a lot of questions. North and Shaw had opted not to answer any of those questions, on the grounds that it seemed like a shitty idea. Jesus had begged for an ambulance. Aldo, when he had recovered enough to talk, had told a story about an intruder.

The St. Louis homicide detectives had wanted to go over it again and again. This was about the thirtieth again.

"One more time," Monzyk said with threadbare patience. "What happened?"

"Well, it all began in 1832 when Old Master Grumplin killed his first beaver—"

"Shut the fuck up!" The shout echoed in the small room. Monzyk mopped his face with the triangle of his tie. "You two think you can skate away from all this. You think you can fuck us, and we'll smile and spread our cheeks and ask for more. You walk off from our scene? Fuck us. You dodge us when we want a statement? Fuck us. You call us with leads we can't follow up on, with stories so full of holes I could rip them apart with one good fart, and a few hours later we've got Reck screaming down the phone at us, telling us you need help. And when we drive across the state to pull your asses out of the fire? When I've got jai alai scheduled with Father Wedge, when it took me a week and a half to get a reservation for the fronton? What do we get? Another fucking. Fuck us, right? Fuck us six ways from Sunday. This story about the intruder, that's bullshit. I know what I saw: two police who'd been hurt, and the two of you holed up in that cell like you meant to fight off the Mongol horde. Whatever went down in there, it wasn't an intruder, so quit spinning me stories and—"

The door opened, and Jadon poked his head into the room, mussed and beach-bum perfect in his tailored suit. "John, Nestor, could I talk to you for a moment?"

"Not now," Monzyk said, his eyes fixed on North.

But Contalonis made a huffing noise as he pivoted at the waist and his back popped and crackled. "Come on."

"In a minute."

"In a minute, my keister," Contalonis said. "Before you blow a gasket."

Monzyk spent another ten seconds glowering, and then he slapped the desk with both hands and stood. When he followed Contalonis into the hall, Jadon drew the door shut, and the shouting began. It went on for a few minutes, the voices muffled. The ending was wavelike—the crest of sharp voices, troughs of quiet, then the ebb into silence. The door opened again.

"Let's go," Jadon said.

"About fucking time," North shouted through the doorway, at the sound of the homicide detectives' retreating footsteps.

"Cut it out," Shaw said.

North swallowed his response to that.

Jadon was carrying two plastic bags as he led them through a squad room. The smell of orange Fanta hung in the air, mixing with lighter fluid—North spotted the sources on one of the desks, an open two-liter and a bag of match-lite with its top furled. Four single-serving Lay's originals and a Dixie plate, the paper spattered with dark spots where oil had soaked in, completed the picture.

A note in thick strokes of Magic Marker said, *Sorry you missed the BBQ, Reck. Enjoy the leftovers.*

"What happened?" Shaw asked.

Jadon shook his head and walked faster. An exit door appeared around the next corner, the hallway dimly illuminated at this hour, the EXIT sign sending a red wash along the walls. Hitting the crash bar with the heel of his hand, Jadon shoved the door open. Then the early morning rolled over them, the air chill with the hint of autumn, the smell of the city—cold concrete and the river—clean and welcome.

"Why are they leaving you out of things?" Shaw hugged himself. The flannel shirt with the grandad collar was probably warm enough, but the bike shorts exposed the goose bumps on his legs. And, yeah, the shrinkage. "Why are they being mean to you?"

"Monzyk and Contalonis got your property back from that piss-ant department." Jadon handed a plastic bag to each of them. "Even the guns. I think they did it because they like being assholes and because they were pissed about whatever went down out there, but you still owe them."

"I'll put them on my Christmas card list," North said as he checked the keys on his ring and then the contents of his wallet.

"He's not joking," Shaw said. "He really does have a Christmas card list. It has four names on it. One of them is me, and one of them is his dad, and one is the Pope, and—wait, do popes believe in Christmas?"

"Why would I have the Pope on my Christmas card list?"

"That's what I wanted to know. It seemed a little insensitive."

"You don't even know what a pope is."

Shaw's chin came up. "Of course I do."

"Tell me what a pope is. Right now. No phone."

For a moment, Shaw made a few ineffectual gestures. Then he shouted, "They have great hats!"

Jadon was rubbing his eyes. "You're done. Do you get that?"

"Of course I'm done." North checked the CZ, but it didn't smell like it had been fired recently, and all the cartridges were still there. "This is total bullshit; he knows what a pope is. He's trying to get a rise out of me."

"No, I mean you're done with this case. This investigation."

North spat. He missed Jadon's shiny oxfords—on purpose, thank you very fucking much—but not by much.

"I'm serious," Jadon said. "You found the girl. That's what you were hired to do. So you're done. You go home, you get back to work on your other cases, and you leave this alone."

"It's nice to have some direction in my life, Jay," North said. "Sometimes I feel so fucking lost."

"Cool it," Shaw whispered, squeezing his upper arm.

"It's our case," North said. "We're done when we decide we're done."

Jadon loosed a disbelieving laugh. "Are you serious right now?"

"We're the only ones who have made any progress on finding out who killed that girl—"

"Oh yeah? Who did it?"

"We've been talking to locals who are involved—"

"The doctor, the lady at the shelter, the owner of the temp agency. Yeah, I know. Do you know why I know? Because Monzyk and Contalonis have talked to them too. Which one did it, North?"

North felt the heat in his face as he shoved the CZ into his waistband.

"They all have alibis—" Shaw began.

"Of course they all have alibis. This thing you walked into, whatever it is, this thing is huge. It's got people everywhere. You saw how far they can reach last night—"

"What the fuck do you know about last night?" North said.

"I know I saved your fucking ass, North." The fury in Jadon's voice, when the detective so rarely lost his cool, hit North like the heat off a furnace. "Twice. By sheer luck, because I got notified of Shaw's live stream and decided to see if he was going to unwrap another of those egg surprises full of Korean skin care products, and when I saw what was happening, I knew it was hinky and hauled Monzyk and Contalonis out of bed. And you are being a fucking dick to me, the way you always are, when I'm trying to tell you that you're in over your head. We're not talking a domestic killing. We're not talking about someone topping their business partner. This is an organization, this is a machine, and they've got money and influence and people. It could have been a hundred different no-name guys who shot that girl in the back."

"No," Shaw said, "because Malorie knew whoever was driving that vehicle, and she got in because she trusted them to some degree."

"You think. You believe. You assume. Did you call the FBI?"

North met Shaw's eyes; then he let his gaze fall, knowing that he looked like he was doing a teenage sulk, not able to help it. He fumbled with his phone and saw the string of missed calls from an unknown number, the voicemails, and a text. A text with an address.

"Of course you did," Jadon answered for them. "And they wouldn't say anything, right? Because they've got a line on that place. They're working it. Slowly. Properly. Building a case with real evidence. What have you two done? You've trampled all over a homicide investigation. Any evidence you've touched, it's tainted. So I'm telling you to stop. Right now."

Again, North was unable to stop the words: "You can't make me."

A little black car, sporty, flashing halogen lights, sped past the station. The beat of subwoofers trailed in the air. A moment later, a cruiser swung out after the car, lights blazing.

"No, North. I can't. But Monzyk and Contalonis can charge you, and they can jam you up and make your life hell, and I'm tired of trying to smooth things out for you—"

"Nobody asked you to stick your fucking nose in!"

"—and maybe you could consider dropping this case because you're a decent human being and maybe, just maybe, you could consider dropping this case because you're going to get yourselves killed, and if you don't care about yourself, then at least you should give some thought to Shaw."

In the distance, the sound of the black car's engine had been swallowed up by the sirens of the cruiser in pursuit. Pretty dumb, North thought, the words detached and floating. Pretty stupid to drive right past the station like that. Kicking the cops in the teeth like that.

"That's not fair," Shaw said quietly. "We're partners. I'm working this too. I'm the one who wanted to take the case."

Jadon worked the knot on his tie down with two fingers, and then he stopped, his hand hanging there. He looked up the street. The wind dragged strands of sandy-brown hair across his forehead. Then, without a word, he let his hand fall, and he headed back into the station.

Shaw put his phone to his ear. North imitated him, but after the first few words of the message, all he heard was a staticky hiss in his ears.

"Nik left a message—" Shaw began and then cut off. "What's wrong?"

"My dad had another heart attack."

Chapter 31

BARNES-JEWISH HOSPITAL was a bulk of stone and glass and light against the false dawn to the east. Visiting hours were almost round the clock for patients in the ICU, the only exception being doctors' rounds, so North signed in, sent Zion home, and let a nurse lead him to his dad's bed. The woman kept giving North second and third looks, and North figured it might have something to do with the pepper spray and the cuts and bruises and the almost being murdered. The space wasn't exactly a room, although it had a partial wall, and North guessed that places like this were called stalls or cubicles or maybe even rooms, with a real fuck-you for the proper meaning of the word. Curtains offered the illusion of privacy, but someone was coughing, and a man with a deep voice kept murmuring something that sounded like bingo numbers.

David McKinney looked like a bad photocopy of himself, all the color gone, thinner than he should have been, the once clear lines blurred and indistinct. He was intubated, and a ventilator made his chest rise and fall with mocking regularity. North sat, put his head in his hand, and let his eyes close partially. Part of him was winding up—a spring in his chest getting tighter and tighter as he replayed the conversation with Jadon, replayed the hours in the cell, replayed the arrest. Exhaustion had scraped thin the barriers he usually kept high, and his eyes kept filling with tears he had to blink away or snuffle into his t-shirt. I'm mad, he kept telling himself. This is because I'm so fucking mad.

"B10," that deep voice whispered in another stall.

Around him, machinery whirred and beeped. The sound was like one vast organism—the hospital itself, maybe—breathing. An astringent, chemical smell suggested disinfectant. Under it lay the stink of loose bowels. His mother had died in a hospital, taken her time about it. That was when North had learned to wash his own clothes, coming home after visits, desperate to get the smell of death off him. He remembered now, with a faint kind of wonder because the memory had been gone so long, squeezing his too-big teenage frame, gangly and awkward, between the washer and dryer so that he could cry while the machines were running. So that his dad wouldn't hear him. Who are we when we're alone? Christ, North wasn't sure he could stand knowing.

The smell of urine, sharp and immediate, brought North's head up. He opened his eyes; a dark stain was spreading across the thin hospital bedding near his dad's waist. The ventilator continued its rhythmic bellows-work.

Twitching aside the curtain, North whisper-called to the nurses' station, "Could I get some help?"

A disgruntled sound answered him. Then, after a delay that had a hint of passive-aggressive power behind it, a heavyset guy in clunky nurse shoes trudged toward him. When he was close enough to whisper, he asked, "What?"

"My dad's pissing himself, that's what."

The guy had caterpillar eyebrows that bristled and unified at the tone in North's voice. "He must have pulled out the catheter."

"He's unconscious. How's he going to pull anything out?"

"Sir, if you're going to be combative, I'll have to ask you to leave."

"F4," the deep voice called.

"I'm not being combative. I don't think it's unreasonable to expect you to do your fucking job."

"Verbal and physical abuse of staff—"

"Are you going to clean him up? Or do I need to?"

The answer—you—was clear in the nurse's face, but the man didn't say it. Instead, he moved to the bed and stripped the bedding, which he wadded up and tossed on the floor. The hospital johnnie was soaked too, but he only rucked it up. North had a couple of vivid childhood memories of walking in on his dad naked, but seeing him now, like this, exposed, was strangely humiliating—emasculating was the word that came next, although North couldn't even have said why. The catheter lay between his legs. The nurse made a disgusted sound as he gloved up. Then he tried to reinsert it. His touch was rough, too forceful, gripping the penis in a way that suggested annoyance and distaste and shoving the catheter inside. Something wasn't right, and he had to try again, and he made that noise of disgust once more.

"Hey," North said, "easy."

The nurse's shoulders rode higher. He jammed the catheter in again.

"I want a different nurse."

"You're not getting a different nurse."

"I surely fucking am." North yanked the curtain back. "Who the hell do I have to hump to get another nurse?"

"Sir, that's enough. You need to leave this unit right now." The expression on the man's face was close to professional, but it didn't hide the glee in his voice.

That deep voice again: "C3. No, C3."

"I'm not going anywhere. Is there another nurse here? Does anybody else fucking work here?"

"If you don't leave, I'm going to call security and ask them to remove you. You're disturbing the other—"

"What's going on here?" She was middle-aged, black, her thick white hair gathered in a bun high on her head. Like the male nurse, she wore scrubs and cushioned shoes designed for long hours on her feet. "Jeffrey, what's the problem?"

"I—"

"This fuckwad can't do his job, and he's hurting my dad."

"We need security down here—" The nurse, presumably Jeffrey, whined. "This man threatened me."

"Go finish up your notes and clock out." When Jeffrey lingered, she said, "Did you not understand something?"

"I'm calling security."

"You do whatever you need to do. But go finish your notes."

Muttering under his breath, Jeffrey sidled past her and trudged toward the nurses' station. The woman, whose name tag said Dora, offered a clinical smile for North. "Tell me what happened."

"That fucking—"

"With a civil tongue."

North blinked. He had that sensation of having fallen into a dream. After a moment, with a kind of precarious watchfulness he hadn't felt in ages, he picked through his words and managed, "My dad's catheter came out. That guy couldn't put it back in."

Dora nodded. She gloved up, and then she had North help her move his dad while she cleaned him up and changed the rest of the bedding and the johnnie. Then she put on fresh gloves, opened a new catheter, and inserted it on the first try. She tucked a clean sheet and blanket around North's dad and stripped off the gloves.

"Miss Dora?" It was a man's voice. He was black, built big, and he wore a gray uniform. "Some kind of trouble?"

"I'll tell you about it," Jeffrey scrambled out of the nurses' station, waving a hand like he was flagging down a bus. "I'll tell you!"

"Sit down," Dora told North. "You look like a wreck. I'll handle this."

The bingo player's deep whisper rolled through the room: "B7."

Dora pulled the curtain closed, the rings chiming on the rod, and low voices continued from the other side. North tried to pay attention, but he couldn't. He moved his chair closer to his dad and held his hand. And then he thought about what his dad would say about that—faggy would be the warm-up pitch—and he moved the chair back. Then he leaned forward, elbows on knees, hands over his eyes, and wondered how people did this by themselves. How was he supposed to do this by himself? Even when it had been his mom, he'd had his dad. That had been awful in its own way, but it had been better than nothing. How was he supposed to handle this shit alone?

The curtain rings jingled, and Dora said, "Mr. McKinney?"

North wiped his face.

"I'm afraid Jeffrey is being…insistent. You'll have to leave. You can come back in an hour; his shift is almost over. I'm sorry for the inconvenience."

"No, I can't—" He gestured at the bed. "I mean, please?"

After a moment, Dora sighed. "I'm going to take your name off the visitor's log. You be quiet, all right? As far as anyone knows, you'll be long gone. Don't worry about security; I've known Randall since he was in Pampers."

The curtain rattled shut again, and the murmur of low voices swelled and then drained away. North tried to find a comfortable spot in the chair. His last thought before sleep was that he was never going to fall asleep, so he might as well invent a time machine and travel back to murder the bastard who invented hospital chairs.

It was the sound of the shoes that woke him: the soft whisk of a sole on the linoleum. He dragged himself upright and degunked his eyes.

"Somebody had a rough night." She was young, brunette, pretty in a Disney-princess way like a sexualized child. She wore the same blue scrubs as Dora. In one hand, she held a syringe. She was doing something to the IV line. "Go back to sleep; I'll be out of here in two shakes."

"What are you doing?"

She frowned at him and then gave a tiny shrug. "This is his antiplatelet medication. It's to keep the stent open. Prevents blood clots. That kind of thing." She went back to working on the IV line.

North closed his eyes, but her arrival had shattered sleep for him. Something nagged at him. He sat up straight again. He looked her over, scrubbed hands through his hair, blew out a breath.

"D1," came that low whisper from far off.

A sound, maybe. North tried to figure out what was bothering him. Something he hadn't liked.

She looked over her shoulder. Huge eyes. A tiny furrow between her brows. "You're not supposed to be in here, you know. Not without signing in, and there's nobody on the visitor log."

It was habit, routine, the kind of bait and trap that had become second nature in his line of work. "Didn't Jeffrey tell you I was in here?"

She hesitated a second too long. "I guess he forgot."

Then it crystallized: the sound of her shoes. The whisk of leather on the linoleum. She had the scrubs right, and she had the attitude, and she talked the talk. But the shoes were wrong: ballet flats. Leather soles. No arch support for hour after hour on her feet.

"Who are you?" North said as he lurched up from the chair.

"I'm Janice, I'm your father's—"

"Don't bullshit me. Who are you? Drop that fucking IV line and get the fuck away from my dad."

"He needs this medication. I don't know what your problem is, but I've got a job to do. You can talk to my supervisor if you want to." She turned, reaching for the line's end cap.

"I said drop that. Hey!"

The roar must have broken her nerve because she turned and ran. North reached out, and cotton whispered between his fingers for an instant; then she was past him, sprinting through the curtain, her steps slapping the linoleum. North launched himself after her. He hit the fire doors to the ICU right before they swung shut again.

The woman—whatever her real name was, it wouldn't be Janice—was already rounding the corner at the end of the hall. She shoulder checked a portly white nurse, who promptly went ass over ankles in a fountain of paperwork.

"Stop her!" North shouted, Redwings pounding out his steps. "Stop her!"

But by the time he reached the corner, she was gone.

Chapter 32

MID-MORNING LIGHT lacquered the old floorboards like honey. In the living room, the rat-tat-tat of gunfire laid down the beat, and Nik built on top of it, a string of swears, moans, and excited shouts. Track number God-only-knows of this particular album, which Shaw was considering titling *I Just Want My Life Back*. The game was called Fortnite, and whatever it was, it meant Nik hadn't bothered Shaw in almost three hours, which felt like a world record. Shaw massaged his aching jaw—he was grinding his teeth again—and sipped his tea: cacao and ashwagandha. He considered the possibility that it was making his headache worse. He considered his boyfriend, who sat across the gate-leg table.

North hadn't come home until after six, and by the time he'd finished telling Shaw all of it—the argument with the nurses, the strange woman, his conviction that she had been trying to murder his dad, and the struggle to get the hospital's security team to review camera footage of the woman's flight— it had been almost seven. Shaw had pushed him onto the bed, literally, ignoring North's protests, and North had fallen asleep while Shaw was still stripping him out of his clothes.

Now, it wasn't quite eleven, and he was trying to leave.

"All right," North said for the fourth time. "I'm going to go back there and make sure everything's covered."

He had greenish shadows under his eyes like bruises. He had real bruises too, plenty of those. His eyes were bloodshot, and he smelled like the energy drink he'd pounded over the sink—it had the chemically green color and, presumably, flavor that was nectar to teenage boys. He kept gripping his jaw, fingers white where they bit into his cheek, palm across his mouth. Some people sat like that when they were holding back a scream.

For the fifth time, Shaw said, "You need more sleep."

"I can't."

"Of course you can."

"I'm going to go straight there."

"North."

He stretched in the chair, one hand sliding over his eyes, the gesture so casual that anyone else might have missed it. "Maybe he'll want something from home. Can I bring him something, you think? A magazine? I should stop by the house."

"North."

"The cats—"

"The neighbors are taking care of the cats."

"You're right." In a stronger voice, he repeated, "You're right. I'm going over there right now."

But he sat there.

With an inner sigh, Shaw stood and moved around the table.

"What are you doing?" North said, rearing back. "I need to go. I'm leaving. I'm—"

Catching his head, ignoring the fractious pull away from his touch, he drew North's head against his bare chest and combed the thatch of blond hair. It was still dark with water. It smelled like the hemp shampoo that North thought Shaw didn't know he stole from under the sink sometimes. The warmth of his body was a rigid line against Shaw for what felt like a long time, and then North turned his face into Shaw's belly and shuddered. Only once, but his whole body. Fault-line movement.

"Zion and Truck are sitting at his bed right now," Shaw whispered, scratching the bristles on the back of North's head.

North nodded.

"The city put a corrections officer in the ICU."

Another nod.

"Hospital security has a man at the unit doors."

A weaker nod, barely a movement at all. "Shaw?" The word was hot against Shaw's bare skin. "I did something."

"What?"

"This morning, I called Truck." More of that warm, irregular breathing wicked along Shaw's belly. "I asked hir—"

Shaw watched the clock until a minute had passed. "What did you ask hir to do?"

North shook his head.

"Do you want to tell me later?"

North nodded.

"Back to bed," Shaw said, trying to find the line between firm and gentle. "You're showered and clean, and you're going to sleep so much better."

"I can't."

"We're not going to let anything happen to him, North, but you're going to drop from exhaustion if you keep pushing yourself like this, and it's going to happen at a bad time. You need to rest now, when it's a good time, so you can push through when you have to."

"No, I mean, I can't sleep right now. I'm wired from that energy drink."

Shaw petted his hair. "You can't if you don't try. That's what my grandmother always said. Clothes off. Then you're getting in bed."

North did a lot of grumbling, but he was surprisingly tractable as Shaw led him past Nik and into their room. Shaw turned him out of the tee, pulled off the boots, removed the jeans. He was on his knees, face even with North's boxers, and he slid them off. He kissed the tip of North's dick, and then he kissed a line up the flaccid shaft, through the thick patch of blond fur, up the trail to North's naval.

"Baby, I can't—I mean, I don't think right now, I'm totally spent—"

"Oh please. I wouldn't let you even if you had a solid steel tromboner. That was because I love you, all of you, and because I wanted to." Ignoring North's muffled complaints, he pressed him back against the bed, with a pile of pillows under his head. He pulled up the sheets. He kissed North's biceps. His shoulder. His jaw. "Sleep."

"I told you—"

"Then have some of your private time. Catch up on the Cardinals. Read about how to build me a bigger deck. Find out what a tune-up is."

"I know perfectly fucking well what a tune-up is."

"Watch some anime."

It was always so hard for him, this part, to let himself be vulnerable after all the years of trying not to. After a moment, he managed, "There's one called *Violet Evergarden* that I've been wanting to see."

"That sounds nice. Get some good sleep, some solid sleep, and we'll talk about going to the hospital for a visit."

North reached up, tracing a hand across Shaw's bare chest, flicking a nipple. His fingers followed the swell of faintly defined abs, teased the trail of russet hair, and plucked at the waistband of the jersey bootie shorts. He cupped the bulge of Shaw's erection, applying pressure as he slid his hand back and forth.

"Let's take care of this before you go out there."

"No," Shaw said, laughing as he tried to turn away.

North caught the shorts' drawstring and tugged him back. The man was a devil with his hands, slipping one up the leg of the shorts, caressing Shaw. "You're wet."

"I'm fine. Stop it. Go to sleep."

"I don't want dingbat out there getting any ideas."

"Dingbat is too busy shooting strangers and creating psychic echoes of digital trauma."

"You're a hazard with this thing sticking out. You're going to knock things off tables and shelves. Let's figure out how to make it go down again."

"Stop," Shaw said with another laugh, and this time he was successful in pulling away. He fished through the clothes on the floor and squirmed into a tank, which he then displayed for North, using his hands to draw attention to the words stamped across the chest: FREE RIDES. "Are you happy? I'm decent now. My body is all covered, which is a way for you to control me by controlling who looks at me."

"You're wearing shorts with a four-inch inseam and one of your sluttiest tank tops. You're basically a Victorian matron."

"Don't say slut. Oh, but actually, that's a great idea. I found one of my best whalebone corsets the other day. I could wear that, and I've got so many crinolines—"

"Never mind, I want my alone time."

"One of them is printed with Victorian erotica."

"I want permanent alone time."

"The things they do with parasols."

"Get out!"

Shaw let himself out of the room with a backward glance; North was trying not to grin, but he looked surprisingly happy for someone who had moments ago done so much shouting.

In the living room, Nik was still playing his game. He had the puppy sprawled across one leg, and the little dog didn't seem bothered in the slightest by all the moving and shouting. Several more of the energy drink cans littered the table in front of him, but when Shaw went to pick them up, the puppy raised his head and issued a warning growl.

"You've got to be kidding me," Shaw said. "First North, now him? I'm the nice one. I'm the one who communes with nature. I've tapped into the earth spirit and channeled Mother Gaia and dream-walked with Jane Goodman's ghost. I'm the one you're supposed to like."

"Huh?" Nik said.

"Can we turn this down? North's going to sleep some more."

"Yeah, uh huh." And then, with the distracted effort of someone pretending they had been following the conversation the whole time. "I mean, yeah, I totally like you."

Shaw reconsidered his words and the tank and the shorts and realized he might have made a mistake. He decided the kitchen was safer.

But the problem was that there was nothing to do in the kitchen. Well, sure, there was a pile of dishes, and the floor was covered in muddy puppy prints, and the fridge needed cleaning out, and Shaw was pretty sure that either a potato had gone bad in one of the lower cabinets or someone had started hiding dirty diapers in their house, but there was nothing interesting to do. He paced. He sat in a chair at the gate-leg table. He paced some more. He gave the dishes a dirty look, but they refused to respond to his psychic demand— imposition of will on inanimate objects was either level forty-seven or level seventy-one; it was hard to get a straight answer out of Master Hermes sometimes. His mind kept going back to North. Alone was never good. Alone meant North slipping away from Shaw. Alone meant new walls and new locks and new bars, securing all the places that Shaw had tried so hard for so long to be given access to. They had broken up once, and it had almost killed Shaw; he wouldn't survive it again.

According to the treacherous clock, which also refused to respond to his will, it had been less than five minutes. Better now than later, Shaw reasoned, although he wasn't sure exactly what logic had yielded that conclusion. He padded back to the bedroom and tapped on the door.

"I'm asleep," North said.

Shaw eased the door open.

North was propped up against the pillows; the sheet had pooled at his waist, exposing the broad planes of his chest, the thick blond fur, the dark buds of his nipples. He was scratching his sternum with one hand; the other hand steadied a tablet against his knees. Voices in Japanese cut off when he touched the screen.

"I just wanted to check on you," Shaw said.

"I told you," North said. "I'm asleep."

"Right, well, yeah, but you are kind of talking to me."

"Sleep talking."

"Oh."

"Go away, Shaw."

"Actually—"

North set the tablet aside and rubbed his eyes.

"I'm going to be so fast," Shaw said. "I'm going to be super-duper fast, and you won't even remember I was in here, and you'll have all this time to be alone and self-actualize and explore being the kind of person you want to be without anyone influencing you. That's how fast I'm going to be."

"It feels really fucking fast so far," North muttered.

"I wanted to give you your birthday present early. One of them."

North rubbed his eyes again, but this time, his voice was softer. "Ok."

"And we'll still do a birthday party for you, or whatever you want, but I thought today, because everything's been so awful, you might want to open one of your presents early."

"Shaw, if it's a tungsten cock ring or a shotgun-shaped dildo or that milking machine you sent me fourteen different AirDrops for, now isn't the right time."

"I'm going to puke," Nik shouted from the living room. "I'm going to kill myself if I keep staying here."

"Then get the fuck out of my house," North shouted back.

Shaw opened the closet, pulled down a shoebox where he kept one of his pairs of Dorothy's red slippers, and extracted the card he'd hidden at the bottom.

"I don't want ruby slippers," North said.

"Don't be mean. Open it."

North opened the card, and his face softened. He seemed to read it twice, his eyes moving back up to the top, and then he folded it closed and looked up at Shaw.

"I don't know if it's any good, or if I'm crossing a boundary, or if you want to be the one who decides how much of that part of your life you share with me, but—"

"It's perfect," North said.

Shaw stored the slippers and wiped his eyes on a peasant blouse hanging there. "Yeah?"

"Yeah. Crunchyroll is kind of, like, the best. I mean, for streaming anime, anyway. They have all sorts of shows that nobody else has, and they—I mean, it's amazing."

"I saw it when I was trying to find something you might like, and then I thought maybe you already had it, and then I went through all your credit card statements—"

"Excuse me?"

"—and made sure you weren't already subscribed, and then I thought maybe the oppressive culture of toxic masculinity had prevented you from getting your own Crunchyhole subscription—"

"Roll, God damn it. Roll, Shaw."

"—and so I thought maybe, well, you'd like it. And they've got a show I thought I remembered you talking about, um, *Made in Abyss*."

North folded the card back and forth.

Video game explosions were interrupted by Nik shouting, "Eat it, bitch."

"Yeah," North said. He cleared his throat. "Yeah, I've wanted to watch that one."

"I'm going to let you watch it, then. All by yourself."

"Come over here. I want to say thank you. One kiss to say thank you."

But the kiss turned into the jersey shorts halfway down Shaw's thighs and his hard cock halfway down North's throat.

"No," Shaw protested, finally managing to extricate himself. "Stop it!"

North drew the ridge of his knuckles under his lips.

"I'm leaving before you…before you seduce me into something wicked."

"It's less convincing when I can see your Crunchyhole," North called after him.

"I hate both of you so much," Nik said when Shaw emerged from the room and pulled the door shut. "Why can't you be normal gay guys and talk about folding laundry and drag shows?"

"That's an offensive stereotype," Shaw said as he adjusted himself in the shorts and then, realizing Nik was watching a little too intently, hurried toward the kitchen. "We don't just talk about folding laundry. Sometimes we actually do it."

More pacing in the kitchen. He tried to think about the case, but the reality was that they'd hit a dead end. Whatever had happened on the last day of Malorie's life, Shaw had no idea how they'd ever find out. Jadon had been correct when he'd pointed out that the number of possible killers was staggering—Big Joe could have used anyone to get rid of Malorie. And while Shaw still held to his belief that Malorie had trusted whoever had been driving the car, their primary suspects all had alibis that, although not airtight, meant that they weren't on Monzyk and Contalonis's radar. He tried to play out the day's events in his head. Malorie had left the shelter that morning. She had told Nik where she was going. Freddie, Jesse, and Alex had all confirmed that Malorie had visited them wearing the clothes she had left the shelter in. Then she had gone back to the shelter. She had changed clothes. And then she had gotten into a car, been shot in the back, and died as she tried to escape.

Another dead end—for her, literally.

Shaw found himself in the living room; he didn't remember leaving the kitchen. He stopped and turned himself back. North wanted to be alone. And Shaw wanted to put North first. And that meant Shaw wanted what North wanted. And that meant Shaw wanted North to be alone. It was as easy as that.

Not that it wouldn't have been nice, Shaw thought, his steps veering toward the front room again, to spend a little time together. Not that it wouldn't be nice to spend a little downtime together. A couple of hours as a couple. Sure, they spent days on days together for work. And they'd been friends for years, hanging out, going out, almost continuously in each other's company. But it would be nice, Shaw thought as he scooped up the puppy, ignoring the warning yip that threatened to pop his ear drum, it would be really, really nice, and it didn't seem outrageous at all, to want to spend some of their limited free time together learning how to be a couple.

"Somebody misses you," Shaw said as he pushed into the bedroom.

"Shaw." North paused the show and fell back against the pillows, arms behind his head. "Do we need to have this talk again?"

"I'm not even here. It's not me, Shaw. I'm just a means of transportation for this little guy." The little guy in question was wriggling in Shaw's grip, trying to bend himself in half so he could nip Shaw's hands. "He was so sad without you."

As soon as Shaw set the puppy on the bed, the puppy hopped in a circle, yapping in Shaw's direction. Then he jumped off the bed, slid on the floorboards, and recovered himself to sprint out to the living room and, presumably, Nik.

"I can tell," North said.

"You didn't see him out there. He was lonely."

"Ok, I guess we need to have this talk again."

"No, no, no, no, no." Shaw backed toward the door and held up a hand. He said again, more firmly this time, "No. I was doing the puppy a favor, but he's an ungrateful little monster, and he's sending mixed signals today—"

"He's not the only one."

"I'm leaving you alone right now, a hundred-percent alone, the perfect picture of masculine solitude and contemplation—"

Shaw barely got the door closed in time before the barrage of balled-up socks began.

As the thump-thump of stockinged artillery fire quieted behind him, Shaw headed back into the kitchen. He considered the room again and said, "Nik, you need to do the dishes."

Whatever Nik answered, it was lost in the sound of his game.

"Does the back door look plumb to you?"

No answer this time.

"Or is it square? Am I supposed to ask if the door is square?" Semi-automatic gunfire. "Nik, I'm talking to you."

"Fuck yeah, bitch, take it up the ass."

"Nikolas Nikita Nikshay, watch your language!"

The answer was a teenage grumble that Shaw decided it was probably better he hadn't heard.

North would know. North would know if you were supposed to say the door was plumb or square or—

No.

Shaw turned and headed for the stairs. He'd do some laundry. That was a nice, ordinary couple thing he could do. A gay thing, per Nik. They were doing nice, ordinary couple things today. He took the stairs down to the unfinished basement; a laundry basket waited at the bottom of the steps, and he used one foot to slide it along the concrete slab toward the washing machine. This was what North wanted, and logic said this was what Shaw wanted too, and so it was great. An ordinary couple thing. Couples did this all the time.

Dumping out the basket, Shaw squatted. He began to pick through the garments. North had a fetish for what he called "separating lights and darks," which Shaw had spent two hours trying to explain sounded a little racist even if North hadn't meant it that way. He'd been pretty close to convincing North to adopt a washing system where clothes were sorted by how interesting their psychometric associations were, but then North had said something like, "Mary, Mother of God," and gone outside and started the lawnmower. Shaw had tried to finish making his (in his opinion, compelling) case, but the engine had been too loud, and North had spent a suspiciously long time cutting the grass. Shaw was fairly sure he had gone over the whole yard twice.

So, Shaw sorted the clothes. This was a nice, ordinary couple thing. He could see lots of days like this. On the rare chances that their work schedules gave them a shared day off, North would want to have some time alone—

which Shaw was totally, perfectly ok with—and Shaw would spend his time picking through boot socks and maybe digging that pit in the backyard to try kalua pig cooking. They'd be like every other couple. That's what North wanted. He wanted to get married. And that was all right, wasn't it? Every other couple spent time alone, and they had separate interests, and they went to dinner parties where they flashed vicious smiles at each other and said things like "There is such a thing as too much time together" and "Giving Roger the den is what saved our marriage" and to new couples, the grins sharpening, "Oh, you still like being around each other?" and then they laughed their little Mary Tyler Moore laughs and went looking for more gin.

He was halfway up the stairs before he realized he was moving, and by then, he was committed. He ransacked the pantry until he found something that would work. He dug through the closet in the guest room for an accessory. Nik was jamming buttons on the controller like a maniac, so intent on the screen that he didn't seem to register Shaw's presence. Across his leg, the puppy lay on his back, obviously hoping for tummy scratches. Shaw slipped into the bedroom.

To judge by the volume and the music, something exciting was happening on the show, and it took North a few seconds longer than usual to notice Shaw. He punched something on the screen and looked up. "I don't want a beer, and I don't want the puppy kibble that you think is a hipster granola mix, and I don't want—"

"North McKinney," Shaw said with a plasticky grin, dropping onto one knee and producing the black velvet box. He cracked the lid to display the ring pop nestled inside. "I want to put a baby in you. Will you marry me?"

Outside, a leaf blower started up.

North pushed the tablet off his lap. "What is this?"

The smile was starting to hurt. "I know you've had a hard week, and I thought—"

"Is it a joke?"

"Well, I mean, we've been saying this stuff all week. It's kind of hot, and it's kind of funny. I mean, the ring pop is a joke, unless that's what you want."

"Great." Pushing back the sheet, North swung his feet to the floor. He stood and started picking through the clothes on the floor. As he yanked up a pair of boxers, he said, "So this is a fucking joke to you."

Shaw got to his feet, knees stiff now. "North, come on. It's—I mean, not the idea, you know, of…"

"Of? Of getting married?" North snagged jeans and stepped into them. "You can't even say it."

"Of course I can say it. I don't know why you're acting like this."

"You don't want to get married."

"Of course I want to get married."

"Do not fucking do this right now, Shaw. I'm warning you."

"Of course I want to. Of course I do."

"Bullshit. You are a liar. You are a fucking liar, and you are a bad one, and you are—" For a moment, emotion crested in North's voice, his control sounding like it might slip. "You are pissing me the fuck off."

"What is going on? I came in here because I thought we could have some sexy times and—"

"You know what, Shaw?" North dragged on a tee; he didn't seem to notice that it was on backward. "It's one thing when we disagree. Hell, it's one thing when we fight. But this—this fucking horseshit act of pretending you're ok with things, Jesus Christ. Do you know what that feels like? Like I'm not even worth talking to. Like I'm not worth an ounce of respect, like I'm not worth hearing what you think and what you want because, fuck, I don't know, am I too stupid? Is that why?"

"North—"

"Am I too heteronormative? Am I too immersed in a culture of toxic masculinity?"

"It was a joke," Shaw said, his eyes stinging. "It was supposed to be a joke."

"It was a joke because you think it's so fucking funny that I want to get married." North shoved a hand through his hair. "You know what's toxic, Shaw? This dehumanizing fuckery of not respecting me enough to tell me the truth. That's what's fucking toxic."

"I don't understand what's happening."

"Do you want to get married?"

"Why is this about getting married?"

"It's about everything," North shouted. "It's about the house, about the chores, about whether we pick up KFC or Hi Pointe. It's about me wanting a few fucking minutes alone. You tell me yes, yes, yes, but I know you want to say no, and that is so fucking hurtful that I want to—" He let out a whistling breath and, after a moment of visible struggle, seemed to master himself. "So here we go. No more telling me what I want to hear. We'll start with an easy one: do you want to get married? Yes or no, Shaw. And don't lie to me."

Shaw stared at him. His jaw worked once, soundlessly.

The leaf blower outside whined, choked, and died with a sputter.

North shook his head and pushed past him toward the door. "Jesus Christ."

The door flew open before North reached it, and Nik stood there.

"What the fuck are you saying to him?" Nik shouted, planting both hands on North and shoving. "You can't talk to him like that, you can't—"

North grabbed Nik's tee and hauled the boy forward. Off balance, Nik stumbled, and the force of the pull sent him crashing into the bed.

"North, holy shit," Shaw said.

"He's been asking for it since the minute he walked into this house," North said. He had his hands on his hips, but his fingers were curled into fists, and his chest was heaving. "I need the fuck out of here."

"Yeah." Shaw wanted to say more, but all he could come up with was another "Yeah."

North's stomps shook the floor. A moment later, the back door crashed shut.

Nik was still untangling himself from the bedding, trying to sit up, but he existed only on the periphery of Shaw's awareness. The rest of his focus was already replaying every horrible moment of the last few minutes. He was trying to track what had happened, trying to understand how a joke had spiraled out of hand so quickly.

"Are you ok?" Nik asked.

Shaw nodded, but he barely heard the question. He barely noticed the arms going around him, barely noticed the warmth of Nik's face pressed against his neck. He wasn't sure how long it was before he heard what Nik was saying.

"He doesn't deserve you. You're perfect, you're so good and perfect, and he treats you like shit." Nik's mouth dusted kisses on Shaw's throat, on his clavicle. "You don't have to worry about him. I'm not going to let him talk to you like that."

"Nik," Shaw said, "stop."

"I won't stop. I love you." He looked up, eyelids lowered, only a glimmer of dark challenge—and hope. "I love you so much. I love you more than he ever has, and I'm going to treat you right and—"

"Nik." Shaw managed to get free, and when Nik took a step, Shaw planted a hand to keep him at bay.

"I love—"

"Stop saying that!" Rein it in, a part of Shaw's brain warned him, but the hurt from North was too great, and it felt good to do this, to be the one hurting. "I don't love you. Get it? I don't love you!"

"You're upset. It's ok, because you're upset, but I'm going to show you how much I love you."

"Nik, I need you to leave. Right now."

Color rushed into Nik's light brown cheeks. His eyes flooded with tears. He turned, took a few stumbling steps, and stopped to turn back. "I'm going to show you." Then he broke into a run.

Chapter 33

NORTH WAS ON I-64 toward Barnes-Jewish when he started shaking, and he pulled off at Hampton and parked in a Hardee's lot and dug his thumbs into his eyes. Hospital. Hospital. Gotta go to the hospital. Dad might be awake. Truck and Zion needed a break. He could smell disinfectant, old bodies, urine. He could hear the unrelenting beeps and whooshes of machinery. The memory was a caul, and for several long moments, he was blind to the brilliant September day. Then he started the GTO and drove to the office instead.

The CLOSED sign hung in the door, with an emergency contact number—North's cell—printed at the bottom. North unlocked the door, and the smell of lamb and spices—cardamom for sure, and clove and cumin—met him. A fresh takeout container sat in the trash, which meant Pari had been here recently. She must have needed to run an errand. Good. North didn't know what would be worse—if she tried to pick a fight with him, or if she tried to be nice.

He washed up in the cramped bathroom. He noticed the tee was on backward and fixed it. HAPY BURG-DAY the shirt told him, and it featured a massive cartoon burger. Yeah, North thought. Right. Happy fucking burg-day to me. If I still have a boyfriend in four days.

After drying his face, he headed for the office he shared with Shaw. The french fry smell was strong today. The water stain in the hall looked like it was spreading. The acoustic tiles sagged overhead, and the faux-wood paneling had definitely peeled back farther, exposing framing that looked like it might be infested with black mold. Take a picture, North thought, rubbing his eyes as he dropped into his chair. This is North McKinney's life. He doesn't get what he wants, he throws a fit, and he spends the rest of his fucking existence alone, unless you counted the ghost of a murdered french fry and the manifestation of Our Lady of the Pestalozzi Street Shopping Plaza (ALDI COMING SOON!!!). This, he figured, was why people probably shouldn't keep guns in the office.

He went through the paperwork on his desk and in his inbox, examining each document before turning to the next page. When he got to the end, he hadn't seen any of it. Then, for a while, he sat there, hands clasped loosely and hanging between his legs. Not thinking. This was better than thinking. North had made Shaw watch *Point Break* a few weeks before, the original of course. He kept seeing, in his mind, Bodhi riding the pocket, the curl of the wave constricting, the whitewash falling in a curtain of spray. This moment, now, in the office, was like that. The only light coming through green-blue water. The water tightening. Green-blue darkening to black. And that darkness reminded him of dreams and the booger woods, that place you don't want to go alone.

The bell on the front door jingled, and North startled in his seat, banging his knee on the desk.

"Pari?"

No answer.

Steps moved through the reception area, coming toward North's office at the back. The part of his brain that he had trained for this job warned him that it could be something bad; the rest of him was too tired and hurt, washed out and empty as the flood of adrenaline pulled back, to do anything.

"Listen, motherfucker," Nik said as he came through the door.

North waited.

Nik straightened his tee—North's tee, actually, from the 2016 Rock 'n Roll half marathon that North had staggered through, thrown up at the end of, and immediately sworn, then and there, to give up smoking.

"Listen up," Nik shouted.

The chronometric time-travel agent on the floor above them started playing Enya. Lots of lutes. At least, North thought they were lutes.

"We're going to have a talk," Nik said, plucking at the shirt as though he were too hot and taking a strutting step into the room. "Man to fucking man."

North held up three fingers.

"What the fuck does that mean?" Nik said.

"It means you've said the same thing three fucking times, and I am at the end of my fucking rope, so get the fuck on with it. Tell me I'm a fucking piece of shit for the way I treated Shaw."

"You're a fucking piece of shit, the way you talk to him, the way you treat him." Nik took another of those nervy, daring paces into the room. "You don't deserve him."

"No. I surely fucking don't. Tell me to get the fuck out of Shaw's life and never talk to him again."

Nik blinked rapidly and looked away. When he looked back, his eyes were still shining. "You should," he said in a thick voice. "You should let…let someone else, someone who would—" Nik cut off, dashed an arm across his eyes, and finished in a rush, "You're a fucking asshole, and he still loves you, and it's not fair!"

Then he started to cry. The sobs were huge and racking, and after a moment, North got out of his seat. He took Nik by the arm and guided him into the chair and pressed a box of tissues into his hand. Then he went out to the reception area and filched a Diet Summit Cola from the mini fridge under Pari's desk. Back in the office, he opened it and pressed the cold brown glass into Nik's hand. Nik was still sniffling into a mass of tissues, and then he took a snotty swig and choked and had to mop at his face with the tissues again.

"That's awful," he gasped.

"Don't tell Pari; she's hooked on it. Sit up. Yeah, like that. Take a few deep breaths. Throw those away because they're fucking disgusting and blow your nose with some clean tissues."

Nik trumpeted into the kleenex.

"Better?" North asked.

Nik nodded. Then he shook his head and wiped his eyes again.

"What happened?" North asked.

"Nothing happened. Because he loves you. He told me—it doesn't matter." Pulling his knees up to his chest, he dabbed with the tissues again. "Everything is the worst."

North surprised himself with a laugh. "Yeah, it is." The glare on Nik's face, full of suspicion that he was being mocked, made North grin. "So you think I'm a fucking asshole who doesn't deserve Shaw?"

The glare intensified.

"So do I," North said with a shrug. "Join the club."

Nik made a noise of adolescent disgust and sniffled into the collar of his—North's—tee.

Above them, Enya was wailing louder and louder. A vacuum kicked on in the suite next door. North watched this kid, who had been through the teenage equivalent of hell over the last year, flexing his fingers around the wadded tissues.

"It doesn't make sense to anyone else either, if that helps," North said. "But we work." Then, face heating, he added, "For the most part."

"Why are you so mean to him?"

North snorted. "Because he likes it."

"He was crying! He was falling apart!"

"That's not what I—I thought you meant something else. Look, it's hard to explain a relationship to someone who's not part of it."

"You want to get married. He doesn't."

"Ok, maybe it's not that hard."

"I don't understand why you care so much. It's so heteronormative, and it reinforces the power of the landed class, and it turns spouses into chattel, and it's part of the system used by the patriarchy to oppress anyone different from themselves."

"I see Shaw gave you some talking points."

"No! I took AP Euro, motherfucker."

North raised his eyebrows.

"And, uh, maybe I heard him talking to some guy on the phone."

"Great. Emery Hazard is giving marriage advice. I should drive into the river now, while I have a chance."

Nik plucked at a loose thread on the shirt's hem for a moment. Then he burst out, "I don't understand. He loves you so much, and it's like you don't even see it. He wants to spend his whole life with you, and all you care about is a piece of paper." The words were tumbling out. "All he wants to do is spend time with you, and you're always pushing him away, finding reasons to keep him away from you. It's like you don't even want to be, you know, a thing with him."

All the closed doors. All the empty rooms. The TV, the books, his phone. Walls you couldn't tear down because you weren't even allowed to call them walls.

"I need a beer."

"You shouldn't drink for emotional reasons," Nik said.

"Shut the fuck up, you little crankhead," North said, but with a grin.

To his surprise, Nik grinned too. Only for a moment. But it was something.

"The last guy, my ex—" North tried again. "I was married. He beat the shit out of me. That's not—I don't know why I told you that. Christ, I don't even know where to start. My whole life, I've been two people: this person on the outside, like a shell, that let me keep people at a distance. If it was my dad, I was a queer. If it was the Chouteau boys, I was this blue-collar kid who still worked construction sometimes. If it was Tucker, it was—" Shaw, he wanted to say. "—other things. And on the inside, shit, I don't know. I don't even know who the hell that guy is some days. I like anime. I like baseball. I like going to art exhibits, but only the ones Shaw picks, that he knows I'll like." He shook his head. "But I'm figuring that stuff out. And some of it I already know, and I'm working on being honest about it. The part that's fucked up, though, is I don't know how to be in a relationship. I know how to hook up—"

"Be a fuckboy," Nik said. When North fixed him with a look, Nik shrugged and said, "Shaw told me about freshman year."

"Jesus Christ. Yeah, ok. I know how to be a fuckboy. And I sure as fuck know how to get my wires crossed and let people knock the shit out of me and think that's good, old-fashioned family bonding. But something real? An actual, honest-to-God healthy relationship? I don't even know where to start. Or who I'm supposed to be. Or how to be me and not whatever version of me I think will keep Tucker from picking up the strap." North shook his head. He opened his mouth, and then he shook his head again.

"That's, like, everybody," Nik said.

"Oh really?"

"Yeah. Everybody has to figure themselves out."

"I'm not talking about 'I like staring at the boys' swim team and then jerking off while I listen to the Jonas Brothers.'"

Nik's legs unfolded, and he stood. "You're such a prick."

He had almost reached the door when North said, "Ok, ok, ok."

Nik stopped.

"Come on," North said. "Let's hear it."

"No. You're an ass."

"Yeah, obviously. Tell me about sharing a sleeping bag with Ricky and the first time you popped wood."

"What is wrong with you?"

"Honestly, I don't know. Sometimes I think Shaw puts off this low-grade radiation."

Nik watched him for a moment, probably considering whether or not to leave. Then he put his hands on his hips. "My parents wanted me to be a doctor. A dermatologist, to be specific."

"And?"

"And they're dead, and I never told them I was working on a web comic and I'd been accepted to a summer program for graphic design. And it wasn't just my parents. I was with Lucas, only he was literally a Boy Scout, and his parents are so Catholic that they have those calendars with all the saints, and Lucas kept telling me he loved me and that we couldn't let anyone know about us. And I just—I just let him do that. He'd stick his dick in my mouth whenever he wanted, but when his friends were around, or my friends, or his parents, or anyone, he acted like we barely knew each other. And then Pranith, my fuckhole uncle, walked in on us one time, and he threw Lucas out, and then he threw me out, and I went over to Lucas's, went around back to the basement walkout because I was sure he'd help me." Nik stopped. He hugged himself. He was shaking. "And he didn't. He wouldn't even come to the door."

North stood. He came around the desk and put a hand on Nik's shoulder.

Nik slapped his hand away and started to cry. "I don't even like you. I fucking hate you."

North drew him into a hug.

After a while, through wet breaths, Nik said, "That's what I miss about Malorie, you know? I could be myself with her."

Chapter 34

SHAW LOST THE WHOLE day worrying. North didn't come home. Neither did Nik.

He took the puppy on a walk, which turned into the puppy taking Shaw on a walk, which turned into trying to cross four lanes of lunch-hour traffic, which snapped Shaw out of his fugue long enough to get the puppy back home.

He watched the news, but when Belia Lopez came on the air, he turned it off.

He cleaned, but he had barely started on the bathroom sink when he realized he was using toxic cleaning products. Then he decided to make his own. Then he realized he'd used all his eucalyptus oil breaking a curse on the GTO, after North spent a whole week working out in the garage, trying to fix something with the carburetor, when Shaw wanted him to watch that special five-night miniseries on mandrake-infused intimacy oils. Then he realized he shouldn't start with cleaning products; he needed to start with tools, so he decided to research how to grow his own sponges. He had filled a virtual cart with a two-hundred-and-forty-gallon reef tank when he started crying so hard that he went downstairs, got his stash of edibles from behind the laundry soap, and proceeded to get himself high enough to tolerate his current situation. His last clear thought was making sure the puppy had food and water before he decided to explore his quilt, because his hands were suddenly a million times more sensitive, and wait, do I still have any of those cookies.

He woke to sunlight bright against his eyelids. Late morning, his brain told him. A weight on the bed made the mattress sag. The smell of leather and American Crew gel and Irish Spring soap. He wanted to open his eyes. He didn't want to open his eyes.

"Quit faking or I'll give you a fucking charley horse so you can't walk for a week."

He decided bravery was one of his essential life values and opened his eyes.

North didn't look great—fatigue showed in the dark raccoon rings around his eyes—but he'd showered, and he wasn't wearing a shirt. The thick pelt of blond hair was distracting, but something else had changed. Something in the way he carried himself.

"How many of these did you take?" North asked, holding up the Altoids tin where the edibles had been stashed.

"How many are left?"

"Zero."

"Ok." Shaw tried to do the math. "How many did I start with?"

"I'm asking if you need to go to the hospital, ass-shitter."

"I don't understand that insult."

"I'm going to take that as a no."

"Aren't we all technically ass-shitters? Unless there's some sort of ostomy situation, I mean."

North's hand was warm as it smoothed the sheets over Shaw's belly. Shaw found himself suddenly hard and, rare in his life, embarrassed at his reaction. North's hand avoided his erection. It wasn't clear if he'd noticed; if he had, his face gave no sign of it, but he was also a surprisingly observant man.

"I'm sorry," Shaw said. "No, wait. Before I keep going, can I pull a pillow over my face?"

"No."

Shaw sighed. "I didn't think so."

"We can talk later if you want," North said. "I brought breakfast."

"Oh?" Shaw asked, sitting up, his woody brushing the inside of North's arm.

There was no way he hadn't noticed, but his expression didn't change. "It's porridge."

"I like porridge. You can put brown sugar in it. And regular sugar. And maple syrup. And chocolate chips. And those little marshmallows. And if you ask them, sometimes they have peanut butter behind the counter. Did you ask them—"

"Vegan porridge."

"Oh. I mean, oh!"

"So, no processed sugars."

"Oh."

"No sugars at all, really."

"Uh huh."

"And definitely no mycotoxins or aflatoxins."

"Umm, of course not."

"In fact, the grain part about porridges worries me."

"North."

"So, I made sure to ask for the grain-free option."

It was obvious that he was waiting for a reply, so Shaw said, "That was unnecessarily thoughtful of you."

"I guess it's really just a bowl of mashed zucchini. Extra watery. I asked them not to strain off the juice—is it called juice?"

"No, I think—"

"Because I didn't want you to miss out on all those probiotics."

The house creaked.

"Unless you didn't want vegan porridge," North said. "Unless you wanted to break your PiYo Fit Forty diet."

"It's a lifestyle," Shaw said with what he assumed sounded like dignity. "Not a diet."

North didn't smile. Then he did, but only with his eyes.

"North, I'm so sorry. About yesterday. About—about all of it. I was trying so hard to give you what you wanted. That's important to me. Not only because I've messed things up in the past by being selfish, but because I want you to know that there's someone in this world who puts you first." Shaw took a breath. "But I overcorrected. Not being honest with you about what I want, yeah, I see that's a problem. A big one. And I'm going to work on it. I made Dr. Farr cancel all her other appointments, and I've got a six-hour session tomorrow, and she and I are going to do a deep dive into this whole marriage thing because even though I don't want to, I think that's maybe my oppositional, um, behavior manifesting, and if I work on it, I think I could make some healthy changes because I want to spend the rest of my life with you and—"

"Stop talking," North said gently.

Shaw shut his mouth.

North's hand moved lightly over Shaw's belly, pressing on the spot below his navel that drove Shaw wild before lifting again and moving on. The woody had progressed to a wetty, the cotton sheet dark where it clung to him.

"I was so scared you weren't coming back," Shaw whispered. "Where did you go?"

"The office. The hospital. To see the lesbians who make zucchini porridge."

"North, I want you to know—"

North shushed him. Then, he slid down onto his knees and laid his upper body across Shaw's legs. It was a strange position, obviously uncomfortable, but it presented his back to Shaw. It took Shaw a few seconds to understand what he was seeing. Then he started to cry.

The tattoo was fresh, shiny under a salve and cling wrap, and the skin was inflamed from the needle and the ink. It was simple: black lines, black dots. An abstract rendering of a constellation. Two constellations, Shaw realized.

"Aquarius for you," North said into Shaw's leg. Even muffled, his voice sounded strangely thick. "And Libra for me."

"North."

"I was going to add a date, that first day in the dorms, but then I wanted to put the date you took me for coffee after class, and then I wanted to put the first time we watched *Buffy* on your laptop in your room, and I figured I was going to have the whole fucking calendar on my back if I didn't keep it simple."

"Oh my God, North."

"I love you more than anyone I've ever known, and I've been so worried about figuring out how to be in this relationship with you that I've fucked the whole thing sideways by not actually being in it with you. I kept telling myself I needed to figure out who I was, figure out how to be myself. But what I really want is to be myself with you. I want to be with you, Shaw. For the rest of my life. If you don't want to get married, that's fine. Fuck marriage and fuck civil unions and fuck all those heteronormative fucks to fuck. You're part of me, and that's never going to change, and I wanted to show you." He shifted slightly. "But don't get any ideas; I'm still going to kick your ass out when I want to watch the Cards. It's important to me, you know. Having time to myself. Not all the time. Jesus Christ, you know what I mean. Also, when I envisioned this, I didn't plan on talking to your leg."

"My leg is very happy," Shaw said, wiping his face. "All of me is very happy."

"All of you is poking me in the stomach, so I kind of got the message."

"North, I want you to have time alone. I do. But then I get worried. I start thinking you're going to…to push me away. That we're going to grow apart. And I couldn't stand that. I'd die if I lost you."

"Please. If I haven't been able to get rid of you by now, what chance do I have?"

Shaw laughed, but it was a broken sound.

"For real," North said quietly, "I'm not going anywhere. Sometimes I just need an hour or two."

"I'll do better. I promised I'd put you first, and I will. If that means giving you time by yourself, I'll figure out how to do it." Shaw reached to touch the tattoo and pulled his hand back at the last moment. "I can't believe you did this."

North shifted again. "It's just a tattoo. But I wanted you to know."

"I'm going to get one too."

"You don't have to do that."

"It's going to cover my entire back."

"No fucking way. I know who would end up applying ointment for a fucking month, so don't even think about it."

"It won't be constellations. It'll be an actual water bearer, with me as the model of course, only they can use Emery's ass for inspiration. And I'll be holding a set of scales—ow!"

"You get to be a fucking water bearer, and I have to be a set of scales that you're holding?"

"It's not my fault. I didn't design the zodiac. Oh! Don't worry, I changed my mind. I'm getting two Siberian tigers, only they'll have our faces—oh my sweet Buddha, North, I think you gave me a blood blister."

"Then quit talking."

"What if we did a lotus tree, and I can be Krishna, and you can be a rakshasa, and Jadon can be—"

"Jadon is not going to be part of our fucking commitment tattoos."

"Wait, you didn't let me finish. John-Henry will be Rati, and Emery—"

"I'm sitting up now. I'm going to have them change this tattoo into a map to the closest Jiffy Lube."

"No, no, no," Shaw said, laughing as he pressed him down carefully.

"I'm going to have them turn it into a fucking crankshaft schematic."

"No!" he wailed before dissolving into more laughter.

Somehow they ended up lying together, North on his stomach, his face pressed into the crook of Shaw's neck. Shaw tickled his ribs with feathery touches that made North shift every once in a while and grumble something quasi-threatening.

"You're going to puncture my spleen," North growled, swatting at Shaw's boner.

"I love you," Shaw whispered.

"No, you're a jerk. You love Emery's ass and Jadon and tigers."

"I love you so much. Sometimes it feels like so much that the universe can't hold all of it. I can't hold all of it. I can't believe you did this for me. I can't believe how lucky I am, lucky that you put up with me when I turn all your socks into mouse tunnels—"

"For the record, I still don't know what a mouse tunnel is."

"—lucky when you don't make me do chores—"

"I do try to make you do chores. I'm just fucking terrible at it."

"—lucky that you didn't run off eight years ago when you realized how crazy I am."

North raised his head. His eyes were wet, and he kissed Shaw slowly and gently. When he pulled back, he said, "If you don't want vegan porridge, I got Donut Drive In."

"North McKinney!"

"What?"

"North Cassidy McKinney!"

"You like donuts, so don't give me another fucking lecture on gluten or refined sugar or—"

"You lied to me twice! You said you went to the office, the hospital, and the lesbians. You didn't say anything about the tattoo parlor. And you made me think I was going to have to eat vegan porridge when you didn't say anything about Donut Drive In."

"You should be thanking me; I could have made you eat that vegan porridge to prove how sorry—

The realization, when it came, went through Shaw like a shock, and he jerked halfway into a sitting position. "Oh my God."

"Chill your nips. I wouldn't really have made you—"

"Oh my God, North." Shaw grabbed his phone to double check the photos North had taken of Malorie in the storm drain, but that was only for confirmation. "I know what happened."

Chapter 35

THEY WAITED AT THE end of the block in a rented Mercury Sable, 1990, the color of acid-washed jeans and despair. St. Rita's of Bevo Mill looked empty, but it wouldn't be for long. North was counting on it.

The pain in his back was moderate—not as bad as he'd feared, although he probably wouldn't have rushed into getting the tattoo if he'd been expecting a stakeout. Oozing blood and being unable to sit back were definite downsides in an experience that primarily consisted of sitting motionless in a car that smelled like cigarettes and something that might have been BO or might have been really foul onions.

"Nik isn't answering."

"He's got a burner; he probably ran out of minutes."

"He didn't come back last night."

"He's butt-hurt because you didn't want to play house with him. He's fine. He'll get over it."

"But—" Shaw began.

The blinds in St. Rita's front windows fell, and Shaw cut off.

"Here we go," North grunted as he levered himself out of the car.

They went around back—prying eyes, and all that—and when North tried to kneel down to have a go at the lock, his back twinged. He must have made a small noise because Shaw took the picks and, after a few minutes of fumbling, got the lock open.

As he passed the picks back, Shaw said, "A little quieter, please. We're trying to sneak up on her."

"Untwist your panties."

"You sounded like one of those porpoises at SeaWorld."

"Ok."

"But when they're unhappy about the quality of chum from the bucket."

"Enough."

"Oh, wait, actually, you sounded like that time the puppy got his tail stuck in the vacuum cleaner."

"This is why huge, romantic demonstrations are a fucking plague on society," North said, stiff-arming Shaw out of his way. "Move, ass-shitter."

"I still don't—no, stop, you're closing the door on me."

North decided, for the sake of professionalism and the urgency of their current objective, to stop trying to crush his boyfriend—life partner? God, that sounded like they played canasta—between the door and the jamb.

They stood in the shelter's kitchen, with the smell of stale grease in the air and sunlight bleeding across the stainless-steel appliances. North took the lead, unholstering the CZ as he moved down the hall. Faint noises from the office told him that he'd been right so far.

When they reached the door, it stood ajar, and he had a perfect view of Ryley. She was crouched down by the computer, examining the cables, her chunky bob swaying as she moved her head back and forth. Jean cut-offs and a cropped tee. Not many places to hide a weapon, but no point in taking any chances.

"Put your hands up where I can see them," North said.

She didn't put her hands up. She whirled to face them. She saw the gun. And a spattering sound and the unmistakable smell of urine filled the room. "Oh my God, oh my God, oh my God!"

"Hands up, Ryley." A beat. "Up!"

Still whimpering half-formed prayers, she put her hands up.

North McKinney motioned for her to stand. The dark spot on the front of the cut-offs was visible. The glistening track on the inside of her leg. North McKinney, hero to the underdog. Faster than a speeding bullet and all that. He can scare the piss out of young girls. How long can you go, North wanted to know, seeing the worst side of everything?

"Ryley, it's ok," Shaw said. "You're not in any danger—"

"Not unless you try something stupid," North said.

"But we need some answers."

"Oh my God," Ryley whispered. Then, tears flooded her eyes and she said, "Can you please not tell Ximena?"

"You saw Malorie, didn't you?"

Ryley stood frozen—a rabbit frozen in the invisible glare from the CZ.

"You came back to the shelter early that day, and you saw her. She wasn't supposed to be in here, but neither were you."

"I don't—I didn't—"

Shaw held out a photo, a printout from the pictures North had taken of Malorie dead in the storm drain. "Those are the smiley-face earrings that Ximena bought you, aren't they? The ones you said you lost? Malorie's wearing them."

Ryley shook her head. "I lost them. I don't—Those aren't mine."

"What's Ximena going to say when we show her this picture?"

Ryley shook her head once more. Then she started to cry and nodded. After a moment, North let out a breath and lowered the pistol.

"Come on," Shaw said. "Let's get you cleaned up, and then you can tell us."

In a clean pair of sweats, sinking into one of the ancient couches in the rec room, Ryley looked even younger. Childlike. Shaw sat close to her. North stayed near the door; he hadn't forgotten Ximena's stunt with her nine-millimeter.

"You've been stealing from the shelter for a while, haven't you? And you never get caught, you never get in trouble, because Ximena is the one putting you up to it." When Ryley didn't say anything, Shaw said, "It's better to get it all out in the open from the beginning, Ry."

"It doesn't hurt anybody." Ryley brushed a pattern into the nap of the upholstery. "There are all these big companies that want to give money, but they won't give it to Xi. She's got a certain lifestyle to maintain. People need to see that she's successful. She's an ambassador—"

"Skip the talking points she sold you," North said. "Tell us what you've been doing."

"I take stuff and sell it and give Xi the money. Computers are good—there's a tech company who likes to give us their obsoleted stuff."

"She gives you some of the money after you're done?"

"What? No. She needs help. She's such a good person, and there aren't many people she can trust."

"And last Wednesday, you were here when Malorie came back."

After a moment, Ryley nodded, keeping her gaze locked on the vinyl flooring.

"Did you get in a fight?" North asked.

Another hesitant nod.

"About what?"

The silence stretched out until Ryley threw up her hands, and the moment snapped. "I don't know! She—she was so awful. She always thought she was so tough. She always got what she wanted. Xi loved her, but she didn't see how Malorie was a bully. If she wanted something, she'd find a way to take it. She was always—always so selfish!"

"What happened?"

"She was getting stuff out of her locker. She saw me, and she went crazy. She shouted at me, told me to leave. When I wouldn't leave, she—" Tears thickened Ryley's voice. "She grabbed my hair and pushed me to the ground. She pounded me in the back a few times. I don't think she knew how to fight, but she kept hitting me like this." She made a clubbing motion. "I just wanted to get away." She stopped, pinching the upholstery, eyes empty and unmoving.

"She took the earrings," Shaw said.

Ryley nodded.

"And she threatened you," North said.

"She said if I told—if I told anyone, she would tell Ximena what I'd been doing. She was going to keep the earrings as proof."

"You knew Ximena wouldn't care."

"But what if she told the police?" A note of despair rang in the words. "I was in care for four months. I don't want to go back."

"When she left," Shaw said, "what did you do?"

"Nothing."

"Bullshit," North said.

"I didn't do nothing! Anything! I didn't do anything!"

"You took the money out of her locker," Shaw said.

Ryley tried to get up, but the sofa was too deep and swaybacked, and after a moment she fell back against the cushions. "She was such a bitch! She took whatever she wanted. I wanted to take something of hers. I was going to give it back. Trade it for the earrings. But then she was dead, and Xi got rid of the registration papers because she was worried, and—and if I told about the fight, people would think I had something to do with what happened to Malorie, and then everything would come out about how I was helping Xi, and she's the best, she doesn't deserve that."

"But Malorie deserved what she got," North asked, "didn't she?"

Ryley ducked her chin, refusing to meet his eyes.

"When you saw her," Shaw said, "that day, when you saw her in the shelter, that first moment, what was she doing?"

"She was changing clothes."

"Quit wasting my fucking time," North said.

"She was! She was going to the movies with Nik, and she was changing clothes."

"You're a fucking liar."

"I'm not lying! I'm not!"

North opened his mouth, but he blew out a tight breath when Shaw made a small gesture with one hand.

"You saw something," Shaw said, "something Malorie didn't want you to see. That's why she hit you. That's why she took those earrings. She wasn't going to the movies with Nik, not right away. She was going somewhere else first, and she wanted to keep it a secret. What did you see, Ryley?"

"I don't know. I don't! She was dressed nice. This white tube top and her good jeans. She's got great legs. These strappy silver sandals. Like in the picture. That's all."

"That's not all," Shaw said, "or she would have let you go."

"I swear to God—"

"Ry, take a breath, and walk yourself through it again. You're inside the shelter, you're coming up the basement stairs—"

"No, I have a key. Xi gave it to me."

"That explains why Nik thought the shelter was empty when we went through that goddamn window" North muttered.

"Ok," Shaw said, "you let yourself in the back, and you're coming through the kitchen, and…"

"And she's standing by the lockers, and I can tell by her face that she's already going to be a bitch." But Ryley wriggled forward, caught up in the moment now. "She's pulling stuff out of her locker and shoving it in a bag at her feet. She hasn't seen me yet."

"What is she putting in the bag?"

"There wasn't a bag with the body," North said.

Shaw motioned for him to be quiet.

Distress twisted Ryley's features. "I don't know."

"Sure, you do. You saw it. You saw what she was putting in that bag. Was it something big? Small? Square? Round?"

Ryley waved a hand, her eyes lost in the memory. "It was clothes."

"Clothes?" Shaw asked, his eyes sliding to North's. "But she'd already changed for the movies, right? Already showered and changed?"

An impatient nod. "They were ugly. This green, kind of turquoisey. Made me think of a hospital."

"Scrubs," Shaw said.

"Yeah, that's what they were. Scrubs. She was putting them in the bag, and then she saw me, and she went out of her mind."

North's mind went to the porno photo, the one of Malorie in the exam chair.

"She was going to do another shoot," Shaw said, voice tight with emotion.

Chapter 36

HAZARD'S VOICE WAS MORE annoying than usual over speakerphone, North decided. The Wahredua detective was trying to convince Shaw about something having to do with mushroom rings. That fairies weren't real, North guessed. Good fucking luck.

When Hazard took a breath, North said, "Your voice is even more annoying over speakerphone."

The line's static hissed in the silence.

"I thought you'd want to know," North said.

"I didn't," Hazard said.

"It's not that annoying," Shaw said. "But it does kind of remind me of those people who have been on Thorazine for a long time."

"I—"

"No, wait. It reminds me of that guy who got kicked in the head when he was a child. The mule kicked him, remember?"

"I—"

"I think his name was Simple Pete."

Shaw's eyes were bright with the fuckery of it all, and North had to bite the inside of his cheek to keep from bursting out laughing.

The silence had a strangled quality to it now. Then Hazard said, "I'm hanging up."

"No, wait," Shaw said, "wait, wait, wait, please!"

The buzz of static said the call was still connected.

"How hard would it be to have someone raid the Big Muddy?"

North wondered, in the pause that followed, if Hazard would figure it out on his own. North hoped not. He was kind of looking forward to explaining their plan in excruciating—and belittling—detail.

But all Hazard said was "I'm in Oklahoma, so I can't help you. But if you're planning what I think you're planning, then you need to talk to John anyway."

"Oh, that's perfect," Shaw said. "I haven't had a chance to tell him about the time that I cream-pied him—"

"What the fuck?" Hazard said.

"We're hanging up now," North said. "Go get stampeded by some buffalo."

"I honestly don't know which of you is more fucking—"

North disconnected the call.

"Sweet," Shaw said. "I think he was going to say sweet."

"I thought he was going to say hung."

"Oh, that one's easy. We'll give Hazard a ruler and then we'll play that part in *Braveheart* where you always pop a rod—stop, stop, stop, you're pulling my hair out."

"Whoops," North said as he rocked back in the office chair and released his boyfriend-slash-life-partner-slash-we-built-our-own-shuffleboard-court-person. He had stacked the cash they'd pulled out of the bank on the desk in front of him. From the reception area came Pari's music, the low throb of the beat. Somebody smokin' like a Rasta. Somebody blowin' smoke. "Now call Jadon."

Jadon, if possible, sounded even less happy to hear from them than Hazard. "Shaw, now isn't a good time."

"Good afternoon to you too, dick shine," North said.

Pari's song changed. Thump thump thump. English. Spanish. El diablo me llama. North didn't know the song, but he felt it. The devil is calling me. Since the case had broken open, he'd felt like he was one of those wing walkers, barnstorming his way across fucking Iowa, adrenaline dripping into his bloodstream in a steady infusion. El diablo me llama.

"What do you want?" Jadon asked.

"Jay, I know you're mad at me—" Shaw began.

"I asked what you want."

Shaw bit his lip. After a moment, he said, "I need a favor."

"I know. That's why I asked what you want."

"Cut it out, ass-munch," North said. "Shaw didn't do anything to you."

"Screw you, North." But his voice was milder when he said, "What is it, Shaw?"

"We need someone to watch Freddie Eggenberg's clinic. An unmarked car, preferably, the kind that screams cop if you know what to look for."

"Or if you're paranoid enough," North added.

"Is this the Walton case? I told you to drop it—"

"Jay, this is it. The whole case. We can hand you Freddie Eggenberg, the Big Muddy, all of it."

"Really? With evidence you and North haven't made inadmissible? How? What part of this case haven't you walked all over?"

"Tell Monzyk and Contalonis we can give them this case on a silver platter. Just make them the offer and let them refuse if they want. All we're asking is a couple of cars, some warm bodies. They can be uniformed guys off duty if you want."

"Jeez, Shaw. Do you have any idea the kind of shit that would get us into? The union would have my balls, and that's after I'd been cornholed by everyone from my sergeant to the commissioner."

"But—"

"You're sure about this? You know who killed that girl?"

Shaw's evasion was so slight that North almost missed it. "We know who's behind all of this—the trafficked kids, Malorie's death, all of it."

El diablo me llama. Wing walking. This was the make it or break it moment.

"They're going to make me eat shit," Jadon said. "They're not going to listen to me."

"Not at first. But they will, eventually, and you can convince them."

"They're going to put me in one of those cars. You know that, right? That's going to be payback. They're going to stuff me in one of those surveillance cars, and there's no way I'm going to pull overtime for it."

"North will pay you for the extra hours."

"Like fuck," North said.

"Please, Jadon," Shaw said.

"I cannot believe I'm doing this," Jadon said in an undertone. "I'll call you back if they say yes."

"Thank you, Jay!"

"If, Shaw."

"Thank you so much."

"Good Lord," Jadon muttered and disconnected.

"This might actually work," Shaw said. "As long as Truck and Pari and Zion don't get bored following Big Joe."

Scooping up the cash, North said, "Of course it's going to work. Now get your phone and come make a video of me burning our retirement money."

Chapter 37

THEY HAD BEEN SITTING inside the cement-block warehouse by the Meramec for eight hours when they heard the first vehicle. A truck, North guessed from the sound of the engine. It was late on Friday, almost midnight, and he figured the driver wasn't looking for the good boys at Kroyer Auto Body next door. Gravel crunched under tires, and then the engine shut off. The night sounds filtered into the empty office where North and Shaw waited: the river, crickets, the shiver of brush as something—a fox or a possum, probably—startled and ran.

North understood the feeling. Standing there, in that empty room with its peeling white paint and its high-traffic carpet and the smell of closed-up, humid air, he felt like he could run straight up a wall. It was that kind of high-wire nervous energy—run straight up a wall and not stop. Shaw brushed a hand down his arm, and North shivered at the touch and let out a breath.

The phone in his hand showed views from the two cameras they had installed: one out front, and one out back. On the camera in front, the heavyset form of Big Joe moved into view. His jeans were too tight. The Big Muddy t-shirt too loose. The Bass Pro Shop hat was cocked back, and some of his thin, greasy hair spilled across his forehead. The revolver holstered at his hip was huge, a cowboy gun that he hadn't even bothered trying to hide. North switched apps and tapped the record icon on the phone; their little meeting was being streamed to a couple of murderously inclined homicide detectives up the road (which North thought was kind of an irony, but not one Monzyk and Contalonis would appreciate), but it never hurt to have a backup. He switched back to the camera app as Joe reached the door.

A moment later, he heard the sound of it opening.

"In here," Shaw called. He was holding his gun at his side; North was too.

Big Joe appeared in the doorway a moment later. He took them in with a long look and then shuffled sideways, his back to the wall. He had surprisingly small feet. Or maybe they only looked small on a man his size. North wanted to giggle, thinking about Big Joe's feet right then. Adrenaline high. It gave him a sour stomach, too, but that never made it into the comic books.

"You boys screwed the pooch," Big Joe said.

"Shut the fuck up," North said.

"Majorly."

"Shut up, or we're done here."

Big Joe's face didn't change, but he stayed silent after that, pulling out a can of Red Man. He packed the tobacco into his lower lip.

A minute. Big Joe spat onto the floor, the tobacco and spittle staining the carpet between them. Two minutes. Five. The puddle of saliva and tobacco flakes refused to be absorbed into the high-traffic carpet, and so it grew into a miniature, grayish-brown ocean.

They heard the engine twenty seconds out. This one was definitely a sedan—smaller engine, lighter on the crushed stone. The Volvo, North guessed. She would have brought the Volvo. Headlights swept the building's front windows, and gravel shifted under tires. On the phone's display, the blue Volvo parked next to the truck. The headlights went out. The engine died. Freddie Eggenberg moved across the lot. She wore sneakers, jeans, and a black tee. No weapon that North could see, but it was hard to tell on the phone's small screen. She stopped, pulled out her own phone, and did something. As though on cue, from Kroyer Auto Body came frantic pounding, metal ringing out.

The sound sent North's pulse racing, and he barely suppressed a start. They'd planned on the auto body shop being empty at this hour. He tried to catch Shaw's eye; a furrow had dug itself between Shaw's brows.

Big Joe laughed. "You fucked up, didn't you?"

The CZ's grip felt slippery in North's hand.

The front door of the abandoned warehouse opened. More steps. Freddie stopped in the doorway.

"Come in," Shaw said. "We've got a lot to talk about."

Freddie's lips guppied for a moment, puckering and quivering and then releasing. Then she pulled red-gold hair over her shoulder and moved to stand next to Big Joe.

"I don't know her," Big Joe said. "I don't know why I'm here. I—"

"Be quiet," Freddie said quietly.

An ugly, patchwork flush covered Big Joe's face. He gave the bill of his hat a savage yank.

"You know why you're here," North said. "We know what you're doing. Freddie's part. Joe's part. The kids that pass through the two of you and never get seen again. We know you tried to do it to Malorie, only she was a fighter. She got away from you, and you couldn't find the body, couldn't cover up what had happened. We know you wash the money through the Big Muddy, which isn't a bad idea, and we know you can't wash it fast enough, so you've got the cash you can't wash in nice little bundles." He flashed a mean grin. "Just waiting for a problem like me to come along. So we're going to start by talking about what we're going to do with all that cash that's sitting around, ready for somebody to put it to good use."

"That's our money," Big Joe shouted. His amusement, his apparent self-possession, had evaporated, and he stabbed a finger at North. "That's ours, and if you think you're getting a red cent—"

"Stop talking," Freddie said.

"They've got my money! You saw the video, the two of them burning that stack of hundreds." He rounded on North and Shaw. "You bet your ass you're going to pay me back. I know how much is there, down to the last dollar, and before I put a bullet in your heads, you're going to pay me back—"

"Will you stop talking?" Freddie asked. "Just stop."

"I'm not going to stop, you dumb bitch. My inside guy, he says there's a shit storm coming. Raid me. Raid the Peach Grove. My place at the lake. Those motherfuckers know about all of it. And then I get that video, my money going up in flames, money I earned—"

"Shut up, shut up, shut up!" The last was a scream. Freddie pressed her hands to her face. "Let me think for one minute."

"You don't have a minute," Shaw said.

"You don't have five fucking seconds," North said.

"All right," Freddie dropped her hands. Her voice was wet and thick. "You got us here. You found the money. What else do you have? And what do you want?"

North grinned. Shaw did jazz hands.

Big Joe's jaw dropped.

Freddie's expression transformed from sick fear into ice.

"I'm going to explain something now—" North began.

Freddie loosed a wet laugh. She scrubbed her mouth, and her thin lips guppied. Then she said, "You don't have anything."

North met her gaze.

"You've got nothing."

"My inside guy—" Big Joe began.

"That was the point of this. Why would you bring us out here, otherwise? Why not turn it all over to the police?"

"The raid—" Big Joe tried.

"Pull your head out of your ass," Freddie snapped. "Jesus Christ, what was I thinking, going into business with you?"

"They're talking about this raid—"

"There is no raid!" Freddie's lips quivered and puckered, her whole body trembling. "It was a bluff. They don't know anything. They don't have anything."

"My money—"

"They burned a stack of hundreds, God damn it. They could have gotten them anywhere."

Big Joe's expression was childishly hurt when he turned to look at North and then Shaw.

"Technically," Shaw said, "only the top bill was a hundred. The rest were ones, which I thought was cheap, but North said that's the way spoiled rich boys who buy emerald-encrusted ball weights talk, and I said they weren't ball weights, they were nipple weights you could use on your balls, and he said that wasn't the point, and I said something about the point being that we could burn a few hundreds if it meant roping in scum like Dr. Egg, and—"

"But my money," Big Joe said. "I saw it!"

North shrugged. "You saw what you wanted to see. Christ, I bet it ate you up, didn't it? You wanted to drive out to your stash. You wanted to check on it. But you couldn't because those guys in the unmarked cars were waiting for you to make a move."

Freddie's smile was cold. "Were they even police?"

"Some of them."

For a moment, she looked genuinely amused. "All those hours I spent fretting. Oh well. Goodnight; you have nothing, and I don't think there's anything left to discuss."

When she took a step toward the door, North said, "You might want to drive around for a few hours. Give the guys who are processing your house and office time to finish. In fact, they're going to get to work here in a few minutes, and you might want to stay around to answer a few questions."

Freddie froze.

"See, the police were not happy with us," North said.

"Jadon said bad words," Shaw said. "Jadon almost never says bad words, except for that one time I wanted to talk about the weekend North and I spent in that bed and breakfast, when I was telling Jadon about how North liked to put me over the back of that armchair, and Jadon said, 'I cannot fucking do this' and had his hands over his ears and walked out of the room."

"You told him about that?"

"I thought it was inventive. And I want people to know that you're a creative lover, and that you're dedicated to your partner's pleasure. What you did with that rope around my ankles—"

"For the love of Christ," North said.

"—and when you borrowed that Boston rocker—"

"There is a raid," Big Joe shouted. "There is a raid! I knew it! I knew it! There is a raid!"

"Thank you, God, yes, let's talk about that," North said. "As I was trying to say, before fuckhead here interrupted me—"

"That's me," Shaw said. "I'm fuckhead."

"Just tell us what's going on!" Freddie screamed.

"You showing up here, that was what they needed to get the warrant. See, we had the picture of the kiddie porn you were making with Malorie, but we didn't have any evidence to connect you directly. So we sent you that video of us burning the money, and you showed up here. We didn't have to tell you the address. In our business, that's called guilty knowledge—something you wouldn't know unless you were involved in a specific crime. A couple of good citizens let the police know about this meeting tonight, and since we're not police or employed by police, this isn't entrapment. As soon as you showed up, they snapped some pictures, got a phone warrant, and had their team kick down your door. Well, not literally."

"Probably not literally," Shaw said.

"I guess we'll find out. By the time they finish with your house, your office, and the porno studio you've got set up here, they'll have plenty to put you away. Big Joe too, I bet. I imagine the Feds are about to squirt right now, gearing up to storm-trooper the shit out of the Big Muddy." North smirked. "Say, settle a bet I've got with myself: was Malorie really pregnant?"

The shock on Freddie's face was too real to be anything but genuine. She barely seemed to hear the question, but she nodded.

"Who cares?" Joe was panting. "Who the fuck cares if that bitch was pregnant?"

"Well, I think the circuit attorney will care when she decides which charges to file. Not that what you tell me makes any difference; they'll figure it out in the autopsy. But I was starting to wonder. Malorie lied to a lot of people. Nik was convinced she was pregnant, but he was also convinced she wasn't using anymore, that she had stopped tricking, all that. She made sure Jesse thought the baby was his, but I bet she told other guys the same thing. Lots of lies all around. But you know what everybody agreed on? The one thing I figured had to be true? Malorie was a fighter, and she fought for what she wanted. And that kind of girl? She doesn't just up and disappear. That was your biggest mistake."

Breathing harder, Joe sidled along the wall.

"Joe, take one more fucking step, and you're going to have some serious fucking trouble."

Joe stalled out, breathing hard. He seemed to have forgotten his cowboy revolver, and he was a sickly gray color, his eyes sliding to the open door.

"I'm leaving," Freddie said. "I'm going to call my lawyer."

"Here's the fun part," North said. "Things look bad for both of you right now. And justice, although implacable—"

"He read that in his power drill manual," Shaw said.

"—is slow, which is why various law enforcement agencies would be thrilled to have your cooperation. In exchange for testimony against co-conspirators, partners, petty thugs. If you could put the finger on who killed Malorie, for example, that would go a long way toward convincing them that a deal might be in order."

"Nice try," Freddie said.

"It really was a good speech, North," Shaw whispered. "Co-conspirators is, like, a million points on that Scrabble crib sheet you keep in your boot."

"For fuck's sake," North said, "I'm the one who graduated college. Me." To Big Joe and Freddie, he said, "I've got a college diploma on my wall. Do you know what he has?"

"Tasteful erotica," Shaw said.

"Four fucking Junior Policeman certificates he stole."

"I didn't steal them."

"You opened boxes of Cookie Crisp in the store until you found all of them. And you didn't pay for anything. That's stealing, Shaw."

"It was Kirby," Big Joe blurted, eyes rolling wildly. "Shane Kirby. He killed that girl. Freddie told him to pick her up. She said the girl wouldn't think anything of it. But she did. She smelled something wrong and made Kirby crash, and when she ran, he shot her in the back. It was Kirby. And her, the doc. They done it. I'll tell anybody who'll—"

Freddie drew the revolver from Big Joe's holster and pressed it to the side of his head. She grabbed the collar of his Big Muddy tee, twisting it until it cut into his thick neck. Then she yanked him back a step. Joe made a moaning noise. His knees looked loose, and the tension in Freddie's body suggested that she was partially holding him up.

"Shut up," she whispered, digging the muzzle into his head. "Stand up and walk. Stand up!"

Big Joe stumbled as she dragged him toward the door.

"Not a great choice of hostage," North said.

"Good enough," Freddie snapped. "Try to follow me, and I'll kill him."

"This is why I told you he was not a great choice," North said. "Why the fuck should I care if you kill him? He admitted to trafficking kids; he's the kind of shit, you throw your shoe away after you step in it. Kill him. And then I'll put two of these—" He tilted the CZ. "—in your chest."

Freddie stopped in the doorway. Color blotched her cheeks. She was panting, and her eyes crisscrossed the room. She seemed to reach some sort of decision; she released the Big Muddy tee and reached into her pocket to withdraw a phone. She tapped it once. Tapped it again. Then she angled it so that the screen was displayed above Big Joe's shoulder.

The night vision camera didn't provide a great image, but it was clear enough that North could identify Nik's face. It was hard to tell because of the green shading to everything, but his face looked bruised and swollen; his lip was definitely split. He was leaning into a metal barrier of some kind, pounding, and in that moment, North understood the series of booming noises that he could hear from Kroyer Auto Body.

"Get it?" Freddie asked.

Shaw bit his lip and nodded.

"You two think you're so smart. But you didn't know about that, did you? He was sniffing around the Big Muddy. Hitched a ride out there. Thought he was some super-secret spy." Freddie laughed, but it sounded dry and forced. "Kirby picked him up, and Joe asked me what I wanted to do with him. I said why let him go to waste. We could use him."

"I didn't have anything to do with that," Big Joe mumbled. "I didn't have nothing to do with the snuff. What she did to those kids, I didn't have nothing to do with it. I sold the videos, that's all."

North's stomach dropped. He thought of the pounding noises they had heard from the auto body shop the last time they had been here. He thought about the stage Freddie had built for her productions. He thought about the fact that she had medical training, that she knew how the body worked. He thought about kids who had gone missing, kids who hadn't been sent out to the Big Muddy, because Freddie did something much, much worse to them.

Freddie pocketed the phone, twisted Big Joe's collar tight again, and dragged him backward. "Tell your friends not to get in my way. Anybody tries to stop me, that place will go up in flames. I press one button on my phone, and whoosh, bye-bye to your little friend. Tell them."

"They heard you," North said.

Freddie grimaced, and it took North a moment to realize she was smiling. She gave a jerk, and together, she and Big Joe backed out of the room. They moved with awkward, shuffling steps down the hall. When North heard the front door open, he caught Shaw's gaze. Shaw nodded.

North sprinted down the hall toward the front of the building. Shaw tore off in the opposite direction.

The front door was still rattling shut on its pneumatic closer. North caught it with his hip, but he stopped when the Redwings touched gravel.

Freddie and Big Joe were halfway to the Volvo. "Stay right there," Freddie shouted, forcing Big Joe's head sideways with the cowboy revolver. "Don't do anything stupid."

Big Joe's head rolled. He was panting like a sick dog. Then he looked up at the flat roofline above North and shouted, "Kirby, shoot this bitch, shoot her, shoot her!

The revolver roared; the side of Big Joe's head blew open, splattering blood and bone and brain against the truck. Big Joe's body fell slowly, Freddie already rushing toward the Volvo. The high-pitched crack of a rifle rang out, and the Volvo lurched as though someone had shoved it. Freddie threw herself into the driver's seat. Another crack. The Volvo's rear window shattered. Red lights. White lights. Reverse. The Volvo backed out, carving an arc across the gravel, thumping over Big Joe's body. Another crack. Freddie was a silhouette against the headlights, and this time, North saw her body jerk. That's one for Kirby.

The Volvo lurched forward, but then it turned sharply, and it crashed into the concrete-block wall just below the sign for Kroyer Auto Body. North's ears were ringing from the gunfire, but he could still hear swearing from above him; Freddie had driven too close to the building for Kirby to take another shot, and now the sniper needed to change position.

Blue lights whirled to life up the hill, and a brown Impala came roaring down in a cloud of dust and gravel. Another shot cracked the night, and even from a distance, North could hear the sound of glass shattering. The Impala swerved, ran through ten yards of brush, and came to a shaky stop on side of the hill. North couldn't tell if Monzyk or Contalonis had been hit. He didn't care; he had bigger things to worry about.

A door slammed, and North turned in time to see Freddie staggering away from the Volvo. She rammed the door to Kroyer Auto Body with her shoulder and barreled inside. A shot rang out, and North lurched into motion after her.

By the time he got inside the ancient auto body shop, Freddie was already a third of the way through the building. Unlike the other half of the structure, which had been divided into offices and storage, the space that had once belonged to Kroyer Auto Body was one large room. North had an impression of the skeletal remains of garage equipment—a lift shrouded in tarps; a rolling tool chest; the smell of engine grease; the clink of metal as something small and shining went skittering across the concrete slab. A single string of bulbs provided weak illumination. It was enough for North to make out Shaw and Nik, both of them crouching behind a workbench as Freddie squeezed off another shot. It was enough for him to process, peripherally, the cages. Hog wire panels. Padlocks. A girl with stringy hair, curled up with her arms around her head.

"Stay down," North shouted, the Redwings pounding the concrete as he raced after her. "Stay the fuck down!"

Freddie turned and fired. North didn't have time to dodge. He didn't have time to react at all. He heard the clap of the shot and, under it, a ping like a kid playing Airsoft. Freddie turned forward again. She was still running, and with one hand, she was doing something with her phone.

"Stop," North yelled. "Stop right there!"

She kept running. A moment later, machinery grumbled to life: a rhythmic, juddering noise. A pump, maybe. And then the tang of kerosene. A click-click-click. Like a lighter trying to catch.

"Shaw, get out of here!"

"The kids," he called back, already crawling to the next cage.

"Get out!" But that was all North had breath for. His side was in stitches, and he couldn't get enough air. Too many alley smokes. Too much pizza. Too many days he'd enjoyed morning fucks instead of hitting the gym. Shaw was already at the next cage, using something—a screwdriver, North thought—to force open the padlock. Nik had moved in the opposite direction, heading toward a cage down the line.

Freddie turned and fired again. This time, North saw it: the bullet struck the floor ahead of him, throwing up sparks and chips of cement. Something stung his face. The sound of the pumps had changed, gotten deeper, as they pulled up the kerosene. The pungent smell was stronger, and ahead, the fuel was already pooling on the floor, spreading out from the pumps, which North couldn't locate on his quick, frustrated scan. Hidden by old racking, crumbling cardboard boxes, a stack of rusted scrap. Where the weak light from the bulbs touched it, the kerosene had an oily, pearlescent sheen.

Click-click-click.

"Stop," North shouted, but then he had to suck in air and fight the urge to stop, double over, and possibly puke.

Freddie hit the crash bar on the exit door and tumbled out into the night.

North counted. One-two-three-four—

At five he slammed into the crash bar. Then he caught the concrete-block wall, jerking himself to a halt.

Darkness. The specters of trees. Old, thin branches weaving a net. Freddie barely more than a glimmer of pale skin and gold hair, already being swallowed up by the night. North's heart pounded in his chest; his stomach flipped over as he tried to draw in enough air to satisfy his body. Part of him was screaming to run—she was getting away. But the part of himself that he'd trained to think even in moments like this, the part that wasn't operating on animal instinct, remembered Kirby.

From the front of the building came men's shouts and demands—North had seen previous performances, and he could tell from the voices that Monzyk and Contalonis were hunkered down, not willing to come out while an active shooter was still on the loose. Shaw was inside the building, and Nik was with him, while Freddie was getting away, which only left—

Jadon came around the side of the building in a long-legged stride that made North hate him all over again. Even in sneakers and jeans and a tee, he looked like he could have run a marathon without breaking a sweat. His pace slowed fractionally as he searched the darkness ahead. Then he took off toward the flicker of movement that marked Freddie's escape.

The rifle cracked.

Branches snapped and rustled.

North shouted, "Dumbass, get back here."

Jadon slowed, but he didn't stop.

The rifle cracked again.

The gleam of gold and white crumpled.

Jadon's pace faltered. He looked back over his shoulder. He was ten yards from North. Five feet from where the brush and trees started at the bottom of the hill.

"Motherfucker," North growled as he ran.

He caught Jadon in a flying tackle just as the next gunshot shattered the night. Something tugged at North's shoulder, and then he collided with Jadon. They hit the ground in a tangle and rolled into the waist-high scrub. North's back screamed at him, but adrenaline fenced it off for the moment. Another shot rang out. The weeds shivered at the bullet's passage.

North dragged himself up onto his knees. Ten yards and change to the flat roof. Kirby lay there, the rifle settled on the asphalt lip. He swung the barrel, tracking North.

North emptied the CZ's magazine. The pistol kicked. The smell of gunpowder filled his lungs, the taste scorching him with every breath.

And then it was over, the CZ's slide locked back, the hot brass rolling to a stop between his knees. Kirby slumped on the roof. Silence rang in North's ears. The rifle tumbled from Kirby's hands and hit the cement apron near the exit door.

"Holy shit," Jadon said; the words sounded muffled after the gunfire. "Holy fucking shit!"

A moment later, Shaw appeared in the doorway, Nik hovering behind him. Shaw glanced around and then met North's eyes. When North nodded, Shaw sprinted out of the auto body shop, heading straight for North. He slid on his knees at the end and hit North at what felt like thirty miles an hour. North grunted, arms tightening around Shaw, Shaw's face hot against his. Over Shaw's shoulder, North saw Nik hurrying kids out of the building. A moment later, there was a click, a rushing noise like a vast breath, and fire roared to life inside. The heat hammered at North; he told himself that was why he hugged Shaw tighter, why he needed to close his eyes.

"Oh my God," Shaw whispered, and then North felt the pain in his shoulder.

He pulled back long enough to consider the wound. Lots of blood, but when he mopped at it with the torn shirt, it looked like a graze—the bullet had barely caught him.

When he looked up, he saw it in Shaw's face. "No."

"Oh my God."

"No, Shaw. Do not fucking say it."

Jadon groaned.

"You jumped in front of a bullet for Jadon."

"That tattoo was the biggest fucking mistake of my entire fucking life," North said, pulling Shaw tighter against him. "I'm taking it off with a belt sander when we get home."

Chapter 38

FOR SHAW, THE end of that night was a slow spooling of the pain and terror they had gone through. By some miracle, he didn't dwell on Big Joe's final words, his comment about the snuff films. He knew what Joe had meant, what had happened to the kids who were too difficult or too risky to traffic. But the labyrinth in his mind didn't open, and he wondered numbly about that. It was like any wound, he decided. There was a gap. A cesura. The span of time when the nerves were still sending the message to the brain.

Monzyk and Contalonis didn't say much about it either, but their reactions suggested that they would be beginning a long and difficult search. The homicide detectives interviewed them at the hospital, where they'd all been taken, even though North was the only one who had been hurt. North had tried telling the paramedics he didn't need to go to the hospital—that he'd hurt himself worse on job sites—until Shaw started listing possible workman's comp complaints, and North's face had gotten red, and he'd let them put him in the ambulance. The most Shaw had been able to learn from the homicide detectives was that Nik and the other kids they'd rescued were being examined and seemed to be stable, although doubtless they were far from fine. Then, after an eternity, they were released—it was sometime Saturday morning, dawn rising like a white banner, when they hit the bed.

Shaw woke hours later to the sound of the Redwings being laced; when he opened his eyes, North said, "You don't have to come. I can handle this."

"No, I'm coming. I'm going to drive separately, though. I've got an aura cleansing with Master Hermes after."

He dressed quickly: vellies, technical pants, a new leather belt, a blue Oxford shirt. Suburban daddy meets college hipster. North retrieved the duffel Truck had left in the garage, and they took separate cars, the Mercedes and the GTO, to Ellisville. It was a suburb near the outer ring, one of those places constantly being voted Nicest Places to Live, and A Tree City, and where Shaw was pretty sure dreams went to die. The house was a mock Tudor, white stucco and half-timbering, a steep gable roof. Shaw parked the next street over and watched the back.

His phone buzzed.

"We might be here a while," North said.

"We won't," Shaw said. "He's sitting on the patio reading the paper." His squinted, trying to make out details, but all he could see was Ronnie's familiar outline. "I can't tell if he's armed, but it doesn't look like it."

North's breathing deepened. Quickened. "Here we go."

Shaw disconnected and got out of the car.

It was mid-afternoon on a Saturday in September. It was a quiet street in a quiet suburb. Kids were safely hooked up to their Xboxes. Moms and dads were safely hooked up to their phones. Shaw jogged between the houses, cutting straight back toward the house where Ronnie was reading the paper. He was halfway there when Ronnie looked up. The squat little man's body stiffened, the newspaper fluttering in his hands like a dying bird. Then he stood and turned for the house.

North came around the corner. He'd surrendered the CZ to the police for the duration of the investigation, but he didn't need it. He carried the duffel over one shoulder, and now he slid a hand inside, and the blued-steel barrel of the Mossberg poked out of one end of the bag. Shaw was close enough to hear North say, "Quiet."

Ronnie's mouth hung open for a moment before he nodded.

As Shaw joined them, North motioned with the partially hidden shotgun. "Hands up."

Ronnie lifted his hands. He looked so much older than the first time Shaw had seen him. He wore flip-flops, cargo shorts, and a Hawaiian shirt—red and blue, like Hawaiian punch. But the fringe over his ears was untrimmed, and his bowling-ball belly sagged against the cotton, and fresh lines scored the corners of his eyes and mouth. Being evil as shit apparently took its toll.

"Check him."

Shaw did. He found only a phone, an older model with press buttons and a tiny display. Shaw removed the SIM card and the battery; he'd dispose of it later.

"Inside."

Ronnie first. Then North. Then Shaw.

"Downstairs," North said.

The treads were bare, the basement unfinished, the light yellow and fuzzy from incandescent bulbs. It smelled like exposed concrete and damp and recirculated air. Ronnie's flip-flops made slapping noises as North guided him toward a support column. Upstairs, something hissed, and then came the sound of running water.

"You boys caught me on laundry day," Ronnie said.

"Stop talking."

"North, my lad—"

GREGORY ASHE

North kicked him in the back of the knee. Ronnie's leg buckled, and he stumbled. Then he fell. He landed on hands and knees and let out a noise— part surprise, part pain.

"Crawl," North said. "Talk again, and I'll make you do it on your belly."

Body stiff, Ronnie seemed to wind tighter and tighter. Then he inched forward toward the column.

When he reached it, North retrieved a pair of cuffs from the bag. He hooked them by the chain to prevent leaving usable prints, and he tossed them to Ronnie. "One hand. The other end goes around the column."

Click. Click.

Ronnie raised up on his knees, rattled the cuffs, and sat on the floor. Then he looked up. Red mottled his cheeks. A spit bubble at the corner of his mouth inflated, shrank, and then swelled to popping. "You have fucked yourself, my boy. You have really done it this time. You've—"

"Ronnie," North said. His quiet voice had the same sheen as the blued steel. "Shut the fuck up."

Ronnie swallowed. The spit bubble was back.

After lowering the duffel to the cement, North drew out a pair of disposable gloves. He pulled them on, snapping them at the wrist. Then he drew out the pistol. It looked cheap, which it was, and hard used, which it probably had been. North hadn't said the words, not all the way, but Shaw understood. He had asked Truck to get it for him. And Truck had known where to get it.

In one quick movement, North pressed the gun into Ronnie's free hand and wrapped Ronnie's fingers tight against it. Ronnie thrashed, trying to free himself, and North let him break away. He got to his feet, moved away from Ronnie until he was out of reach, and set the pistol on the ground.

"What are you doing?" Ronnie asked. "You don't have any idea the kind of trouble you're asking for. I've been patient with you, North McKinney. I've been tolerant of your—"

"You went after Shaw," North said in that same cold voice. "You went after my dad. I warned you, Ronnie."

Ronnie yanked on the cuffs. "What is this? What do you think you're doing? What is this, what is this, what—"

"This is a first-degree murder charge. And it's assault on a law enforcement officer, which is another Class A felony. This is you going away for life. No parole. No good behavior. Nothing but concrete and steel for the rest of your life. Once I make the call, the police will be here in five minutes."

"You can't prove any of that. I didn't do any of that!"

"The cop that got killed a few weeks ago? That's the gun. The ballistics will match. And your prints are on it now."

"I'll have an alibi." Ronnie yanked on the cuffs again. Steel jingled against the support column. "This won't work."

"You'd better hope it does," North said. "If it doesn't, your buddy Vinnikov is going to put you underground. Goodbye, Uncle Ronnie."

He stood, jerked his head at Shaw, and shouldered the duffel. When they got outside, the air smelled like autumn leaves and standing water. The bird bath, Shaw realized. And a birding book on the patio table. He must like birds. Shaw squeezed North's hand.

"I'm ok," North said.

Shaw squeezed harder.

"I'm ok," North said again, his voice thick. "That fucker deserves so much worse." He drew in a breath. "I'm really ok."

"Ok," Shaw said.

"You don't want to process this? You don't want to talk it into the ground? You don't want me to tell you all my feelings, how shitty this is, how shitty I am for doing it, the fact that I'm a fucking coward?"

Shaw stretched up on tiptoes and kissed his cheek. "You're North Cassidy McKinney."

North smiled and wiped his eyes. "Something like that."

"Let's go home."

North headed toward the front of the house. Shaw walked between houses to the next street. He got in the Mercedes. He went around the block. He made sure the GTO had left. And then he parked again and went inside.

Downstairs, Ronnie was rattling the cuffs, letting out savage strings of swears as he jerked on the chain. He must have heard Shaw's steps because he glanced up. "What? Did North forget something?"

"Hi, Ronnie," Shaw said with a smile.

"What the fuck do you want?"

Shaw drew out a pair of disposable gloves. As he pulled them on, he asked, "Do you know what shadow work is?"

"What?"

"I didn't think so. See, I'm new to shadow work myself. It's probably because I'm not a natural-born witch. North is, in case you're wondering, but he can only identify tool belts by brand. Something like that. I forgot what he said."

"Do you know what I'm going to do to you when I get out of here? The Laguerre kid, what he did to you? That's going to be cheesecake compared to what I'm going to do when I get my hands on you. You tell North that. Tell him I'm going to make him watch."

Shaw undid the new leather belt from around his waist. He wiped it down with the tail of the blue Oxford. He laid it out on the floor, and it made him think of a dead snake.

"Shadow work," he said, "is dealing with aspects of yourself that you've repressed. You know those parts of yourself that you ignore? Or that you try to hide? Or that you're ashamed of? That's your shadow. And shadow work means recognizing those parts, acknowledging them, and coming to terms with them. It's a process of becoming self-aware—and, of course, as a result, it's incredibly empowering."

"I knew you were nuts. Nutso. I knew it."

"Yes," Shaw said. He took a second set of cuffs out of his pocket. "North would agree, I think. But for some reason, he's willing to put up with me, and, of course, I love him because he's the best man in the entire world, even if he does push all his boot socks to the bottom of the hamper, and sometimes it builds up down there like swamp gas. Let's see your hand."

"Fuck off."

Ronnie tried to resist, but he was already halfway restrained, and it only took Shaw a moment to secure his other hand to the support column.

"See," Shaw said, "I don't think you've ever done shadow work, Ronnie. I think you keep all those parts hidden and locked away. Maybe you think you've buried them. But they don't stay buried. Me, on the other hand? I've been doing shadow work. And you know what I've figured out?"

"You're insane. You're a fucking lunatic."

"Exactly." Shaw squatted so that he was eye to eye with Ronnie. After a moment, Ronnie looked away. "We've got a problem, Ronnie: you're much, much more dangerous than North is willing to believe, aren't you?"

Ronnie bared his teeth in what was probably supposed to be a smile.

Upstairs, the washing machine sang out a cheery tune. Time to switch loads.

"You wiggled out from under those industrial espionage charges. And you came after us through Tucker. And you got to North's dad in prison. And even though North likes to pretend he's tough, he's actually surprisingly gentle. He thinks he can put you away on this murder charge without having to hurt anyone. He's trying to self-actualize right now, and I think part of that is coming to terms with how gentle he is." Shaw grinned. "I'm rambling."

"If you let me out, and if you do exactly what I tell you, I might not kill you. North will still need to be taught a lesson, of course, but—"

"No, Ronnie. You're going to try to kill us. You've made that perfectly clear." Shaw extracted a plastic bag from his pocket. He unfolded it as he spoke. "I wasn't there for North when Tucker was hurting him. I didn't know, but that's no excuse. I should have known. I should have helped him. North needs someone who is going to take care of him. He's fundamentally incapable of taking care of himself; you should see how much dairy he eats. But I'm here now, Ronnie. And I'm not going to let you hurt him."

"What do you think you're doing? Stop that. Stop!"

He tried to jerk away, but Shaw pulled the plastic bag down over his head. Then the belt. He drew it tight. Ronnie shouted. Then he screamed. He jerked and thrashed. His heels drummed on the concrete. After a while, he stopped. Shaw counted to sixty. He counted it again, five more times. He released the belt. He unlocked both sets of cuffs and pocketed them. He examined Ronnie's wrists—there might be minor bruising, but if he were lucky, there would be nothing. He unbuttoned the top of Ronnie's cargo shorts and tucked Ronnie's flaccid hand behind the waistband.

Then he left.

Chapter 39

THE BANNER SAID, HAPPY BIRTHDAY, CASSIDY! Shaw had already hidden all of the ladders.

"That's ok," North said as he headed for the garage. "That's perfectly fucking fine. I don't need a ladder; I'll pull it down with a rake."

Shaw sprinted ahead and framed himself in the doorway. "I gave away all the rakes. To a charity. Um. For homeless people."

"What do homeless people need with rakes?"

"They use them to clean up Forest Park."

"Move, Shaw."

"No rakes! The rakes are all gone."

North stopped. He folded his arms. His eyes narrowed. "Breezi has a blowtorch."

"Breezi is under strict orders not to lend you any tools."

If possible, North's eyes narrowed even more. "Fine."

North turned and headed back toward the house. It was a beautiful Monday evening—the smell of the coals and the brats, the old grass clippings baking in the heat of an Indian summer. Fat sizzled against the inside of the kettle. On the speakers Shaw had brought outside, somebody was singing about speeding through the friend zone; North had already complained twice that it was giving him douche chills.

"No," Shaw shouted after him. "What are you doing?"

"Simple," North said without looking back. "I have a gun. I'll shoot it down."

Shaw caught him at the door, and wrestling turned into kissing, which turned into wincing when Shaw pulled on North's shirt.

"I'm sorry, I'm sorry, I'm sorry."

"It's fine," North said. "It's a bitch of a place to get a tattoo, though, and I'm going to repeat again that I would have waited if I'd known—"

"Hello?" Jadon had stopped at the gate. He was carrying a six-pack of Schlafly's summer ale in each hand. Shaw was careful not to look for too long at how tightly his tee fit because sometimes North had the silliest ideas about things.

"Just go over and squeeze his tits," North said, but he didn't release Shaw's waist. "Then you'll know if they're real."

"Oh, they're real," Shaw said. "One time, when Jadon and I were first dating, I found out he likes it when I do this thing that's half biting and half—"

"Never mind," Jadon said, reversing course, "I'm going home."

At the exact same moment, North said, "If you want to chew on his tits so bad, why don't you go home with him?"

"God, no," Jadon said.

"Well, if you think that would be best," Shaw said. "I've been wanting to talk to you about sexual tourism, which is when partners remain emotionally committed, but—"

"I wanted to date him," Jadon said to the empty backyard. "And then, by some miracle, I got out, and I keep coming back."

"No sexual cruises," North said, grabbing Shaw's sleeveless shirt—which had been totally basic until Shaw had covered it in pink rosette sequins—and giving him a shake. "No sexual walkabouts. No sexual moon landings. Jay, either ice that beer or get the fuck out of here."

Jadon carried the six-packs to the galvanized tubs filled with ice. "Other people have friends who are actually nice to them."

"Other people don't have the personality of shit leaking out of a dog's anus. What did I say about icing that fucking beer?"

North left Shaw then, heading straight for the tub to harass Jadon some more, which turned into both of them holding beers and laughing, with lots of looks at Shaw that Shaw found vaguely insulting.

Shaw decided the best punishment would be to deprive them of his company, so he checked the brats, moved them to the warming pan, and laid fresh ones over the coals.

North and Jadon were talking now, Jadon animated, North listening and shaking his head and then launching into a counteroffensive. They didn't seem to notice their deprivation.

"I'm depriving you of my company," Shaw shouted to them.

North waved a hand, his attention still fixed on Jadon. Jadon didn't even seem to have heard.

"North."

The song had changed. Fever dream. Quiet night. A bad, bad boy.

"North, I'm depriving you!"

North glanced back, scowling, and snapped, "Can you deprive me a little more fucking quietly?"

Shaw had an answer to that—it involved pouring North's craft buttermilk down the disposal while North watched—but Pari and Truck arrived, with Pari immediately asking if this was a work function and, if so, where she should clock in. Then the rest of the guests began trickling in.

Breezi and Nita came next. "She's been doing calculations," Nita warned Shaw as they passed him, "something about engine displacement, so get ready for North's head to explode."

Then Zion came, and he hung around near the beer and looked at Jadon approximately every fifteen seconds. Jadon's attention stayed fixed on North, but his posture got better, and he was holding a beer in a way that made his biceps look huge (which, to be fair, they were), and he touched his hair and laughed a lot more, which seemed to confuse North.

Shaw's parents came, and they stopped to chat with him at the gate.

"I can't tell you how many phone calls I'm getting," his father said. "There's lots of interest in funding a new shelter and improved anti-trafficking programs. Your mother has been doing all sorts of research."

She scoffed in a pleased fashion and took Shaw's hands. "You did something wonderful, dear, helping those children. We're so proud of you."

Shaw nodded. But he ran up the tally—Nik, all those other kids, the dead bodies left on the banks of the Meramec—and he had to focus on a spot in the background, behind his parents. His smile felt like four-color process.

"Wilson," North said as he approached, using what Shaw had come to think of as his man-to-man voice. "Phoebe. Thanks for coming."

"Happy birthday, North," Wilson said, shaking his hand. "And congratulations. You and Shaw did an amazing thing."

"Many happy returns," Phoebe said. She produced a card from her purse. "I hope you don't mind, but Shaw said you'd prefer to have your gift in the garage."

"You didn't have to—" North cut himself off. "Thank you. That was very kind of you."

"You don't even know what it is," Shaw said. "It's one of the Swedish saunas I wanted to buy at Costco, only they made it out of old bourbon barrels, and it's infused with the angry wraiths of all the bourbon makers who died in the Great Bourbon Fire of 2014."

North looked at Wilson, who was lighting a joint, and Phoebe, who was smiling at Shaw the way she had after he'd gotten first place at the science fair in fourth grade.

"Come on," Shaw said, taking North's hand.

"Do they really not notice stuff like that?" North whispered as they moved toward the garage. "It just rolls right off them?"

As they moved toward the garage, Shaw smiled the smile he knew would make North crazy.

The short version—which was also the for-TV-and-small-children version, with the pornographic moans of amazement and delight tastefully edited out—was that North loved the rolling tool chest that Shaw's parents had bought him. Breezi wandered in, and she and North seemed to take an unreal amount of pleasure in showing each other the drawers. Open, close. Open again. Look at this one. They were all drawers, Shaw wanted to say. They all looked exactly the same.

"They don't look exactly the same," Breezi said, hands on her hips, which was Shaw's first sign that he might have accidentally expressed his opinion out loud.

"This one has dividers," North snapped. "It's a six-inch." He yanked open the next, slightly larger drawer. "Does that look like a six-inch?"

"It has dividers too," Shaw said.

North stared at him, his expression flickering between outrage and disbelief.

"Don't listen to him," Breezi said, rubbing North's shoulder.

"Sometimes," North said, "it's like he's trying to be mean."

The cooing and ooing might have gone on for days, except a horn blared at the front of the house. North checked his phone, swore, thanked Shaw's parents again, and jogged toward the gate. Shaw followed.

North's dad had hitched a ride with a neighbor, who looked like a slightly stockier version of David McKinney, albeit with jet-black hair that was obviously dyed. North got the wheelchair out of the back, set it up—Shaw's efforts to help with setting up the chair earned him a few "I know, I know," and one "I said I know!" at which point he decided to let North handle things— and helped his dad into the chair. The neighbor drove away, and North wheeled his dad toward the gate. The ride over the grass looked bumpy, but it smoothed out when they reached the backyard.

When North got his dad set up, equidistant between the beer and the grill, Shaw waited for it: the carping, the criticisms, the corrections. But David McKinney only sat there, watchful, examining the people who must have been strangers to him. He looked waxy, blue smudges under his eyes, and in spite of the warm September evening he wore jeans and a Mizzou sweatshirt. When North went for a beer, Shaw grabbed his wrist and mouthed, *Puppy*.

Gratitude cascaded down North's face, and he trotted across the yard to liberate the puppy from Pari's embrace. The puppy squirmed and wriggled so enthusiastically, trying to lick North's ear, that Shaw suspected the poor thing had been half smothered.

With a beer and the little dog, North's dad looked slightly more relaxed— one knobby hand stroked the ruffled fur, and he laughed to himself and muttered soft reprimands when the puppy tried to chew on the cannula's tubing.

"Uh, North," Truck called. "I think I did something to the grill."

"Jesus," North muttered. He cocked his head at his dad, catching Shaw's eye, and Shaw nodded. "Be right back."

The signs were propitious. The gods inclined their favor. The time was now or never.

"Hi, Mr. McKinney," Shaw said, stretching out a hand. "I know it's been a while."

David McKinney's eyes came up. He stared at Shaw. He took in the rosette sequins on the sleeveless shirt, the rumpled white linen shorts, the woven sandals. One hand remained on the puppy. The other lay in his lap.

Heat started in Shaw's chest, ran up his neck, and filled his face. He looked up. His parents were watching from across the yard, and that was even worse, so he returned his gaze to David McKinney.

"I'm—"

"I know who you are." David McKinney's eyes jittered up to Shaw's and then slid away.

The kettle grill boomed—struck by the tongs or the turner, Shaw guessed—and Truck laughed loudly. Nita was saying something about work, but the words buzzed and turned to dust before Shaw could process them. David McKinney was coiling some of the puppy's fur around his finger, and the collar jangled, sun flashing off the bronze tag.

"Mr. McKinney?" Shaw glanced up at the sound of his father's voice. Wilson Aldrich stood in front of the wheelchair, introducing himself while Shaw stared. North's dad was staring too, his expression so closed that it was impossible to tell what he was thinking. "It's a pleasure to meet you," Shaw's father finished.

David McKinney nodded.

"I wanted to tell you that North and I—" Shaw began.

"I was hoping I could have a minute of your time," Shaw's dad said over him. "North told me that you're a union man. Pipefitter's."

Another nod, but this time, with sharpened interest.

"I'm having a hell of a time with the carpenters," Wilson Aldrich said, casting around for a seat. Shaw grabbed one of the folding chairs and brought it over. His dad sat, adjusted the seat, and continued, "We invested in a construction company, and the jackasses saw it as an opportunity to renegotiate. I tried to let middle management handle it, but they botched the whole thing. They tell me we've got sites where nothing has happened for weeks."

With what seemed like grudging agreement, North's dad said, "The carpenters always try to grab with both hands." Then, as though the question were being dragged out of him, he asked, "What's this about construction? I thought you did medicine or science or something."

"We're a private equity firm. We invest diversely." Wilson frowned and checked his phone. "They've got a guy named Joe Ackerman handling things on their end."

"Who?"

"Ackerman. Joe Ackerman. He's the one giving us all the grief."

"He's nobody." David McKinney coughed, a dry, rasping noise, and leaned over the arm of the chair to spit. When he sat up again, he said, "You talk to Cy Kosselka."

"I don't know that name."

"He's the one you talk to. Cy ran the local for twenty years. He does plants now, putters around on his porch, but the guys still listen to him. You talk to him, and then see what this Ackerman kid says."

"Interesting," Shaw's father said. "What's your view of their situation long term?"

It was a softball question, and David McKinney went for it, launching into a spiel on union politics and the disappearance of the middle class. He was still talking, Shaw's dad nodding and asking the occasional follow-up, when North came back with a smear of ash along one cheekbone.

"Don't ask," North muttered. "Truck is driving me out of my mind, and Belia won't quit calling for a comment about Ronnie's death, even though the police say it was auto-erotic asphyxiation, and if it wasn't an accident, there's no way I'm telling her I think Vinnikov—" He stopped, and in a strange voice he asked, "What's going on?"

"I have no idea," Shaw whispered.

"Back away," North suggested, "and don't make eye contact."

They were almost out of earshot when Shaw's father asked a question that Shaw couldn't hear, and David McKinney said, "I wouldn't say no." A silence passed, contorted with an emotion Shaw couldn't trace, and North's dad added, "I guess they're all right for each other, aren't they? North can't get enough of your kid. You did something right there."

Shaw looked at North. North's lips were parted, and he looked like he'd taken a solid right hook to the jaw.

"Oh my God," Shaw whispered.

"No," North said, the word sounding automatic.

"Oh my God."

"No." A little stronger this time. "Whatever you're thinking, no. Don't go offer to braid his toe hair or shave his armpits or stitch decorative feathers around the crotch of his jeans."

"Your dad likes me."

"Nobody likes you," North said, pulling Shaw into a hug so tight that Shaw thought he felt a rib crack. His face felt hot against Shaw's cheek, and his eyes were puffy when he drew back, his voice thick as he said, "We all just put up with you. Now leave them alone before you ruin everything."

In retrospect, Shaw should have seen it coming. Jadon and Zion and Truck had been squirrelly for fifteen minutes, the three of them huddled together like overgrown kids, giggling and whispering and throwing lots of looks at North and Shaw—at North in particular. When it happened, it happened fast.

Jadon sprinted toward North and Shaw, while Zion and Truck whipped out—seemingly from nowhere—matching water guns. Jadon was laughing and shouting, "No, no, no," and Truck was laughing like a maniac, and a huge grin split Zion's face.

"What the—" North began.

It was all he had time for. Then Jadon reached him. Jadon spun, the way the players sometimes did on the football games North coerced Shaw into watching with him, pulling North in front of him as a human shield. The water hit North, and to judge from the sound and the spray, these were some serious, high-pressure models.

"Motherfuckers," North roared, batting at the water, trying to shield his face. "You are all dead, you sons of bitches!" But Jadon was still holding him as a shield, and North was so busy trying not to get blasted in the face that he couldn't break free.

When the jets of water finally died, Jadon wrapped North in a hug and kissed him—a huge smacker—on the cheek. "My hero," Jadon said, in dreamy, starlet tones.

Zion laughed so hard he had to sit down.

Truck grinned and was visibly sporting a chubby.

Pari, Nita, and Breezi made identical noises of infinite disgust.

Shaw's dad was trying not to grin.

North's dad wore the beginning of what looked suspiciously like a smile before he turned his attention down to the puppy.

Shaw's mother was staring at Truck, and Shaw knew she had found her latest muse.

North, finally, elbowed Jadon in the gut and got free. He rounded on Jadon first, stabbing a finger. "You think that's funny, motherfucker? Fine. Next time, you can catch your own fucking bullet!" Then, turning on Truck and Zion, who was still rolling on the ground laughing, he said, "Yuk, yuk, yuk, you fucking imbeciles. Those are fucking Soakzookas. Did you fucking think about that? Those fuckers can put out a fucking eye!"

"He's always grumpy when he gets wet," Shaw said, taking North's arm. "Don't pay any attention."

North pretended to try to yank his arm free. "I do not get grumpy when I get wet."

"He jumps over puddles," Shaw told everyone, which made Nita burst out laughing before she clapped a hand over her mouth. "It's dainty."

Jadon had what Shaw thought was the biggest grin he had ever seen on his face.

"Payback, motherfuckers." North turned in a circle. His tee clung to him, exposing the hard, sculpted ridges of his body. His hair lay flat and dark on his head. "Pay. Back."

"He fluffs right up when you dry him," Shaw told everyone as he towed North toward the house. "You'll see."

North grumbled all the way into the bedroom. "They think that's funny? I'm going to show them what's funny. How funny do they think it's going to be when I pull their spark plugs?"

"Arms up," Shaw said, turning him out of the tee. "The tattoo looks ok. Jesus, they really soaked you, didn't they?"

"It's called a Soakzooka, Shaw. It's not called a lady-parts spritzer."

"I have one of those if you ever need it," Shaw said as he knelt to work on North's boots. Then the jeans. Then the gray trunks. By the time he'd finished, North was more than halfway hard. "You're supposed to wait until I fluff you."

North grunted. In a rusty voice, he said, "What if I say not right now?"

Shaw raised both eyebrows.

"What if I say I want to be alone right now?" North asked.

It was a joke, but it was also a test, and Shaw had to think for a moment. When he spoke, he kept his face and voice as neutral as he could. "If you want alone time, I think technically you have to get married and then put porny posters in your garage. Someone told me that once."

North smirked. "Not worth it. Do you know how much a wedding costs these days? Why buy the cow when the milk is free? If I want time by myself, I'll just make you go play with your dolls in your oxygen tent in the basement."

"They're not dolls. They're Fashionista Fillies." Shaw licked the tip of North's dick. "And they're collectibles."

North's voice was even rougher as he asked, "What do you think you're doing?"

"It's like the old commercials said: wetter is better."

With a fresh grin, North grabbed his hair and pulled him forward to use his mouth.

They went slow at first. Then faster, until Shaw had to back off, choking and wiping spit from his chin. North's eyes were blue-black, the pupils dilated, a flush glowing on his cheekbones.

"God, you're beautiful," North whispered. "Get on the bed."

"We've got a party to get back to."

"Fuck the party. Get on the bed."

"It's your party. It's your birthday party."

"Happy birthday to me. On the bed, baby. Now."

Shaw stripped—too slowly, apparently, because North started yanking on the sleeveless shirt, and rosette sequins went everywhere—and then he was on the bed, and North was already lubed and pressing into him. Shaw bit his fist through the first stinging moments, until North was seated, and they were both still. He put a hand on North's chest, fingers digging into the thick blond fur, tracing warm skin over muscle, following the rhythm of North's racing heart. He nodded, and North began to move.

Shaw lost it first, coming with a pillow over his face to muffle the sharp, breathy noises he couldn't hold back. North lasted longer, the intensity of sensation escalating until Shaw's nerves felt raw and electric, and then North gripped his shoulders and whispered, "I love you," as he drilled into him with short, hard thrusts, his face crumpling under the weight of his orgasm.

They lay together, sweat-slick, shining in the light that rose and fell like waves as the curtains stirred in the breeze. North's breathing was vast and deep, his body a furnace. Shaw closed his eyes. At fourteen, he had stood on the edge of the Grand Canyon, feeling the fall—the possibility of it—in his gut, the sun hammering the side of his face, painting a line of heat down his side, the smell of sweat and the desert air licking it up. For a few moments, he tumbled, the long drop. When he woke, he tried to sit up, only to find North's arm heavy across his chest. The last few days came back to him, everything he had processed in bits and pieces falling on him at once, and he started to cry.

"Are you ok?" North asked in a sandy-sleep voice. "What happened?"

"Yes. Yeah. I'm fine."

North roused, propping himself on an elbow. His hand stroked Shaw's chest and belly, and he kissed the hollow of Shaw's shoulder.

Shaw closed his eyes. He wiped his cheeks. He had a baseball in his throat.

North touched that spot of hair, the one that he always touched, although it didn't look different from any other part of Shaw's head as far as he could tell.

"Why did he run away?" Shaw asked. It was the question he couldn't wrap his mind around—those hours on the phone with the police and child services, thinking at first it had been a mistake, and then confusion turning into hurt.

With a sigh, North strummed Shaw's abs. "Nik is dealing with a lot, Shaw."

"We were going to help him. We saved him, and not just by getting him out of that cage. We were going to let him stay here a while. We were going to investigate his uncle and figure out what happened with his parents' money. And instead he ran away again."

North drew up the sheet. His hand flattened it against Shaw's stomach, a warm weight.

"I just don't understand why," Shaw said.

"We don't know why," North said. "But he's a kid. And he's been through a lot. And to be honest, he was probably embarrassed because he tried so hard to impress you and ended up getting his ass handed to him. And he's been using, maybe for a while, and he's scared you'll make him stop."

"I didn't care about that. It wasn't his fault. He didn't know what he was getting himself into, and all I wanted was for him to be safe and—" Shaw drew in a shuddering breath. "Never mind. I'm sorry. I wasn't going to talk about this today. I wasn't going to ruin your birthday."

"You didn't ruin my birthday." North's mouth was like that desert sun on Shaw's shoulder again. "You got me the perfect birthday present."

Shaw rolled to face him. "I was going to wait until tonight. Now everybody's out there wondering what we're doing—"

"I don't think they're wondering," North murmured.

"—and you got your present way too early."

"I wasn't talking about the sex. I can have sex with you whenever I want. I was talking about the tool chest."

Shaw sat up a little. "Excuse me?"

"The tool chest. It's perfect. It's better than the one Breezi has."

"I gave you my heart and my soul and my body."

North blinked. "The fuck? We fuck all the time, Shaw. We fuck like rabbits."

"You are unbelievable."

"Come on."

"No, you're completely unbelievable. I'm done with you."

Shaw tried to sit up, but North snared him and pulled him tight, kissing his cheek and jaw and neck until Shaw relented. Then they lay together, breathed together, the curtain dancing, the last light of day pulling out like the tide.

"—incredibly rude to disappear in the middle of their own party," Pari was saying as she passed under their window.

"They didn't disappear," Truck said, "they were playing hide-the-sausage."

"No," North shouted, "we weren't."

If they heard, they gave no indication.

Zion said, "Have you ever heard the two of them? It's not hide-the-sausage."

"Please stop," Jadon said.

"When North goes at it, it's more like slam-the-sausage."

"God," Jadon said, voice growing distant, "I'm going to have nightmares."

"Twelve-year-old virgins have more finesse," Zion said.

"What the actual fuck?" North bellowed.

Jadon might have laughed, but by then, they were far enough from the window that it was hard to tell.

More silence, the rustle of the cotton sheet, the scratch of North's hairy legs against Shaw's.

In the purple twilight, Shaw touched North's jaw. "I love you."

"I love you too."

"Happy birthday."

North made a contented noise as he tweaked Shaw's nipple.

"What are we going to do?" Shaw asked.

"I've got a few ideas. They start with closing the window."

"North," Shaw said, wrapping a hand around his wrist.

With a huff of a laugh, North kissed his knuckles. "We're going to find Nik and make sure he's ok. We're going to solve crimes that Jadon fucking Reck is too incompetent to handle. We're going to be crazy in love. What did you think we were going to do?"

Shaw crawled across the bed. He slid the window closed, and when North raised his eyebrows, Shaw smirked. As he dropped down next to North, he said, "I don't know." He kissed North's palm and pressed it to his cheek. "But we'll figure it out together."

RELATIVE JUSTICE

Keep reading for a sneak preview of *Relative Justice*, book one of Hazard and Somerset: Arrows in the Hand.

CHAPTER ONE

OCTOBER 31
THURSDAY
11:26 PM

THEIR FLIGHT OUT of St. Thomas was delayed, and they had to run through Atlanta's Hartsfield-Jackson, Terminal I to Terminal S, to make their connection.

Vacations were all right, Hazard thought. Honeymoons were pretty great. Travel, though, was a bitch, especially when all you wanted was to get home.

"Noah and Rebeca called," Somers panted as they ran, phone in one hand.

"What'd they say?"

Holding the phone to his ear, Somers made a face. He didn't seem to see the custodian with the trash cart ahead of them, so Hazard snagged his elbow, detouring both of them toward a bakery. The aroma of cinnamon pretzels wafted toward them. Then the unmistakable fragrance of cheese dip. Hazard's stomach rumbled.

"Something kind of weird is going on," Somers said, parroting the words from the voicemail. "Could you give us a call back when you have a chance?"

"That's all?" Hazard asked.

"That's all."

They reached the gate, where a heavyset young guy had six kids on a leash and was taking advantage of the family boarding.

"What if it's about Evie?" Somers said.

"Evie's with Cora."

"I know, but what if it's about her?"

"Call them before we take off," Hazard said.

"It's almost midnight there."

"Then don't call them."

"But what if it's about Evie?"

"John, if it were about Evie, they would have left a detailed message and said it was an emergency. It's something weird. That's it. That's all. Maybe somebody broke a window. Maybe there's a package on the porch."

"Yeah," Somers said, smiling, the line of his shoulders softening. "Ok."

Hazard slept on the flight to St. Louis, and he was groggy as they waited for their bags and rode the shuttle back to the parking garage. Their driver was the same ancient man Hazard had tried to help with his whiteboard diagram when they had flown out; he noticed the old man hadn't taken any of his advice. Tonight, he was wearing a t-shirt that said MY OTHER CAR IS A GO-KART. After they'd gone up and down every aisle on three floors at an average speed of five miles an hour, Hazard would have been happy to trade for a go-kart.

Somers kept checking his phone.

"Did they call again?" Hazard asked.

"No."

"Did they send you a message?"

"No."

Hazard studied his husband.

"What?" Somers asked.

"Normally I'm the one who worries."

Somers's grin flickered in and out. "I guess I'm just tired."

"No," Hazard said slowly. "That's not it."

"Ok, I don't know. I just feel weird."

"Is it your tummy?"

Somers put his face in his hands.

"Are you gassy?" Hazard asked.

"I think it's actually worse," Somers groaned, "that you're a hundred-percent serious."

"Of course I'm serious. The digestive system is one of the major invisible factors affecting our overall health. And many people experience some sort of irregularity after traveling outside the country. Do you need to—"

Somers put a hand over his mouth.

Before their flight had gotten delayed, they had planned on driving straight back to Wahredua; when Hazard asked if Somers wanted to get a hotel, he shook his head, so they hit I-70 and went west. The highways were deserted, and they made good time. A couple hours later, they were pulling into their neighborhood. The Arts-and-Crafts homes were dark, and the streets were quiet. A possum shot out in front of the Mustang, and Somers tapped the brakes, and then it disappeared beyond the headlights.

When the house came into view, Somers let out a breath.

"It didn't burn down," Hazard said.

Somers laughed, but it wasn't a real laugh.

The garage door rattled up, and yellow light made an apron on the driveway. As Somers turned in, the headlights bounced across the porch, and Hazard saw someone sitting there.

"John."

"I saw him."

They parked in the garage next to the Odyssey, and Somers shut off the engine.

"Gun?" Hazard asked.

"Locked up inside."

"Go get it," Hazard said, reaching for the door.

"No." Somers shook his head. "Let's just see what's going on. It's not like he was trying to hide; he could have been waiting inside the house if he wanted to hurt us."

Hazard nodded, but he still grabbed a baseball bat from the pile of sports gear before heading out to the front of the house. Somers walked at his side and then took Hazard's free hand and squeezed it once. Hazard gave him a look, but Somers just shook his head.

"Hello," Hazard said.

The guy was sitting on the porch steps, his knees pulled up to his chest, shivering in the early morning chill. At Hazard's voice, he stood, and Hazard realized his first impression was wrong: this guy was really just a kid, probably still in high school, but tall and lanky. His hair was buzzed short, and his eyes were a dark amber that glittered in the distant light from the streetlamp.

"Can we help you?" Hazard asked.

The kid's eyes went to Somers first, held there for a moment, and then followed their joined hands to Hazard. This time, his gaze lingered.

Somers drew in a sharp breath. "No fucking way," he muttered.

"What?" Hazard asked.

Somers didn't answer, but he was clutching Hazard's hand hard enough to hurt.

"Who are you?" Hazard asked the kid.

"You're Emery Hazard?" the kid said. He had a low baritone voice, smooth and assured.

"That's right. Who are you?"

The kid smirked, displaying a crooked eyetooth. "I'm your son."

CHAPTER TWO

NOVEMBER 1
FRIDAY
5:06 AM

"WHAT THE FUCK are you talking about?" Hazard asked. His voice boomed up and down the empty street.

Somers squeezed his hand.

The kid met Hazard's gaze. He was wearing a half smile.

Hazard's head pounded from hours of travel and a sleepless night. He rubbed gunk from his eyes and wiped his hand on his jeans. The sour smell of sweat, of too many bodies crammed inside a tin can, mixed with the morning's cool humidity. Light from the porch glittered on dew-bright spiderwebs. Part of Hazard's brain catalogued the need to get out later that day with a broom.

Still that stupid half smile.

"Well? I asked you a question: what the fuck are you—"

"Ree," Somers said, his free hand coming up to take Hazard's arm so that he was holding him with both hands now. "Let's go inside."

Hazard tried to yank his arm free. "No. Whatever the fuck this is—"

"You're shouting."

The silence rang in Hazard's ears. He took a deep breath. Then he peeled Somers's hands off him. He clomped up onto the porch, shouldering the boy out of his way, and tried his keys. He couldn't find the house key. Then he dropped the ring, and they clinked against the porch's cement slab. When he bent to recover them, Somers beat him to it, and the blond man offered a tight smile. Hazard curled his hands into fists while his husband opened the door.

The house had a stale, closed up smell, and it was almost as chilly as outdoors. The lamps and lights on timers had all turned off hours ago, so Hazard hit the switches as he stepped inside, and the bulbs overhead shivered to life.

"Why don't you—" Somers began.

Hazard moved past Somers, heading deeper into the house. Evie's rideable unicorn stood in his path; he shoved it, and it wobbled on its wheels until it hit the wall. A pair of Somers's sneakers and socks waited near the couch in the living room, victims of a last-minute fashion change before the wedding. A can of Pepsi, hopefully empty, sat on top of a stack of *Missouri Conservationist* and *ESPN* magazines on the coffee table. On one of the armchairs, someone had left behind a crumpled gas station receipt.

"You left your shoes out," Hazard said without looking back as he passed through the living room and into the hallway.

Somers was speaking quietly, presumably not to Hazard.

Hazard adjusted the thermostat, and a moment later the furnace clicked to life, and air whooshed through the vents. He made his way back to the living room. Somers and the boy were standing there. Now the boy was carrying a backpack.

"And you left a can of Pepsi on the table."

"Ree, this is Ares."

"We could have gotten ants."

Somers let out a controlled breath. "Let's start with introducing ourselves. Ares, I'm John-Henry."

"His name isn't Ares," Hazard said. "Is that your receipt on the chair?"

"My name is Ares," the kid said, flashing a look at Hazard before returning his attention to Somers. "Why is he acting like this?"

Hazard grabbed the wadded paper and flattened it against the arm of the chair. It was from the Kum & Go on Market Street. "This is yours," Hazard said. "The last four of the Visa match."

"Ree, this is a stressful situation. I'm stressed. I'm sure you're stressed. Can we deal with the receipt and the shoes and the pop and whatever else— can we deal with it later?"

"It's from a week before the wedding. Why didn't you leave it in the office for me to reconcile?"

"What's his problem?" the boy asked. "Is he a retard or something?'

Hazard turned on him. "In the first place, dipshit, don't use that word again. Not where I can hear you, anyway. In the second place, I don't know who the fuck you are or what the fuck you think you're doing, but you are not my son."

"I am."

"You surely fucking aren't!"

The boy took a step forward, his chest puffing up. "I am! I can prove it!"

"Are you out of your fucking mind—"

Somers closed the distance between them and stood in Hazard's line of sight. When Hazard tried to step around him, Somers shook his head and caught a handful of Hazard's tee. "Let's take a minute, you and I. Let's talk."

"I don't need to talk. I need to get this—this kid out of our house."

"Emery Francis Hazard."

Somers said the name calmly, evenly, but worry lines marked the corners of his eyes.

Hazard didn't trust his voice, so he made a noise.

"We're going upstairs—" Somers said to the boy, but he kept his gaze on Hazard.

"No." Hazard cleared his throat. "He might steal something."

"I'm not a thief," the boy said.

Somers frowned. "He's not going to steal—"

"I'm not going upstairs, John."

"What's he going to steal? Evie's unicorn? My Adidas?" Then he shook his head. "Ok. Ok. How about the kitchen?"

In the kitchen, Hazard paced, staring at the boy through the opening that connected with the living room. Four steps. Turn. Four steps. Turn. The boy was chewing a thumbnail, watching him back.

"Stop looking at me," Hazard called.

"Jesus Christ," Somers muttered.

"He's trying to start something."

"Ree, sweetheart." Somers took his face in both hands and stopped him. "I know you're exhausted. We both are. I know this is out of left field. But you are starting to freak me out."

"I'm fine."

"You're not acting like it. You're acting—" Somers stopped himself. He softened his voice. "You're acting like you're out of control."

Hazard closed his eyes. He took a deep breath. Then another. He opened his eyes and found Somers looking back. His husband was a beautiful man: perpetually rumpled, hair always looking like he'd rolled out of bed, eyes tropically blue. Blue like the waters where they'd gone for their honeymoon. They had spent almost a week on the beach. The sound of the waves rolling in had filled their room. Almost a week of coconut drinks and suntan lotion and the inescapable grit of sand. Hazard ran a hand up his husband's arm, along the dark whorls of the tattoo sleeve.

Somers's eyes held a question.

Hazard gave a fractional nod, and his husband released him.

"Let's start—"

"He is not my son."

"Ok." Somers bit his lip. Then a giggle escaped him. Hazard stared at his husband, and Somers clapped a hand over his mouth. He struggled for a moment and then peeled his hand away to whisper, "I'm sorry, I just—" Another giggle slipped free. "I'm just thinking of you with a—" Another giggle. "I'm sorry. I'm not laughing at you. I'm tired and loopy, but I keep thinking about you with a woman—" He dissolved into laughter again and tried to smother it with his hands.

"I'm glad you think this is funny," Hazard said, turning away.

Somers's expression cleared, and he caught Hazard's shirt. "Ree, baby, come on. I'm sorry."

Hazard looked past his husband, studying the boy in the living room. Ares—or whatever his real name was—was flipping through the DVDs, pausing on the action movies that Somers liked. *Die Hard: With a Vengeance* was the current object of his attention. The height and build were right, Hazard thought. He had been skinny like that when he was a teenager, and he hadn't filled out until his twenties. The dark hair. The amber eyes.

But there were a lot of tall, skinny kids with dark hair and light brown eyes.

"Talk through this," Somers said, with that way he had of reading Hazard's mind. "He looks like you. Let's start there."

"I've read articles about expectations and perception. They've done studies with neuroimaging and electrophysiology. We see what we expect to see."

"Are you talking about the kid?"

Hazard stared past Somers, his gaze still locked on the boy.

"Is it even remotely possible—" Somers began.

The words pulled Hazard's eyes back to his husband. "With a woman?" He could hear the horror in his voice, but it was too late. "Jesus Christ, John."

"Ok," Somers said, lips quirking into a grin that melted away. "That answers that. What about, you know, like a donation." His lips trembled again. "Maybe a turkey baster. No, no, no, stop." He moved into Hazard's path, stroking his chest again, urging him away from the living room. "I'm sorry. Bad time for jokes. But he looks like you—"

"Expectation, John. Expectation and perception."

"Right, but he looks a lot like you. It's uncanny. That's not just expectation."

"It's a coincidence."

"He was sitting on our porch. Whatever it is, it's more than coincidence."

Frustration knotted Hazard's voice; he sounded reedy when he forced out the words, "He is not my son."

"I believe you. Hey, come on, we'll figure this out."

Hazard nodded jerkily. He had to look away from the tenderness in Somers's face, but then Somers pulled him into a hug, and Hazard let himself lean in, his nose buried in Somers's hair. Somers rubbed his back.

After a few moments, Hazard broke free and cleared his throat. "I'm tired."

"We're both tired."

"I should have handled this better."

Somers's eyes narrowed. "I don't think there's a script for this kind of thing."

"I should have been logical about this."

"Oh Lord."

"And logic says that this son of a bitch—"

"I can hear you," the kid called from the other room.

"—is lying." Hazard took off for the living room.

"Ree, let's slow down—"

But Hazard had moved beyond his reach, and he didn't look back. When he got to the living room, he swatted the DVDs out of the boy's hand. They hit the floor, the plastic cases clattering, and the boy let out an indignant noise.

"Who are you?" Hazard asked.

"Ares Hazard. My mom—"

"Bullshit." Hazard spun. Somers was coming into the room, trying to get in Hazard's path. Hazard stiff-armed him out of the way and grabbed the backpack. He yanked on the zipper and dumped the pack's contents onto the couch: a pair of jeans, several pairs of white briefs that had been washed until they were gray, a small cardboard box with an ethnically ambiguous man on the front and the words *Who's Your Daddy?*, two t-shirts (one for Budweiser, one with the picture of a buck caught in crosshairs), and a paperback of *Catcher in the Rye*.

"Hey!" the kid shouted.

"Ree, Jesus," Somers said.

Hazard turned the backpack inside out. In silver marker, someone had written the name COLT in the bag. He grabbed a pair of briefs, where in the same letters someone had used a black marker to write the name again.

"His name is Colt." Hazard tossed the briefs at the boy. "Not Ares."

The boy—Colt—batted the underwear away and lunged forward "That's my shit, you freak! That's mine!"

Hazard yanked the pack away, holding it out of reach.

"You motherfucker," Colt said. His face was splotchy, and his voice was thin and high. "You can't do that to my stuff!"

"Ree, for the love of God." Somers snatched the backpack and moved over to the boy. He dropped into a crouch and began loading the clothes back in, but Colt elbowed him out of the way and ripped the backpack out of his hands. Somers rocked sideways and landed on his ass.

"Did you just lay your hand on him?" Hazard shouted, stepping in toward the kid.

Somehow, Somers was back on his feet and faster than Hazard. He caught Hazard with his shoulder and forced him back a step.

Hazard pawed at him. "That son of a bitch knocked you down!"

"Jesus Christ," Somers said, shoving him back another step.

"Don't touch my stuff!" Colt screamed.

"I'll touch whatever I fucking want," Hazard roared back. "This is my fucking house!"

"Enough!" Somers shouted.

In the lull that followed, blood howled in Hazard's ears. He pressed into Somers's shoulder and tried to force his way forward again.

"Cut it out," Somers snapped at Hazard. Then, to Colt, he said, "Kid, this is going to shit fast. Everybody needs to cool down."

Colt was breathing so rapidly that he sounded on the verge of hyperventilating. Red stained his cheeks. His eyes were wet, and as Hazard watched, the first tears rolled down his cheeks. The boy wiped them away furiously, blinking and trying to fix them both with a glare at the same time.

"He is my dad," Colt said. It sounded like he was having trouble getting the words out. "My mom told me. She saw him on the news and told me."

"That's fucking bullshit."

Somers rounded on him. His eyes were wide with what Hazard recognized, distantly, as disbelief. "Ree, shut up."

The words rang through the house. Hazard's face prickled. Below them, the furnace chugged and groaned. One of the ducts boomed hollowly as the metal expanded.

"I'm sorry," Somers said in an undertone. "But you're making this impossible."

Hazard stared past him. The shelves needed dusting; he could see where Colt had moved things, where he had rested his hand. Somers touched his arm, and Hazard angled his body away.

"All right." Somers scratched his eyebrow. He stared at the floor. Then he turned back to the boy. "Go ahead."

Colt worked his jaw for a moment. Then he rolled one shoulder. "That's all. I told you: he's my dad."

"What's your mom's name?"

"Mary McDermaid."

When Somers checked over his shoulder, Hazard kept his gaze on the bookshelves, but he shook his head.

"Make him take a test," Colt said. He fumbled through the pack and came up with the cardboard box: *Who's Your Daddy?*

"I can't make him—" Somers began.

"Fine," Hazard said.

"Ree, I don't think—"

"Let's get it over with." When Colt turned the box over, Hazard's brain kicked into gear. "Wait. I want to see it."

Colt made a disgusted noise, but he passed the box to Somers, who inspected it briefly before handing it to Hazard. Hazard took longer, checking the seal on the box, checking the box itself for signs of tampering, before opening it and inspecting each item individually. Nothing looked like it had been altered or contaminated. The swabs, tubes, and envelopes were all still sealed in their packaging.

"I didn't mess with it," Colt said.

Hazard ignored him and continued to examine each item. Finally, he looked at Somers.

"It looks fine to me," Somers said with a shrug, "but why don't we wait until we've had some sleep and—"

"No. You're right; I'm making this more difficult than it has to be."

Somers scratched his eyebrow again. He was studying that same spot on the floor. After thirty seconds, Hazard ripped open the packaging on a swab and ran it back and forth on the inside of his cheek. He sealed it in the tube, and then he sealed the tube inside a tamper-evident envelope. He tossed the remaining swab to Colt.

"Now you."

Colt tucked the swab inside his cheek.

"Open your mouth," Hazard said. "Let me see."

"You're such a freak," Colt said, but he pulled out the swab and opened his mouth. As far as Hazard could tell, there was nothing unusual. Hazard didn't even know how someone might fake a DNA test, but he imagined some sort of patch held inside the mouth where the imposter tissue could be collected. He couldn't see anything like that in Colt's mouth. "Well?"

"Go ahead," Hazard said.

Colt finished with the swab. He sealed it in the tube, and then he sealed it again in the envelope. He collected Hazard's sample and swung his backpack over one shoulder. Then he took off toward the front door, his attention fixed on the bag as he juggled the samples and tried to stow everything. He had to stop twice, shifting everything around, to get it all stowed.

"Hold on," Somers said. "Colt, where are you—"

"Not so fucking fast," Hazard said.

Somers tried to stop him, but Hazard elbowed him aside and grabbed the backpack. He tugged on the zipper. Colt spun in a circle, trying to get the bag free.

"Give me those," Hazard said. "I'll send them in for testing."

"Bruh!"

"You're not walking out of here with those samples." Hazard gave another yank, and the backpack came free from Colt's grip. Hazard reached inside, found the two sealed envelopes, and extracted them. He shoved them into his back pocket. Then he tossed the cardboard packaging from the test onto the coffee table. It hit the Pepsi can, which rolled off the table and dinged softly against the floor. "I'll expedite them."

"You are seriously fucked up," Colt said.

"Then you'd better hope it's not genetic," Hazard said with a chilly smile.

"This whole thing was a fucking mistake."

"Yes, it was. And the test will prove it."

Colt's eyes were red. "Fuck you, man."

The kid grabbed his backpack, zipped it shut, and headed for the door.

"Hold on," Somers said again. "Where are you going?"

Colt didn't look back. "I can take care of myself."

"You heard him," Hazard said. "He can take care of himself."

Somers cast him a look, and Hazard felt his face heat. With a shake of his head, the blond man jogged after Colt and caught up with him at the door.

"Where's your mom?"

Colt shook his head. Then, in a thick voice, he said, "She's dead."

"Where have you been living?"

"I'm fine. I've got my own thing."

"Colt, where have you been living?"

Colt glanced away and shouldered the backpack higher. He ran his arm under his nose. "He doesn't want me here."

Hazard nodded. "I sure as fuck don't."

"Ree, Jesus," Somers said, but he sounded tired now instead of angry. He moved slowly, bringing his hand up, resting it gently on Colt's shoulder. The boy quivered like a wild animal. He was still staring off into the darkened front room. "Come on," Somers said, squeezing once. "We've got a guest room. Have you eaten anything?"

"He can't stay here," Hazard said.

"See?" Colt snuffled into his sleeve again. "He hates me."

Somers looked over the boy's shoulder; his eyes locked with Hazard's, and Hazard broke first. "We'll talk about this after I get Colt settled."

"He's not staying, John. It's not safe for any of us. It's not safe for him to stay with two strange men—"

"I need you to drop this."

"It's not safe for us to have a teenage boy we don't know sleeping in our house."

"I'm telling you to let it go, Ree. We're all tired. Let's pick up tomorrow."

"It's not safe for Evie. It's unbelievably irresponsible of you to endanger her by letting a stranger stay in this house."

"Unbelievably irresponsible? Of me?"

Hazard shifted his weight.

"He's staying, Ree." Somers's voice was flat. "End of discussion."

"Fine," Hazard said. He shot toward the kitchen and the door out into the garage. "Then I'm not."

CHAPTER THREE

NOVEMBER 1
FRIDAY
5:29 AM

IN THE GARAGE, the smell of gasoline, motor oil, and old grass clippings met Hazard. The light was on, and the garage door was still up. They still hadn't even gotten their bags out of the car. Hazard opened the trunk, pulled out his roller bag, and set it on the cement slab. He had a moment of doubling, of seeing himself as a child, running away from home because his dad had beat his ass with a belt for talking back, because that was the scrap of power he had left.

He dragged the bag out onto the driveway, hit the garage door control, and started down the driveway as the door rattled closed. He stopped at the sidewalk. It was like running away all over again, because where the fuck was he supposed to go?

The house—his house, his and Somers's house—was bright with lights. In other houses on the street, lights were flicking on. The sky was brightening to the east, a distressed gray like someone was taking off the black with sandpaper. No moon.

The roller bag's wheels chittered on the cement as he followed the sidewalk. In the distance, someone still had sprinklers running, even this late in the year. Chi-chi-chi-chi-chi-chi-chirp. It was almost as good as white noise. Just enough to keep his brain from backtracking and playing the whole scene over again.

At the next house, Noah and Rebeca's house, the front door opened. A wedge of yellow light spread across the porch, then across the lawn. A familiar, gangly outline filled the doorway.

"Hi, Emery," Noah said.

Hazard stopped. His hand felt like lead on the roller bag.

"Want to come inside for a minute? Sounds like, um, maybe you guys are having a rough night. Morning. Whatever."

Down the street, the sprinklers hissed and then faded into silence. Hazard flexed his fingers around the bag's handle.

"Come inside, Emery," Noah said with surprising firmness.

Hazard dragged the bag up to the porch. Noah took it from him. He was skinny and tall, and he was wearing a matching pajama set with some sort of *Star Wars* character printed on them. He held the door and tilted his head for Hazard to go first, and then he followed him inside.

In the kitchen, Rebeca was making coffee. She was wearing a t-shirt and shorts, and her dark hair was up in a ponytail. She had some sort of green gunk on her eyes. Upstairs, children's voices told him that at least some of the six kids were awake.

"Did I wake them up?"

"It's been a weird night," Rebeca said. "Sit down."

"I'm sorry I woke them up."

"Emery, you didn't wake them up. Sit down." When he didn't move, she pressed him down onto a stool at the bar.

Noah cleared his throat. "You did kind of wake up Raquel, but only her."

"Noah," Rebeca said.

"What? He did."

Hazard propped his elbows on the granite. He put his face in his hands. Coffee dripped and filled the air with its acrid smell. After a moment, he asked, "How much did you hear?"

"We just heard voices," Noah said.

"Noah talked to—" Rebeca's hesitation told him what he suspected. "To that young man."

"He's not my son."

"Right." Noah laughed nervously. "I mean, we knew that."

"Oh my God," Rebecca said under her breath.

"We did. We totally knew that." Noah swallowed. Loudly. "What happened? I mean, I told him he could wait inside—here, I mean—if he wanted, but he said he wanted to talk to you as soon as you got home, and, um, yeah. What, like, happened?"

Hazard dropped his hands. "He, like, turned my husband against me, Noah. He, like, fucked up my entire life. That's what, like, happened."

"Hey, man, I'm sorry, I didn't mean to sound like—I don't know." Noah rubbed a hand through his hair. He looked at his wife.

"Why don't you make sure everybody's getting ready for school?" Rebeca asked.

"Yeah," Noah said. "Yeah, ok. Um, Emery, I'm sorry if I—I'm really sorry."

Hazard closed his eyes. Footsteps moved away. The coffee dripped a few last drops, and then the only sounds were shrieks of protest from upstairs. The fridge door opened. Bottles clinked. Rebeca set something on the counter—

milk, he guessed—and then the sound of the carafe bumping a ceramic mug. Then came the sound of ceramic sliding on granite.

When he opened his eyes, a mug saying WORLD'S BEST DAD sat in front of him, three-quarters full of coffee. In spite of himself, he smiled. "I'm such an asshole."

"It sounds like you're exhausted and walked into a really fraught situation," Rebeca said as she leaned on the bar opposite him.

"I'm a terrible neighbor."

"I've been wanting to talk to you about the parties and the loud music."

A smile tugged at the corner of his mouth again. When she lifted the jug of milk, he shook his head. Then he took a sip of the coffee.

"Want to talk about it?"

He tried. But he'd been awake for almost twenty-four hours, and he kept tangling the emotional threads of the story with the narrative sequence, his throat constricting when he tried to explain Somers taking the boy's side. Finally he had to stop because his eyes were stinging and his face felt like it was being pricked with pins and needles. He sipped coffee for a while. He traced patterns in the granite.

"First thing, John loves you," Rebeca said. "And he's on your side."

Hazard nodded.

"He is, Emery."

His jaw cracked when he opened his mouth. "I know."

"You get the paternity test, and you see what it tells you."

"He's in my house. Right now."

"So call family services."

Hazard blinked. He did a search, found the Jefferson City office, and placed the call. It went to a recorded message asking him to call back later.

"They're not open yet."

"Hold on. I did a panel with a social worker." Rebeca grabbed her phone, scrolled through it for a minute, and then displayed it. The contact information was for Ramona Andrews. "She works around here; maybe she can tell you something."

He didn't have any luck with that call either, but at Rebeca's prompting, he left a message. When he disconnected, he took a deep breath; some of the weight on his chest had eased.

"It's going to be all right, Emery," Rebeca said.

From the opening to the living room came the sound of someone clearing his throat. Hazard looked over. Somers leaned against the wall. He looked as tired as Hazard felt and, of course, because he was John-Henry Somerset, he still managed to look gorgeous, even with bags under his eyes and wearing a t-shirt and shorts and slides.

"I'm here for the firing squad," Somers said. "Do I get a blindfold?"

"Hey," Hazard said.

"Hey."

"I'm going to leave you two alone for a minute," Rebeca said. The shrieks from upstairs had changed to sounds of laughter, but it didn't sound like much progress, if any, was being made toward getting ready for school. "If I'm not fast, he'll promise them another Xbox."

"Godspeed," Somers said, and his smile when she bussed his cheek broke Hazard's heart. So much weariness. And, of course, pain. Pain that Hazard had put there.

"I called family services," Hazard said into the stillness between them. "And a social worker Rebeca knows. No one answered, so I left a message."

Somers nodded. "I got him settled in the guest bedroom."

"That was good of you." Hazard had to stop and gather himself. "You're always very kind."

"Not always," Somers said with a worn-out grin. "I'm sorry for how I handled that. I don't like how I talked to you. I just—I felt like I was at the end of my rope, not that that's an excuse. I can only imagine how much worse it is for you."

Hazard nodded. "You were right. He's a kid. We can't put him out on the street."

"This isn't about being right or wrong, Ree."

Hazard nodded again.

Somers came across the room and slid an arm around his shoulder. After a moment, Hazard let his head rest on Somers's arm.

"Why don't we go home?" Somers asked.

"Ok."

"Before he steals all my *Die Hard*s."

"You noticed that too?"

"I guess if he takes them, I could buy the boxed set with all the extended editions and the director's commentary. It wouldn't be a totally bad thing."

Rising from the stool, Hazard said, "Extended editions?"

"One of them is, I don't know, four hours."

"Christ, let's hurry."

Somers's grin looked a little less tired.

They walked home, Hazard towing the roller bag behind him. Somers had unloaded the car, and Hazard left his bag with the rest of their luggage in the kitchen. When they reached the top of the stairs, Somers stopped him, and Hazard listened. The boy—Colt—was moving around inside the guest room.

Hazard shook his head.

"It's going to be ok," Somers whispered, stretching up to kiss him.

"Gross." When Hazard looked, Colt was standing in the hall, staring at them.

"I'm gay," Hazard said. "In case you missed it."

"Uh, yeah." The words were full of teenage scorn. "I know."

"Is that a problem?'

Colt's answer was nonverbal contempt.

"So?" Hazard asked.

"You're old. Nobody wants to see old people kissing." Colt then added, in the tone of someone providing clarification, "It's disgusting."

"You can stay until we talk to a social worker. Then you're leaving."

Colt crossed his arms.

"Let's all get some sleep," Somers said. "Colt, I put a new toothbrush in the bathroom for you. There's toothpaste in the cabinet. Do you need anything else?"

The boy was still trying to match glares with Hazard, but after a moment, he shook his head.

Somers tugged Hazard toward their bedroom.

Hazard washed up in their bathroom. Then he listened again, straining to listen over the sound of Somers's splashing. He couldn't hear Colt, but that didn't mean anything. The kid could have come up with this ridiculous story for any number of reasons, and Hazard didn't like any of the possibilities. He waited until Somers was washing his face, and then he moved around the bed and opened the gun safe. He took out the Ruger Blackhawk and chambered six rounds. When he looked up, Colt was watching him from the hallway, staring through the open doorway.

Hazard stood. He spun the cylinder and slapped it closed. He raised an eyebrow.

With a sneer, Colt shook his head. Then he turned and walked into the guest room.

Acknowledgments

My deepest thanks go out to the following people (in reverse alphabetical order):

Wendy Wickett, for braving so many things that Granny Prechtl wouldn't have approved of, for that 'unicorn,' once-in-a-lifetime hyphenation of shit-dribble, and for being so generous with her time and support even though she was raised in the Orthodox Pepsi Church.

Jo Wegstein, for teaching me (again—I promise, one of these days, I will remember!) the correct way to put on a pair of Redwings, for teaching me (yet, yet, yet again—I promise, one of these days, I'll get them right!) how to use a semi-colon, and for helping me to eliminate so many distractors and focus my writing.

Dianne Thies, for backing me up on those truck stop cheesy dogs, helping me calibrate the banter (too much, sometimes, especially in certain moments!), and (among a million other errors), catching when I switched the spelling of a name mid-book!

Tray Stephenson, for spotting so many errors that nobody else saw—including an absent cedilla, several missing words, and some extra letters—as well as for his insight into the full circle of the character arcs, especially Shaw's.

Cheryl Oakley, for prompting me to think much more carefully about Shaw's actions at the end of the book, for cheering me on (even when she was dealing with plenty of stuff in her own life), and for giving me a great idea about where to take some of the consequences from this book in future stories.

Steve Leonard, for helping me with (and knowing!) Richie Hofmann, for giving me the absolutely perfect idea for the vegan BBQ conversation between Hazard, North, and Shaw, and for pointing out the original inequity in how North and Shaw addressed their competing needs (and the underlying issues driving them).

Austin Gwin, for showing me that shelter policies for biological sex grouping are much more complicated than I made them sound, for all the help (and inspiration—car talk!) with Breezi and North's rivalry, and for suggesting a more satisfying resolution to the relationship arc at the end of this book.

About the Author

Learn more about Gregory Ashe and forthcoming works at
www.gregoryashe.com.

For advanced access, exclusive content, limited-time promotions, and insider
information, please sign up for my mailing list at
http://bit.ly/ashemailinglist.

Made in the USA
Las Vegas, NV
27 August 2021

29109527R00169